BLINDING REVELATION

BOOK 2: ARMOUR OF LIGHT SERIES

DONITA BUNDY

JOURNEY
PRESS

Editor - Belinda Pollard
Proofreader - Alix Kwan
Cover Design- Donita Bundy
Cover Images - Adobe Stock
Copyright © ABCDstock, Nejron Photo

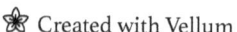 Created with Vellum

In memory of Margaret:
for your courage and testimony, thank you.
For Ron:
for your wisdom and perspective, thank you.

CONTENT WARNING

Dear Reader,

I want to alert you to some of the topics covered in this book which might influence your decision whether or not to read it.

Child prostitution:

The work of the young British woman, Amy Carmichael (1867–1951), inspired some of the context and characters in this book. She worked in India to rescue children sold to the temples and forced into child prostitution. Amy rescued, housed, educated and cared for over a thousand girls. In my teens I was inspired by her, and a number of years ago I came across Destiny Rescue, a not-for-profit organisation currently working around the world pursuing the same goal. This is still a prevalent reality in the world today.

Self-harm:

While all the characters and context of this work are completely fictional, some issues faced by the characters are inspired by children I met during my time as a school chaplain. Self-harming is touched upon in passing as it is a real issue and a tool used by some young people as a way to deal with emotional pain and suffering.

Reasoning:

My goal is not to glorify these issues or to use them gratuitously.

As a writer, I marry my life experiences to the fiction in order to create a three-dimensional work. And it has been my experience and prayer that when the grace, hope and love of our Lord meets with pain—physical, emotional and psychological—it is transformational.

He has the answers. His is the way, the truth, the life and the Light. And He is for all.

Sincerely,

db

TO THE CHURCH IN LAODICEA

[15]I know your deeds, that you are neither cold nor hot. I wish you were either one or the other! [16]So, because you are lukewarm—neither hot nor cold—I am about to spit you out of my mouth. [17]You say, 'I am rich; I have acquired wealth and do not need a thing.' But you do not realize that you are wretched, pitiful, poor, blind and naked. [18]I counsel you to buy from me gold refined in the fire, so you can become rich; and white clothes to wear, so you can cover your shameful nakedness; and salve to put on your eyes, so you can see.

Revelation 3:15–18

1

INDIGO: ON THE BRIDGE

Seven Years Ago

"Why are you so keen to fly?"

"What the—! You frightened the life out of me."

"Saved you the walk then, yeh?"

"Smart aleck."

It was understandable she hadn't seen me. I'd been propped up by the heat-sapping steel of the girder attempting to blend into the unforgiving concrete of the bridge when she'd climbed over the railing. Not only was I hidden by the shadows of the beam, the wind racing through the streets far below was whipping her long hair into a frenzied golden halo. I was surprised she'd seen anything at all. The weak reflections of the night sure as frack weren't doing anything to help.

Watching her ease her way onto the ledge caused an iron fist to clench the skrat out of my heart. She leaned out, her toes over the edge with only one hand anchoring her to the safety of the strut. A hand decorated in reptilian scales marking her as an acolyte of the goddess Ashera. The chick was drop-dead gorgeous. Her long flowing dress flicked and lifted, allowing the dim streetlights to bring the blue, purple and gold scales to life. They shimmered, merged and snaked up her body as far as the eye could see.

A High Priestess.

She shuffled back from the edge. With her free hand she swept back her mane and tried to hold it in place. "Why are you here? I've never seen you on the ledge before."

"Come here often then?"

She huffed a chuckle. "Seriously, if that's not the lamest pick-up line ever. Not that men need to be too creative where I come from. Normally, cash does the trick."

"Well, a man's gotta do what a man's gotta do when he doesn't have cash. And when he's from my neck of the woods."

"Whatever. But you haven't answered my question. What are you doing up here?"

"I'll show you mine if you show me yours, eh?"

"Seriously?" Her free hand flew to her hip, thankfully she still clung to the strut with the left. "I'm off-duty. You'll have to talk to one of my... handlers to sort that out. But then you just said you're strapped so, yeah... good luck with that."

"Calm down princess, I was talking about answers, yeh?" I didn't know her from Adam but was glad she'd stopped teasing the drop. It'd be a sad waste if she flew, unintentionally. "You show me your truth and I'll show you mine."

"Droll."

"Deep."

"Whatever."

A silence settled, separating us from the city below. In that bubble of time the girl had given me what I'd needed to trip my mind out of its endless, hopeless loop—the cluster bomb that was my life. She was a gift I intended to make the most of. "Well?"

"Well what?"

"For goodness' sake, girl! What are you doing up here? Tell me why the Temple's finest, one of its pampered prizes for the privileged, is playing on the edge of death. You after a thrill, or the real thing, eh?"

"What does it matter?"

"Cos it looks to me like you're keen to fly. And from where I sit, that's a hell of a waste. So, I'm thinking something's either screwed in your head, or in your life. Which is it?"

She stared into the shadows, not seeing me. Even if she could have pierced the darkness, she was miles away. Her gaze shifted to the canal below then drifted to the city beyond. I thought I'd lost her. That she wasn't going to answer. But then the wind carried a hint of a whisper, so soft I almost missed it. "What's the point?"

"Of answering my question?"

"No, smart aleck. Of life? What is the point of fighting? To keep going?"

"You trying to tell me that with all you got, you can't find anything worth living for?" I mean, I knew what she did for a living, but it couldn't be that bad. Where I'd come from, it was a part of life—the way most girls survived. And this chick would be getting well cared for in exchange, yeh? She had no idea of how hard life could be.

She didn't answer. She just searched for me in the shadows again, but this time her eyes swam in tears. The wet scales on her left cheek glinted, reflecting the play of lights. I knew Temple prostitutes were enhanced to bait mere mortals like me. To draw men in and entice them to spend time "*communing* with the goddess"... for a fee, yeh? The scales indicated the level of experience a handmaiden had. And by the look of it, this "girl" was top of the top.

She was way out of my league. But even if there was any doubt, the scales made her even more beautiful, unreachable, unreal. The Temple's scarring had claimed half of her for the goddess. The other half was for humanity. I knew she'd be spoiled rotten at the top of the food chain, but I did kind of wonder if there was any part of her left for... her?

She gracefully folded herself and sat on the concrete. Reptilian scales and white hair played with the glow from the lights of the bridge, as her legs hung over the edge, swinging, like a normal person would. Sitting on a bench. Not like they were sitting on the edge of death-drop like she was. I was relieved to see that with one hand, at least, she still held on to the railing beside her. But I'd lost her to silence.

I figured with nowhere to go and nothing to lose, I'd fill the void with some noise of my own. "Well, I find myself with the opposite dilemma. I am here because I have just landed in this godforsaken city and I have been given life at the expense of the only two people I have ever loved. But right here and now, living seems to be a very hard thing to do. I just don't know how I can keep fighting."

"Love? What is love?"

"Well, princess, I have come to think, contemplating this fracked city of yours, that love is sacrifice, yeh? Perhaps, love is... choosing to sacrifice yourself for someone else."

"That's a big ask. That means you can only love once, and then... that's it. That can't be right."

"No. I think the act of making a sacrifice for others, doesn't have to be your life. Offering up something, anything, that costs you is the actual love bit; giving your life is the ultimate act of love. I don't know, I'm still trying to figure it out. All I do know is that I feel obliged to live, but all I want is to not... be. I don't want this pressure, here"—I thumped my chest—"anymore. But how can I? That'd dishonour their gift and spit in the face of their sacrifice."

Being hidden in the dark and speaking to a stranger somehow made it easier to confess the mess inside. Who cared what she thought? She was no one to me except a neighbour on the edge, yeh?

"Having had someone to love and having been loved in return is..." Once again, she was lost.

I finished her sentence. "Precious. But it takes away the choice."

"What choice?"

"The choice to give up."

"Then don't give up."

"This from the girl who wants to launch herself off the bridge. Nice one."

"Well, it's different for me. I might have everything given to me, but it's still hard."

"Poor little rich kid, eh?"

"What would you know? Yes, I have access to the nice things, but it comes at a price." She swept her hand down her body.

"All I know is that I would swap with you any day, princess. Life's not nearly so generous when you come from my hometown and look like me, yeh?"

"Where is that? And why are you hiding? Why don't you come out from the shadows?" If she'd been standing, I'm pretty sure she would have stamped her foot.

"No thank you! Believe it or not, I'm actually enjoying being treated like a normal human being. So, for now, if you don't mind, I'll stay hidden. I'm not in the mood for hysterics. I'm tired, I'm hurting, and I'm not ready to run again."

"Come off it, it can't be that bad. Don't you think you're being a bit dramatic... princess?"

Silence came and joined us again. But this time it wasn't easy.

To reveal or not to reveal, that was the question.

Ha, Dan would have loved that. The book freak.

But before I could decide either way, she bought me some time. "So, what's your name anyway?"

"Indigo. It's a nickname but it stuck. What about you?"

"To my face, Mother. Behind my back, Razor, or Raz for short."

"What the...?" Mother or Razor? She couldn't have been more than eighteen... twenty tops, only a year or two older than me. Mother? Yeah nah, not likely, but Razor? "What kind of name is that?"

"I'll show you mine if you show me yours."

"What are you on about?"

"I'll show you my truth, if you show me yours." She waited. Her cockiness swept away by the wind. Her right hand going back to her hair.

My heart was pounding like a steam train. What would she do when she saw me? When she knew? "Listen, if you're going to freak out, just take off and do it somewhere else, yeh? I was here first, so..."

She smiled into the darkness. It softened her face, and the wall of my fortress cracked a bit more.

She twisted her body, so one knee rested on the ledge. Holding her right hand over her heart she vowed, "I, Razor, promise to either not freak out, or freak out quietly in another location, leaving Indigo to dwell in his depression, alone and in peace."

An involuntary grunt of laughter escaped my lungs and immediately the tension evaporated. I was going to miss her when she ran. It was heaven to have a normal conversation with a normal... beautiful... human being. Carefully, I edged my way out of the shadows to sit with her in the light, painfully aware that she was still close to the edge.

She gasped. "What happened to ... your face?"

"The old wounds are from living life in Gomorrah." I paused and waited.

Her eyebrows rose. "I thought I recognised the accent."

"The new ones are courtesy of the welcoming committee in Laodicea. Seems this place is not fond of people who look like this and are from my hometown, yeh?"

"It's not just Gomorrahans. Folk from Sodom are just as welcome." She winked.

"We're not all like that, you know."

Again, with the eyebrow, she challenged me.

"I mean, it is pretty bad. That's why we made a run for it, Dan and me. It was that or go under. We'd survived by being in a gang. But after a while, me and Dan knew we were in too deep. Trouble was, once you're in they don't give you up." The wounds were still fresh and the loss of my best friend and my dad were still raw. I tried to swallow the grief that threatened to choke me.

"What happened?"

2

INDIGO: REVERIE

I looked over the city. The lights flickering on the water below reminded me where I was. Out of there. It still hadn't had time to sink in. I was free.

"The Commander trusted us. Or so we thought. We were sent to mug an old fella in a shop. It was supposed to be a simple smash and grab, yeh? Way below our normal standard. We never planned to actually go through with it." Stealing was one thing. But attacking innocents—yeah nah, innocence was a myth. I should say "attacking the underdog" was a whole level of not-okay.

"With some of the bloods, we'd scoped the shop earlier in the day. The old guy had been front and centre, sweeping out his pawn shop. He wouldn't have much cash in there. Not in the till anyway. Dan and me both knew it was time to split. We'd not signed up for that skrat, eh? But we couldn't just hand in our resignation and walk away. The gang owned us.

"At sundown we left the compound, knowing we weren't going back. We strolled through the streets toward the pawn shop. The plan was to slip our tail, hide out nearby, then ride the train out of town. Simple. But not so easy.

"There's this place where the tracks make a sharp turn before heading out of town. All the trains slow right down to make the turn. If you run like a juvie, you can jump on the freighters and Bob's your uncle. We didn't care where we was headed. We just wanted out. I'd hoped to see my dad again before bailing, but too many bridges were burned, and we had run out of options. It was literally down to the wire—life or death, yeh?"

Like purging pus from a wound, once I'd started it was almost impossible to stop. The girl just sat and listened as the memories flooded and words flowed. "It was a set-up, yeh? Before we even got close to the shop, all the bloods were waiting for us. We were trapped but made a run for it anyway. If we turned ourselves in, they'd kill us, but play with us first. If we fought, we might get out, or die trying. Either was better than being hauled back to the compound to be fodder for the Commander's psychotic pet, Soldier.

"We bolted, but they'd set the noose tight. We were surrounded. We knew we weren't going to make it. So, Dan stopped."

A mountain crash-tackled my heart. It stole my breath and snuffed out my thoughts. Pain held me hostage. But I couldn't stop. I had to tell her, yeh? She might be the only person on the planet who would know. I had to honour my best friend.

"He stopped, but screamed for me to run. To run for my life. To run and not look back. Yeah, nah. No way was I going to leave him. I yelled at him and cussed him out. But he just stood there. Looked me in the eye. Silent. Then turned and walked back, falling under the scrum, disappearing under fists and kicks.

"And then I ran. I made it to the train and got on the next freighter heading out of town. I hid in a corner and planned on staying there forever. I was so lost. Weightless. Cut loose. No ground beneath me, no air to breathe, nothing to hang onto." It had been a new feeling: numb. Scary at first, but now I just wanted it to come and take me again so I could escape, and never have to feel like... *this* ever again. But I guess there was just too much pain.

"I almost fell out of the carriage when a voice spoke out of the darkness, yeh?" The memory brought its own warmth to the chill inside and out.

"It was my dad. He'd sent the rest of our mob away from Gomorrah earlier, but stayed to try and find me and Dan, and get us out too. But he'd given up and just managed to get himself out." A fresh wave of grief filled my lungs, and my swollen, smashed hands started throbbing again. "We got off here, in Laodicea, hoping to make a fresh start, eh? We asked around, looking for digs and work. Then later, when it was dark, outside the pub where we'd had dinner, we were met by a welcoming committee.

"And, for the second time in twenty-four hours, I was again being told to run. My dad took the brunt of the attack and screamed for me to run. To find the Light and run for my life. And... I did. I left him and ran for my life. But guilt had me on a short leash. I hadn't gotten far before I had to go back to try to find him. To help him, yeh?

"I carried him to the closest hospital: the one in the city centre. They took him in, but he died soon after. When I told them I had no home, no money, they said they'd take care of things. But from the moment they'd laid eyes on me and heard me talk, they'd suggested it might be best if I kept on moving right out of town. But I'm sick of running. And I'm tired. Just so fracking tired."

It was done. I was no longer the only one carrying the story. I still felt like skrat, but I was drained. Empty. The raging storm had stilled.

So lost in my own world, I'd forgotten the girl sitting next to me and jumped when she spoke.

"My parents work at that hospital. It's their life. I was dropped off at the Temple when I was three years old so as not to interfere with their 'civic duty'. And just so you know, I am in complete control of my senses, and in no danger of freaking out." She hitched one side of her mouth. "I hate to tell you this, Indigo, but you're just not that scary."

"I'm on my best behaviour, yeh?"

"I'm honoured."

Another silence settled, this time a bit awkward. But then time stretched and yawned, and a forever passed. A chill, bone deep, brought me back to the bridge. To my companion. She was still there and, true to her word, hadn't run. "So...?"

She came out of her trance. "So, what?"

"So, what's with the name? Razor?"

Careful-like, she released her hand from the rail and turned her arm over so I could see.

My exhaustion helped me not to react. The soft flesh on the inside of her arm, free from scales, was scarred with a web of healed cuts and raised white lines. A fresh, blood-soaked strip covered her latest fix. Wordlessly I asked the question.

She answered. "I'm sick of feeling numb. This helps me feel; reminds me I'm alive. That I *can* feel."

"But why this way?" It was a whisper.

"Because I don't have many options. We are monitored by minders all the time. We are medicated, educated and manipulated... constantly. But I'm sick of hurting, I'm sick of cutting, I'm sick of sacrificing. I'm not really keen on 'flying' as you put it. I just like to push into the edge a little."

She looked back over the city and her focus came to rest on a hill rising above the whole city. Lit up like a beacon, the Temple mount was home to the three gods who apparently ruled Laodicea: this chick's goddess, Ashera; some other chick-god, Artemis; and Dad's god, the Light. "As long as it doesn't interfere with my job or turn the worshippers off, no one cares. And believe it or not, the *worshippers* aren't interested in my wrists." She gave me a humourless smile. "They couldn't care less, so my minders don't care either." She turned her attention back to the Temples set on the hill. "Escaping into the night, on the other hand, is a definite no-no. I can't risk being seen by the public. And, if I'm ever discovered, out here or back there"—her chin indicated the high point of the city—"there will be hell to pay. But I have loyal acolytes who protect me and help cover my... leaves of absence." This time warmth from her smile reached her eyes.

"What's your real name, eh?"

She looked at me. Sized me up. Then, satisfied by what she saw: "Izabaal."

"Izabaal, I kind of know what you're saying." I held out my hands and made fists for her to inspect. My knuckles were freshly swollen and openly wounded from bearing the brunt of my latest burst of anger and pain. Not all had been caused by hitting flesh and bone.

"Ow! That looks... painful."

"Ha, I thought you'd understand. That's the whole point, yeh?"

She huffed her agreement and rolled her eyes with a twitch of her lips.

Silence fell again, this time in comfortable companionship. From opposite ends of the food chain, we'd found common ground in pain.

Time passed and I had come to understand that she really didn't want to jump, she just wanted to flirt with death. "Look, Izabaal?"

She smiled from the eyes when I used her real name.

"I'll make you a deal, yeh? I'm new in town and I'd appreciate a local's advice. So, instead of taking a walk over the water, how about you walk me to a place where I can get a cheap feed. The canal's not going anywhere if you change your mind. But for now, I could really use your help, yeh?"

The smile reached down and lifted the corners of her perfect mouth, causing the stars to come out in some alternate universe.

"I don't really know my way around, but I'd happily to show you a place I know between here and the Temple that's open twenty-four hours. I've never been in there, so I can't say what it's like, but I can point it out so you can give it a try." She looked up at me from under her lashes. "Looks like that pick-up line worked after all, eh?"

We both laughed.

With one hand grasping the rail like a vice, I stood and stretched my cramped, stiff body. Sitting still for too long had robbed me of feeling and flexibility.

She stared up at me. What was it on her face? Surprise? Fear? Her eyes then travelled down my body to where my shirt was still lifted by my raised arms. Admiration? I smirked, then reached down to help her up. "Come on princess, where can a boy get a feed in this joint, eh?"

She looked to my hand, then up to my eyes. Her hesitation threw up a wall. "I'm not going to sleep with you."

The shock of her statement overrode my fear of falling and both my hands flew into the air. "Whoa, princess, I'm just after a coffee and a cheap meal, yeh?"

"All men want to sleep with me. I'm the Jewel of the Temple. The Prize of Laodicea."

If she wasn't so ridiculously gorgeous and so depressingly serious, I'd think she was joking, or at least completely full of herself. But it was the sadness sapping all her lightness that made me believe her. "Izabaal, I'd have to be blind—and deaf—for your beauty not to flick my switches. But I think I have enough self-control to hold myself back, yeh?"

The doubt was still plastered in bold letters all over her body.

With one hand over my heart and the other firmly back on the rail, I vowed. "I, Indigo, promise to not ravish, attack or have my evil, manly ways with Izabaal, unless she asks—very politely. Then, if she's very lucky, I may think about it. But until that time, I guarantee her virtue is safe with me, yeh?"

At this she actually snorted. "Virtue? Does such a thing even exist?"

I squatted down in front of her on the edge of the bridge and looked her straight in the eye. "From this day on, it does." I stood and once again offered her my hand.

A watery veil covered her eyes. She grasped my hand and then, like a jackrabbit, jumped up. Her total disregard for the danger of the drop forced my heart into my mouth.

She laughed. It was golden. Then she pulled me back over the barrier onto the roadway and started across the tarmac, heading for the safety of the walkway on the other side of the bridge.

Three steps out onto the road, light beams hit her.

My heart stopped.

A speeding car swerving all over the road lined us up, and locked on course.

My heart thudded once.

Frozen in shock, Izabaal couldn't even scream. Paralysed by fear, she watched the car come straight for her.

My heart boomed again.

"Iza!" Still holding her hand, I pulled her back and threw her into the guard rail. She was safe.

A third beat.

The car hit. Screaming wasps swarmed, stung my brain and broke my body. Then, finally, the darkness came and drowned the world.

3

IZABAAL: TRUTH AND DARE

"Okay honey, time for us to roll him." Indigo's main nurse, Ruth, interrupted the nightmare that was consuming my waking—and sleeping—life. What was I going to do? I was completely lost and alone in a hostile world.

I shuffled into the corner, away from his bedside, and allowed the concert of beeps and alarms and the wheezing of Indigo's artificial breather back into my consciousness.

Ruth and I had an agreement. I was allowed to stay, to hide out, if I kept out of the way.

For now, hiding had become my major concern. I knew the Temple were looking for me, but after three days their enthusiasm was waning at last.

Alain, my father, had forbidden any major reconstructive or restorative surgery for Indigo, but Audette, my mother, had intervened. Their clashed horns met in the middle of a strained compromise that left Indigo lying in ICU on an angled bed, with no internal treatment and a limited stay.

A hole had been burred into the side of his head to remove a big pocket of blood, and now a narrow tube allowed excess fluid to drain.

His dislocated shoulder was strapped to his chest... gingerly, on account of his three fractured ribs. His lower right leg was in a cast so his tibia and fibula could mend.

And that wasn't even the worst of it.

With my hands buried within the front pockets of a borrowed jumper, I twisted the huge watch draped around my wrist. It had miraculously survived the crash and been stripped from Indigo on admittance. I hid under the oversized hoodie that Ruth had brought in for me.

The nurses here were amazing. They snuck me meals, brought me fresh clothes, and let me use the bathroom and the showers. All without saying a word. Not to the authorities, the Temple, or, most important of all, Alain.

For the past three days I had been in a stasis, much like Indigo's induced sedation. They monitored his vitals and progress while I tried to come to terms with my new reality. I needed to make some decisions, to make a plan... But all I could come up with was over-whelming nausea. My cuts and bruises were healing, but as healing came, clarity still eluded me. I had nothing, no one, and nowhere to go.

I had run out of time. Today they were removing his breathy-tube-thing and reducing his sedatives. Today, I was going to have to confront him and his new reality.

Indigo stirred. "What... where... what happened?" His free hand rubbed his face. He flinched when his fingers coasted over the shaved wound on the side of his head. An eye cracked open and confusion cloaked his face. Scrunching his eyes, he looked around the room, squinting in the glare of the dim lights.

I bolted to the bathroom just in time as my anxiety purged my stomach. Again. After rinsing my mouth and washing my face, I went back into the stall, bolted the door, pulled my feet up onto the lid of the toilet and tried my hardest to disappear. Maybe I could just stay here forever?

Ruth found me on my journey of denial and told me it was time.

He had to be told and I'd asked if I could be the one. I didn't want to tell him. But, since I was responsible... I dug into the depths of my scant reserves and sought the confidence of my Priestess persona: distant, cold, safe.

When I returned to his bedside, his eyes were closed again. His right hand, the hand I had held for three days, moved slowly back and forth across the bed, his fingers grazing over the blankets and sheets. I watch amazed as his body relaxed; he smiled and exhaled. Peace settled and erased the hard lines from his face.

No, Indigo. I am afraid you really aren't that scary at all.

I continued to stare uninhibited at his marred features. I had memorised every scar, peak and valley. Fascinated by the way his blue-black hair couldn't decide whether to spring up and out, or droop in a mop of curls around his exquisitely dark, extensively damaged face. Quietly I had admired his incredible physique, the richness of his skin's deep dark colour and wondered at the many scars on his body. Well, those I could see above the sheet... I hadn't gone looking for more.

This unusual stranger had saved my life. He had appeared from thin air and stirred within me a hint of feeling, a desire for life—and birthed hope. This young man who, by his own definition, had "loved" me.

Wasn't that what he'd said? "Love is choosing to sacrifice yourself for another. Giving your life—the ultimate act of love." Isn't that what he had done for me? Involuntarily, my hand ran down the side of my body over the bruising from the bridge barrier, as my eyes were drawn to his broken body.

I had dreaded this moment when he would regain consciousness. I wiped away the evidence of my grief on my already damp sleeve. Grieving his loss. Selfishly grieving my imminent loss when he knew the truth and discarded me. We'd spoken mere moments, yet I didn't want to live without him.

His head lifted off the pillow. "No! I'm not done." His eyes rolled, then he crashed back into unconscious. But this time his eyelids jumped and pulsed.

I pulled my chair closer. The temptation to take his hand was strong, but I fought it now that he was coming round. This space was closing, and I had to get ready to let go.

"Where am I?" This time he croaked, more conscious but still unsure. A dry tongue ran over his cracked lips. I poured a cup of water but held it close to my chest until he was ready to drink.

It was time to confess. The sooner he knew, the better. "Please don't be angry."

He rolled his head toward me and squinted. As I came into focus, he nodded slightly. "Iza... Izabaal? What happened?" The words got stuck on their way out between his pasty lips.

I reached over and held the straw between his lips. His huge hand covered mine as he strained to inhale the water. Well, not literally, of course. I had to pinch the straw to stop him. He was only allowed sips for now.

Eventually he gave up straining and relaxed. "Any meds with that?"

"Hello, Indigo. Glad you're back in the land of the living." Ruth introduced herself and after a brief negotiation about pain, adjusted the controls on his drip. She smiled at me, then left me to face the firing squad.

I locked on to his beautiful black eyes and gave myself a pep talk. I inhaled, ready to give full disclosure—as his eyes drifted shut and peace reclaimed his features.

Relief, grief and adrenaline swirled as that bullet grazed past. But I knew it was a temporary reprieve. I was running out of room in my emotional closet. I had told him I was numb. I had played on the edge in an attempt to feel. But since Indigo entered my life, I had done nothing *but* feel. Emotions were bursting out of me.

If I didn't tell him soon, I would quite literally explode.

TODAY WAS A NEW DAY. It brought another opportunity to reveal the truth.

He'd slept fitfully through the night, and this morning he was more alert, more aware, and full of questions.

This was it. My stomach was tangled in knots. I was going to be sick... again. But since I'd not been able to eat, it was an empty threat.

Take two. I stalled by offering him another sip of water. Heat prickled every inch of my body and I gripped the cup with both hands, trying to stop them shaking.

It was no good. I just had to come out and tell him. I'd deal with the consequences later. "I am so sorry, Indigo. A car came. You pushed me out of the way... you saved my life... but you were hit. Do you remember?"

He lay still, eyes shut, and nodded his head minimally. "Pain. So much pain."

Ruth bustled over. She brushed the hair from his forehead and spoke soothingly. She played with the controls on his drip, then gave me a gentle smile and a knowing nod. "You won't have long; the meds will kick in soon."

Indigo unclenched his eyes and rolled his head to face me. "Where are we?"

"At Laodicea Private Hospital. I'm so sorry I didn't believe you. I was so naive. Please forgive me."

He slurred, "What are you talking about? And can I have some more water?"

I held the cup for him to sip, but my hands shook so badly it sloshed over the side, wetting the blankets. Thankfully he was in no state to notice.

"Why do you keep apologising?" He rubbed his eyes again and gently ran his hand over the new swab on the side of his head. With a scrunched face, he gently rolled his head in fierce concentration.

"Oh Indigo. I don't know how to tell you. Please don't be angry at me, I didn't know what to do."

He closed his eyes, his face cleared. Breathing deeply then exhaling slowly, he spoke in a growly whisper. "Just tell me."

I steeled myself... then faltered. How could I tell him?

"Just. Facts."

Oh no, he was fading, and I was running out of time. I tried again. "You were hit by the car. It didn't kill you, but it would have. I rang my mother who sent an ambulance. You had a bleed in your head, a dislocated shoulder, cracked ribs, a broken leg, and... and..." I couldn't do it.

His eyes worked to stay focused on me.

"Your back was injured... about halfway. They called it a T9 injury? But all I know so far is... it means, it's very like you won't walk... again... ever... without aids."

He shook his head as his eyelids grew heavier. I could see him fighting to stay awake, to stay alert.

I put the cup down before I either broke it or my fingers, then raced on. "The staff at the admin recognised you from earlier. They knew you were from Gomorrah. And when my father found out, he forbade anyone doing anything more than keeping you alive. No reconstructive or reparative surgery. He... my father wouldn't treat you. I begged him to fix you. He told me to let you die. I pleaded with him. I told him how you saved my life."

Indigo lay perfectly still, his eyes closed. Was he asleep again? I couldn't waste this opportunity, I had to tell him before I burst into flames of shame.

"Sadly, because I am already dead to him, that was irrelevant. Mother stepped in and organised treatment. But he prohibited her and his staff from doing more." I couldn't look at him. I was so ashamed. "Living at the Temple my whole life, I had no idea what it was like on the outside."

I looked at him then. His face was blank. Watery, unfocused eyes fixed on the ceiling. Tears pooled, then cascaded into the crisp white pillow. He fought to stay awake, his eyes shutting for longer intervals.

I'd done it. I'd told him, and now the truth trapped me in its claws. I was a prisoner of the consequence of his decisions. Indigo's chest laboured to rise and fall rhythmically. I collapsed back into the chair.

"Leave."

My heart jumped out of my chest. I had thought he was asleep. "Oh Indigo, I'm so, so sorry, I—"

"Now." He turned his head away, shutting me out.

I placed his watch on the bedside table and left the room.

4

IZABAAL: YOU OR THE BRIDGE

Wandering blind through the halls of the hospital, I found a nook in the sunlight. It was furnished with large leather chairs facing wall-length windows overlooking the city. I chose the furthest one. I let my hair form a curtain to hide my profile and pulled my feet up under my skirt, wrapping my arms around my knees and tucking my hands down the opposite sleeves, ensuring my scales were covered. Curled in a ball, I stared blindly at the city that lay below.

I was truly alone... again. I couldn't return to the Temple. I was officially dead. Well, that was the rumour they were spreading. If I were to show up now, I may as well be. The repercussions would be significantly unpleasant. Audette would've taken me back, but that too was impossible now, since I was officially dead to my father. And once again, she'd chosen him over me.

From the age of three, I had looked forward to her visits and the gifts she brought me. As a child, I remember being happy. But then, too soon, childhood vanished and reality arrived. I had begged my mother to take me home. To get me out. She couldn't. Wouldn't. In the end I refused to see her. I knew she still came by regularly with her offerings. Not for the goddess, for me. I gave them to my sisters. I refused to accept anything from her when she refused to do the one thing I needed.

It was Amina, not much older than me, who had raised me inside the Temple. Indy thought I didn't understand love. But I did.

Amina had chosen to step down from the coveted position of High Priestess to protect me—to guarantee my safety. The high priestess was the only one given any semblance of choice. On occasion, it was her right to pick her consorts, thereby bestowing greater honour to those she consented to "commune" with. What a joke.

The one thing that gave me peace was knowing she was safe. Apparently, there was a way to enable our medicated bodies to fall pregnant. No one chose this option because it led to expulsion and a life of destitution on the streets. But with her man's help, Amina had escaped Laodicea to Benin, where they could raise their child safely.

I missed her so much. But I was glad she was safe. And happy.

Maybe it was time for me to leave. To just take off. But I had nowhere to go. No one to go to. And I was a prisoner of my scales.

The bruising was not enough to dull the internal pain. I slipped the razor out of the folds of my top and played with the blade. Even though I was anything but numb, the sharp, familiar edge soothed my despair.

"Iza? Is that you?"

The blade disappeared back into its pocket. I checked my scales were covered and turned. It was Mother.

"Excuse me, Felix." She was talking to a tall crow of a man immaculately groomed in a perfectly tailored suit. He looked at me, his face a cool mask. Mother spoke quietly to him. He nodded to her, and then me, before turning and gliding away.

Mother approached and perched on the edge of the seat next to me. "Iza, ma cherie, how are you holding up?" She knew I wouldn't accept her touch. But even still, her hands reached out. Then dropped back in her lap.

I didn't know what to do. Where to go. I was lost.

"It will be okay, my darling."

I looked at her. Really looked at her. Her eyes were heavy and shaded by black circles, her perfect make up not concealing her washed out complexion.

"I have organised all I can. Once Indigo is released from hospital, he is booked to receive treatment at an old rehabilitation clinic based at Laodicea University. He will get preferential treatment from the best, as paraplegia is no longer... common."

Anger swirled in me and my ears rang with fury. "He wouldn't be a paraplegic if Father had allowed surgery."

"What do you want me to say, Izabaal? I have done all I can. You can stay in an apartment on campus and visit with him each day. Then when he is released, he can stay with you for a further three months for day clinic. I have paid the bill and organised catering and care.

"Afterwards, an apartment near here is leased and paid for, a further six months. So Indigo can stay nearby for check-ups and help if he needs it." She held up her hand at my protest. "I insist. Yes, I am doing this for you. But I am also doing this for that boy... young man." Her face dropped and tears ran.

"He saved your life, and I will never be able to repay that debt. He is alone in a foreign city, crippled and with no one to help him." Her eyes lifted and through a watery veil, they burned. "I have to do what I can. The specialists and therapists will be able to see him and treat him in the apartment until he finds his way." She pulled a delicate handkerchief from her pocket and dabbed her eyes. "Of course, my darling, you are free to do as you wish. You can make use of the apartment, or not. It is already leased and paid for. But he has no choice, he needs time to learn and heal. If your father—"

"That man is not my father." I fingered the comforting edge of the blade in my hidden pocket as heaviness grounded me to the earth. I too owed Indigo a debt. But unlike my mother, I had no way to pay.

It was hopeless. From a toddler, I had been groomed to be a handmaiden of the goddess. I had never been responsible for anyone or anything apart from pleasuring men. And I vowed I'd never do that again. I had nothing, could do nothing. I searched my mother's face. "I don't know what to do."

"Just be yourself. And think. Use that wonderful intelligence that is in there." Mother's hand caressed my hair.

I let her.

"This is your time, Izabaal. You are free. Find yourself, stick with this boy, and know, ma cherie, that my door is always open."

"What of Alain?" I spat the words.

Fire sparked in her eyes and brought colour to her cheeks. "I will take care of him."

I was grateful for what she had done. I knew she would suffer for it. Just like everyone who defied the man. Like I had when I'd had the audacity to be born a girl.

"I am so proud of you. I know you refuse to believe me, but I do love you. And I am here if you need anything. Anything at all..."

Letting her run her hand down my hair was one thing, but accepting her help, allowing her to ease her conscience for abandoning me was another. "No."

Her brokenness sent a shaft through my heart. "Thank you. I appreciate all you have done. Thank you for saving Indigo. But we'll be okay," I lied.

Her pager snagged her attention. And just like that, another priority stole her away.

I SPENT the rest of the day hiding in the back halls and another restless night in the nurses' lounge. I delayed the inevitable for as long as I could. But after waiting yet another twenty-four hours, I was going insane. I had to know one way or the other what he was going to do. I returned to Indigo's room.

The numbness continued but I was done crying. I could not change the past. Indigo could hate me, but at least now he knew. I wordlessly returned to the chair by his bed. He was now on the ward and we had more privacy. We stared at each other for eons, both trapped in our own hopelessness. My rabbit warren of woes had me pursing the worst possible scenarios, all of which ended with me battered and beaten and left for dead on the streets.

Eventually his red, swollen eyes pulled me back to the here and now. It was hard not to be selfish when that was how I'd been trained. I had no way of understanding what he was dealing with. I shook my head with nothing to say, then took his hand.

He let me.

I stared at the wounds cloaking the knuckles he'd shown me almost a week ago. Running my fingers lightly over his brokenness, I asked, "Are you in pain?"

"I have meds." His hand lay still under my fingers. "So, your mum came by."

I held my breath.

"Yeah. Well, apparently I'm some kind of anomaly." He huffed. "I've not ever been called *that* before. But, turns out, those who can afford therapy are the kinds of people who have access to regenerative surgery, who are the kinds of people who don't end up paraplegics. The poor suckers who can't afford therapy never see the hospital and end up figuring this skrat out on their own, yeh?" He fell silent and inhaled a long watery breath.

I still couldn't look at him.

"Anyway, she— your mum came by with some people who reckon they're gonna help me learn to live a full and active life." His snuffly voice was edged with cynicism.

Staring at our hands, I nodded.

"She explained what she'd set up."

I shrugged.

"So, seems I have a choice: adapt or die."

The bluntness of his statement demanded a response. Finally, I dared to look into his red, puffy eyes. They matched mine—tired, swollen and awash with tears.

"I told you how dying isn't an option, yeh?"

I nodded.

He drew in a ragged breath. "Well, this is fracked."

I hated swearing, but I couldn't help my laugh.

He turned his hand over under mine and held my fingers. "What are you going to do?"

The wretched tears started again. "What do you mean?" Was he shutting me out? I withdrew my hand and wrapped my Priestess Cloak around me as a shield.

"Well? You going home to your parents?"

"My father has denounced me." *You are the High Priestess of Ashera.*

"What?"

"Alain sold me to the Temple when I was a baby. Last week when I approached him for help was the final straw and the slammed door on our joke of a relationship. He ordered me back to the Temple—immediately." *You don't need anyone.*

"What about the Temple?"

"Burned bridge." *People come from all over the globe to worship the goddess through you.*

"Friends?"

"The High Priestess has acolytes, servants and... worshippers." *You are above all.*

"Hey, careful. You promised me to either *not* freak out or do it quietly, leaving me to dwell in my depression alone and in peace, or something like that, yeh?"

It was enough to crack the wall and take me back to the bridge. "Smart aleck."

"Good to have you back." He held out his hand again.

I studied it. This boy had saved me. With that hand he'd pulled me to safety. He'd loved me. It was enough to loosen the cloak of lies.

He went on, "Now, do you have anywhere to go, anyone who can look after you?"

I just shook my head and looked at our hands joined on the bed; purple, blue and gold wrapped in wounded, black and broken. What a pair. "Apart from what my mother has set up, I have nowhere for us to go."

"Us?"

The abyss swelled in my stomach and threatened to swallow me whole. "Do you not want me either?" I swallowed my lips.

"Nothing about what *I* want princess. I thought you'd ditch me faster than a busted balloon."

Warmth broke through and I dropped the cloak altogether. "Well, it's you or the bridge. And like you said, the canal isn't going anywhere, so, if you turn out to be a disappointment, I'll try my luck there." My attempt at lightness was as transparent as glass.

"Gee thanks. Talk about bruising a boy's ego."

"You'll live." The smile started in my heart and worked its way to my toes.

"So, apparently, I'm on the ward for a couple more weeks, then I start rehab?"

I nodded. It was happening. We were making plans. We... us.

"Hey, Iza. Um... thanks." He laughed at me. "I bet you don't use that face at the Temple."

"How on earth can you be thanking me? I caused this mess."

"You reached out to your parents to save me. That was hard, yeh? You're not running or screaming. I hate hysterics. So, thank you."

"You saved my life, Indigo, and I don't know why. I am no one to you."

"Not anymore, kid. We're partners. You know this city—"

"No, I don't. I live in the Temple."

"You don't get out? At all?"

"We can't, it's not safe. Not without our keepers."

"But you know the lay of the land, yeh?"

"No. I know where the Temple, the bridge and the hospital are. That's it."

"Right then. That settles it. We're well and truly fracked."

5

INDIGO: THE FACTORY

One Year Later

The handle turned and the door eventually yielded after Iza gave it a decent shove. She disappeared inside and soon a dim light shone through the filthy windows, inviting me through the front door. I manoeuvred my chair up the two stairs and came in out of the rain.

Dank, musty air welcomed us. But it was a shelter from the building storm outside. Iza had found it a few days ago. Our time at the unit had run out and we needed somewhere to go. But since Iza couldn't go out in daylight and I'd been tied up with rehab, it was tough going.

I still fought the rage that overwhelmed me when I remembered the blood and bruises she'd come home with that first time.

It'd been that much worse because I'd sent her out... because I was an invalid. She'd tried to warn me. But I hadn't listened. So, knowing what was in store, Iza had gone out in search of somewhere for us to live. People'd seen her scales and she'd, once again, became public property to be consumed.

Yeah, nah. After that day, she only ever went out at night.

Covered.

From head to foot.

And in spite of all of that, she had found us somewhere to live.

"This is great, Iza. Perfect, eh?" The building was a small box with a kitchenette behind a partial wall. A radiator was installed at the top of one wall and the floor was covered with thin-but-tough carpet.

She beamed. Her split lip had almost healed but the bruise on her right cheek was still blooming purple. It matched the scales on the other side of her face.

I gritted my teeth. Never again. I'd kill the next kret that touched her.

"It's okay, Indy." It was hard to keep secrets from her. She had been trained in reading body language from a young age. Iza ran a cool, perfect hand down my face. "Look what I found." Twirling away, she disappeared around the divider and came back with two mugs. "Dishes."

It was like the girl had discovered gold. But I shouldn't think of her as a girl. She had three years on my sixteen, and was well and truly accustomed to the brutality of the world. Yet, at times like this, her joy at such simple things stripped the years away and settled my toxic soul.

She vanished again and I heard the distinct sound of an electric kettle boiling.

"And this place was open, eh? Unlocked? With electricity?" I gave my head a quick shake. Partly to get rid of some of the water, but also in disbelief. "How could a place like this just be sitting here? Unused."

"I don't know, Indy. But it's perfect. And you wait till you see all of it. It's huge." Her smile cracked her lip again and a thin trickle of blood began down her chin. She didn't notice. "There's a huge wall all the way around the outside of the property." She knelt by my side and placed her head in my lap, wrapping her arms around my dead, useless legs. "We're going to be safe here. I can feel it."

She'd already shown me the wheelchair-accessible bathroom, fitted with a shower, in the main warehouse, close to the cabin we now sheltered in. I'd wanted to ask why we weren't set up over where the bathroom was. But it was early days, and I didn't want to rain on her parade. By some miracle she'd found this place, and for some unknown reason, she'd picked this building out of the lot. Now wasn't the time to argue the point. But I would have to bring it up eventually. I needed that bathroom close by.

My life was now divided between before and after. For a while it had been before and after Gomorrah. Then, for a heartbeat, it had been before and after losing Dad. But now it was permanently split between before and after the bridge. Before the bridge I was carefree. I hadn't known it at the time, but I'd had the privilege of only having to care about myself: to do what I wanted, when I wanted, how I wanted, eh?

Now, I was completely and irrevocably trapped. Iza was incapable of taking care of herself. Which was a sick kind of irony. She was able bodied, intelligent, and had far too much experience in the ways of the world, or I should say, people. But she was so utterly naive and helpless. Without me, busted or not, she wouldn't survive.

I was trapped in this fracking chair. I knew I was better off than some of the other poor krets who were out there on their own with no help. I'd been helped, trained, kitted out and could now take care of myself. With the chair Audette had arranged, I was mobile, independent and capable. But it was a constant reminder of what I'd lost, what I'd become, and who I wasn't able to be.

But most of all I was trapped in routines. I was now a slave to a schedule. Every day I had to do my stretches, exercises, strength training and cardio. Every day I had to check and maintain my chair. Every day I had to go over myself with a fine-tooth comb looking for injuries I couldn't feel. And at specific times every day, I had to take myself to the bathroom. My system and I had an agreement. If I stuck to my schedule, it wouldn't embarrass me in public.

So, believe me when I say, now wasn't the time to argue about Iza's choice of bunkhouse. Now was the time to be ridiculously grateful we weren't on the street. And for the ancient biscuits and disgustingly stale coffee we'd just downed in celebration. I knew which camp I was planted in, yeh? And it didn't grant me the privilege of being a "chooser". Iza had found a mattress in one of the old staff cabins— yeah, don't ask, I don't know why we weren't there, either—some cushions and a throw in one of the cupboards, and made a nest on the floor.

And now she slept in my arms.

It had begun the night of the attack. That afternoon she'd come in broken, battered, and abused inside and out. Wordlessly she'd showered, changed, thrown her torn clothes in the bin and led me to my bed. Climbing in and scooting over to the wall she'd held the blankets high, silently inviting and patiently waiting for me to manoeuvre my way in. After I arranged my body and got settled, she rolled to face the wall, pulled my arm around her and backed her body into mine.

Since that night I had become the wall between Iza and the world. And for the first time since this whacked mess erupted all over us, right now, in this manky hut, I felt that maybe, just maybe, we might be okay.

~

"FOR FRACK'S SAKE IZA, can't you read?" I knew it was harsh, but seriously. Yes, she'd found the place at night, but hells-fracking-bells.

That made her angry. Tears swam in her eyes. I knew she hated me swearing, but it was more than that. She munched on her lips and fisted her hands. "No, Indigo, I can't."

That pulled me up short. "What? For real?" How'd she hidden that?

"What do you think we do at the Temple, Indy? Funnily enough, learning to read and write is not part of the curriculum."

The tears flowed. Iza had confessed to me in our first week that after burying all her emotions and hiding her tears for so long they now had a habit of escaping. She simply couldn't hold them in. Any emotion—from happiness to... anger, by the look of it—the girl leaked like a tap.

"We were not taught to read or write, we were not taught to sew, or cook, or even clean." She shot her arm up and threw it out, indicating the mess of the old run-down factory we were standing in.

The contaminated factory, yeh?

"The untouchables do that for us. The Temple is a place that traps girls into serving and sacrificing till they are no longer desirable. Ashera forbid that one of the priestesses actually learn a skill beyond sex, because then they may actually start thinking about options."

She started pacing and building up a real head of steam. "And we can't have girls thinking, Indy, because then they may realise that maybe, they might just be able to make it beyond the walls." She stopped, fists planted on her hips, rivers leaking from her eyes, fierce, wild and beautiful, eh? She got right down in my face. "And that can't. Ever. Happen. Because, Ashera help us if the meal ticket starts thinking. Worship the goddess, my butt. The only worship that goes on in that place is the worship of money and men's lust."

The Temple's prestige came from its vast wealth. It had nothing to do with the goddess. Even I knew that, eh? But Iza hadn't finished. "There is no goddess. There are men." The rage was a savage storm that burst the banks and was well out of control. Saliva flew, tears ran, and clenched fists jabbed to punctuate each point. "Men who use us, men who enslave us, and men who become very rich because of us."

Fire consumed her pale skin. Even her scales glowed in her fury. "So no, Indigo. I. Cannot. Read."

I nodded. And I'll admit, I was fully impressed by her rant. By her. "Okay then. Do you want to learn?" Ha. That took the wind out of her sails.

"What?"

"You wanna learn?"

"You'd teach me?"

"Sure, why not. Not like we got a lot of other things we gotta do."

Her smile was so big, her lip started bleeding again.

"Damn it, Iza. You gotta stop smiling. That thing will never heal."

She did that knee-hug thing again, and I was growing to... get used to it. "Although, we may have a bit of a problem, yeh?" She looked up at me. Her hair still wild, eyes wide. "The signs all over the place say this factory was shut down because it's contaminated."

Iza sat back on her heels and gasped. The tears returned. I felt the same way. To have hope ripped away was worse than having no hope at all.

"But you know? I reckon we give this place a good going over and check it out. The cabin you found is out in the open. So, if it's in the air, we should be okay. If it's soil contamination, that won't affect us. So, how about we give it a go, eh?"

She pulled her lips in to stop the wound bleeding again, but watery sunshine burst from her eyes.

"Look, there's a cafe. And a laundromat."

That night, under the cover of darkness, Iza and I had started a tour of the area. We'd wanted to know who our new neighbours were and run a bit of a risk assessment. I was looking for street life, signs of gangs, territorial boundaries and tags.

Iza was window shopping.

"Not that we need a laundromat. Can you believe it? Those old staff accommodation-demountable-building-thingys having a bathroom and a laundry? With a washing machine? That works? Why would they just leave everything, Indy? Not that I care, it makes it perfect for us." Iza waltzed. Yep. Waltzed beside me along the deserted street. "Oh. My. Goodness." She'd stopped dead.

"What is it?" Immediately I was on guard. "Get behind me." I pushed her into the alcove of the shop entrance beside us and scanned the shadows. Edging my chair between her and the street, I locked my brake and set myself to block any attack.

"No, Indy. Look." She was staring through the large windows of an enormous shop.

I could barely make out the name. "Good to Go." It seemed some sort of charity shop. The window was full of all sorts of household items. The faint glow in the shop showed it had clothing, furniture, books and pretty much anything you could think of. "What time does it open?" Not that I was going to show it, but it was gold, and exactly what we needed.

With the money Audette had given me, we had enough to set up home and get by for quite a while, until we found our feet. The trouble would be getting back here in the daylight. Iza couldn't come by herself. And I still hadn't managed to lose my telltale Gomorrahan accent... or keep my mouth shut.

"Um, seven?"

Damn it. Nice one, idiot. I'd forgotten she couldn't read. I looked to where she was staring. She was right but. "Do you know numbers?"

"Yes, and some letters, but I'm not too sure."

We sat there for ages as I got her to point out the letters she knew. I helped her figure out the ones she didn't. The fancy shape of the letters made it a bit tricky. "Okay, what about the numbers, then?"

When we'd used up all the writing at Good to Go, we moved on to the next window. And that started our nightly routine of walking the streets learning letters.

The next morning at six-thirty, with Iza covered as much as possible, we made our way back to Good to Go, just in case they opened early. The sooner we got this mission over and done with, the sooner we could go back to safety. I still wasn't confident of fighting from my chair, eh.

I looked up from checking my father's watch when chills fingered my spine and danced across the bridge of my nose. "Iza, stand in the alcove of the shop. Now."

"Why? What's wro—?"

"Just do it and pull your hoodie up and stick your hands in your pockets, yeh?" I flicked my eyes over her. Damn it. I could still see her scales. "Can you make yourself as small as possible. Curl up in a ball and sit in the corner of the doorway. Keep your head tucked in your lap and cover your feet with your skirt. Quickly."

A group made their way toward us, ripe and ready for trouble. I kept my head low but turned my chair to face them.

"Indy?"

"Hush Iza, it'll be okay. Stay tight in a ball, yeh?"

"Don't leave me."

"I'm not going anywhere sweetheart. Hush now."

Breathe out the emotion. Breathe in the calm. I am a rock. I am the ocean. Breathe out the heat. Breathe in the ice. I may not have legs, eh, but I was damned if I was going down without a good fight. And it'd be good to smash something other than walls. It was a truth Dan and me learned early. Smashing heads—other people's heads—was the best way to feel better, yeh?

"Hey Gimpy, nice chair. Whatcha doing on our turf this fine morning?"

I remained silent but looked them over. Five: four guys and a girl. Ranging in ages from... thirteen? to maybe a bit older than me, I'd say seventeen/eighteen? Not that it mattered. The leader was a weedy little kret in the front flanked by two pieces of meat. It was the bloke at the back I was most worried about, eh. A glimmer of intelligence sparked from his hooded eyes. I wouldn't overlook the girl at his side either.

My eyes came back to the mouthy weed out the front.

"I asked you a question."

I remained silent.

"What? You dumb as well as frack-ugly?" He turned to share a laugh with his muscle.

Sharp as skrat.

"What was that, gimp?"

Damn it, that was supposed to be on the inside. Since there was no escaping the inevitable, I locked the brake on my chair, ready to stand my ground.

I'll hand it to them, the thugs were fast. They both moved in quicker than I was expecting. But the good news was, they weren't used to fighting someone in a chair—a shorter target with a lower centre of gravity. Two quick jabs to the jewels and they were vomiting dinner from last week. I gave a quick word of thanks to Jeremy, my physio, for making me slave on my upper body strength, then smiled at the witless leader.

I stopped smiling when he dropped a metal pipe from the sleeve of his oversized jacket. Intellect and the chick just watched, expressionless. Witless brandished the thing around with enough confidence to make me think twice.

"Indy?"

Damn it.

"Well, well, well. What have we here?" He moved to step past me.

Yeah, nah. I intercepted.

He sneered and swung the bar back in a wide arc. I raised my arm to save my head. I couldn't afford another crack. It'd been about six months since the accident and I still hadn't got over the headaches. His blow didn't come. Something behind me had caught his attention.

"Indy!" Iza screamed.

"Stay back, Iza."

Witless stood frozen, arm raised, his eyes focused on something behind me. He must have seen her scales. The whole skirmish had only taken seconds, but while I held the advantage of surprise I launched myself out of the chair, using my head to ram the weed in the gut. I was taller, heavier and stronger. His advantage was his mobility and that bloody bar. On the ground, I had him. And was making short work of him. But Iza was defenceless against the other two.

Self-defence was another skill they hadn't taught the girls at the Temple. It was going on the to-do list.

Dad, if you're up there... help!

Iza screamed again. I had to finish this off. I grabbed the bar dropped by Witless, raised it and went to bring it down onto his head, when it was ripped from my hands.

"Damn it." Witless lay moaning below me. Intellect and the chick were hightailing it down the street. A new enemy was above me. I rolled and came out swinging. My opponent leaped back. I searched for Iza. She stood in the doorway in the arms of a woman. She was safe.

"Easy now, laddie." An old man stood a safe distance away and took hold of my chair. Using it as a block between us he brought it to my side, clamped on the brake, and stepped back till I had climbed in. "Breathe it out boy. You're safe now. They're gone."

I raked Iza with my eyes, giving her the once-over, looking for injuries. Her lip was bleeding again. "You okay?"

She nodded.

I looked between the couple. "Thanks." Not father and daughter... husband, wife? Didn't matter. They'd saved us.

"I don't know, son, you seemed to be taking pretty good care of yourself before we arrived." He chuckled. "We're not due to open for a while yet. Would you like to come in and join us for a cup of coffee?"

I looked to Iza. She was still nestled in the woman's arms. She gave me a nod.

"Thanks. That'd be sweet." I checked the street. It was clear. Witless had scampered with his tail between his legs, and as far as I could see, no one else had seen Iza or knew she was here. "Just a quick one though, we can't be out too long, I need to get Iza back before the streets get busy, eh." That and I was on a tight schedule. This place didn't look like it was kitted out with a wheelchair accessible bathroom.

"Come on, dear." The woman led Iza through the shop and into a huge living area out the back. I followed as the old man locked the door and trailed behind me.

6

INDIGO: LIFE HAPPENS

It was still dark when I dropped Iza off at Good to Go. It was her morning for cooking lessons with Kerm.

The old guy was pretty cool. Said at his age he didn't sleep much, so getting up early one morning a week was no skin off his nose. Helen, his wife, was a fair bit younger and made it clear that she was definitely *not* a morning person and would not be joining them, "Thank you very much". But, would have her turn catching up with Iza over her morning coffee when she was better equipped to be sociable.

Iza never failed to gush over her time hanging out with them and how Kerm had taught her how to make Helen's coffee. Before I came and picked her up after the lesson, she would take Helen her "morning starter" and they would "chat". Whatever the hell that meant.

It was the making of her, yeh? We'd bought some second-hand kids' books from the shop to teach Iza to read. But because we went through them so quickly and because we were really careful with them, Kerm and Helen let us just borrow and return them. Kind of like a library.

Iza was crazy-happy learning to read and cook. And not only that.

The old guy had a thing for sewing. Had a back room full of contraptions that looked more like torture devices than sewing stuff. Anyway, he'd promised Iza he'd teach her how to drive them as well... at some point.

She also loved the fact she could pay for her lessons by helping sort the cartons, bags and loads of items that were donated. We'd go after dark when the shop was shut. Or I'd drop her off on my way out to get supplies early in the morning. She was also really good at scouting out things that would help us at home. The whole set up was sweet as.

This morning I was running a bit late on my return trip from the city. Now that spring was officially here, I'd miscalculated the time. I'd seen my contact, conducted our business and given my order for tomorrow. Then with my supplies loaded into the bag strapped to the back of my chair—another find of Iza's from Good to Go—I was... good to go, yeh?

The tingling over the bridge of my nose told me I was in trouble. Ever since it was broken in a fight in Gomorrah, it'd become a warning beacon. It was like I was caught in the early stages of a sneeze... but not. Not that it really mattered what it felt like, the main thing was, it never let me down.

It'd been months since I'd had any trouble from Witless and his crew. I couldn't see who was following me, but as my nose twinged and tickled, I knew someone was out there gunning for my tail. I didn't want to take trouble to Good to Go, and I didn't want to reveal our home at the Factory. So, even though it was getting lighter, I turned left on to Crown, leading them away. Heading west on to Regent, I worked up a sweat hightailing it to the top of the hill with the plan of gaining speed and losing line of sight, if they had one, on the other side.

I told Iza the reason I went out each day was for fitness and upper-body strength. To stay healthy and capable, I had to keep moving, keep exercising. We both knew I could've easily picked up enough stuff to last a few days. But it was to keep me sane. I needed to get out... regularly, eh. Don't get me wrong. The Factory was our safe haven, and I was super grateful. The wall allowed Iza freedom, but it was my jail. So, I compromised, eh. Each day before dawn I escaped. And each morning before sunrise, I came back.

Iza needed me, so I needed to stay at my optimum. What I'd lost in muscle in my legs since January, over the following nine and a half months I figured I'd more than doubled in my arms and chest. And for this I was supremely grateful. Especially now I was on the run. I was cooking under my layers and sweat threatened to run into my eyes. Stopping to wipe my face was a luxury I couldn't afford, I had to keep working. But it didn't matter how hard I pushed; they had the advantage on me going up. I just hoped I could make a break on the other side.

Dawn was breaking behind me and I was getting further away from home. Queen's Park was at the top of the hill, but sticking to the tarmac was my best bet with road tyres.

I made it to the top and chanced a look behind me. Cold grey light marked the city as a silhouette. I could make out the buildings around me but couldn't see what they were.

Before I saw them, I heard pounding feet on the road behind me and someone who was doing it hard up the slope. At least one of them was heaving like a steam train.

Gulping in a lungful myself, I brushed my face across my shoulder, took a right and set off as fast as I could. I'd start making my way back round in the general direction of the Factory. Even though I didn't want to lead anyone there, one way or another, when this was over, I still had to make it back before full light to get Iza.

Flying down the other side, I was looking for a path that would take me due north. Lanes and alleys flew by on the south, each one a missed chance of escape. I needed to get off Edwards before they crested the hill.

Dad, if you can hear me up there, a little help with directions would be seriously helpful. Please?

Tears from the icy predawn wind were streaming down my face, chilling the sweat to crust. I bent down low over my legs trying to gain as much speed as possible. I felt the start of a wobble in my castor wheels. But a bigger problem was trying to figure out how I was going to control a turn at this speed.

Damn it. I was going too fast. Making the turn was going to be tricky. If I applied the break fully it would stop the wheels and send me flying. I saw a turn up ahead, a dark hole between two imposing shadows. Finally, an alley heading north.

With no idea whether the crew had made it over the crest of the hill, I wrapped my left hand inside the sleeve of my jumper, veered over to the right-hand side of the road and used my upper body to lean into the turn. I grabbed the left rim to slow the propulsion and pulsed the right brake on and off in order to slow down and make the turn.

The left wheel lifted. I was going to go over. I tried to sit up to counterbalance. Damn it. Too much. I'd made it into the alley, but I'd turned too fast and was heading for the wall of the nearest building on the corner.

My left hand was heating up within the cloth of my jumper guarding my hand. I tried righting myself, and overdid it. The left wheel hit the ground and the right came up. Momentum carried me. I couldn't fight it and was launched into the air.

Without thinking I protected my head with my arms and tried to roll. But in that split second, I'd forgotten I didn't have legs and the ballast of my weight pulled me up short and hard.

My chair bounced over my head and crashed into the wall of the alley in front of me. I slid to a stop leaving half my face and shreds of my jumper and skin on the concrete. Time froze. It was that precious second before the pain hit. The echo of the crash faded but the silence was broken by feet running past the end of the alley. I held in the groan that was building. I hurt like hell and had no idea if my chair had survived the crash. My only hope was that Audette's gift of an imported carbon framed chair with solid rubber wheels had withstood the impact. I still needed to get home when this was over. But in the dark, I didn't even know where the bleeding thing was.

The only positive was that the chasers had kept going.

"Found him lads. Oi. Back here."

Yeah nah. No positives.

At all.

This was going to hurt. More than it already did. A lot more.

Before the voice behind me had a chance to be accompanied by his mates, I started pulling myself along the ground on my smashed elbows. If I couldn't get to my chair, at least I could try to have the wall at my back.

"Where do you think you're going." A weight pinned my legs.

Damn it frack to hell. Frack. Frack. Frack.

Dad? Help me! I'm broken and fracking useless... a worm, on my belly.

Even though the kret had his foot on my legs, I still pulled and made a bit of ground. Inching my way to the wall, barely visible in the dark alley.

The gravel under my hands bit into the fresh wounds, making it harder to make ground.

I know I'm not going to win, but I can't even bloody fight.

"Determined little kret, aren't ya?" The guy reached down and grabbed my shoulder.

Well, frack it all to hell, Dad. You said there was Light. But you lied.

I scooped as much gravel as I could and twisted, throwing it in his face.

He swore, then growled.

I was back to squirming along the ground trying to find my chair or something that could help. I threw my hands out wide feeling for anything. A metal bar? A bottle? Anything?

Nothing.

There's something very distinctive about the sound of a knife flicking open. It's neat, clean, and the click of it locking in place is very satisfying. If you're holding the knife. If, however, you're not, that little flick and click has the power to slash all hope.

Adrenaline upped a notch and I fairly scrambled to the wall, twisted and pulled myself up to sitting.

The guy was alone. I guess he was so focused on revenge, he'd forgotten his friends. And, thankfully, they'd forgotten him.

That was one for the losing side.

He spat, swore and slowly approached.

I edged my hands out, constantly looking for anything I could use.

"Well done Gimpy. But now you gotta pay."

My fingers found part of the frame of my chair. I had no idea which part and I didn't care. It was cold, hard and very reassuring. I hoped my pack had come loose in the crash. I didn't need the extra weight just now. I had to swing high and hard.

Okay, so I'm gonna thank you for the lightweight frame. But that's it.

I didn't take my eyes off his looming figure. It was still as dark as sin in the alley, but the light coming in from the street gave me enough of an outline to line the kret up.

He lunged and I swung with every desperate, frightened, frustrated and angry fibre of my being. It smashed him in the side of the body. But most importantly, it hit his hand and he dropped the blade. The way he screamed and fell to a crouch, clutching his head, I'm guessing it hit more than just his arm.

The guy wouldn't shut up, but it gave me the distraction I needed. With the chair upright, and no idea what damage it had sustained, I put on the brake and hauled myself in.

Okay, so if the wheels work, I'll thank you for that too.

"Dray, where the hell are ya?" Voices crowded the end of the alley, the echo mocking my hope.

Damn it.

The kid kept screaming and I rolled away. There was a distinct wobble in the front right wheel, but I was mobile. Now all I needed was for this alley not to be a dead end. One-on-one, in the dark, with the element of surprise, I could handle myself... apparently. But more than that and I was a goner. For sure.

And right then, when hope was doing its best to get up off the mat, I heard the worst sound in the world. Footsteps. A horde of footsteps. Running toward me. I was too high on adrenaline to feel the full dose of pain yet, but when this group had finished with me, I was going to be in real trouble, eh. I wasn't too worried for myself. But what would happen to Iza?

A door burst open behind me. I stopped and turned. Light

flooded the darkness bringing with it the smell of coffee and bacon. Somewhere inside, a child cried. I could relate. Right then, crying seemed like a really good idea.

"Oi, what's going on here and what's with all the racket?" A man... a very large man... with a baseball bat... stood in the doorway between me and my pursuers. His eyes landed on me. "What the hell happened to you?"

I nodded to the crew gathering in the alley around my attacker. His hand was not very effective in stemming the river of darkness covering the side of his face.

Baseball Bat Guy stepped out into the alley with his back to me, loosening his shoulders by swinging the bat.

I'll be honest, if he did that in *my* face I'd be scared, yeh? The kid and his seven thugs were in agreeance. Appears they weren't so dumb after all.

"So, eight on one... in a chair. Doesn't seem right to me. How about I even the odds a bit." The child's cries from inside the open doorway started to quieten. Someone was shushing it and cooing quietly.

"But he's a gimp."

My saviour, Baseball Bat Guy, answered. "He might be in the chair. But you're the only gimp I can see here, boy."

"What are you, dumb, or just blind?"

"I don't have time to deal with this. Skitch off or I'll call the authorities... *after* I have some batting practice." Now the bat swung in big arcing circles. It whistled quietly in spring's fresh morning chill. He tossed it from hand to hand then lined up, two-handed.

One by one the gang left, pulling the walking wounded with them. I was very happy to see the kret unsteady on his feet as he was coaxed and led from the alley.

"Thank you." I nodded but kept my distance. He'd just saved my skin, but he still held the bat, eh.

"Seems like you were doing alright by yourself."

"Yeah nah, it was about to get pretty ugly, eh. My time had run out and taken luck with it."

"Well, you'd best come in and get cleaned up."

"Thanks man, but I really need to get back before it gets too much lighter." I wheeled past him and started looking for my bag. It was in the shadows, still done up, but I didn't want to think about the state of the supplies inside.

The guy followed me. I put the bag on my lap. If he decided to take a swing at me, I could use it as a shield.

"Listen, son, my wife and I understand, and we'd like to help." Behind him, standing in the light of the doorway was, apart from Iza, the most beautiful woman I had ever seen. Golden skin, long, straight black hair, and grey scales down the left-hand side of her body. She held a quietened child in her arms, legs hanging limp against the woman's side.

I hadn't even realised I'd moved until a hand rested on my shoulder. "Steady, son."

I dropped my hand, and looked up at the woman. "You're like Iza, but with grey scales."

"You know Razor?"

"Her name is Izabaal." I didn't mean to growl.

"Sorry. Izabaal." The woman's voice was quiet, deep and warm.

I looked at the child. Brown hair and golden skin. Entranced, I answered, "Yeah, we live at the abandoned Factory near here. I was out getting supplies when those goons found me and hunted me—" I froze.

Damn.

I looked from the woman to the man.

Damn it. Damn and... just damn. "Umm, no one knows we're there, eh."

The woman handed the child to the man and squatted down in front of me clutching my legs. "Is Raz... Izabaal a Greyscale?" Her eyes wide and voice rushed.

"What? No. Her scales are coloured." I couldn't take my eyes off the woman and her child.

The guy hustled her inside and held the door for me. "Come

inside mate, you're a mess. The girls will be here soon, and Lottie can fix you up."

"But I need to get back, eh. I need to pick Iza up before it's light, she'll be worried. I have to get her back to safety. It's already getting late. And... um... I need a bathroom." The adrenaline was leaking like a sieve and my head was throbbing like a tribal war-cry. Pain was making itself known but possibly worst of all was the humiliation of feeling so fracking vulnerable.

"We'll sort it out, son. Come on in."

Baseball Guy... Ben, phoned Good to Go and I spoke to Helen.

I heard her muffled voice. "It's for you."

Silence, then a tentative, "Hello?"

"Iza. It's me."

She burst into tears.

"Iza, I'm alright. Listen. Someone's going to come by and pick you up and bring you here. His name is Ben, and you can trust him. Okay?"

Silence.

"Iza?"

7

IZABAAL: EXTENSIONS

A mountain of a man knocked on the glass doors of Good to Go. Kerm spoke to him and called me through from peeking around the frame of the door onto the deck. With the extra time we'd been given, Helen had invited me to join her on their back verandah, waiting for the sun to rise, waiting for news. Any news. I'd been worn to a frazzle waiting for Indy to arrive.

He'd been late. Indy was never late. He might swear, lose his temper, have a crude sense of humour. But he was never late.

I checked my scales were covered and my hood was up. The meal I'd made was packed and wrapped in tea towels. Clutching the warm dish to my chest like a shield, I approached the shop entrance. Kerm gave me a brief one-armed hug and handed me over to the stranger. I stopped in the doorway and tried to breathe.

Indy had said I could trust him.

Behind him on the street, a white van waited. The exhaust created billowing clouds in the chilly morning air. It was light now, the sun's beams creating rays of light across the street as it peeked through the gaps in the buildings behind us. Normally by now we'd be home, safe behind the walls of the Factory. I just couldn't seem to make my legs move toward the stranger.

The mountain rumbled, "It's alright, lass. Tomiko said to say hello."

I almost dropped my pie dish. "Tomiko. You know Tomiko?"

"She's my wife, girl. Now come on, Indy's waiting, and a mite distressed about you being out in the light."

I leaned into Kerm's gentle kiss on my cheek. "Thank you for everything."

"How about you both pop in tomorrow morning, usual time, and tell me all about it."

Ben held the van door for me, and I shuffled into the seat. I wasn't used to travelling in vehicles, seeing as we never left Temple Mount—with permission.

Hot, thawing air swirled around my ankles as Ben made sure I fastened the buckle on the seat harness. And with a quick wave to Kerm, we were off. I was only just getting the hang of the feeling when the van pulled into an alley and stopped. Even though the sun was working its way over the buildings, it was still dark and freezing cold in the shadowy lane.

Ben let me out and guided me through a door into a storage area. Boxes were stacked in tall, neat pillars. We made our way into a warm kitchen that smelled like bacon, eggs and coffee. I'm ashamed to say my hunger had returned and I started salivating.

But then I forgot my stomach.

I may have even forgotten to breathe.

The pie dish crashed to the floor.

Indy, covered in blood, fresh wounds, and bandages sat lopsided in his damaged chair.

And three women rose from their seats, dropped to their knees and bowed their heads. "Mother, heart of the Goddess, Arm of Ashera," they intoned.

"Stop it. Stop. Get up at once. I have nothing to do with Ashera. I am no one's mother and I do not deserve your reverence." I was half on the seat next to Indy, one hand running over his damaged body. One knee on the ground half embracing my sisters. My brain stopped functioning, overloaded with concern for Indy, and shock, and joy at seeing the priestesses. These women had been discarded by the Temple because their bodies dared to defy the will of men and the medication we'd been fed. Greyscales, each of them. Judged guilty for the sin of falling pregnant.

"Lottie, I can't believe it's you." I fell into the old woman's embrace and sobbed. Where Amina had been my mother, Lottie had been my —and everyone else's—grandmother. Beyond her years of service to men, she'd been used in service to the girls. The aging woman had been trained in basic medicine and health care. Then, once she had trained her replacement, they kicked her out to the streets. No longer attractive to the punters, getting too old to be considered an asset, menopause turning her scales grey.

I pulled the older woman to her feet and sat her back in the chair. And looked at the other two. Shauna and Tomiko, each abandoned during Amina's reign as High Priestess. Each left to fend for themselves.

"Mama?" A small golden girl wheeled herself into the room, her hair a wild nest of toast crumbs and spread. An old chair seat had been attached to a board with four small wheels attached to the corners. The curved edges of the seat stopped her falling out, but the girl propelled herself along with golden hands protected by leather gloves. She scooted over to Tomiko, who scooped her up and kissed her cheek. "Mothe— Izabaal, meet Kazi."

I approached the angelic child. "Hello, Kazi. My name is Iza and I am very pleased to meet you." Kazi hid behind the curtain of her mother's hair.

Ben approached the girl. "Forgive her, she's not used to people."

Kazi held her arms out to him. "Papa."

He tickled her and she squealed with laughter. "How about we go up and get you ready for the day while these folk have a catch-up." Ben nodded to the closed blinds in the front of the cafe. "We open at nine o'clock. I can run you two"—he bounced his eyes from Indy to me—"back home but I have to be back before then." He then retreated through the doors into the kitchen and we heard screams of delight and heavy footsteps climbing stairs.

"Her spine was damaged at birth." Tomiko answered my unspoken question. "In that alley, actually." She looked through the kitchen to the way we'd entered. "I was just trying to find a safe place out of view, and out of the weather. It was a... complicated birth." Her arms crossed her middle, then she smiled. "Ben found us."

"Ben found all of us." Shauna spoke up.

I was scared to ask the question, but I could see no other child.

"Jade died young. He became ill very soon after he was born, and I... I couldn't..." Silence sat heavily as Shauna's words dried up.

My heart dissolved in a mist of pain. An ocean of sadness threatened to engulf me. The grey scales marked them as easy targets.

But finally, the tide broke and so did I. The horror of their realities drowned me. How they had been robbed. The way they had been treated. Their loss. It was too much. I collapsed on a chair behind me and didn't even try to stem the river of tears that swelled. I felt Indy's hand on my shoulder before it travelled down and took my own.

How could I be so selfish as to think my lot was hard? How could I even begin to be as strong as these women? And Indy?

My attention was then drawn back to him and his extensive wounds. "And what happened to you?" It wasn't actually meant to be the accusation it sounded like. I was scared for him. But angry as well. "Were you careless?"

"No, of course not. I just need to leave earlier or work out another way, that's all."

I was about to respond when there was a sharp rap at the door. Just the one.

Shauna and Lottie smiled. They looked at each other, then at me.

Tomiko had just returned from the kitchen after cleaning up my dropped pie. "Glad you're sitting down, Mother." She cupped my cheek with her soft, warm hand on her way to the door.

"Yes, I know we're late. There was trouble on the way. Have you gluttons left anything for me and Joko?" A fourth woman entered the café and my heart stopped.

I couldn't see her clearly through the flood of fresh tears. I couldn't speak. All I could do was sob. Loud. Ugly. Violent sobs. My whole body shook as my heart threatened to give out utterly and completely.

It was an awkward tangled hug. I was wrapped in her arms as she knelt between my knees with her head resting on my shoulder. Her tears mixed with mine. The mother of my heart was here. Amina.

It was quite some time before I noticed a small boy staring at me with the eyes of an old man and the rich, dark skin of his mother.

He studied me.

I gave him a trembling greeting. "Hello, young man."

"I am Banjoko. I am three years old and a warrior like my mother."

"It is a pleasure to meet you, Banjoko."

More coffee was served and a brief catch-up started. But all too soon, Ben brought Kazi down the stairs. "Sorry folks, but I need to get you home. We have to open, and you need to be safe."

My heart shredded. I looked to Indy. "Do you think we could... I mean, there's enough space for everyone?"

He nodded. He already knew what I was thinking. He'd probably been thinking it longer than me. It was then I realised just how completely I needed him in my world.

I stood, walked to his side, and very gently kissed his treated cheek. "Thank you." While we had tried to squeeze years of news into minutes, Lottie had done a good job of cleaning his wounds and medicating his pain from Ben and Tomiko's first aid kit.

In short order it was arranged. Ben would take us all back to the Factory and the ladies could decide if they would like to stay with us, or if they wanted to return to the places they had previously made their homes.

"Shall I keep Joko here?" Tomiko spoke quietly to Mina.

Amina looked around the group. Her eyes rested when she came to Indy.

He stared back unblinking through a battered face.

Whatever she was looking for she either found it or didn't. "No thanks, Tomi." She took Joko's hand and led him through the kitchen out to the back. We followed in her wake.

I embraced Tomiko as I passed her. "Thank you so much for finding Indy and taking care of him. Thank you for being here. Thank you for finding the others and opening your doors to us all." I tried to keep going, but a ball had lodged itself in my throat and my emotion was leaking out my eyes again. It was not an easy hug. By tradition, I was not to touch any below my elevation. But I wanted to show I was done with the Temple and everything it... *they*, stood for.

Tomiko returned my embrace with passion. With a bit of help from Ben, we manoeuvred Indy and his damaged chair into the van. Amina, Joko and Shauna joined him in the back. Up the front with Ben, I tried to navigate the way. Thankfully, he didn't need help. Indy had already told him where we lived. If he had been relying on me, I'm afraid we may never have arrived.

Silence travelled the short trip with us. I had already started organising the accommodation and where everyone could fit in. The demountables would be perfect. Two rows of five cabins, two beds in each, with a bathroom at the end of one row, and a laundry at the end of the second. There was a bigger kitchen facility and enough seating in one of the old staff areas in Warehouse One.

I jumped with fright when Ben spoke. We'd pulled up at the Factory and I hadn't even noticed. What was I thinking? I was so frantic looking up and down the street for watchful eyes, Ben had to repeat himself... again. "Tell that man of yours to come by and see me first thing tomorrow morning after he's dropped you off at Good to Go. Okay?"

"Yes. Yes, of course. Thank you so much for everything. For rescuing Indy and finding my sisters. I just can't thank you enough—"

"How about you pop out and let them out, so you can make a start in there and we can get everyone off the street. Okay?"

"Yes... yes... of course. Thank yo—"

"You'd best get a move on now."

I stopped my stuttering, finished struggling with the seat harness and got out. Ben knew the area well enough to use the western entrance that was off the main street. We ushered everyone in behind the large rolling gate and breathed a sigh of relief when it rolled back into place, blocking us from the world's view.

I watched as they looked around and took in the facility. I couldn't believe it. After so long being alone, I would have these people back in my life. Amina and her son, Joko. Lottie and Shauna who had been well entrenched in Temple life and able to settle the younger ones as each of us had arrived.

Indy and I led the women through the Factory and showed them what I'd been thinking and how they could use the facilities if they decided to stay. We made it clear that during the daylight we had to stay within the cover of the multiple warehouses. The bridge that rose above our eastern wall gave commuters a clear view into our grounds.

However, the ladies were so used to hiding and keeping to the shadows they didn't mind at all. The warehouses were all joined by large sliding doors and open spans, giving us endless space to move and live freely. Well, as freely as we could, hiding behind our walls. One of my favourite places was Warehouse Two, or the Sunroom as I called it. With most of the roof removed it was open to the sky, allowing the weather to bathe the whole space, including a huge hole that had been dug through the concrete floor. It wasn't too hard to deduce this was the site of the contamination. But now grass and flowering weeds had fought their way through the clay and dirt, creating our own private garden.

Joko loved the space... and Indy. Being so young, the boy had the gift of brutal honesty and asked bluntly for what he wanted. As a result, he was sitting on Indy's injured lap coasting through the huge, empty warehouses. But after this morning's adventure it was a bumpy, tender ride, with at least one wheel askew. Joko soon dismounted and took up the role of "driver" and navigator, deciding it would be more fun to push Indy's chair. But since he was too small to see over the back of the wheelchair, it was more of a mystery tour. And I'm not sure who enjoyed it more.

Mina watched, not forbidding, but on alert.

From a window in Warehouse One, I pointed out the bridge and how we were visible to cars driving into the metropolis. We had to circumnavigate the car park and approach the cabins from the cover of the enthusiastic bushes that lined the exterior northern wall. At night we were free to move around, but during the day we clung to the shadows. Obviously, this was nothing new for my sisters: they were Greyscales.

We went through the cabins, and the women each picked a room. Amina assured me there were more of us out there. She'd explained how every morning she left Joko with Tomi and Kazi and went searching. Amina had been the true mother at the Temple. She should never have advocated for me. But I was still puzzled as to why she was here. She should have been safe in Benin with her man, raising Banjoko. She promised she would explain, later.

But for now, she and my sisters were happy to join us at the Factory. They each picked a cabin in the front row of demountables. But Lottie took two, claiming the one next to the bathroom as her "hospital".

We were going to need bed linen, pillows, and blankets... among other things. Like our hut, each cabin had a small air conditioner and radiator at the top of one wall. We tried not to use too much water and electricity. It was a miracle that services were still connected, but we didn't want to draw attention to ourselves with the usage level spiking on a radar somewhere.

Joko wasn't the only fan. The women loved the place. Apart from Lottie, they couldn't read, so they didn't know about the contamination. Lottie brought it up though. And I used the same argument that Indy had used and gave them the option to leave.

They didn't.

The women had each brought all they had with them, and lined up to take turns in the shower. I had enough soap and shampoo to go around. But before Lottie did anything, she checked Indy over once more. Sadly, apart from giving him another dose of mild pain killers, there was nothing more she could do for him. Now all he needed was rest and time to recover.

As the women were getting themselves sorted, Indy and I started making lists of all the things we'd have to get as well as a better-equipped first aid kit. We then had to break it up between what we could afford to buy from Kerm and Helen, and what he would have to source from wherever it was he got our daily supplies.

I was frustrated he wouldn't carry a larger load. I knew he was capable. There wasn't much he wasn't capable of. But he was determined to go out daily. I died an anxious death each morning he went out, unable to settle until he returned at daybreak. But he insisted that he was fine. So, we made our lists, left the ladies to their discovery, and then I led Indy to our hut, shut the door and put him to bed. I checked his wounds and climbed in behind him and for once became *his* wall, holding back the world as he rested and recovered.

He didn't say it, but I knew he was hurting pretty bad. I made sure no one troubled us for the rest of the day.

I was kicking myself for dropping the pie. Now we didn't have anything for dinner. I guess it wasn't the first time we'd gone without. And it definitely wouldn't be the last.

8

IZABAAL: NEW GUESTS

Three Years Later

"What is this?" Amina spat at me. Her fierce grip strangled my arm, turning it over, exposing the new wounds on the underside. When I didn't answer, she shook my arm then threw it back at me. "I did not raise you to be weak."

"I'm sorry, Mina."

"I tell you this, my girl. If I see this again"—her hand pointing to my wrist—"I will take Joko and we will leave."

"No. You can't leave me, Mina. Not again."

"I did it before for your own good. I will do it again. I will not stay and watch you do this."

"But it's so hard."

"Well, you get harder girl. You are twenty-three, it is past time you grew up. Put this childish way behind you. You were raised to be Mother. Now more than ever, you are needed. Stop thinking of yourself only."

"How can you say that. You of all people know that I am the weak one. The weakest. I am the only one here who is *not* a mother."

"Silly girl. Mother is more than birthing children. Mother is protector, provider, carer. I protect, you care."

Indy rolled past with three-year-old Hiro in his lap, Joko pushing from behind. Now that he was seven, Joko loved to "drive". Hiro was still a littley, but made it known his position was riding shotgun on Indy's lap.

"Even this one is more Mother than you. He provides and cares for children." From anyone else this could have been taken as a compliment. But, if it came from Mina's mouth and involved a man, best to take it as the insult it was intended to be.

"But Indy has protected us all and provided for all of us since the start."

Amina spat on the ground. "Men have one use. Provide us with children." We watched as Indy, Joko and Hiro played. "Your man is no man. The one thing he is required to do, he cannot do."

Indy threw Hiro into the air and caught him as Joko spun them around in the chair. "I love you too, Mina," he drawled as they cruised past.

She looked down her nose, nostrils flaring, but didn't acknowledge him with a response. Amina had to accept that this place was founded by both of us. Indy protected me and provided for us all. As much as she begrudged his presence, she had to acknowledge that he played a vital part in our survival.

At night, he worked alongside her taking turns at patrolling the premises. And each morning before light, Indy would head out with the trolley Kerm had adapted from a golf buggy to get our daily supplies from his undisclosed source.

Mina used to go with him. But now, word of us had spread through the underground grapevine at the Temple. Any who were abandoned knew they could join us, so she only went once a week, to keep tabs on what was happening at our old home.

But still Indy went out every day, sometimes taking Joko with him. I wondered at Amina allowing it. But neither she nor Indy would speak of it. The two of them didn't get on, but in this they had some iron-bound truce. I had tried a number of times, and ways, to find out what was going on, where Indy went and who his source was, but with no results. I guess it didn't really matter. I just made him promise me he wasn't stealing or doing anything illegal.

What I did know, though, was that what we were doing was working. The week after Mina and Shauna had settled in, Helen brought Vashti by. She'd been living on the outskirts and only came into the city when she was desperate. Helen had found her a few years before and had been supporting and keeping regular tabs on her. She'd tried to offer Vashti more, but the woman had declined. However, when she heard about the Factory, Vashti had agreed to meet us. Of course, Lottie and Shauna knew her: she had been a contemporary of theirs. But she'd been evicted while Mina was still a young girl and I was even younger.

Vashti was a quiet woman whose life's ambition was to be invisible. Which was a bit tricky. The harsh trials she had survived throughout her thirty-two years had not dimmed her exquisite beauty or diminished her regal grace. But she had no desire to leave the grounds, happy to settle in a room next to Lottie and serve in whatever way she could. I don't think she ever got over the grief of losing her baby to malnutrition. We loved her dearly and only wanted the best for her, but after twelve years on her own, her only desire was to blend into the background.

Earlier this year Aiko arrived, pregnant with Hiro. Her scales had started fading, but not enough for the Minders to notice. Before she could be evicted from the Temple, Amina was ready to collect her. Aiko was proof our system was effective.

The vibrancy of our scales was affected by the pregnancy hormone, HCG. Once it was released in a girl's system, her scales began to fade. Apparently, some women knew before the Temple became aware. But in the past, they stayed as long as possible and were only cast out when it was obvious. The keepers didn't care what happened to us, as long as there were no Greyscales on site.

Now, because there was somewhere to go, arrangements could be made. But the Temple must never know about us. They would shut us down and see us ruined to make sure their dirty laundry was not aired to the general populace.

Due to Amina's diligence, the sisters knew they could come here. Aiko was our first successful withdrawal. She had been able to stay at the Temple long enough to ensure a good diet in her early weeks, then pack what she could and arrange to meet Amina in the early hours of the morning. The expectant mother was safe and settled within the Factory walls before the horrors of morning sickness hit. Lottie was able to care for her, Indy continued to provide, and Amina kept watch. I was able to find enough of the equipment we needed for Hiro's arrival from Good to Go, while Shauna and Vashti looked after us and the premises.

When it had been time for Hiro to be born, it was within a safe environment, off the streets, into a brood of overprotective grandmothers and aunts, and a fierce big brother and doting sister. Joko had not left Hiro's side in his first year. Each night he had to be dragged away—bribed sometimes—so he could sleep properly in his own bed. Kazi had become a regular visitor with us here, and since there was a living doll she could play with, she begged Tomi and Ben to bring her over as much as possible. Not that we minded, of course. It was wonderful for all of us to see them.

Now Hiro could crawl, it was easier. And Indy was adored by both boys and Kazi. The feeling was mutual.

Everything was perfect. So, I don't know why I still fell into my old ways. I knew we were safe. I knew we were doing a good thing. I was no longer numb. But I couldn't fill the hole that ate me up from the inside out. I had Indy, I had Amina, I had my sisters. Kerm and Helen were teaching me and had been adopted as grandparents alongside Lottie. So why did I still ache? Why was I still so empty?

"Are you listening to me, girl?" Amina was in my face again.

"Ease up Mina, give her a break, eh?" Indy stopped in front of us, the boys crawling all over him, giggling, totally unaware of the tension.

"I will not ease up. She has to grow up. It is time. Past time. Now, she must put this away." She turned back to me and looked me in the eye. "I promise you, my child, I will leave if I see you do this again."

"Mama?"

"Hush, Joko." Amina did not reduce the heat of her gaze. She drilled into my soul. "Do you hear me, child of my heart? This"—she took my wrist—"must stop."

I couldn't speak, the words were captured in my strangled throat. The emptiness that had been threatening me all week was gathering. I could not lose Mina again. Stupid tears ran, cutting a deeper crevice in my soul. So many tears. I nodded.

"Joko, Hiro, come." Amina stalked off. But as she went, I heard the words fall over her shoulder to Indy, "See to your woman."

Indy rolled toward me and took my hands. He turned my wrists over and kissed below the fresh wounds.

I looked into his deep, dark eyes, and within their depths I found an anchor I could hold onto. "You won't leave me, will you?"

He didn't answer. He just placed my hand on his shoulder and guided me to our hut. Inside, he waited by the bed. I crawled in, scooted over and held the blankets up as he manoeuvred his body beside mine. Instead of facing the wall, I curled into his chest and let his warmth chase the emptiness away.

"How could I leave you, Iza. You're my home, eh."

THE SPRING SUNSHINE broke over the Factory. Indy had returned from collecting the daily supplies and we'd gathered in the dining room of Warehouse One. A collection of flowering weeds sat in a pretty blue, glue-repaired vase on the table. Earlier that morning, Joko, Kazi and Hiro had helped me gather them from our weed garden in the Sunroom of Warehouse Two. Vashti and Aiko had helped me make scones from a recipe Kerm had taught me in one of my very first lessons. They were a crowd favourite. And Tomi had brought some sandwiches from the cafe.

It was still early, and we were expecting both Helen and Kerm to arrive any moment. Hopefully before Amina arrived with our newest sister. Shauna had made a large pot of tea and, as everyone waited, I decided I needed to speak, before I lost my nerve. Brushing a finger over the edge of my blades in their hidden pocket calmed me. "I was wondering if you could all help me, please." I had to cough to clear my voice. Before I could think too much about it, or change my mind, I pulled the blades out and put them on the table.

The silence built and magnified till it boomed. The room stilled and every eye was trained on the small metal rectangles.

"I am throwing these out." I pushed them a bit further away from me, into the centre of the table. "I would like help, please." I looked to each of my sisters, then to Indy. "I would like someone to throw them in a bin or a place I don't know, where I can't get them back." I swallowed the lump in my throat. "I know you all know what I have tried to keep hidden. But I don't want to do this anymore."

From where he sat beside me, Indy took my hand and kissed my knuckles.

Shauna quietly came and hugged me. As did the others, except Lottie. "I admire you girl. But you know this isn't the end of it. It's not going to be that easy." The truth was as harsh as her voice. But her heart wasn't. Lottie knew more than most. She'd worked with Temple acolytes for decades.

"I know. But I am bringing it into the open and I would like your help." I looked around the room at my family. "All of your help. To keep me accountable."

These women had suffered so much more than me. They had been put into situations far worse than mine through no fault of their own. Yet, I had been given a privileged position among them. I did not deserve to lead them, but I could serve and care for them as in turn each served this community in some form or another.

Shauna looked after the kids when their mums or Indy couldn't. Vashti and Aiko cleaned, washed, and helped me prepare meals. Lottie watched over our health and wellbeing, advising Indy on what foods were best, and what the new mothers and babies needed.

Amina protected us and kept watch for any new sisters who needed a sanctuary.

And I did nothing.

But not anymore.

Amina was right. It was time to grow up.

"I have not done a good job in my role as..." I still could not say "mother" to these women; the word dissolved into dust in my dry throat. It was hypocritical. "...Carer. But, with your help, you can show me how best I can serve you and—"

Voices from outside interrupted me. I was glad. I didn't know what else to say. I didn't know how to put it into words. But they were all amazing women, older and more experienced than me, and I was sure that they loved me and understood. Lottie looked me square in the eye, puffed on her used cigarette butt, and rasped, "That we can, my girl. That we will."

The others murmured their agreement as Amina opened the door and led in a girl, wide-eyed, pale skinned, with caramel coloured hair.

The shock froze me momentarily. "Carley! Welcome." The girl had been sixteen four years ago when I'd left the Temple. She'd been full of life and lip that was always getting her into trouble with the keepers, but won her favours from the Worshippers. I was sad to see that life had drained her energy, but glad to see that she was safe.

"Mother." She dropped to her knees. "Heart of the—"

Amina pulled the girl up from the floor. "Stop. That is not our way."

Carley looked around the room, her eyes growing as she caught sight of all the women she'd known at the Temple, two ex-Mothers, and Lottie. Her lips trembled and her hands shook. Our natural mother hen, Shauna, clucked over her, Aiko and Tomi wrangled the kids, and Vashti swiped my blades off the table and hid them out of sight.

"Are we going to have a new baby brother, Mama?" Joko broke free from Aiko's grip.

"More than likely, my boy." Amina caught her son as he launched himself into her arms.

Joko looked at Carley as she wept and was partly hidden, enfolded in the arms of his aunt Shauna. "Do not worry, we will take care of you. I am Banjoko, I am seven years old, and I am a warrior. My brother Hiro, sister Kazi, Uncle Indy and Mama are all warriors like me. We will protect you."

Hiro squealed his agreement from his prison on Kazi's lap. But it may also have been because at that moment, Kerm entered the room. Helen was with him, but the kids only had eyes for Kerm when it came to their adoptive grandparents.

"What's this? You started the celebration without us?" Kerm had not even got through the door before Hiro was in his arms and Kazi had wheeled her way to the door, in her new chair, chasing him. Thankfully, it was Helen who held the cake.

Introductions were made and Vashti took the cake, cut it up and served it with the scones and sandwiches. I greeted our newest guests with a kiss on the cheek and received a full embrace from Helen. Kerm was then pulled into some interesting investigations involving the kids and Indy. The five of them grabbed some scones and scooted out of the room before anyone could pretend to be too cranky.

Once the chaos had receded, we all sat and had an opportunity to catch up with Carley and to introduce her to the Factory. Each new member was invited to stay, but there was no obligation or expectation. The only thing we asked, if they stayed or not, was that they kept the Factory a secret. It didn't surprise any of us that Carley agreed to stay even before she'd had the opportunity to look around.

And just like that, we were ten, soon to be eleven. Sometimes it felt like the previous four years had passed in the blink of an eye, and other times it felt like we'd been here forever. I didn't know what the future held, but I did know it was time to figure out what my place in it was to be.

9

FELIX: INTRODUCTION

I worked for an incompetent baboon.

The nasal whine of the Overseer droned down the line. "I simply can't make the meeting today, something has come up."

I looked at my watch. Half an hour. The man had rung and cancelled thirty minutes before the meeting began. I didn't gratify him with a response. It was a given, and becoming more and more the norm. I would take his place.

"Felix?" A few tones lower, but none the less irritating.

I squeezed the phone tighter.

"I really am sorry. But you understand. Just fill me in on any details I need to be aware of at our next meeting." And... he hung up.

I do believe that was a first. A whole phone conversation, brief as it was, and I had not said a word. I doubt he'd even noticed. But then that was my job: to do, not be heard: to be, not be seen. But to be perfectly honest, I preferred it that way. It was the Overseer's job to be the face of the Community. It was my job to *run* the Community.

I buzzed Marlene. My PA ducked her styled grey head through our adjoining door. "Heading out? I'll reschedule your two-fifteen to three-thirty. And you've a dinner meeting with Bertrand at the

Atrium. Six-thirty. A car will be out the front in five minutes. Shall I organise another for this evening?"

I didn't mind that all my calls were... open. I had no secrets from Marlene. As I saw it, we were a team. Marlene was my enabler. I'd willingly admit to being an obsessive workaholic. But I was a successful obsessive workaholic due to Marlene's contributions. I had brought her with me from Systems Corp. A spinster married to the job. The woman was sharp, subtle, and intuitive in Manolos. In Marlene I found a meeting of minds I'd not come across with any other.

"Thank you. Traffic on a Friday evening will be... tedious."

She held my jacket as I prepared the papers necessary for the nightmare I was about to endure. It wasn't the meeting I dreaded. It was the board. No, that was not entirely true. It was one or two of the members who left an... unpleasant taste in my mouth.

I flicked through the agenda in preparation. But as she stood in my peripheral vision, I was once again drawn to the mystery of Marlene. At fifty-six, she was still fit and lithe. She never spoke of exercise and I knew she didn't belong to a gym. She definitely didn't have the time for... extra-curricular activities. Maybe it was her genetics? But most baffling was her green armour. It was the elephant in our partnership. Ever-present, never mentioned, always brilliant emerald. Again, it flashed as she spun out of the room to do my bidding.

All who were associated with the Light had it. Mine was orange... I believe. It was in fact a gauzy veil that could have been orange, gold or yellow. Why Marlene's was so... intense, I couldn't fathom. But in all seriousness, it was of no consequence. She was a marvel, and was the unseen anchor that kept me secure, the legs swimming madly below the surface that kept me afloat.

"Felix." Even after living in Laodicea for two decades, Audette maintained her French accent, exceptional looks, and St Laurent heels, despite their impracticality for a surgeon. Albeit one who worked mainly in research these days.

"Audette." We air kissed. She insisted.

"You are here for the meeting?"

"Sadly, yes. The Overseer is... tied up." We had intersected in the hallway outside the corporate offices at Laodicea's leading private hospital. Audette and her husband, Alain, were chief surgeons who had broken the ceiling of the medical world. They and their research team had pushed our city to the front of medical and surgical advancements worldwide. I say "had"; for the past four years, their outstanding progress had... slowed somewhat, to say the least.

"Sadly? Are you grieved to see me, Felix?" She pouted. It was an act. She knew damn well it was my father, Charles—the head of the Board—I'd rather not see. But it was a game we played. Audette was a no-nonsense woman... mostly, and I enjoyed her company.

I returned a flat stare.

She laughed. Then wisely changed the subject. Dropping her voice as we travelled along the carpeted hallway, "I am glad you are here. It has saved me a phone call. I have such wonderful news." The woman practically bounced. Rare for such a cultured creature. "The deal has gone under contract. Finally after four years of red tape and nonsense, with your help, and letters of recommendation, it looks like it will all go ahead. I am so excited." Her fingernails dug into my arm. "I will never be able to thank you enough. If there is anything, anything at all, please let me know." She exhaled and shook her head. Then turned her attention back to me. "How are you going with your medication? Is your, how do you call it... 'Crow'... under control? Do you need another script?"

"Please don't mention it, I am happy to help and, thank you. No. I have been well." My debilitating illness was currently subdued and for that I was supremely grateful. As I was for Audette's sensitivity in helping me manage my anxiety disorder. Not something I was keen to advertise. Much like our new... partnership. "Have you had news lately?" Like my anxiety, Audette's daughter was a sensitive topic. Both necessitated cards played tight to the chest.

Light flashed across her face and settled in her eyes. "Yes. She is well, and I believe she is content." A shadow passed across her face, she leaned in close to whisper in my ear, "To the best of my knowledge she is safe and still hidden. Not long now, and things will be better."

We had done what we could to make it so, and I hoped it was still the case. "Is Charles here yet?"

Business formality sapped all humour and talk of hope. "He arrived earlier and is meeting with Alain in the conference room."

How... convenient. My two thorns, ready and waiting. "How is Alain?" Audette's husband was cut from the same cloth as my father. What she saw in him, I had no idea. But really, I didn't care. I didn't have to live with the arrogant fop.

"Alain is... Alain." She smiled sadly.

All too soon, we arrived at the closed conference room door. Unrehearsed, we both stopped, stepped apart, and inhaled. I braced myself, shoulders squared, mask in place.

Audette followed a similar routine. After exhaling she subtly rolled her head and shoulders. Her long golden hair, restrained in a clasp, sashayed down her back. There was no doubt about it, she was an exceptional woman: intelligent, resourceful and beautiful, and one of the few I considered a friend.

At her nod, I went to open the door, but paused when an argument forced its way through the gap.

"...tell me you still can't find her?" My father's growl was intimidating to most, but independence and distance had made me immune.

"You know I need her found as much as you. More than you. My life's work is riding on this, Charles."

Not one who made a habit of eavesdropping, I went to push the door wider for Audette to enter. But stopped when she placed a slender hand on my arm.

We listened as Charles returned to the battle. "How hard can it be, damn it? I am losing money. A lot of money, every year your research dries up."

"And I'm starting to lose credibility." Alain's shout forced us both to take a step back.

We almost missed Charles' whispered rebuttal. "Whatever it fracking takes, you find her and get her back to the fracking Temple. You made a deal with the goddess: your daughter for medical genius. Thank your fracking stars that the blessing hasn't turned into a curse —yet. How much longer do you think Ashera is going to be patient with you? You do what it takes to get the goddess's favour back on board and fix this mess, Alain. I am not a charity. And my patience is running out. Find your daughter and get her back where she fracking belongs."

Audette's hand dropped from my arm. She'd managed to dampen the glee from her face but was incapable of dimming the light of victory in her eyes, nor the new steel in her spine. She had the confirmation she craved. After a moment's silence she nodded, and we entered the room.

Now seated, yet separated by several spaces at the table, both men had composed themselves... mostly. A hint of heat remained in their pallid faces.

Charles assumed a relaxed position, lounging with an arm eased across the back of the chair next to him, one ankle resting on the other knee, revealing to the world he was a Minyetti man.

Alain attempted to mirror him, but his clenched jaw faulted his facade. "Should I be worried you arrive with my wife, Felix?" The pompous fool. He had been imitating Charles for years, but still fell short of reaching truly distant, narcissistic egotism. But at least he had the right shoes.

You could tell a lot about a person by their footwear. I have noted, in general, there is a spectrum running from those who choose style in preference to budget, through to those who choose comfort in preference to style. However, regardless of where one sits upon this spectrum, shoes are indicators, status symbols, identity markers, cultural statements.

Alain and my father were a case in point. Charles had been a Minyetti man his whole life, as his father before him. His shoes a subtle yet blatant flag for wealth, social status and a subdued alliance to societal and cultural norms. There was nothing wrong with Minyettis of course. On the contrary, the brand crafted quality products. I, however, wore Berlins *because* my father chose Minyetti—my statement of disassociation.

Not taking his eyes from mine, Charles tsked. "Alain, this is Felix you're talking about. He wouldn't know what to do with a woman even if the Temple opened its doors and offered him a smorgasbord." Sharp, lethal, and insensitive as ever.

"Father. Alain." I entered the room and held a chair for Audette to take her place at the conference table. She blushed furiously and clenched her jaw. Her earlier victory had dulled, yet her spine remained ramrod straight. I turned my back on their feigned laughter and went to the drinks table. Returning, I set a tall glass of chilled water in front of Audette and took mine to a seat two down from hers.

The old man's eyes burned. "Such a waste." The pretence was dispatched, the show was over.

I sat very still and responded to his glare with an impassive mask and followed my own personal thread. Graduated dux from Laodicea Grammar a year early. Achieved Honours in a double degree of Finance and Business at LU. The youngest to rise to the position of general manager of Systems Corp. Moved sideways to manage all aspects of Laodicea's Community—the largest on the Northern Seaboard. I had nothing to be ashamed of.

Charles often bemoaned the fact I hadn't died instead of my brother. It wasn't that he loved my brother more than me. He was incapable of loving anyone other than himself. No. I suspect what he meant was, he was sad I didn't die *alongside* my brother. I believe the man harboured hostility to any who might outlive him. I suspect he'd even hated Mother. Although she'd had the grace to die before him.

Charles's ire was stacked against any who reminded him that he was aging and mortal. His peak had passed and there was no denying the best of his life was behind him.

So, I did my best to live well and excel in a field he hated: the Light. It was Mother's gift to my brother and me before she succumbed to cancer. I was not one who rapturously consumed the faith, but I ticked along in my own way. I pursued a career within the organisation because its benefits were twofold: the role suited me, and Charles hated it. Thus, serving as both an invigorating challenge and a useful weapon.

Collecting weapons to use against each other was a game I was forced to learn from an early age. Stand and engage, or fall by the wayside along with the other flotsam in Charles's wake. Stacked in my arsenal were my refusal to go away and my insistence on doing well. In fact, I was close to committing the greatest sin of all: outdoing him.

I would be lying if I denied enjoying the benefits of wealth. But rather than pursuing money for money's sake, it was a consequence of the ladder I had climbed. I saw it as a vehicle that offered choice. It provided opportunity and options otherwise not available. And it was a tool. Considering my new clandestine venture with Audette, a powerful tool in the game.

However, Charles saw it as a way of keeping score. And since coming under my management, the Community had flourished and had earned a place at this table, among others. As had I. It was another great wound in his side. To be outdone in his own field, using his own weapons, by progeny, was unforgivable. His barbs and attacks were evidence of his angst, and therefore to be taken as victories.

I smiled. "You're looking... well, Father?"

He burned.

The door opened as other members of the board and the Heads trickled through.

All weapons were sheathed for now, and the four of us pretended to be civil human beings working together from our lofty height for the betterment of humanity who swam at our feet.

10

MARCUS: ENOUGH IS ENOUGH

The Crew Arrive

The sun dragged its claws across the surrounding mountains like a belligerent cat moving on for the night. Orange exploded across the plain then slowly melted as dark velvet reached down to haul it into tomorrow.

A pillar of fire had been set like a carrot dangling in front of us through the night as Kait drove us out of Sodom. When the sun rose, our glowing guide had turfed its insides out and become a pillar of smoke. After a pause of three hours, it charged on, daring us to stop or rest and miss out. Not the types to back down from a challenge, we hadn't.

Instead, we'd travelled due north for about ten hours. For the following ten we traced the coastline and headed due east with Kait and me doing most of the driving. We'd tag-teamed every two hours when the tiredness had pinned us to the mat. Then finally tapped out at one-hour intervals. But you could bet your bippy, we'd neither one of us got much left in the tank.

The cold had numbed the pain in me hands and arms but, as I gripped the wheel of the truck, blood forced its way through me veins and beat a tedious tattoo. Raph had worked wonders healing the acid burns caused by demon blood. But they weren't one hundred percent better yet. I was with the cow and fiddle it wasn't worse and tried to be thankful that the pain had helped keep me awake on the final leg of this journey.

As we passed the signs to Laodicea, our guide dissolved like scotch mist, and the uglies came out to play. Demons of all makes and models: humanoids, Morro-mashups, giants, creepers, crawlers and flyers had been vomited from the bowels of hell to welcome us to Laodicea. And they looked as angry as a pack of wet wolves. I guess this meant we had the right address. They wouldn't've bothered with the extravaganza if we weren't in for a party.

"Well, happy birthday to us." It was a whisper, but it was enough to cause a stir. I didn't dare take me eyes off the road or our welcoming committee. Icy stillness had joined the stench of sulphur that had invaded the cab, alerting me to the fact Kait had woken up and was taking in the horror that surrounded us. The twins stirred from their nook behind the seats. Truth be, I'd rather they didn't see this, but it was going to happen sooner or later. So maybe sooner would give us more time to prepare for the fallout.

A cat tiptoeing over plush carpet would wake Val, so if she had been asleep in the back of the truck, she'd not be now. And I doubted the other two had slept much in the past twenty hours either. Sounds of life came through the "hole in the wall" joining the cab to the back of the truck as furniture moved.

"What the hell?" Daniel was obviously awake.

"What... what do we do?" Tessa too.

"Nothing." And Val made three.

Slowing down wouldn't serve our purpose. And speeding up wouldn't make them go away. So, like parting sand in a vast desert, I cruised through an ocean of ugly as we entered the outer suburbs of our new home.

Eyes ahead, I kept a true course and did me best not to sink below the waves of despair. I knew our guard was set about us and suspected a few more may have joined us for the welcome parade. Kait's hand found me leg and took a firm hold. I was tired to the bone, as was she, and the thought of taking this lot on sucked the wind from me sails.

Not only had we been driving for nigh on twenty hours, we were all still like dish cloths from the fight and wrung out from grief. Odd snippets of news had leaked through our dodgy radio and we'd pieced them together with snatches of information from fuel stations. The carnage had been restricted to Sodom and Gomorrah. I'd not realised Gomorrah had also gone the way of the dogs. All I knew was that the Light knew what He was doing and, for now, He was leading us into Laodicea. Which evidently was hell's home away from home.

I hadn't heard much of the city except the medical miracles they had been able to work at the research hospitals. Or so Kait told me. Apparently, they'd a pretty significant reputation.

Bully for them. Truth be, I couldn't give a continental. All I wanted was to bring this bus to a stop and sleep for a million years.

We navigated what turned out to be one of the three main arterials heading into the city. Streetlights did a great job of darkening shadows and completely disorientating me. I had no idea where to go, what to look for and how to find it.

I know you've got a place for us somewhere, but please don't let me mess this up and miss the signs. Please help me get me family to our new home.

We were sucked into the evening traffic like it was quicksand. It closed around us and did its best to assimilate us into its system. Which made it hard for us to go at our own finding-a-place-to-stay pace. It also made it tricky, not knowing the lay of the land, to stave off an attack if one should happen along. On the brighter side, the closer we moved toward the city's centre, the faster the demons evaporated. Which suited me just fine.

I suspected we would be given time and space to recover from our battle in Sodom. But truth be, we wouldn't be coming here without reason and that reason typically involved a fight. I just hoped we'd have time to recover from the last one before we were supposed to engage in the next.

"Okay love, I guess now'd be a good time to start looking for a place to stop." I took me eyes off the road long enough to study Kait. She looked terrible. "How'd you sleep?"

"Like I was sitting in an uncomfortable seat, one side of me frozen to the door, the other side stuffy from the heater, but I slept a lot better than you." She laughed. "Are you okay?"

"I will be when we can call it a night."

"Probably best if we start our search in the inner suburbs. That way we can see what we're up against, and we'll have easier access to supplies." Her focus was already scanning for a potential place to pull up.

"Sounds gold to me." I could barely keep me eyes open and me brain was hardly functioning. She could have told me to drive up to the nearest park bench to camp, and it would have been an invitation I wouldn't refuse.

We sailed along, eyes peeled for signs of a Soteria House. It wasn't just the feel that gave them away. Typical old-school Soteria Houses had a particular look: box-like building, large front doors, usually single storey and sometimes a spire—depending on the era and culture—and an off-street car park.

When we were able to ditch the highway and move through the suburbs, we'd have a better chance. The first one we drove past showed signs of use. That was promising as far as the climate of the city went, but it wasn't any good for us. We kept moving.

Families were settling in for the night. Cars were parked in drive-ways. Yards were still. And families were roosting in their coops behind pulled curtains. Again, without taking her eyes off our surroundings, Kait's hand found me leg. We were driving through what had become our barren pipedream. Instead of taking flight and bearing fruit, it had flushed our hopes away instead. A home with two-point-four kids and one-point-eight dogs was never going to be our reality. Not that I was too broken up about the dogs. But we'd always craved kids of our own.

It was hard not to hurt. This was what we'd been hungering for from the day we met. We knew we were in the best place possible and neither of us would have traded a day. But still, the what ifs had their way of gouging a hole in the guts of hope, starting again in a new town.

After we'd driven past the fifth in-use Soteria House, I'd had enough. "The next one, we're taking. I don't give a flying wet hen what it's being used for, we need to stop and rest. Whoever finds us can direct us to a place we can set up permanent camp."

"It's exciting to think they are all being used. Can you imagine the Community they must have here? It is the polar opposite of Sodom. I just can't believe it. But I agree. We need to get off the road and rest. The sooner the better." Kait removed her hand from me leg as she upped her focus on finding the next Soteria House.

"There!" She almost jumped through the window.

I had already put on the indicator and slowed for the turn. "I see it."

"Maybe you should park off the street, there seems to be room."

"Kait, I can find me own car park."

"I know, but look, there's more space around the back. We'd have more protection."

"Kait..." I turned to glare at her only to be met by her wicked grin and a wink of her tired eye. She was out of the cab as soon as I had pulled into a secure spot at the side of the building. While I turned off the engine and stretched, she went round and released the others from the back. Clouds of warm diesel fumes blended with chilly fresh air swamped the cabin in her wake. I took a moment to sit and look at the scene before me. On a slight hill, I could see down across much of the city, lit up like a carnival.

From me take on things, we were a stone's throw from the Central Metropolitan District. Bright multicoloured lights from high-rises dotted the night sky. It was a huge city. And now the truck's fumes had died down, I could identify a blend of fried food and a soft floral perfume tainted by a hint of exhaust in the frigid air. The others were moving and sorting things in the back, but me hands ached, me butt complained, and me neck cried out in protest. I could have shut me eyes and slept the sleep of the dead where I sat.

But there wasn't much point getting to a place of rest and not using it. So push came along and shoved me out of the truck. I went round the side and met up with the crew. We decided to set up the basics first, then bring the twins in to let them continue their sleep as uninterrupted as possible. We'd deposited the poor chooks in a fully fenced kid's play area at the back with fresh water and feed. I didn't take much notice of anything else apart from setting up me cot between the front door and the space where the others would eventually settle down. Punching me pillow into shape took the last of me energy before spending quality time with the inside of me eyelids in the land of Nod.

11

KAITLYN: NOT QUITE HOME

Everyone was exhausted. Pushed to the limit of coping. What we needed most was time and space to grieve, process and recover. Thankfully the long bench seats that typically filled a Soteria House of this style had been removed and the box-like room was lined with warm carpets and brightly painted walls. Numerous good-quality chairs were stacked in columns in the back corner beside a collection of small, collapsed folding tables resting on their sides. The alcove, which would have originally housed a piano or an organ, had been converted to a well-stocked kitchenette. And children's art populated the four walls. Nowhere near the quality of Sariah's, but it was bright and fun, and created a happy atmosphere.

Three radiators were spaced along each side wall. On my initial exploration I turned them all on, giving thanks for the warmth and joy of the space. As the chill decreased, remnant scents of cooking were released into the room: tomatoes and garlic? The kitchenette was too small for serious cooking, but a meal was recently created or consumed in this space. Blessed to still have leftovers from Raph's preparations made... was it only thirty hours ago in Sodom? I couldn't believe so much had happened in such a short time. I put some food aside for Marcus when he awoke for his turn at the watch, and made sure everyone else had something to eat and drink before bedding them down for the first night in our new home.

Despite the challenges we now faced, I was excited to meet this Community and hopefully be a part of what they were doing in this place. And until someone came along, this was a welcoming, cosy pit-stop. It was hard to believe that less than twenty-four hours ago we were in Sodom, fighting the enemy, losing Abbot and Ebony, and just making it out before the city fell. Or went up in a blazing inferno, as it turned out. It was no wonder we were all operating on autopilot.

Tessa and Dan had insisted Val take Abbot's chair for the journey, preferring to sit squeezed together on the floor. Despite padding the minuscule space out for them with blankets, Val was far more rested than they were, and offered to take the first watch of the evening.

We'd pulled two of the armchairs out of the truck as well as the cots. It would make it easier for those on guard but, in truth, none of us could muster the energy to repack them after clearing a space to access what we needed.

Val came in from checking the truck, the chooks and the perimeter. I couldn't help running my eyes over her knife-free body and marvelling at this wonderful oddity. We didn't know how long her respite from the Dark Lord's thorns was going to last, but I asked the Light that He'd allow her this freedom for as long as possible.

The doors were locked, and our regular guard was in place. We'd received extra reinforcements on our way in, but they had all disappeared by the time we pulled up. So, we were under the impression that we'd not be in too much danger. But we were ready just in case.

"Coffee Val?" I offered quietly while the others slept. I was tired, but since I'd dozed most of the last leg, I had volunteered to keep her company.

She took the cup from me and smiled. Moving freely, she stalked around the room before settling into the armchair next to mine. I knew she was tired, but I suspected she was making the most of pain-free movement. Something she couldn't afford to get too comfortable with, but a gift to be made the most of, nonetheless.

After a blessedly uneventful night, the sun rose over us and I was able to turn the radiators down and open the back door to let some fresh air in. I held off making morning drinks for as long as possible. I didn't want to wake anyone; they were all still dead to the world.

Marcus had taken over watch from Val and me at midnight. Then Dan and Tessa had relieved him at three-thirty. Then Val and I had stepped back in at six o'clock.

But we needed to be ready and packed up if someone came along this morning. I let them all sleep till seven-thirty, then boiled the kettle as Val studied the noticeboard hanging by the front doors. As I handed her a morning brew, she nodded her head toward the advertisements. "I don't think we have long. There is some sort of class due to start in just over forty minutes."

"Pity they couldn't have slept a bit longer, but the sooner we get introductions over and done with the sooner we can set up in a place of our own."

"True—" She stopped abruptly as a key started worrying the lock in the front door. Frozen, we looked at each other before the doors burst open.

"Who are you, and what do you think you are doing in our building?" A tall, shapeless woman—I assumed she was a woman by the outrageously coloured Lycra outfit she wore, and the oversized, floor-length fur coat hanging open over the ensemble—accosted us the moment the doors slammed open. Her narrowed eyes and severe face scanned and scalded us in turn.

"Oh my... oh my... oh my..." A smaller woman, clad in an equally garish costume, peeked out from behind, blanching at the sight of all seven of us standing on guard with blazing swords of Light drawn and ready to attack.

"Careful Irene. He has a knife," Woman One warned her smaller companion.

Eight sets of eyes looked from where she stood commandeering the entrance to where she was looking. Dan had not only drawn his sword, but his shiv was also out.

"What?" he responded matter-of-factly. "I didn't know what we'd be up against. I wanted to be prepared."

"Good thinking," Val responded.

Shaking her head and relaxing, possibly sensing she wasn't about to be mugged, Woman One continued her rant. "Who are you? How did you get in here? And what do you think you are doing? You can't be here. We have Zumba in half an hour."

"Oh my. Shelby? Perhaps we should cancel Zumba this morning? And ring the Overseer? I think he might like to meet these people?" Woman Two, still shielded behind her companion, tried to speak reason to her blind friend.

"Don't be ridiculous. We will not waste the Overseer's precious time with the likes of these. Look at them. Ragged, filthy squatters. Not only that, we have a performance to prepare for, the fair is just over three weeks away. We can't afford the time," said Woman One.

Apparently, it was now Marcus's turn to start a rant. "Who are you? And what are you doing here? You shouldn't be able to get in here without a sword or armour." He was exhausted, wounded, had been woken abruptly—without coffee—and had very little patience. His eyes narrowed and his fists clenched, now free after re-sheathing his sword.

"What on earth are you talking about, you stupid man. Sword? What sword? I. Have. A. Key." She held up the key in question. "Is he soft in the head?" she asked the rest of us. Then turned to her friend. "Do you think he's soft in the head?"

She was obviously blind in more ways than one. Even if she couldn't see the armour, Marcus's body language was screaming for her to back down. If he wasn't about to do them bodily harm, it might have been funny.

Please bring some sense to this situation. Please help us get this sorted so we can rest.

"Shelby. Go outside and ring the ladies now. We are cancelling this morning's classes. Then ring the Overseer and invite him to come here and join us immediately." Having discovered her backbone, Woman Two stepped out in front of her friend and attempted to take charge, her faint yellow armour flickering.

"Irene? What do you mean by this?" As previously demonstrated, Woman One was not easily deterred.

"Now, Shelby." It seemed Woman Two had discovered she had matching claws. When her friend continued to stare at her with a gaping mouth, Irene physically turned her around and gently pushed her on her way, shutting the door behind her. "I am so sorry. Please forgive us?" Irene bowed her head and talked to her feet. "My friend is not of the Light and cannot see you as you are. Otherwise, she would not have been so rude?"

"Irene...?" She nodded when I confirmed her name. "Thank you for your intervention. It was both timely and wise." The roundness of her body mirrored her plump cheeks and short, curly, grey hair. She didn't look up; she merely bobbed her head.

Val spoke softly. "We understand that you have something happening here soon and we'd happily move to another location if you could just tell us a suitable place to go? Or wait to meet your Overseer."

Irene shook her head, her short curls bobbing wildly. "No. It's okay. Really. You look like you have travelled far, you can wait here where you've already set up?" Her face darkened to a rose blush. "I don't think it matters how much practice we do; our performance is going to be a bit of a comedic routine at best." She bustled her way to the kitchenette. "May I get you something hot to drink and warm to eat?" The words tumbled over each other, hit the floor, and landed soothingly in our ears.

"Finally, someone's speaking sense," Marcus barked out.

I glared at my husband. *Careful! Can you not see how precarious this situation is?*

He continued in a milder tone, "That'd be great Irene, thanks a million." He looked back at me. *Better?*

I winked.

How about this then? "Excuse us, Irene, we might take the kids out to the bathroom to wash up." He tilted his head and ducked, trying to make eye contact with her. But she resolutely refused to be drawn, she merely nodded again.

Marcus, Dan and Tessa took the twins out the back to the toilet block while Val and I went to help Irene in the eatery. She still wouldn't look at us, and whenever Val came close to her, Irene flinched.

"I might pack up the cots and reload the truck," Val suggested, aware of the discomfort she was causing. But I sensed she was also eager to get going.

Once I was alone with our host, I introduced myself and told her a bit of our story, leaving out the gorier details. Once again, I thanked her for her help. It didn't seem to warm her up much. When I said we'd escaped from Sodom, she risked a glance. I was presented with a round, white face and huge brown eyes for an instant, before I was once again talking to the top of her curly head. Whoever this Overseer was, I hoped he got here soon so we could put this woman out of her misery.

"We really appreciate the meal and your hospitality. We've been on the road for twenty hours and crashed here last night. And we truly are sorry to put you out, but we didn't know where else we could go."

"That's not a problem at all, the ladies will be happy for the morning off. And we store meals in the freezer for families in need. I had one thawing in the fridge from yesterday to give to one of the ladies this morning in class. I can easily get another one out and give it to her frozen." At this she looked up to me again with a hint of a genuine smile. "I guess the Light knew we'd need it this morning."

The others stayed outside for as long as possible, but they were cold, tired and hungry. By the time they made their way back in, we'd made hot chocolate and coffee and the meal was almost heated in the oven. Sadly, it was a meat casserole, but I would just have to eat what I could. I had a strict vegan diet to help me discern Words from the Light, and I was hungrier for information and guidance in a new place than food, but I would not rebuff hospitality. I would just make up for it when I could.

"Should we invite Shelby in for a hot drink?" Val asked Irene.

"I could, but she won't come in. She'll wait outside in her car until the Overseer arrives so she can fill him in." Again, she risked a rueful smile. "I think it best if we just leave her be for now?"

The meal was devoured, the plates were cleaned and dried and returned to the cupboard, and all traces of our visit were removed. Irene put out some chairs and invited us to sit while we waited. Raph came to sit in my lap and I sensed the heaviness of his heart. I cradled him as best I could, allowing him freedom to grieve. I knew his struggle in the wilderness between wanting to be a man and still needing to be a child was made all the worse by his need for comfort.

Riah walked to where Val sat, off to one side. Normally she would have gravitated to Abbot, and it was in this quietness that we were all hit by the tsunami of his passing. Val opened her arms and Riah climbed onto her lap and together they shared a time of silent tears. Tessa and Dan sat close, her head on his shoulder, his arm around her. Marcus stood on guard. It was evident that while this was a Soteria House, it was not safe enough for us to rest. We needed to find the place the Light had set aside for us here and, until we did, we couldn't fully let our guard down.

Irene, no longer being able to bear our company, decided to wait outside for the Overseer's arrival. The twins had quietly cried themselves back to sleep and we all dozed in our seats waiting. I was trying to maintain my enthusiasm for meeting the man, but it was waning as the day wore on. We no longer had need of the heaters and I was thinking about what I could scrounge for our next meal, when Irene came back inside.

"I have just received word. I'm so sorry, but the Overseer has been held up and he can't meet you here, he has asked that I take you to his office?"

"Of course. We understand." The man must be very busy overseeing the Community of Light in such a large city. We were happy just to be here and didn't expect preferential treatment. We just wanted a vacant building to call our own and an oar to pull in this ocean. We packed up the kids and the chooks and made sure all evidence of our stay was removed. Marcus, Raph and Riah volunteered to go in the back while Val and Dan took the front seats with

Tessa easily sliding into the nook behind for the short trip into the city centre.

Shelby, having given up the wait, had driven Irene home so she could get her own car, and thankfully a change of clothes, so she could pilot us into Head Office. I couldn't suppress a bubble of excitement as we approached a large historical building with a grand stone facade. "The Community must be doing really well here in Laodicea if it can afford to rent space in a building like this."

"Um, yes? But actually, the Community owns the building. This is Head Office for all our organisations and Heads of Staff?" Irene's face flushed at our open stares.

"The whole building? As in the whole"—Tessa craned her neck to count—"seven floors?"

"Yes. We've been very blessed with an extraordinary administrator." Irene turned and continued leading the way.

"I'd say more than blessed," Marcus growled out the side of his mouth.

I shoulder bumped him. *Behave yourself.*

Seriously, Kait? Check this place out.

I have. But we've only just arrived. Can we please wait to start offending the locals?

Eight sets of shoes echoed in the cavern as we walked across the vast white marble floor. Reflected light bounced around the opulence making me feel small and, considering my state—filthy, ragged and exhausted—a blemish on the perfect surroundings.

All the kids were a bit on edge as we were herded into a lift. Thankfully, they were too tired to take much of it in. Raph's eyes grew and Riah turned and buried her head into Val's side at the new experience. The tight squeeze enabled us to subtly hold them close as we rose to the seventh floor. A chime announced our arrival and the doors opened, releasing us into a lavish foyer carpeted with lush cream carpet that absorbed all noise.

12

FELIX: OVERSEEING OPPOSITION

"Sodom. They've come from Sodom. I don't want that filth in my city."

I tried breathing slowly and counting to ten. But I was fed up with the Overseer and his narrow-minded perspective. And to be perfectly honest I was rapidly tiring of the man's infantile behaviour. "Perhaps, before you judge them unworthy of... your city, it might be prudent to meet them?"

"You know damned well I have just got off a conference call with the High Council. Four don't approve of us accepting them."

"Yes. I am aware. I was part of the conversation. However, it is my understanding that leaves seven members who approve of us welcoming them?"

"Disgusting filth, the lot of them. Good riddance to both Sodom and Gomorrah, they were a blight on the planet. We don't need the likes of them here, Felix. I don't like it and I don't want the problems they are going to bring."

"What problems might those be, Overseer?"

"Well, I don't know man. For goodness' sakes. They'll probably start infecting people with their... practices." Finally, the Overseer stopped pacing and stood looking out the massive window surveying "his kingdom". "The Gerent is scheduled to tour our city in two months. What if these vagrants cause a disruption? What if they tarnish our reputation? You know very well how hard we are working to be accepted as a reputable religion on this continent by the Gerent and his Delegates. Their approval means everything to us: life or death, Felix. We can't afford any slip-ups at all. We are only here and prospering because of the Gerent's goodwill and his generous offer of a trial period." He huffed like a child.

"Do you fear the past fifteen years' credit means nothing to our liege?"

"Don't you see? Fifteen years, Felix, and we still haven't been given official accreditation. We are stuck in provisional status. Why do you think I am working so hard to lift public opinion of the Community? We need our Gerent's endorsement to be safe. We are vulnerable until we can get his final approval. All of this is for nothing if we can't get ourselves over the line. And we most definitely don't need any trouble coming in from Sodom."

"May I suggest that, as our Gerent's visit is still two months away, and the majority of the High Council are in favour, that you take the risk of welcoming these people? Then, after a while, see if in fact they are a negative influence on the Community—before the Gerent arrives. If needs be, you can take whatever action you and the Board deem necessary at that point in time."

He fell into his chair and turned to look up at me, his eyes pools of hopelessness. "I don't know, Felix. I just don't know. Raymond, Nyle and Edward strongly suggest I don't allow them to stay. And quite frankly, I agree with them." He swivelled his chair until he was looking back out the window. "And where would I put them? I don't want them too close to the Temple of Light or Head Office in case people learn there's a connection. Heaven forbid people think we're like them... behave like them and... do what they do." He turned back to me. "I just want to protect the name of the Community, Felix. We've both worked so hard to raise our profile and reputation within the city and the wider region. Your work with the hospital and universities could be damaged because of this association."

I had a passing moment of sympathy for the man. I did understand his quandary and our predicament with the Gerent. Yet, to be perfectly honest, I felt he was making far too much of the situation. "There is a recently vacated house in the Jacaranda district, and I believe the cleaning crew should be finished with it by now. It will be suitable for them. An acceptable distance away from the Community's centre, it's still close enough to keep an eye on them. It could be an ideal solution if you saw fit."

Another weighty sigh.

I didn't need to follow any threads for the Overseer, I just needed to work at reining in my frustration at the man's weakness and short-sightedness. "I believe this small group, two of whom are children, will fit well there. Also, the Community here is several thousand strong, and the city of Laodicea has a population of almost five million people. I do believe the odds are stacked in our favour if something were to go amiss with this group of seven. But, as always, the decision is in your hands. We will follow your lead."

He looked thoughtful, as if he were actually doing the math.

I dared to add, "We could always petition the Light for guidance?"

His rebuke was cut off with a buzz from the foyer. They'd arrived. His time was up.

"What is your decision? Be guided by the majority of your High Council or stand with the minority?" I had just pinned his tail to the wall, and it looked like he felt every bit of it.

"Yes, of course. The majority is always our priority. You'd best go greet these... visitors."

13

DANIEL: FINAL COUNTDOWN

Would this freggling day never end? Bone weary, famished, and fed-up, I'd had enough.

We stood in awe, looking out the ginormous windows of the top floor at the city below us. We were bunkered in lush, cream luxury. The thick carpet, high walls, the desk and the chick who sat behind it —it was a bland, silent, cream cocoon.

Val's whisper carried to the edge of our group. "Incoming."

I squared up behind her. Kait was caught off guard, and jumped, but still kept one arm wrapped around Raph's shoulders, her other hand in Marcus's. All three looked done in. I couldn't blame them. Kait and Marcus had had hardly any sleep after driving pretty much non-stop from Sodom, after an epic battle against the spawn of hell, and losing Abbot. I was surprised they were still standing.

A hawk nose, beady eyes and a blank face appraised us like something the cat dragged in. I guess, in a way, we deserved that. Irene stood in front of us torturing a hanky, repeatedly twisting and wringing it into a ball, her focus on a piece of carpet in front of her curling toes. The silence... the surroundings... everything in this place was whacked.

"Irene." The baritone greeting was at odds with the crow-like appearance of the man who acknowledged the old girl. Her mismatched get up was dead set opposite to Crow Man's immaculate suit, tamed black hair and expensive shoes. His faint orange armour also warred with my memory of Abbot.

"Felix?" Irene squeaked in response. I'd only been around the woman for a millisecond and didn't know her from squat, but seeing her cringe like a mouse in the claws of a crow had me seeing red. Val loosened her limbs in front of me as she guided Riah behind her left hip. Not a good sign.

This caught Felix's eye. With his focus firmly locked on Val, he continued to address Irene, dismissing her in action and words. "Thank you, that will be all."

Handed her "get out of jail free" card, Irene turned to face us, still not looking us in the eye. She mumbled something about helping us out if needed, then high-tailed it to the waiting lift. The standoff was maintained until she was safely removed from the field.

"The Overseer is expecting you, if you'll follow me?" Turning a super shiny heel, he glided down a short hallway and stopped outside a non-cream coloured door. When we all arrived beside him, he tapped once, then, without waiting for a response, let us in.

"Ah, Felix, there you are." A fat, bald dude rose from a humongous desk and held us at a distinct disadvantage, silhouetted against the setting sun exploding through the windowed wall. I couldn't get a read on him.

I didn't know about the others, but the whole thing put me on edge: the mouse, the freak, the luxury, the smell of sulphur everywhere... everywhere... and the dim armour these goons wore. I'm pretty sure my first day in the Light I had brighter armour than these guys. Even though we weren't in enemy territory, I was not happy about walking into a room, blind to my opponent. Hopefully this guy would help us out. I just wanted to go home, any home, lock the doors and pass out.

"Come in, come in, have a seat. Felix, please ring down for refreshments." The Overseer seemed nice enough... accommodating and all. If only he'd move out from behind that fortress so I could see him. Crow dude reached across and used the Overseer's phone to put the order through, then stood behind Baldy's shoulder. Great. Now they were both hidden by shadows.

Silhouetted arms waved to the sides indicating we should sit on the couches and chairs scattered throughout the huge room. No one moved. We looked at each other and it was then I really noticed the strain on Tessa's face. I guided her to a comfortable looking armchair and, placing my left hand on her shoulder, encouraged her to sit. Leaving my hand in place, I stood guard beside her.

On the same wavelength, Kait led the twins to one of the couches and pulled them down, one either side of her. Sariah's head fell into Kait's lap while Raph was tucked under her other wing. Marcus stood guard at the end of the couch between her and the Overseer, and Val covered the other side of the room. Obviously, we were in agreement about the situation. I still wasn't comfortable, but it made me feel better.

"Come now, you can relax. You're with family and in safe hands now. Irene has told me a bit of your story. You must be exhausted. But believe me, we'll take good care of you."

No one moved.

With a sigh, the Overseer repeated, "Please, be comfortable. Relax," his head moving from Marcus, to me, then to Val. And back again when we didn't accept his invitation.

"Thank you." Val, as always, was polite when she wasn't trying to be blunt. After travelling in the back with her all the way from Sodom, I knew she was walking on broken glass waiting for the Dark Lord's knives to come back. We would all be happier when we could go somewhere to lick our wounds in safety. It wasn't time to stand down yet. But we couldn't... shouldn't refuse the guy's hospitality. Val sat on the edge of a big armchair. I looked to Marcus, and he looked at me. We both looked back at the Overseer, still on our feet.

The tension was disrupted by a quiet tap on the door. Before any of us could react, it was opened by a young woman wheeling in a trolley with all the makings for tea and coffee, and plates of sandwiches. I almost wept as the heavenly aroma of espresso coffee hit me. I was seriously hanging out for the real deal.

Cheers for that!

"Thank you, Beverly. Just leave it there." The Overseer still didn't move as he gave the instructions.

"Yes, sir." The chick bobbed her head like a robin then walked out.

Crow dude and the Overseer still didn't move.

I looked around the room. Kait was held hostage by the twins, Tessa was sinking, Marcus and Val weren't moving, so I guessed it was up to me. I "played mum", as Grandpa used to say, and poured coffee and hot chocolate and handed out sandwiches.

The Overseer continued trying to melt the ice. "I believe you've met Felix?" His soccer-ball head turned, so at least we could see his profile. Felix stayed perfectly still. "And you know I'm the Overseer..."

"Yes... yes, of course. My name is Kait, this is my husband Marcus" —who was now perched on the arm of the couch where Kait sat— "my sister Valarie, and our kids, Tessa, Daniel, Raphael and Sariah." Without removing her hands from the twins, Kait used her chin to indicate who she was introducing.

"Thank you, Kait, it's a pleasure to meet you. As I said, I've been told a bit of your story and I look forward to hearing more. But first things first. I believe you escaped Sodom with not much more than the clothes on your back." He waited for confirmation before continuing. "You are safe and among family here. We'll take good care of you. We have been abundantly blessed by the Light and have a number of properties. After hearing your story and now meeting you, I can confirm that we have the perfect house for you to make yourselves at home in. I've had a team freshening it up for you and stocking it with supplies. When you have finished your snack, Felix will show you the way."

That did the trick. The tension evaporated like drinks at a free bar, and for the second time in as many minutes I almost wept. The food was inhaled and the drinks sculled, with the promise of a place to put our heads. Within moments we were ready to go.

Marcus and Kait offered for Tessa and me to travel up front with them. Marcus drove, Tessa sat across the back, and I was on the passenger side with Kait in the dicky-seat—the narrow perch between the two front seats. I was in a daze, but not enough to miss the fact that Felix guided us through the maze of Laodicea in a supremely sweet black sedan. And there was not a demon in sight despite the ever-present stench of sulphur. It wasn't long before we left the city centre and entered the flash suburbs. A bit like where Ebony lived back in Sodom... or what used to be Sodom... but without the huge walls.

This whole place was warped. Everything was so clean. What city didn't have litter, for crying out loud—garbage, graffiti, or human? Man-made canals wove their way between the spotless buildings. They even had gardens lining the streets, some in the middle of the road. This place was unnatural. We turned into an avenue decorated with huge trees. They reminded me of the jacarandas back in the park I'd called home for seven years before hitching up with this crew. Even naked they were impressive... along with everything else.

Felix pulled up against the kerb in front of a white mansion set on an emerald lawn. I was surprised to see him jump out and wave for us to pull into the driveway. First, because he moved so quickly, but mostly due to the suspicion that these were our new digs.

Well, fregg me. Thank you.

And thank you very much Mr Overseer. This was definitely a step up.

We poured ourselves out of the truck and, after letting Val and the twins out of the back, started grabbing bags.

Felix joined us and looked in the back of what had been our mobile home. "Just bring what you need for tonight, then..." He froze. "What on earth are you doing with chickens?"

Not realising the question was most likely rhetorical, Raph spoke slowly and clearly. "Chickens lay eggs. They eat our food scraps. Their manure is very helpful for our vegetable garden. Not only this, they are our pets. Do you not have chickens where you come from Mr Felix?"

It was pure gold. I had to pay the guy some credit though, after the initial shock, he didn't sneer like I expected him to. But he wasn't very encouraging either. "Hmmm." He closed his eyes and breathed deeply through his nose. "Thank you... Raphael, wasn't it?" Raph nodded. "Do you have any other livestock in here?"

Raph shook his head. Felix then turned and led us into the house. Everyone grabbed a bag, and I grabbed the cage and some food for the girls. Out the back was a fenced off pool area, perfect for the chooks until we could figure out something else. After that we all slipped into autopilot: a quick tour, dumping the bags in random rooms, showers, devouring a pre-cooked meal. And then, finally, at long last, sleep.

I WOKE TO SEE A THREE-HEADED, multi-limbed creature draped over the bed next to me. Tangled arms and legs somehow managed to find space and comfort enough to sleep.

The master bedroom had been taken by Kait and Marcus. And even though there were enough rooms for everyone to have their own, Raph and I shared a twin room. Val, Tessa and Riah shared a medium sized room with the women each taking a bed, while Riah chose to nest in her beanbag.

During the night, however, there'd been a change of plan. Sariah had come to get Raph and had insisted I join them. Seeing her so lost broke me and I couldn't refuse. But this morning it was utter chaos. I could just discern Sariah's outline nestled under the covers of the bed Val had started out in, with a mop of Tessa's hair up against the wall beside her. Raph was curled up in a ball at their feet, covered in blankets from his original bed. Somehow, I had ended up partially in Sariah's beanbag, partially on the carpeted floor.

"Good morning."

I jumped at the whisper and turned to Tessa's original bed, not surprised to see Val had managed to get a space and keep it to herself. I expected it would take the twins a while to recover from the cluster-bomb of Sodom and the upheaval of Laodicea. It was going to take us all time to get that skrat sorted. But I voted for working out better sleeping arrangements for tonight.

The wounds on my back protested when I tried to unfold myself. Still tender from where I had been slashed by the mother of all demons back in Sodom, I was especially stiff this morning. Marcus had been right: I would have some pretty cool scars. Was it wrong to be proud? I saw them as a trophy and a reminder of what and how we'd survived.

I rasped, "Morning. How'd you sleep? Or should I ask, did you sleep?"

"Enough, thanks. Still pretty tired, but nothing a good coffee won't fix." Val stretched her limbs, and I made a quick note that they were still knife-free. So, the Dark Lord hadn't been permitted to turn up the heat just yet.

"Ditto to that. So, what's the plan? Do we reconnoitre while it's still quiet or do we wait till someone wakes up?" I tried to reposition myself to get comfortable in the bean bag. It wasn't working.

"Well, the Overseer said to help ourselves and, as far as I can see, someone else is up."

I looked around trying to see who she was talking about, before I twigged she was referring to me. "Oh yeah, right. Let's go."

It was weird sneaking around the foreign house when everyone was asleep. But the thick carpet and lush furnishings made it easy to go stealth. A burglar's dream. I'd never experienced such luxury. They even had some funky heating system that came up through the floor and warmed the whole house. It was colder here than Sodom, but the rich kids wouldn't have to worry about that. Made me think of the poor suckers doing it tough on the streets. Not that I'd seen any on the trip here. Maybe there were no poor people in Laodicea.

We made our way to the kitchen and Val put together the makings of coffee while I hunted for seven mugs and some sort of tray.

"I thought I heard someone." Kait joined us and gave Val a morning hug and a quick examination. With a nod, she moved to me and gently embraced me, thoughtful of my back.

"Go ahead." I nodded after she had indicated that she wanted to check my wounds.

"It's an absolute miracle. You should be dead. But not even two full days since your attack and there's no sign of infection and only slight swelling. It's closing over nicely, Dan, but still be careful, and just light training and duties for a couple of days, okay?"

"Sure thing, Mum." She cuffed my shoulder then embraced me again, before helping with the drinks.

"Cool scars though." Val smiled over Kait's shoulder. "And you survived your initiation. We're really proud of you, Dan."

"Thanks, Legend."

Val chuckled and returned to the coffee, humbly acknowledging my complement. Where the rest of us merely survived the battle, she had totally kicked everyone's butt and served them up on a platter.

"Are you worried about when the knives'll come back?" I had to ask.

"No use being worried about it, they'll come when they come. Although, to be honest, I'm a bit on edge about the timing." She stopped and looked out the back doors for a beat, before addressing me. "But there's nothing I can do but trust the Light: that He'll see to it that it won't come at a time where it will put any of us in danger. Won't lie and say I'm not enjoying the break though." She winked then poured the brew.

I had found a tray, so I carried the drinks back toward what had become our room. Kait went to rouse Marcus and invited him to join us, and Val ducked ahead to wake the others, so they were ready when their morning mojo arrived.

Soon we were all perched up, sipping away. The window was small—well, small compared to the glassed wall we were used to in Sodom, and it looked out over the road. So, this morning, instead of sitting quietly contemplating the scene, we quietly took turns sharing things to give thanks for: Raph's gift, Sariah's song, Abbot's life and sacrifice, Val's kick-butt-i-ness when it came to battle, Kait and Marcus driving us safely, and Tessa, just for who she was. That was mine. But I shared it with the group. The cool thing was no one made fun of me for saying so. They all just agreed.

"And for Dan," Raph added.

I looked down where he sat next to me and wrapped my arm around his shoulder. "Thanks, Little Master, that means a lot." Looking around the group I continued. "I really do thank the Light for bringing me into His world. And you guys for taking me in and saving me from the nightmare that ate Sodom whole." An involuntary shiver rattled me. I still couldn't get my head around the fact that Sodom was completely gone, or the terror of its destruction. It was too much to comprehend. I put it in the too-hard basket for now. I'd pull it out and think about it later. Maybe.

We were in a strange city, in a stranger's house, and we'd all slept late. But it didn't mean we couldn't maintain a semblance of routine. Returning to our original rooms, we rugged up in warm clothing, dropped our cups off in the kitchen, then met at the back doors for our... late... morning sets.

The chilly air was damp and sweet. As we got into our places, I took the chance to properly check out the massive garden. The chooks were still huddled up in their make-shift hutch. Smart birds. I wondered what they thought of all the moving around and being confined... if they thought anything at all.

I then turned to check out the imposing back of the house, noting that our Warrior guards were relaxed, and wondered again that people in the Light could live like this.

14

DANIEL: WELCOME TO LAODICEA

Reality Bites

The night was still. But something had woken me. In the bed across the room, I could hear Raph breathing deeply. Sulphur burned my eyes and singed my nose.

Skrat.

The end of my bed dipped.

Frack.

The pounding of my heart drowned out every other noise, but I could feel something working its way up my bed.

Frackety frack.

Sweat prickled my whole body. My eyes watered and blurred the moonlit room. A face emerged out of the darkness.

Frack a fracking skratty cat.

"Hello, gorgeous. Did you miss me?" She was back. I mean "it". Apparently, demons are neither he nor she. But since I had an issue with fighting women, and the Dark knew my weakness, my personal demons tended to be dressed up and served as chicks.

"Well, aren't you going to say hello?"

It was purring.

It was drinking up my fear and bloody purring. The twik.

"No need for name calling. I just dropped by to say hi and to personally welcome you to Laodicea."

She had been one of a group who had confronted me on the streets of Sodom. It hadn't ended well. My eyes flew around the room. She was alone. My guard stood by the door. His face was hard and cold, yet with arms crossed and sword sheathed, I figured this wasn't a life-or-death situation.

"That's right, sweetie, you're safe with me."

Okay. I wasn't in mortal danger. But I wouldn't go so far as to say I was safe.

She chuckled. A sinuous hand reached out of the darkness.

Fighting to stay calm, I made an effort not to overreact. That's what she wanted.

She reached for me.

Stay calm, she's not going to hurt you.

A talon caressed my cheek

I was going to hurl. She reeked of death.

Her face leaned in.

I couldn't breathe. My heart hurt, it was pumping so fast. I was a pool of sweat.

"I'll be seeing you, gorgeous."

And she was gone.

Oh God, oh God, oh God, oh God...

That was the frackiest fracking fracked up frack... ever.

My guard's body language comforted me. He wasn't happy either, but he and his ridiculously impressive sword weren't going anywhere. I was safe. But I couldn't sleep. I was so pumped I couldn't sit still. My heart wouldn't listen to my head, no matter how rational my internal screaming was.

I had to get out into my comfort zone: the streets.

I crept out of the house with my guard at my hip and we went for a run. A long, hard run.

15

CONTESSA: MEET THE TEAM

Oh. My. Word.

How could they expect us to live like this? We'd finished our sets and walked in to find a team of people sitting in our. Flopping. Lounge. And, not only that, they'd made themselves at home to our. Flopping. Supplies.

I know. Seriously. It was just plain rude.

I actually had to stop and check that I'd walked into the right house. I mean, they kind of all looked the same from the front, so I guessed they'd look the same from the back too.

"Can I help you?" Marcus stepped forward and we all gravitated into formation. Swords weren't drawn... yet. Although, these guys were mortal. I flicked my eyes to Dan to see if he'd drawn his knife. He hadn't. But his hand was hovering behind his back where it lived. We were ready for a fight.

Teacups rattled as the group stopped their chatter and stared. Their faces paler than their pathetically faint armour.

"Ah..." A high-pitched gurgle came from one of the suited men. He coughed then tried again. "Good morning. We knocked but no one answered." He looked to his crew for confirmation. They all nodded like bobble-head dolls. "You looked busy, so we thought we'd wait till you finished."

Like that made up for being impolite. Right? I mean, who did that?

"How did you get in?" I hope they realised Marcus's bark was nowhere near as bad as his bite.

"Silly"—he shook his head like he was addressing a toddler—"we have a key." They all tittered like a flock of old chickens.

Oh my.

These guys were, like, all kinds of stupid.

Marcus marched forward and shoved his hand out very near the speaker's face. It was open. Palm up. Not like he was going to hit him or anything. But still, the man fell back into his chair and threw his hands up. "What? Don't hurt me." So maybe there was some sense swimming around in there after all.

"Give me the key." Marcus's growl was almost a purr but laced with pure threat. Classic Marcus.

"I can't do that. I need it. How can I get in without the key?"

"Where we come from, if you walk into another man's house without an invitation, you could wind up dead. Give. Me. The. Fracking. Key." Eeeks! Marcus never swore off the battlefield. His growl lost all purr, and barbs wrapped their way around the acid. I could barely hear him, but Stupid did. He handed over the key.

"I will report this to the Overseer."

"You do that." He eyeballed the group of five. "Now." I don't think they understood that Marcus's "now" meant they should leave, now. Not like he was moving to the next thing on the agenda.

They didn't move. Their faces were set in horror. So, he helped them clarify his meaning. "Do you need me to show you the way to the door?"

On cue, the doorbell rang. Without taking his eyes off the group, Marcus gave the order. "Dan."

I gave Dan's hand a quick squeeze before he dashed off. Moments later he returned with Felix.

"Do I need to call a cleaning crew?" Felix's droll tone spread through the tension like water seeping across tissue paper. When his words sank in, he had our confused attention. His eyebrow rose a millimetre, then he explained. "For the blood." He peered around Dan. Marcus was still standing over Intruder Spokesperson. We hadn't stood down, and the rest of their crew were frozen. "Well done, Marcus, I applaud your restraint." This pulled a low chuckle from Val, and the tension eroded another degree.

"Welcome, Felix." She walked across the room and shook his hand.

She was so cool. Not only was she completely scary in battle, she was also a supreme tactician. But then again, for Val, maybe it was all the same thing. Life was warfare.

"Forgive the intrusion. These... helpers"—Felix's voice dripped with sarcasm—"were instructed to wait for me outside."

"We never wait outside, Felix. We have a job to do, and we were kind enough to wait till they finished their"—Stupid Intruder flapped his hand in the direction of the backyard—"dance routine. But, for crying out loud, this house belongs to the Community. Everything belongs to the Community and it's only by the Overseer's grace they have been given anything at all. They own nothing and owe us everything." His cheeks gained colour as he gained momentum.

"That may be, Ty, but you were given specific instructions for a reason. These people have travelled far and are used to a different way of doing things. We owe them our respect." Felix remained calm and quiet, but by the tick in his temple and the response of the group, it looked like he wasn't used to being challenged.

"Are you serious? Look at them." The flapping hand was now directed at us.

"Oh, I am, Ty. Are you?" The standoff stilled the room. The atmosphere was so tense you could bounce a ball off it. Felix broke away and turned back to us. "My apologies, again." Perhaps droll was his default mode. "We might adjourn outside and give you time to freshen up. If it suits you, we'll be back in half an hour to introduce you to the team. They are here, believe it or not..."

Oh. My. Word.

I can't believe the guy just rolled his eyes. But, like, not with his eyes, with his voice. I know. It was actually kind of cool. Not that I would admit it to him, but I was quietly going a bit fangirl. I could definitely learn a thing or two from him. No wonder he was so high up in the Community. He was all kinds of skilled.

"...to help get you settled into life here and make that transition as smooth as possible." He turned to face the five, in various states of shock, disbelief and offence. He held out his arm, indicating the entry and, like a line of ducklings preceding their mother, they left the house.

I tried not to listen to their heated argument that continued outside, but when I opened the window and leaned against the screen, I could hear snippets of conversation. "Ignorant" and "clueless" seemed to be the theme of most of what Felix had to say. But I couldn't hang around too long, I had to take my turn through one of the showers.

Yes, you heard me, *one* of the showers—plural.

One of the hot, hard-pressured, large showers.

In one of the three over-sized, luxurious bathrooms.

This was going to be hard to get used to. Not.

In half an hour... and a few minutes... maybe ten, I was back downstairs with the others, ready for round two.

And all of a sudden, the Light rose, shone and sparkled like diamond fairy dust on our lives in Laodicea. Kari, a girl oozing all kinds of chic, and Jason, a young man carrying a serious trend card, were going to take us shopping for a new wardrobe.

Yes, you heard me.

Not just a new outfit.

A. New. Wardrobe.

Squeal and happy dance. But only on the inside. It would be completely uncool for them to see that. So anyway, apparently the Community had a high profile in Laodicea, and we weren't to let the team down by looking like "vagabonds".

Dan groaned, but when Kait and I exchanged glances, I may have let a giggle escape. And a bit of a squeal. But it was very quiet.

Riah edged her way over to hide beside Val who sent me her side-eye squint. But Kait gave me the secret high five. She was also doing the happy dance. She was so cool.

Even Raph was bouncing on his toes. But when he saw Marcus and Dan's shoulders slope, he tried to play it cool. It didn't work. So Kait told the Laodicea crew that Raph, me and her would join Kari and Jason and shop for the rest.

I flicked a glance at Jason. He winked. Eeeks.

Then I accidentally caught Kari's eye. I hoped they weren't dating. I didn't want to ruin this opportunity of a lifetime by getting in serious trouble by making her jealous. I mean, I wasn't interested. At. All. Except, I had to admit, the guy did know how to wear clothes. But instead of going green-eye territorial, she smiled. A warm, friendly, totally-non-fake smile.

And all of a sudden, it seemed Laodicea was not such a horrible place after all.

Carl, not quite as young or gifted in the trend department as Jason and Kari, but definitely no slouch, was head of logistics. He informed us about the team who would come in and take care of our house, garden and meals.

"But cooking the meals is my job. And Sariah takes care of the garden. Thank you, but we do not need your help with this." Raph had been swept up in the excitement of the proposed shopping adventure. But he was all business when it came to protecting his responsibilities.

A deep voice entered the conversation. "That is admirable young man, but you and your sister will be at school and won't have time for this anymore. But don't you worry, we'll send someone in to take care of it all for you." It seemed that Waide, the fifth member of the team, was here to enrol the twins in school.

"We do not go to regular school; we learn at home with Kait and Abbot."

Oh dear. Raph's breathing quickened. His shoulders rose and his face darkened. There had been so many changes and he'd done so well. But I guess the invasion into his territory and the reminder of

Abbot's loss was his limit. I needed to remember how tough this was for him.

Kait was on her knees gently cradling Raph's face. "It's okay, sweetheart, we'll sort it out."

Riah held his hand, but her face was mirroring his distress.

Val intervened. "We might talk about this later."

"But term has already start—"

"Later." Yeah. Waide would learn. You don't argue with Val. Well, not twice.

"Right, later. I'll leave the papers for you to look at—" He munched on his lips, but eventually, the words sprang out like silly string. "But the Community School, the city's best and most prestigious school, is expecting them to start as soon as possible. The Overseer has pulled significant strings to get them in. This is a significant privilege. Significant."

Val stood beside Riah and wrapped an arm around her shoulder. "Thank you, we appreciate all that the Overseer has done for us. You can be sure we will look at these forms... later."

Waide took a back seat for the rest of the proceedings, chewing his lips and flicking his eyes to Val.

And that left Ty. While a hot shower and some time to process had improved my impression of these people, it was going to take a lot more than that to improve my impression of Ty.

A lot more.

"I have questionnaires for you each to fill out to determine what team you'll be assigned to. Fill in your past experiences, qualifications and expertise."

I winked at Dan. "Wonder if they have need of your specialty?"

"Tessa." Kait scowled and shook her head.

"What?" It's not like anyone could have heard.

Except Ty. Like, did he have some kind of snitch-radar or something? "And what would that be?" He raised his pen ready to take notes.

I looked around the room, but no one stepped forward to save me, so, I dived in to fill the hole I'd just dug. "Before Dan joined us, he lived on the streets." I looked to Dan's stony face. "He managed to survive, alone, for years in a very hostile environment." This may not have started well, but I wanted these people to know. "Dan is a survivor." I couldn't and didn't even want to hide my pride.

"And what exactly does 'being a survivor' entail?" Ty's keen interest caused the room to focus on Dan. My friend. My *best* friend. "Fighting?" He almost gushed.

"Yeah, a bit." Dan had been defensive all morning. But with this, his castle was well and truly reinforced.

"So how did you survive, find food, clothes, accommodation?" Ty seemed genuinely interested.

"Busked."

"You were able to protect and support yourself doing that? Impressive." The whirring calculations were almost audible.

Dan dropped his eyes, then scanned the room red-faced. "Mostly."

"But that's all in the past now? Now that you're in the Light and are off the street?" Ty didn't even look at him, too busy scribbling notes.

Slightly more audible, "Yeah, that's right." Standing taller, "New leaf, an' all that." Dan had every right to be proud of his achievements and how far he'd come. He was completely amazing.

"Excellent, how long ago was this?" Ty lifted his eyes, pinning Dan for an answer.

"'Bout four weeks."

"That's a mighty big change in such a short amount of time." His disbelief was only outdone by his cynicism.

He was a nasty piece of work.

And I did not like him.

At. All.

"Yes, it's called transformation. Maybe you should try it someday." I shuffled closer to Dan and took his hand.

Ty looked at me like I was dog skrat on his snake belly. He then looked at all of us, not even trying to hide his sneer.

"Tell, me Ty, how long have you been in the Light?" Val walked to

Dan. Unsheathing his sword from its home down his back, she handed it to him.

Dan smiled.

Ty blanched.

Until Val drew her own sword.

Then, Ty turned a sickly shade of terror.

"I believe Dan would be happy to demonstrate how far he has come as a Warrior of Light. Being as seasoned as you are, it should be a fair match?"

"Right, I think that's about it." He completely ignored her challenge. "I'll leave these questionnaires for you to fill out. Kari and Jason will make a time to meet up for shopping. And Waide will be in touch about school. The Community meets at the Temple of Light Saturday afternoons at three o'clock." The jerk was too busy gathering papers and cramming them into his case to notice Marcus approach. He squealed when a firm hand clapped him on the shoulder.

"We'd really like to thank you for coming over and making us feel so welcome. In fact, perhaps next time we have our... dance session, you should join us. Dan in particular would enjoy that. In fact, we all would." The lasers coming out of Papa Bear's eyes sliced Ty to pieces. "But be sure to knock first."

"Are you threatening me? Did you hear that?" Frantically looking to his team. "He threatened me." My impression of our guests improved a touch more when, all of a sudden, they were too busy packing up their own belongings to back him up. The guy was pathetic.

"Not at all, Ty, just trying to protect you." Marcus widened his eyes in mock innocence. "If someone were to walk into this house unexpected, we may have flashbacks to Sodom and think we were under attack. I would hate to mistake you for a demon."

A low chuckle came from the corner of the room. Felix had blended in so well, I'd forgotten he was there. Ty's nostrils flared, he grabbed his case, spun on his heel and made for the exit.

The air seemed sweeter in his absence. I nestled under Dan's arm. "And you thought I was the stuck-up twik princess."

Dan kissed the top of my head. "Honey, that guy ain't got nothing on you."

I jabbed him in the ribs, but not too hard. After all, I had, once again, left him out to dry. And he was right. Ty needed to up his snark if he wanted to be a true TP. Although, he was well on the way to being a pro. The less we had to do with him the better.

16

DANIEL: THREE'S A CROWD

As wicked as this city was, I would never be ungrateful for this shower. Thankfully the steam and jets of pure heaven hid the tears of gratitude and bliss that still escaped every single time I could come up with an excuse to indulge. It'd been a week now and I still broke each time. No one had said anything about me taking two a day. I just made sure I worked extra hard each morning in our training and sets and went for a punishing run each evening.

Pulverising hot water in a palatial bathroom of absurd proportions was a flagrant demonstration of sickening wealth and waste. I kept telling myself that. But somehow, I couldn't make myself criticise the shower. I'd pack it up and take it with me everywhere, if I could.

After seven-plus years of living on the streets, sheltering in a clump of trees, not having a roof or a bed, a shower was something I'd never take for granted. But discipline was part of our job description. That meant using the gifts we were given but knowing when enough was enough and when to pull the plug. Ha, get it? Or turn off the taps.

Stepping out of the ridiculously large shower "room", I stretched for the ridiculously soft towel and froze. The temperature plummeted from high thirties to single digits in a second. The mist in the air dropped like a lead balloon.

"Well good morning, gorgeous. Aren't you looking fine today?"

The steam and posh soap smell had masked the sulphur.

"Do you need a hand with that?"

I scrambled to wrap my towel around me. I looked to my guard. He was scowling, his fists were clenched, but his sword was sheathed.

"Oh sweetie, when are you going to learn, you are perfectly safe with me." She winked at my guard.

He may have growled. I had never heard him make any sound before. But today, he growled. I think I might have joined him.

"I just came by to offer my condolences." She turned and leaned over the sink, checking her face in the mirror. She offered me a view of her perfectly proportioned butt. Tight, shiny black leather stretching over a firm peach. She caught me ogling. Like a cat she stretched, turned and then slowly folded her arms under her epic rack, pushing them even higher. Her eyes darkened and, not releasing me from her stare, she leaned forward offering me a view of what she had to offer. "Like what you see, darl'n?"

Girls were all the same. They wanted to manipulate, use and control you with their body and what they had to offer. It made me sick. Because it worked... mostly.

Except Tess. She was different.

"I still make you sick? Now you've made me sad." The pout was fake. The gleam in her eyes wasn't. "Tessa isn't different, you know. She really threw you under a bus, didn't she." Twisting her waspish waist, she made a show of checking her perfect butt in the mirror. "You thought she was special, that she would stand up for you. That... what?" She snapped back round and pinned me with her demon eyes. "You actually thought she loved you?" At this, she bent in two laughing.

Twik.

Her falsetto stopped. She jerked up and prowled over to me. Leaned in. Her sulphur stung my nose and burned my eyes. With a tilt of her chin and a wink, she offered, "She is, isn't she." Then disappeared.

"You. Not her." She'd gone, but still.

Her throaty chuckle danced in the clearing mist.

Like I said. Twik.

17

FELIX: FAMILY MATTERS

I was surrounded by incompetents. It was a disappointing yet unavoidable truth I had discovered at a young age. As I had grown, this truth had not been challenged. However, in the twelve years I had been working for the Community, I had managed to weed most of them out of management positions. My oversight of the employment of people for leadership roles had seen a significant improvement in not only the functioning of the organisation, but, as the Overseer kept commenting, our financial health as well. And as vulgar as money was, it was an unquestionable indicator of success.

My team sat around the table. As was expected, they arrived early, but I made sure it was worth their while. It has been said if you build it, they will come. I have learned that if you feed them, they will not only come, they will arrive on time. Therefore, I insisted on quality catered refreshments being supplied prior to all my meetings. This would ensure Bertrand at least would be present.

We were waiting for our youngest recruit to arrive. Kari had joined the team as Bertrand's offsider and grown to take on the significant portfolio of Events Coordinator. She was young, ambitious, and capable. Unlike her Line Manager, Kari was not motivated by food.

Therefore, she was always last to arrive. But to her credit, she was always on time... just.

It shouldn't have irked me. But it did. It was a power play. And that was fine. I would let her play her games and have her minor victories because it was indicative of the victories she was claiming for the Community.

However, when it came to playing against me and my team, there was a line. Cross it and she would learn what it was to... play with the professionals.

As per usual, we were all seated and ready to begin when she marched through the door at fifteen-twenty-nine and fifty seconds. She took her seat to Bertrand's right. Petite, well presented. Overtly high, animal-print heels. Only spoke when spoken to, polite and to the point. But there was no mistaking the hunger in her eyes.

And, as they say, without further ado, the meeting began.

There would be no surprises in any of the reports. I'd already been informed of everything that was going on in all departments at my weekly one-on-one "touch base" meetings with each Head. I was fully aware of what was going on and how each arm was managing, the areas in which they were succeeding and where we needed to problem solve. This time was more about the team being kept in the loop and having the opportunity to step back and see the big picture.

I looked around the room and pondered. How would a newcomer see my team? An overweight jovial fool in Bertrand. A severe spinster in Fleur. Alex, a fidgeting bundle of nerves. Clyde, doing his best to be invisible. Griffin, shrewd, sharp and savage.

Masks, all of them. Each of them efficient and essential members of the overall running of this organisation.

Perfect?

Hardly.

Excellent at what they did and unified in overall focus?

Absolutely.

Fleur had just handed over to Craig when Marlene stumbled into the room with a shadow pushing at her back. Immediately I was on alert, as Marlene never stumbled... never. "Excuse me, Felix, but—"

"Get out of my way woman."

Charles. What on earth?

Marlene stood her ground, one hand gripping the door frame, the other, white-knuckled, clutched the door handle. "Felix, I'm sorry for the interruption"—Marlene forged on despite Charles' attempt to speak over the top of her—"but your father requests an audience."

"There's no bloody request about it, woman, I demand to see him. Immediately."

"What would you have me tell him, sir?" I knew she added the "sir" to further irritate Charles.

"Thank you, Marlene, I can tell him myself that if he doesn't stop making a nuisance of himself, I shall call security and have him removed." I would not have him coming in here, pushing around Marlene... or anyone for that matter.

Venom, brewed from genuine dislike, spewed from Charles. "You wouldn't dare!"

As I said, Kari could play her power games, but I had been trained by a pro. "Thank you, Marlene, you may show Charles in. If he has not willingly left the building within ten minutes, call the police."

She smiled, nodded her head, moved aside and with her left arm, ushered my bane into the room.

With him came the Crow.

It settled in my stomach, ruffling its feathers, setting my teeth on edge and my gut into motion. With one claw nesting near my heart, the tips of its talons pricked and warned of what was to come. The other claw took purchase in my brain. Hot shivers shot down my spine. Why now? It had been years since Charles had elicited this kind of response. Was it because he had breached the walls of my sanctuary? In the fifteen years I had worked for the Community, Charles had never stepped foot in my territory—Community Head Office. Whatever the cause, I didn't have the capacity to deal with the source of the problem. I was too busy surviving the symptoms.

The Crow and I had come to an agreement. A binding contract, if you will. If I sat very still, and followed threads, it would wait till we got home before it unleashed its full, debilitating attack.

"How dare you!" Charles righted himself and stalked into the room. With a cursory glance around the table, his eyes came back to settle upon me. "Where is the Overseer?"

The Crow rattled. But gave me a reprieve. "If you had been able to ring ahead, you would have learned he is presently out of town." I worked hard at keeping my mask in place: open faced, slightly curious, eternally patient. Meanwhile, underneath, I was a besieged island in the ocean's storm.

"Irrelevant. I know you're the one behind it."

Slowly inhaling, not wanting to disturb the mutinous Crow, I parried. "I'm sorry Father, but we are in the middle of an important meeting and your time is running out. Could you please be more specific?" I switched my mask for one I hoped resembled a serene smile. I certainly didn't feel serene, with the Crow cawing in my head. But the shade of puce engulfing Charles's face and the throbbing in his temple proved I'd hit my mark.

"The hospital requested an increased donation this year. You turned us down."

"The High Council agreed that since our annual support of the hospital was generous, substantial, and sufficient that we would continue to donate at the same rate as per normal, with a two-point-five percent increase in line with GDP for this financial year."

"Don't play coy with me, Felix. I know what you're doing."

The waves buffeted and threatened to overwhelm, but I changed masks again, this time attempting concerned innocence. "You give me too much credit, Father. I do not control the High Council. I am merely a facilitator of their wishes." Again, the serene smile. "Thank you for dropping by. However, if there is nothing more, we'd best be moving on. I do not want to hold these good people up any more than necessary." I looked at my watch then smiled again. The need to repeat the threat to have him forcibly removed was unnecessary. Father knew it was not idle.

Puce deepened to crimson and the ticking pulse looked ready to explode, but thankfully Charles spun on his heel and left.

The tension in the room was cataclysmic. Nausea coalesced like a brick in the pit of my stomach. I didn't waste energy changing masks, I believed the one I had in place would do nicely: serene smile. The Crow had me in its clutches and, by agreement, I sat motionless and breathed deeply through my nose.

"I bet Lightmas lunch is a blast at your place." Griffin's droll humour shifted the Crow's claws enough for warmth to infuse my smile.

I nodded my thanks, then moved on in an attempt to resume our meeting. "Craig, I apologise for the interruption. Please continue."

As still as a statue, I tuned out the room around me, clutched at threads in my grasp, and followed them like my sanity depended on them.

Bertrand. Wingtips. Co-ordinator of the fifty-six Shepherds of the Laodicean Community. Eleven new graduates from the seminary entering service this week. Three within the city, eight from different corners of the continent. Three main worship teams leading services at the Temple of Light. One for each service: 7 am, 9 am, and 5:30 pm.

Hand over metaphorical hand, I followed the thread. Fleur. Blazing red armour. Black, wide-heeled, low pumps. Head of all our cleaning crews. Fifteen for domestic and nine for commercial.

Craig. Quality hiking shoes. Fleur's assistant. Oversaw the eleven gardening teams working on management domiciles and corporate buildings, inside and out. With the end of the school year, we had taken on six new members for the cleaning teams and three for the gardening and maintenance. Two members were preparing for retirement. Presently they were undergoing an equipment audit, the results of which would be presented to me at the end of the month.

The thread continued. Clyde. R.M. Williams boots. Our property manager, responsible for purchasing, selling, renting and leasing all properties in the Community's portfolios. Our employment policy detailed that all management received accommodation as part of their payment package. His team took care of insurance, bonds, rental agreements, cleaning and maintenance, in partnership with Fleur and Craig.

Clair. Mid-range, high, wedged pumps. One of Clyde's assistants.

Oversaw management of the fleet of vehicles in service of the Community. Every year one third of the fleet would be turned over. Clair ensured all vehicles were serviced, registered and insured. She also managed the drivers and oversaw logbooks. She was new to the role, having moved up from being a driver herself. She was on probation and doing very well. Craig was now grooming her to take his position when he retired in three years' time.

I followed the thread. Alex. Doc Martens. Head of administration overseeing the business side of our organisation, including wages, insurances, superannuation, bonuses, leave for Heads. His team of ten worked out of the offices here in our city headquarters. He also ensured that all management underwent regular professional development. Alex was a young man, engaged to be married to a girl, Linda, who headed one of the worship teams at the Temple of Light. March. Soon. I must check if Marlene had got a gift.

Alice. Birkenstocks. Alex's second would step up while he was away on his honeymoon... the Greek Islands?

The thread continued. Griffin. Living with his partner, also in media. Managed our Community awareness project, Eye on Laodicea. Sharp as a tack, cunning as a fox, and a man I enjoyed sparring with... in Berlins. Brown. Mine were charcoal. His teams broadcast the advancements of the three main industries of our city: agriculture, textiles and medicine. They also followed the journey of the successful applicants of our extensive scholarship program.

Hand over hand, thread by thread, until eventually the nightmare was over and I was alone.

18

FELIX: THE CROW

The car deposited me at the doors of my apartment building. I hid the trembling of my body in long strides and made it to the lift. There I camouflaged the tremor in my hands by strangling the handle of my briefcase. Head still, I followed the thread: ride the elevator to the top floor. Get my medication. Have a shower. Call Marlene. Go to bed.

Ride the elevator...

I didn't have to share the lift or select a floor; it was the private carriage for the penthouse. I placed my hand on the sensor, but the shaking and perspiration smudged my print and the scanner failed.

Breathe in, breathe out and follow the thread.

Ride the elevator...

I couldn't call the elevator.

Breathe.

Carefully placing my briefcase on the floor, I fumbled for my wallet in my inner suit pocket. After several attempts with trembling, sweaty fingers, I removed the key. Two-handed, I managed to slide the plastic card into the slot to call the lift.

Follow the thread.

Ride the elevator. Go to the cave. Take my medicine.

The Crow cawed in my head and clutched my heart with its claws. Its talons painfully manipulated my heart like a cat sadistically toying with its prey. Its beak pecking my eyes from the inside out.

We had a deal. A binding deal. Stay still, follow the thread. Until I was safe at home. I just needed my tablets, then the Crow could have its way. I was almost there. I was almost safe. The lift was silent and smooth. Like a needle, it delivered me to the security of my home.

The doors opened. My foot tripped on the tread and I fell to the tiles. For a moment, I embraced the cool stone and allowed it to absorb my heat.

Ruffled feathers swirled in my gut. Pushing myself to my feet I raced to the bathroom and ejected the contents of my stomach.

Now... follow the thread. Take the medication. Have a shower.

I rinsed my mouth and reached for the cabinet above the sink. My hands wreaked carnage, destroying order and logic. Contents flew and scattered around the room. Replicating the meeting of magnetic like-poles, everything fled from my fingers. The objects from the medicine cabinet spilled to the sink and scattered across the bench and onto the floor. From the pool of detritus accumulated in the sink I found the bottle.

Not long now. Take the medication. Have a shower. Go to bed.

I yelled in frustration as the push, twist, and turn of the child safety cap was beyond me. I held the answer in my hands, yet it was beyond me. It may as well have been at the office.

The thread broke.

I was going under.

Breathe... Breathe... Damn it... Breathe.

I had to pick up the thread. Call Marlene. Follow the thread. Marlene. Fifty-six. Patent Manolos. My personal assistant. Qualified from LU with a bachelor's in Business. Worked at Systems Corp until I left and brought her with me to the Community.

I had to call Marlene. My phone escaped from my inner pocket through my slippery hands and fell to the floor. The screen cracked.

Breathe... Breathe... Breathe.

Call Marlene. Marlene would come.

I sat on the lid of the toilet and scrabbled for the phone across the desert of white tiles. Call Marlene. Fingerprint recognition. Finger too sweaty. Face recognition. I hit speed dial. Call Marlene.

"Felix. I'm on my way. Hang on. I'll be there in five minutes. I am pulling up to the building now. Felix. You are okay. I am on my way."

I heard the echo of her shoes through the foyer over the phone. She was here. She would be here any minute.

Follow the thread. Breathe.

My body was going into lockdown. The tremors had taken control. Rigid and shaking uncontrollably, I tried to relax. My mouth-guard lay useless in its sterile case somewhere in the chaos. In an attempt to reduce the tension, I laid my head on my arms and stayed seated on the lid of the toilet.

My phone once again slipped and clattered onto the tiled floor. Possibly useless now. It didn't matter. Marlene was coming. My teeth chattered, then clamped like a vice. It was unlikely they would crack. I hoped. It was too late for the guard anyway. My body alternated between spasms of shaking and locking like a rock. The Crow cawed and rattled behind my eyes. It pecked and clawed at my insides. My heart was in ribbons, my brain was dancing with electricity.

The elevator doors chimed.

Chanel No. 5. Emerald green, patent leather pumps. They matched her armour. A black hem resting over stocking clad knees.

"It's okay, Felix." Marlene prised the bottle from my clawed hand.

Still curled in a ball wracked with spasms, I listened as water filled a glass. I heard the bottle open and the pills jostle into her hand.

Soon. It would end soon.

Convulsions gripped my body, and I was held prisoner by their rage. I couldn't unlock my jaw to take the tablets.

"Right you are then. This is what we're going to do." Marlene squatted in front of me so I could see her face. "I am going to run a warm shower. It will help you relax. When you're underway, I'll bring in a change of clothes. When you have relaxed enough, you can take your tablets and get dressed. I will leave the water and the tablets on the sink." Her soft, warm hand cradled my clenched jaw. "Can you hear me?"

I grunted.

"Do you understand?"

I grunted.

The shower door opened, water flowed, moisture dampened the air. She was back. Marlene removed my shoes and socks and quietly left the bathroom.

I fought the Crow and made it into the shower and vomited bile. I stood. I shook. I soaked until the hot water worked its magic on my trembling body and broke the back of the spasms.

My muscles eased and eventually I was able to move without a fight. I washed. I cleaned my teeth and worked my jaw enough that I could open my mouth. Reaching across, I threw back the tablets and gulped the water.

It hit my stomach and rebounded. But I gritted my teeth and forced it to stay down.

By the time I'd made it out of the shower, Marlene had bundled my clothes for dry-cleaning, and made us each a cup of tea, mine laced with bourbon, hers with brandy, and settled herself in the spare room. Which was really her room. No one else ever stayed there. No one else ever came up here. Just Marlene and her cat, Gem, on nights like this when I needed a bit of... assistance.

She sat in her armchair, Gem curled up in her lap purring, gazing out over the city through the wall of windows.

I joined their comfortable silence, settling in my armchair.

"That was a bad one."

I didn't need to reply. It was obvious.

Gem opened his gold-green eyes, blinked, then continued to ignore everything except the comfort of Marlene's lap.

"You worried about your father?"

I sipped my tea and waited for the alcohol to meet up with my medication and take me away.

"He's full of himself... and hot air. But you have nothing to worry about, dear."

I huffed a laugh as warmth started spreading and untying the last of the Crow's nest in my mind.

We sipped in companionable peace until my eyes grew heavy. I rose, took Marlene's cup and mine to the kitchen. As I passed her on the way to my room, I dropped a kiss on her head.

"You're welcome, dear." She patted my hand, then bent down and pulled out a novel from her bag. "I think I might just stay up a bit and read and enjoy the view."

"Good night, Marlene."

"See you in the morning, dear."

I shut my door and fell into bed, welcoming the oblivion that waited.

19

RAPHAEL: TEMPLE LIFE

Laodicea looked like it had just been unwrapped. Everything was shiny and new and crisp as a freshly washed and ironed shirt. It even smelled nice. It was very neat, and clean, and... odd. There were no demons anywhere. I do not know what happened to them. We saw oceans of them when we arrived. Every kind of evil roared, hissed and spat as we passed the city limits. It was horrible. After the happiness of surviving the tidal wave of darkness in Sodom, my heart was squashed when I saw that those that were killed were not even a drop in the bucket. So many more waited to take their place. I don't know where the Dark Lord got them from, but he seemed to have an endless supply.

But that is what was so odd. We had not seen another demon since that night. I looked. We all did. I had kept expecting them to jump out from around corners and attack. But they had not. And still, they did not.

Marcus drove the big fancy car the Community had given us. They did not like our truck and said it was too big to be driving around the city streets. But the way they scrunched up their noses when they looked or spoke of it made me think there was more to it. But I was happy to be in this very comfortable car. We all got to sit in the body part together and everyone could look out the windows. Even when we were in the back seats.

We travelled through the maze of perfectly straight streets— under, over and beside the aqueducts and canals—taking us to Saturday's gathering. Light bounced off the water, making shimmering patterns on the white walls of the city. But still, I could not find any demons.

One of the first things you learn when you walk with the Light is that there is a world of Others living in the shadows, illuminated by and drawn to His presence. I had to keep checking my armour just to make sure someone had not turned the Light off. Something was not right.

The maze straightened out into a long straight stretch of road that took us up a steep climb to the Temple Complex in the city centre. As the road climbed, it widened, and the buildings either side of the street seemed to lower themselves. It was like they had all agreed, no one would be taller than the Temples. I wondered if they competed among themselves: who's the tallest? which is the grandest?

We followed Felix's car into a huge underground cavern and joined a queue of vehicles corkscrewing their way down to the centre of the earth. I lost count of the number of levels we dropped. Kait pointed out big fans which pumped air in and drew fumes out. She also showed us the special reflectors that captured the sunlight and released it under the earth, turning the darkness to day. It helped. But still, I was not happy being this far down.

Felix parked near a row of elevators and we found a space nearby. After piling out, we went to join him. He was holding the doors of a lift open, waiting for us. Another group approached, but deviated when they saw his face and when he did not move aside. As we joined him, I made sure to fill my lungs to bursting with each breath. I did not know how they did it, but I could only taste fresh air. It helped calm my heart. I also made sure not to think about how far down we were.

The ride up was very quiet. Maybe I was not the only one who was thinking of all that concrete, and dirt, and cars, and machinery, and weight, and darkness above us. We rocketed up and were delivered to the middle of a gigantic square decorated with gardens and trees. Three huge temples each claimed one of the sides, leaving the fourth side of the square open to the wide avenue leading down into the city.

Felix led us along the beautiful paths, our shadows stretching out straight in front of us. Val, Kait and Marcus walked with him. I held Riah's hand and we edged closer to Dan and Tessa who were trailing behind. We all slowed to look down the hill to the regimented forest of buildings below us. Perfectly aligned, tall, light-coloured buildings with walls of clean glass reflected light to every corner of the city. Canals ran along several of the main roads, and aqueducts snaked through the tops, like a vine holding everything together. Gardens full of plants exploded with life on rooftops, sidewalks and street centres. Darkness and dirt had no place here.

I had never been anywhere like it. And for some reason it made me very uncomfortable. I looked up at Dan. I caught him screwing up his nose and scanning the horizon before he saw me. We turned back to see that the others had gained a distance in front of us, so we trotted along the large square-stone path to catch up.

We were heading towards The Temple of Light on the eastern side of the Temple Square. It was a mountain. Tall, thin spires in pale yellow stone rose so high, they poked the sky. Felix had explained that the temple had been previously used by worshippers of Aphrodite. But Aphrodite had lost popularity when Ashera had told her people she required a different kind of worship at her temple. Felix did not explain this to me. But as a result, the Community of Light was able to move in and use it to hold all the people who now worshipped the Light. I thought that was very generous of the Aphrodite worshippers. But Felix explained the Community had been exceedingly generous in return.

Stone pillars were carved with beautiful patterns. Leaves and flowers wound their way up the front wall. It was like a three-dimensional carving of one of Riah's pictures. Pointy-arched windows filled with coloured glass were spaced in rows up to the pointy roof. Everything about it was detailed, expensive and big—bigger than Ebony's mansion. But not as big as the temples next door.

Artemis's green, yellow and red exploded across her dwelling behind us. I did not know much about this goddess; she had not been popular in Sodom. But she had her fair share of patrons mingling in her colonnade. The gentle breeze bringing the scent of Artemis's Temple to us was clean and fresh. It did not stink here like Sodom. But I did catch Dan screwing up his nose a number of times.

Ashera's Temple sat on the northern side. Her spires, the tallest of the three, hung with purple, blue and gold banners waving a shy "hello" from flagpoles. Her building was bright white with large open doors and wide inviting steps. Unlike her temple at home, there were no bodies lying unconscious in the streets spilling from a stinky, over-crowded building. Here, well-dressed people talked with members of the Community and Artemis followers before each went into their own building.

Everywhere I looked, colour, beauty and perfection competed for attention. No wonder they wanted to give us new gear and "flash wheels", as Dan called them. I got the feeling these people did not feel comfortable around things in their natural state.

Dan winked at me and threw his arm around my shoulders. He did not care about the way he looked or what he wore. But Tessa had bought him clothes that made him look very tidy. He wore them to make her happy. But I think that he would have preferred to wear his normal clothes to make Ty unhappy.

The people of Laodicea must be very grateful to live in a city where there was housing, food and clothing for all. We had been told that everyone had a job. But Riah and I were sad to lose ours. The grown-ups said that maybe we should give the Community's school a go. But if it did not work out, we did not have to stay. We did not know how long we were staying in Laodicea, but they said it would be good to have a chance to meet some other kids in the Light.

We did not want to go. But we had agreed because we had no choice. Everyone had been given a job and a uniform. Except Dan and Val. The Overseer was not interested in warfare, so he had no use for them. And we were too young to be useful. We were told that Dan was too much of a risk because he had not been in the Light very long. He had to prove himself before they would let him join a team.

They were not interested in our Badges. This made me sad. Since the Light had increased my Badge in Sodom and I had more power now, I would have liked to experiment to see how it had changed and what I could do.

We were almost at the Temple of Light, but I was not ready to go in. There was too much to see and take in. No wonder seats were dotted around the paths and gardens. I could sit here for hours just watching and learning. I tugged on Dan's sleeve. "Who are those pretty ladies?"

"The ones in blue, gold and purple?" After I nodded, Dan continued, "They are the goddess's acolytes."

"Why are they covered in scales?" The people of Laodicea were not as scarred and disfigured as in Sodom, but at home it was not uncommon to see people with scales. These ladies were all marked on the left-hand side in the tricolours of the goddess Ashera. Some just a hand and ankle, others a sleeve and leg, and a couple, not venturing beyond the vast portico of the building, even had the left-hand side of their faces transformed by scales.

Dan coughed. "These ladies are priestesses. When someone wants to meet with the goddess and enjoy... ahh... communion with her, they meet and commune with a priestess. The more scales, the more experienced they are at... communing."

"Well, that is nice of them, but I think they must be cold, their dresses are very thin."

"Communing isn't cheap so, to encourage people to... spend money they... entice worshipers with their... uniform."

By this stage we had both stopped to watch a group of acolytes who had come to mingle with the crowd heading into the Community Temple. But we were given a hurry along by Felix, so we turned to go inside. But I noticed one acolyte who did not look happy. I was sad for her, so I went to talk to her.

As I came close, I noticed she was just a girl, not much older than us. She hugged herself and looked at the ground as she trailed behind the others. She reminded me of the time Riah used to have to get dressed up for our owner's guests and perform. Riah had loved the beads and sparkly bits, but the dresses made her feel uncomfortable.

Then it became clear. Men were using the acolytes like the bad men had used Sariah. Heat started rising and the Dragon snorted. I saw the way men looked at the girl and it made me angry. I took off my coat. "You look cold, would you like my coat?"

"The goddess only accepts money and anyway, you are too young." I looked into her red-rimmed eyes and felt a washing machine of pain.

"I do not want to meet with your goddess, thank you. I just wanted to give you my coat because you look cold. I can get another one." Tears leaked from her swollen eyes. A shadow came round behind me. The girl looked up and cringed.

"Raph, we're going to be late." Val put her hand on my shoulder.

"But I want to help her."

"Does she want your help?" Val was not unkind, but she was right, I must not assume that all people want to be assisted. We both looked at the acolyte, waiting for her response.

"I can't accept your coat." Tears were making rivers down her cheeks. "But thank you, you are very kind." She went to go.

"Wait." I looked to Val. "What about my Badge? Can I give her that?"

Val squatted down so she had to look up to the girl. "Are you in pain or unwell?" She had to lean in to hear and then, with the smallest of movements, the acolyte indicated that she was. "Would you like to be healed?"

Again, the smallest nod.

"You must not tell anyone what Raph can do. Do you understand?"

"Believe me, I can keep secrets. It's what I'm trained to do, apparently." A harshness settled on her and her back straightened.

Val looked to me and indicated I should go ahead.

"I think I need to hold your hand." I held out my hand as an invitation. Her icy cold fingers settled into mine. I shut my eyes and pictured her whole, and well, and pain free. I asked the Light to come into her and warm her in His way, that she would be free of suffering.

A shout echoed across the square. "What do you think you're doing?"

Val stood.

I opened my eyes. I was met with the girl's look of wonder.

The bellow, closer now, resounded. "I said—"

"Time for us to go, Raph. It was nice to meet you...?"

Shoes were slapping their way toward us. I could see people turning to stare.

"Amber," she whispered.

"Remember, please, for Raph's sake, don't tell."

A set of burly arms came around Amber's shoulders. "Time is money. You want time with her, you pay." The gorilla looked down at us, grunted, then whisked her away.

We made our way across the square to join the others waiting for us. Riah took my hand and Val stayed by my side. She did her secret language with Marcus and Kait, but I did not care, I could not stop thinking about the acolytes and remembering our time in Sodom before we were rescued. I do not think what they made the goddess's priestesses do was good, especially if they did not want to do it.

Soon we were inside and ushered into a row of seats at the back. But no one was sitting down. It was very cramped and becoming overly warm. I was dwarfed in a forest of people who were all talking, crowding my ears with chaos. Dan pointed to my chair and held out his hand, helping me climb up so I could see. Riah copied me and rested her arm around Val's shoulders. Dan steadied me until I could rest my hand on his shoulder, so I did not overbalance as I swivelled to take in the enormity of my surroundings. Bright colours beamed across the chamber from the glass windows. Beautiful flowers were everywhere. The scents of jasmine, rose and chrysanthemums were carried through heating ducts in the floor.

At the front of the building a wooden stage had been built. On it were arranged chairs and stands and lots of electronic equipment;

long chords wove their way around the platform like octopus arms. A group moved to their places behind microphones. A hush settled over the claustrophobic theatre. Then the music began.

It was like nothing I had ever heard. At first, I was scared as the vibrations rattled from the chair under my feet to up inside my chest. But then sense came to it all, and order and rhythm worked their way through. A unifying beat demanded conformity and all the instruments fell into line. The audience was drawn into the compelling uniformity, moving as one under the command of the beat. A singer blended words into the music; words everyone knew. They joined in. They sang about how good it was being in the Light. I found it puzzling, though, how few had armour of any quality.

I did not know the words, so I used the time to study everything around me. The sun was dropping outside and the lights inside were triggered, bouncing off a few bright sparks of blazing armour. It was like looking at a jumble of fairy lights dropped in a mass on the floor, some bulbs shining brightly, some flickering, but most not working at all.

20

KAITLYN: COUNCIL INSPECTION

"Well, that was an experience. I have never been crowded in a Temple of Light before." I wasn't really speaking to anyone in particular.

"That's because we've never been in a Temple of Light before, Kait." Trust Marcus to state the obvious. "This doesn't seem like any Soteria House we've ever visited. Imagine living in something this big." He still had his arm around my shoulders. It could have been because we were packed as tight as sardines, or maybe because he was in uncharted waters. "What about you Val? You seen anything like this before?"

She didn't answer, as such. Her eyes constantly skirted the crowd and, almost imperceptibly, she nodded. She wasn't smiling, so I guess that was a story for later. A less populated later.

I didn't think we'd planned to meet up with Felix again, so we were on our own. "Well, maybe we should wait till the crush has passed then try to navigate our way back to the car?"

Again, no one actually answered, but with all eyes cast to the crowd, Marcus and Val murmured their agreement.

I threw my arm around Raph standing on the chair behind me and gave him a squeeze. Riah stood on Val's chair behind her, arms resting around Val's neck and her chin nestled on her shoulder. Both of Val's arms wrapped behind her around Riah's legs. They appeared relaxed but, considering the circumstances, I doubted that facade.

It was interesting to see how the kids were managing their loss of Abbot. Each had transitioned their affection around the family. We were so grateful for Dan, who, in a very real sense, filled the gap. While Raph doled himself out evenly to everyone, Riah seemed to have "adopted" Val and Dan to fill the cavern created by Abbot's absence.

"Hello. I'm so glad I caught you. I have heard so much about you."

We all turned to see a small, balding man swimming with the tide of the crowd. As he passed us, he jumped out of the river and threw his arm out and started shaking our hands indiscriminately. "Jarvis. Welcome. How are you? How are you settling in?"

When the words stopped tumbling, his bright eyes jumped from one to another of our group. I guess it was our cue to start speaking. I unhooked my arm from Marcus and offered my hand. "Kait." Then I introduced the others.

"Such a pleasure." He eyes sparked and his faint violet armour danced. "Listen, we are heading to a meeting of the High Council and we would love it if you could join us and share some of your story." He lifted his eyebrows and again bounced his eyes between us. With a beaming smile, he breathed deeply and gave his head a small shake.

With the flow easing behind him, Jarvis managed to step back and give us all a bit of room to manoeuvre and start shuffling into the brighter light of the aisle. It was then his eyes widened marginally, then did a double take and paled.

Was it our armour that'd thrown him? It wasn't our guard. They had taken to the roof when we entered. During this past week, the number of our Warriors had dwindled. We were now each just accompanied by our one constant companion. Jarvis's eyes rested on Val and his tone changed. "We, um, we would be honoured, if you would consider, that is if you have time, to join us to, um, share your story. It... we... would be utmost... privileged." He then started nodding his head enthusiastically.

Out of the corner of my eye, I saw Tessa turn away. Hopefully he didn't see her smirk. Or Dan's look of, *What the...?*

"We've got no immediate plans." Marcus turned away from Jarvis and considered the rest of us. *What do you think? Do I pull out an excuse or do we visit with these guys?*

Val gave a hint of a nod. I squeezed his hand. Dan gave a slight shrug and Tessa ate her lips. Riah sized him up from where she still lazed across Val's back and Raph returned Jarvis's enthusiastic nodding.

"Sure. We'd love to meet the High Council. Thanks for the invitation." Marcus returned our verdict.

"Excuse me, sir," Raph jumped in.

"Yes, Raphael."

"Where are all the demons?"

Well, I guess there was no time like the present to attack the question we'd all been puzzling over.

Jarvis, however, may not have agreed. After a choke he managed a splutter. "There are no demons in Laodicea, young man. You don't have to worry about that kind of thing here." He looked to me, Val and Marcus for... support? I couldn't tell. But since we wanted to know the same thing, we had nothing to offer him.

"But there are always demons. Even in Soteria Houses. This is a big Soteria House with Temples of Artemis and Ashera next door, so there are bound to be demons."

Raph was right.

Jarvis didn't agree. "That's preposterous, of course there are no demons in the Temple of Light. And I assure you, there are no demons in Laodicea." His face softened and he leaned forward. "I understand you have had a very difficult time, but believe me, you are not in Sodom anymore, young man. You are safe in Laodicea." He stood upright and looked at all of us. "You are all safe here. Now, if you'll follow me?"

He turned and led us against the tide of the dwindling flow of people to the business end of the Temple, where we could see that the inside of this grand stone building had been dressed with wires, scaffolding, curtains and speakers. Closer to the front, the crowd changed in look and function. No longer mixing with the observers and consumers, we were among the operators and performers. Huddles formed around clipboards, possibly assessing the performance?

No one acknowledged Jarvis, but a few flicked their eyes to us as we passed. The covert evaluation was mutual. Not only was the lack of demons throwing our equilibrium, so too was the lack of armour. Well, in truth, the abundance of insubstantial armour. It was both worrying and perplexing. But there was no time to linger, Jarvis picked up his speed and headed to a camouflaged door to the left of the stage area.

He waited for us, holding the way open, inviting us into a smaller anteroom furnished with an expansive rich timber table and twelve chairs around the perimeter. The echo of the smaller room was absorbed by a lush rug taking up most of the floor space. Rainbows danced through the glass windows, painting the pale stone walls with a kaleidoscope of colour. Despite the volume of the 'smaller' room, it was warm, comfortable and welcoming.

The Overseer sat at the head of the table, Felix to his right. An assortment of people took up most of the other chairs.

"Welcome." The Overseer was first to speak and introduced us to the group. As he did so, Jarvis pulled over some extra chairs and council members shuffled to make room for us to join them at the mammoth table. "We're so glad you could join us. We trust you have settled in well? How has your first week been?"

Before we had a chance to answer either question, the Overseer continued. "Three of our councillors send their apologies but be sure we will pass on anything pertinent to them. Now, have a seat and, that's right, make yourself comfortable." He grinned and nodded as we arranged ourselves. "Felix, refreshments?"

Without responding, his right-hand man made the call. Before the phone had returned to the table, he continued. "Once again we welcome you to Laodicea and thank you for taking time out to join us." The Overseer took a moment to inhale, ready to launch into his next tirade.

I thought I'd see if I could get a word in. Not because I felt I needed to. But things had been a bit quiet and I was up for the challenge... any challenge. "We would like to take this opportunity to formally thank you for all you've done for us and acknowledge your hospitality and generosity." Once more I saw Tessa turn aside. The Overseer forgot to shut his mouth at my interruption. "And yes, we've settled well and had a wonderful week of recovering. Thank you for asking." I offered him my most sincere smile.

He'd managed to shut his mouth and I noticed that Felix was very interested in something on the floor off to his right.

"Right, well, shall we continue?" Once he'd regained control, his colour returned to a healthy peach.

"Refreshments" arrived. It was going to take us a long time to get used to the changes here. I had tried to explain that I was vegan and that Raph had chosen to be vegetarian. This had not gone down well, nor had it been respected. Everything on the trolley was extravagant and nothing was suitable. At least Raph could eat, and the coffee was good.

I managed to get Dan off to the side during the melee of this late afternoon tea. "You okay?" I'd noticed him screwing up his nose and putting everyone under intense scrutiny. He'd not been subtle, and members of the Council were giving him a wide berth.

"Can't you smell it?" He didn't look at me but kept scoping the room.

"Here?" I knew he must have been speaking about the stench of sulphur. In Sodom we'd learned that Dan had a Badge for... smelling demons. Sounds crazy, but that's pretty much what it amounted to. Demons gave off their distinct scent and Dan was able to pick up the faintest traces of it where the rest of us didn't notice a thing.

Like Raph said, we expect to not only see demons pretty much everywhere, we'd also expect to see them in Soteria Houses, and I guess Temples of Light. Not that I'd been in any before this, but it made sense.

But that their scent was evident everywhere, and I mean everywhere, even in the Council chambers, yet there was no other evidence, was baffling to say the least. Especially since Council members, and the Overseer himself, kept saying there weren't any demons in Laodicea.

We knew they were here. They welcomed us in. And, since I'd received my sight, I'd learned that there were not many places the devil's agents weren't. And for them to be completely absent was more than unusual: it was beyond comprehension.

Once we'd all gathered our refreshments and retaken our seats, we were given the opportunity to share our story. Our initial statements were met with blatant disbelief, but then as each of us were given opportunity to share, our audience turned to stone as they absorbed the weight of our experiences. By the end, not a whisper of breath was released as we bared our grief and shared our scars.

They graciously waited as we gathered ourselves after shedding tears and collapsing into grave silences. Some Councillors even shared tears of empathy. Then the questions began. Respectful. Solemn. Genuine.

It was a time of bonding, not only for our family, but for us and the Community's High Council. There seemed to be some reasonable, level-headed men and women, each with various degrees of armour. But none fully Lit. Another mystery to puzzle over.

However, despite the rocky start we'd had with the Overseer and Felix, and the "welcoming committee" in our house, it was cathartic to talk through the incredible trials, triumphs and torments of our last moments in Sodom. They had offered us a fresh start here. And it had done a lot to repair the initial damage.

We'd not been in the best place—on edge and ready to jump at the slightest niggle. But now, after time to relax and repair, we too were more reasonable and ready to engage in our new lives here. It would still take some adjusting to fit into a totally different culture, but we were up for the challenge. Not for ourselves, but this was where the Light had led us, and He had work for us to do here. For that to happen we had to get along with the Community that He'd established in Laodicea.

Who were we to come in and challenge the way they did things? We were guests. It was our place to ask, "How and where may we serve?" To fit in as best we could and to find our niche and pull our oars however the Community saw fit.

So, I was grateful for the opportunity to start over. In contrast to our rocky start at the house, now on an even keel, we'd just been welcomed in and accepted. Our story had encouraged them, but it had also helped to explain our situation. They graciously accepted our differences and saw that we too had something to contribute.

And if a side effect of that was to be blessed with material blessings, who were we to complain? Not that we could afford to get used to it. We could get moved on at any moment. But until that time came, we would happily make the most of the provision of a beautiful house, a lovely car and a luxurious wardrobe. After so many years of doing it tough, it was just so refreshing to have a moment in the sunshine, acknowledging that the Light was not biased in His blessing; He shone on all.

21

CONTESSA: OUT ON THE TOWN

W ell, this turned out to be all kinds of awesome. I was not expecting that. At all. I mean, seriously, after the flopping debacle in our sitting room a week ago, who would?

Not me.

That's for sure.

Anyway, on our way out of Council chambers, I was as red and puffy as a blowfish. All kinds of not pretty. Grief was brutal to my complexion. And after remembering everything that had happened in Sodom... well, I needed a moment.

Lots of moments.

Long moments... to recover.

The pain of losing Abbot was still physical.

So, blotchy skinned, watery eyed and trembly lipped we emerged from the meeting room. I was hiding under Dan's wing. This was one of the ways we were completely different. Situations where my heart decided to expose itself messily all along my sleeves were situations where his upper lip stiffened, his spine hardened, and the Great Wall of Dan emerged. I was beyond blessed to have been offered a privileged place behind that wall. Which is where I now hid.

So, it took me a while to realise we'd been stopped on our way out and Kait was running intercept for our team. All of whom were a bit rough and ragged after the meeting. She was speaking to Kari and Jason, style queen and king of Laodicea.

Oh. My. Word. How embarrassing.

They stood there in all their fashionista glory, perfectly turned out and I was...

Not in rags.

I was not wearing second-hand clothes.

I was wearing, the. Most. Amazing. Pair of boots.

I peeked out from under cover.

"We just wanted to catch you to see if Tessa and Dan wanted to join us? A group of us normally head into the city after Temple for dinner." Kari tilted her head and leaned down so she caught my eye.

And smiled.

A real smile.

Then she looked at Dan.

And smiled.

I stood tall and smiled some fashion of trembly-watery smile back. It may not have been as nice.

Dan's arm tightened around my waist and I relaxed.

The silence became awkward, then I realised they were waiting for us to respond. "Uh, thanks, but I don't know. We only have one car, and we don't know our way around." I looked up to Dan to gauge his response and then to the rest of our group.

"Kari and I will take care of you and drop you home later if you'd like to join us." Jason smiled.

A lovely smile.

Dan's arm tightened.

The grown-ups did their secret conferencing and Kait delivered the verdict. "Why don't you two go ahead and start finding your way around the city and meeting people. We'll take the twins home and see you when you get back."

I looked to Dan. He shrugged.

"Okay, thanks." It was only then I remembered I was wearing

make-up. Or had been before I cried it off. "My face." I just wanted to die. "Do I have racoon eyes?" Why hadn't anyone told me?

Kari held out her hand. "Come with me, we'll sort you out quick smart and then head out."

"Okay. Well, then. See you at home."

Marcus stepped forward and swallowed me into a hug, sneaking a covert, "Love ya kiddo, have fun," into my ear.

He then stepped in front of Dan blocking him from the rest of the group and placed his hand on Dan's shoulder. After a moment they both nodded, and Marcus stepped away.

Then it was Kait's turn. She laid her hand on my cheek, and kissed the other. Then embraced Dan. She didn't need words.

Val wasn't so "touchy feely". But then she never was. Except with Riah. She pierced each of us with her eyes and gave a small nod. *Watch yourselves. Watch out for each other. Watch your backs.*

Then they left, dragging the twins with them. "Why can we not go into the city too?" Raph voiced their joint complaint.

"Because you weren't invited." Marcus didn't have a problem helping them see the light.

Kari then took my hand and pulled me to the side where the toilets were. The harsh lights of the bathroom were as tactful as Marcus in revealing the reality of my situation. The blotchy puffiness had reduced. But the panda eyes were not a good look. Kari produced a small recovery kit out of her bag and went to work.

The girl was my new hero. With a few wipes, a splash, a dash and a brush, I was as good as new.

Actually, that's not true.

I was better.

Now, not only did I have amazing boots, I had a great face.

Thank you.

Then we went back out. And... oh dear.

While I had been put back together, Dan looked like he was ready to take things apart. He stood with his arms crossed. His indigo armour on fire. And his wall thicker and higher than ever. Jason stood to the side, perched on the back of a chair. They weren't talking and the air was thick as mud.

Looking at him from a distance, I saw him in a different light. My heart softened. Dan was so far out of his depth and completely alone. I raced over and grabbed his hand. He must have been miles away because he jumped, and when he looked at me, his face was blank. My heart faded a notch. But then he tucked me under his arm, and we were away.

Kari led us to her car. A very sweet little red convertible. I have no idea what make or model it was. But I did like it, especially because it was a bit squishy smushed up next to Dan in the back seat.

Laodicea was a beautiful city. No doubt about it. At night, the city's lights bounced off all the water artificially channelled via the aqueducts overhead and canals on the ground to create an amazing light show.

With my face glued to the side window, and my hand anchored in Dan's, I was reminded of our second last night in Sodom. We'd taken the time to clear the air and define our friendship. What had started out as being all kinds of awkward had turned out to being close to one of the best nights of my entire life. I tightened my hold on his hand and hoped he was remembering too.

Dan was more than just a friend.

He was my best friend.

Dan understood that attraction was dangerous. It couldn't be trusted. People who were motivated by "attraction" were self-seeking and dangerous. They used you and hurt you in the worst possible way. I had suffered a lot at the hands of guys in the gang I took refuge in, back in Sodom. They had all been governed by desire.

Never again.

Dan and I were attracted to each other. And that was okay. I could deal with his attraction because I trusted him. And we were taking the time to explore that trust and respect. Actually, the respect part was easy. The more I knew him, the more I couldn't help myself respecting this amazing human being.

But the trust part was a bit trickier.

To be that vulnerable was hard.

Really hard.

But Dan understood this. He understood me. And that is why he was worth being vulnerable for. And that was why he was my friend. One day I hoped that we'd move into being the kind of best friends Kait and Marcus were. That exclusive, lifelong friendship that you covenanted.

But for now, he had my respect, and he had my trust. So, it kind of went without saying, he also held my heart.

"Hey, 'bout time you guys got here. We were about to start without you." Yet another clothes horse draped himself out of a cafe window and waved us in.

Kari had manoeuvred her matchbox car into a sliver of a carpark, and we'd mingled with the growing crowd hitting the city. Dan's armour was flaring, and his eyes were darting. Our guard, just the two of them, were also scoping the scene. By now the constant hitching of Dan's nose had become the norm. The scent of sulphur was everywhere. And I mean everywhere, even in the Council chambers, but there was not a demon to be seen. I wasn't complaining, but it was weird. Everyone was on edge, waiting for the big reveal. Especially after our welcome to this unreal city.

We were led into a stylish cafe with retro photos plastered around the walls. Music played through speakers hung in the corners, but I had no idea what the tune was over the buzz of the room. All the booths that lined the front windows and assorted sized tables littering the room were occupied. It sure was a popular place. Jason pushed his way through the clientele, and we followed in his wake.

He stopped and we had a small pile up as we waited for some occupants of a booth to stand and manipulate their way out of their seats. As soon as there was an opening, we were bustled in. Keen faces and eager eyes leaned in over the backs of our seats and gathered round us.

All of them were staring.

All of them silent.

Waiting.

"Okay, back off everyone and give them some space." Jason came to our rescue.

I had no idea what these people wanted or what we'd gotten ourselves into. I thought we were just here for dinner and to meet a few of the "gang".

Dan stiffened beside me. Another reaction that had become a norm since moving here. I had to keep reminding myself that just over one month ago, he'd been a Loner living on the streets. And before that? He lived in a gang in Gomorrah with his friend Indigo—Indy. Things had gone really badly for them, but he'd survived. He still hadn't shared much about it, but from what we could figure out, it had been all kinds of horrible. I mean, the *worst* kind of horrible.

Moving in with us had been a serious adjustment. But moving to Laodicea and the new world we'd been adopted into must have been completely alien to him. Who wouldn't be a bit on edge? Right?

Taking Kait's example, I tried to run cover for him. "Hi. Um. It's great to meet you all." I scanned the group but ignored those standing directly behind me. I'd have to have turned my head one-eighty degrees. "And thanks for inviting us to dinner. Ahhh. All of the changes and trying to learn how you guys do life here has been a bit crazy. But we're really grateful for all that you've done."

Smile self-deprecatingly, and nod.

There.

That should do it.

But no. They all just stood around us and stared. Smiling open faces, eager for... I had no idea what. I looked to Jason and Kari. Maybe they had some idea of what we were supposed to do.

"Rad. It's an honour to meet you and your... boyfriend?"

"Oh, we're, not boyfriend/girlfriend." How could I explain we were so much more? I looked to Dan and smiled. But he just shook his head slowly and rolled his eyes.

Yep. You heard me. He rolled his eyes.

Here I was being nice, and he was bordering on rude.

This time Kari spoke. "That's it, folks." The crowd looked at her. "The show's over." They didn't move. "Back off." While she didn't have a thing on Val, or Kait for that matter, she produced enough steel to get us some space.

I leaned across the table and tried to whisper, but had to repeat myself so I could be heard. "What do they want?"

"They're waiting for some kind of show, I think. You're kind of urban legends around here now. Word has spread about your story: with very little truth, I suspect." Jason eyed us both. "And, of course, your armour helps sell the myth."

"The myth?" Dan almost growled.

"Yeah, you know"—Jason looked at Kari and scoffed—"the story about fighting demons." They both laughed.

I was speechless. But not for long. "What part of that do you think is a myth?" I also had nothing on Val and Kait. But unlike Kari, what I'd hoped would be steel, came out as a squeak of indignation. But at least it wasn't a snort.

"Are you trying to tell us you fought demons?" Kari was incredulous.

"Come on. Let's get out of here." Dan had grabbed my hand and was struggling to get out of the seat. But with the crowd pushing in and the room packed, it was a tangle of limbs and bodies.

"Wait. Wait. Sorry man, I can see this is not the time or the place. I guess these folks are excited to meet you, but we can do all of that another time." Jason tried to rise and face Dan in an attempt to ease the tension. But because he was shut in beside Kari, he was stuck.

"How about we go over and order a drink?" Kari slid out and went to lay her hand on Dan's shoulder. But the laser beams shooting out of his eyes pulled her up short. And not only her. When the beam fell across the rest of the group, and he rolled his shoulders and shook out his arms, they melted out of the way.

He looked back over his shoulder at me. "You want something?"

"Just a mineral water, thanks." I smiled at him and tried with all my might to send him some brain-wave message. But when I realised that wasn't working, I launched myself out of my seat and grabbed his hand. Talk about looking desperate. Well, I guess in a way I was. But not in the way it looked. I just wanted to grab his hand and give it the double squeeze which was the twins' secret language for "love you". Half lying across the table, gripping the tips of his fingers, I managed to relay the message.

He screwed his face up and looked at me like I had grown another head.

So, I tried again.

With a quick shake of his head, possibly trying to get rid of the image, he turned back to face me fully. "You alright?"

Talk about awkward.

And I mean... completely. Awkward.

"You know..." I took a firmer hold of his hand and slowly and firmly squeezed it twice accentuating each squeeze with an exaggerated blink, and a nod of my head, just to make sure the message got through. Seriously. I looked like the freak everyone by that time suspected I was.

But then his eyes grew. Then softened. His shoulders dropped and the edge of his mouth hitched. He returned the gesture, and my heart melted a bit.

Well, maybe more than just a bit.

Alright, it was a flopping puddle.

But at least I'd made it clear, he wasn't alone. We were in this together.

Then he was gone, and the tide came in.

Guys surrounded me and one even took Dan's place. They squeezed me in. I was trapped. Jason didn't notice, his eyes were glued to his phone. My heartbeat ramped up and the temperature in the room rose. White noise increased in my head blocking out their voices. They were leaning over me, trying to speak. Touching me. To ask me things. To... I don't know... I couldn't hear. I couldn't think. I was trapped. I was back in Sodom... guys pawing at me... I couldn't breathe. I had to breathe.

I could breathe.

I could do this.

In: We were in Laodicea.

Out: I had been saved from the Dark Lord.

In: I was a child of Light.

In: I was loved, and I had a purpose.

In: I had survived, and I had overcome my own demons.

Out: I was not alone.

The room was coming back into my peripheral vision, but I was still shaking.

I knew I could do this. Focus on the Light. I had survived. It was over. A new start.

The now began swimming back into focus with snippets of conversation leaking into my consciousness. The temperature was finally coming back down to normal... just before it plummeted.

"Back off. Now." A blizzard blasted through the room.

"Hey man. It's okay, we were just keeping her company—"

"Back. Off. Now." It was hardly more than a whisper, but in the silence that spread like the plague it may as well have been shouted from the rooftops. With the desperation of a drowning girl, I threw my eyes to Dan and locked onto his armour. His beautiful, distinctly unique, armour. That was on fire. Ornate patterns danced in indigo flame with hints of the most beautiful gold and red.

I was able to breathe. His presence had brought me back.

"Calm down, man. We didn't want her to get lone—"

The silence was deafening. Dan hadn't moved but the fire had spread to his eyes, removing the need for words. All arguments and weak excuses fell flat.

I really wanted to get away from these people. "Excuse me. I would like to get out." They were supposed to be fellow Children of Light. But they were rude, pushy, self-seeking and... well, I was having a hard time liking them. I wanted to go home. But the guy sitting next to me was too busy being intimidated by Dan to hear me.

"Excuse me. I would like to get out." I gave him a nudge, but he was frozen in place. They all were. Looking around the room everyone—and I mean everybody—was stilled and waiting to see what would happen.

"Oh, for goodness' sakes, would you move out of the way, please. I want to get out."

Nothing.

They were sizing Dan up as a space cleared around him.

Some were scared—those ones were smart. Some were calculating—those ones were not so smart.

This was ridiculous. I couldn't slide out under the table, there wasn't enough leg room. I couldn't get past the guy sitting next to me. I was not going to walk across the table. But, when everybody shuffled their places for a better view, they'd left gaps in the seats behind me. Once again grateful for my new wardrobe and the fact that I was not wearing a skirt, I climbed over the back of the seat into the booth behind us. Dan held out his hand to help me down.

"But she said you're not dating?"

"Irrelevant. You shouldn't have crowded her."

"If we'd known she was yours, we wouldn't—"

"Contessa is no one's property. She is her own woman."

"That's rad man. But you two—?"

"Have an understanding. And now, we're going."

"Um, thanks for inviting us to get to know you all, but we might just pick up something on the way home." I tried to smooth over the mess. But seriously, I was not impressed. And I just wanted to get out of there. I didn't know what we were going to do, or how we were going to get back to the house. But we'd work something out.

"Come on, I'll give you a lift." Kari scanned the group with a serious case of stink eye. The most potent dose for Jason. Spinning on her awesome wedge heels, she proceeded to lead the way. Once free of the chaos, she spoke over her shoulder, "Sorry about that. You guys are the hottest things on the scene for quite some time." She pointed her keys towards her car and the lights flicked. "But that doesn't mean they can behave like brats."

22

DANIEL: TANGOING THROUGH THE MINEFIELD

"Bunch of frackling morons if you ask me." The three "adults" were waiting up for us when we got home. Thankfully, that Kari chick seemed okay. She'd pulled into some chain restaurant on the way home and the three of us had debriefed over burgers.

We were sitting in the lounge room drinking coffee as Tessa came downstairs from changing and washing all the skrat off her face.

Miss Sunshine herself tried to defend them. "They weren't that bad."

"So, you were okay with the hoard and the way they were all over you like a fresh steak?" She had a short memory.

"Well, no." She shivered and ran her hands up and down her arms. "But apart from that, they seemed okay."

I pulled her down into the couch next to me and threw an arm around her. She sank in and her cold body slowly began absorbing my warmth.

"What do you mean, 'fresh steak'?" I knew Marcus would pick up on that. That'd been my plan. I wanted him on side to speak sense to her. Let him be bad cop. Not only was he good at it, he got a real kick out of it.

Tessa screwed up her face and nestled deeper. She was evading the question, so I painted the picture for them. "Well, when they'd gone fishing to figure out what our connection was, Contessa decided to clear the air and told them we weren't dating--"

"I didn't say that." She rounded on me.

"In their language you did, and I quote: 'Oh we're not boyfriend/girlfriend.' And then the sharks circled."

"But we're not. We're more. You know that." The cold steamed from her body and anger heated her nicely.

The silence grew heavier as I sensed the Three were pretty keen to hear where this was going. I needed to roll out damage control, again, before Marcus produced a shotgun from thin air.

"I know that. These guys know that we have an understanding. But those chumps didn't."

"What kind of understanding?" The lock and load were loud and clear in Marcus's growl.

"Calm down, Papa Bear." I explained what Tessa and I had discussed the night before we left Sodom, where we were going, and how we were planning on getting there. "All based on mutual trust and respect, Dad. So just breathe, would you." I leaned back into the lounge and once again Tessa settled against me. All was good again. Well, at least for the next five minutes.

"Alright then." Marcus tried to look gruff, but the deepened creases at the corners of his eyes were a dead giveaway. That plus the fact that Kait was openly beaming and Val's lips quirked, her eyes sparking like diamonds, was as good as their formal approval.

I tried to play it cool, but my heart was beating like a rampant rabbit. Man. I was glad that was finally out in the open. I knew they kind of knew, but they'd been pretty cool not pushing things. But having their official blessing took a mountain of weight off.

And with nothing more to say, we turned in for the night.

TOSSING AND TURNING, I just couldn't get comfortable. Just hearing myself think those words turned my stomach. I'd gotten soft quick.

Too quick. I'd have to be careful. If I didn't keep my guard up, this easy ride would rob me of my edge, my ability to survive. The enemy here was insidious. It may not have been a direct assault from Suit Dude and all his mates... well, apart from my own private hell-whore, but it was everywhere. In the environment, the attitudes, and sure as hell, it was in the air. Subtle, hidden and deadly.

And the people here were complete jerks. All of them. Except Felix. And maybe Kari. She seemed okay. But the rest could take a flying leap. I still didn't get how they'd all got dim to no armour at all. What the frack was their deal?

Hanging out in this freaky city at the weirdo concert, meeting with the creepy Council, then going to their zoo for "coffee", was a complete joke. All of them salivating like a pack of dogs, treating Tessa like a fresh kill and me like the new attraction at the freak show. The whole lot of them, and this freaked out city, was doing my head in.

The anger sizzling through me made it impossible to calm down enough to get anywhere near sleep. I didn't want to wake Raph, but damn it, I needed to burn off this buzz. The house was silent. An occasional car cruised along the street. We'd shut everything up against the cool spring evenings, but a chill still managed to creep its way in.

Barefoot, but rugged up in tracky-daks and a hoodie, I snuck downstairs to the adjoining garage where Marcus had hung the punching bag. I didn't want the gloves. I wanted to feel the sting and bite of the leather to help release the beast eating me up from within.

What you want from us here, I've got no flaming idea. How you're running this Community with these fools? Ditto. I don't know how to take their crud, but you do... so... any help right now would be appreciated. Cheers.

Checking that my guard was in place and watching my back, I let loose on the leather and pounded the skrat outta the thing. After the initial jar and bite, I sunk into the rhythm. My body heated, and the pain, frustration, burn and anger dissolved into the beat and comfort of the known pattern. Soon I was in the zone, miles away.

Sweat streamed into my eyes. I stopped long enough to rip my hoodie off, using it as a mop in the process. Once I was free of it, the night air did its job and I relished its refreshing kiss, instantly bringing relief from the heat.

Then I froze as the temperature dived.

Sulphur.

Skrat.

"Mmm-mm. You are looking mighty fine there, gorgeous." Dressed for the situation, she sauntered out of the shadows in minimal lycra. Yeah, like she was going to "work out".

"Oh, but I wouldn't mind a workout with you, Dan." More of that fracked purring.

"What do you want now?"

"Is that anyway to treat an old friend?"

"You ain't no friend of mine." I didn't want to turn my back on her, but I wanted the protective layer of my hoodie back, and I wanted to see my guard. Bless the being, he'd moved so I could see them both. I nodded to him in gratitude. Face like flint, he nodded back.

She turned, eyed us both. "Hmm, this could be interesting." A sly smile lit her dead eyes.

"What do you want?" What I wanted was not to play her games. And for her to sketch off.

"Considering how your 'best friend' treated you tonight, I thought you might want a replacement." Again with the pout. "She left you high and dry... again. She declared to the pack of suitable replacements that you were nothing to her. Was it any wonder they were salivating over her?" Running her hands down her ribs and settling them on her hips she sauntered closer.

I put the bag between us.

She chuckled. "You knew as soon as there was competition, she'd ditch you. The only reason she picked you was because you were the only meat around." Another step closer. "Now there's competition, she's dropped you faster than a..." She dropped her eyes, sweaty jockstrap. Another step.

The temp was still low but sweat prickled.

"And why would you care? Look around Dan. You could have anyone you want." If she'd stretched out her arm, she could have touched me.

I readjusted my hold on the bag.

"You could actually pick someone who suited your taste. Not a twig, like Tessa, but a real woman, like I know you prefer." She caressed the bag, her hand running close to but not touching mine. "And honestly"—her dead eyes pinned mine—"would you have picked her if you'd had a choice?"

My mouth went dry. Blood drained from my head and I grabbed the bag for support. She leaned around my barrier and whispered in my ear. "You know it's true." She kissed my cheek.

It was a whisper. But images from a past life and... way of life, flashed through my mind. Urges and heat that I had pushed aside burst from the coffin I had buried them in.

Frack.

"Any time you want, gorgeous." Then she was gone.

I needed another shower. A cold shower.

23

DANIEL: REALITY'S FANGS

K ait had been making her way from the kitchen to the sitting area when she saw me. "What's wrong?"

I was the last to arrive for morning coffee. Wrecked, hardly able to stand, I collapsed on the bottom step, shut my eyes for a bit and let the wall hold me up. I was aware of movement in the background, but the static thumping in my head shut everything else out. I couldn't even smell the frackling sulphur for once. And for that small mercy, I was grateful. All the other skrat I would happily give up. It'd been so long since I'd had a new dream, I'd softened up.

Gentle hands took my shoulders. A warm presence filled the space beside me. I cracked my eyes to see Val's face in front of me and Marcus alert and on guard to my left.

"What is it, Dan?" Val's whisper was a blend of steel and concern.

I tried to let them know it wasn't a big deal. It'd pass. I'd be okay. But I just struggled to find the energy to say anything... at all. "Dream. I'm shattered."

"Do you want to go back to bed. I'll give you—"

"No!" Yeah, well, apparently, I had enough energy to fight that fool idea. "Not going back to sleep. No... thanks."

"I've just made him a coffee. Bring him to the lounge."

"I love that wife of yours, Marcus. Just as well you married her."

Tessa hovered behind me. "He's obviously delirious."

With Marcus's arms around my shoulders, we made our way to join the others.

I could have walked by myself, eventually. But the couch was a hell of a lot more comfortable than the stairs. But that was the danger. I didn't want to go back to sleep.

Sun broke through the large open doors heading to the back garden. A light tang of wet grass, damp soil and new morning feathered the air until it was blown away by fresh coffee. Light bathed everything, transforming dew into diamonds. Each colour and tone fought to blind me with its brilliance. The garden was pretty epic, in a grand, restrained way. But it couldn't hold a light to Riah's. Mainly because it wasn't Riah's. I loved Sunday mornings, our day to sleep in and coast through the morning on the tide of laziness. I had no idea what time it was, and I couldn't give a fig.

Tessa curled up beside me and voiced the question that was bouncing around the room. "What was it, Dan? The House again?"

Tessa had overheard me sharing my House dream with Abbot and Val in Sodom. She knew it was beyond a nightmare.

"No, that one's finished." I nodded to Val. Then shut my eyes and laid my head back on the cushion. She had told me I wouldn't have it again and I hadn't. I started drifting off and snapped my head up. Everyone was staring, waiting. "This was a new one." I took hold of the cup Tessa gave me and welcomed the burn in my hands, the comfort of the aroma, and the gift of not being alone. I'd never had the perk of having a family to help me through the torture.

"I was—"

There was a knock at the door. A very distinct, loud, rapid beat.

"Who the frock would have the gall to visit at this time Sunday morning?" My exhaustion morphed into anger. "What the hell time is it anyway?"

The idiot was at it again. Unless there was a fire, flood or fighting raging down our street, I'd happily teach the twik a lesson.

Kait jumped up. "I'll deal with it. Just relax honey, we'll sort it out as soon as I get back."

She hadn't even finished speaking before the knock turned into pounding. I was ready to explode.

"This really isn't the best time, Ty. Maybe you could come back later?" Kait was trying to head our intruder off at the pass.

"I don't have 'later' Kait. Tomorrow is the start of the new work week and you all need to know what you'll be doing."

As inevitable as a hangover after a night on the tiles, Ty marched through the hall and made his way to where we sat, and I seethed.

"Good. You're all up." He looked at me. "I heard all about your adventures last night." His eyes giving me the once-over, his scoff dismissing me. "I won't keep you long." He walked to the coffee table, pushed our cups to the side and planted a pile of folders. "Now—"

"Excuse me, Ty. We've just made a brew. Would you like to join us for a coffee?" Just as well I wasn't sipping mine. I would have sprayed it at the shock of Val's words. Her face was open, and her offer was genuine. Maybe she'd seen something the rest of us hadn't.

For a moment Ty's facade cracked, but then he was all business again. "No. Thank you. I won't hold you up for long." He nodded to the folders. "Everything is here. But I'll be happy to answer any questions you may have, now and later. If needs be."

It may have been my imagination, but the guy seemed to soften. I looked around the room trying to see us as he would. I guess we could be pretty intimidating. That was a lie. We were very intimidating. Maybe the guy was scared. It then occurred to me that Riah had squeezed her way between me and the end of the couch. I looked down at her and raised my eyebrows, *Was that you?*

She smiled. Her gift of Peace had slid under my radar and lowered my hackles. I took her hand and gave it a quick two pumps. She beamed.

"Would you like a seat?" I followed my leader's lead and genuinely tried to make him feel welcome.

I only got an eyebrow disappearing act and a look, *You have got to be kidding?*, In return. Well, at least I tried. Shrugging and throwing my arm around Tessa's shoulders and holding Riah's hand, I waited for the verdict.

"Okay, well. As you know, Raphael and Sariah have been enrolled at Community College, the most prestigious school in Laodicea, and they are expected tomorrow at 8:30 am. Waide will be dropping uniforms and school supplies off later this morning." He looked to the adults. "If that suits?" I couldn't believe it, but I detected a drop in the level of sarcasm. Maybe we were getting through his defences. He held out the twins' information folder, looking for a recipient. Kait took it.

Raph's face fell and Riah burrowed into my side. Poor kids.

"Tessa." He turned to her and handed her another folder. "Originally you were down for one of our cleaning teams, but Kari has requested you join her events committee. Planning and preparing for the events the Community runs, or sponsors."

Tessa squeaked and jiggled. A hint of a smile ghosted across Ty's face. "Any questions, Kari's number is in there." He indicated the yellow folder she held.

He looked at the next name on his list and breathed deeply. "Marcus." With his shoulders set, Ty continued, "The Overseer has personally requested your assistance."

None of us, least of all Marcus, could hide the shock of that bombshell.

"We understand you have expertise with maintaining and driving a variety of vehicles?" Even though it was a question, Marcus wasn't given the opportunity to respond. "The Overseer would be extremely grateful if you stepped into the role of his driver. He has many important meetings and events that take him not only throughout Laodicea, but to other major cities in our region. His last driver has just taken retirement."

Again, Marcus opened his mouth to make some comment, but Ty continued right over the top of him. "We understand that you are a close family, and this job would take you away for some time, but the Overseer feels that with your background and experience, he will be safe with you in the driver's seat, so to speak." Ty gave a huff of amusement at his own joke. But then all humour left his face, and we saw... fear? He was afraid of Marcus. Understandably.

Marcus didn't respond. Probably waiting to see if Ty had finished and he was safe to speak. As the awkwardness continued, it seemed he was.

"Please thank the Overseer for the honour. This is very unexpected, but I will have to speak to me family first before I can agree." He stood and as he accepted the folder, he clapped Ty on the shoulder. Ty was still standing, so it was friendly. Seemed we'd all called a truce. It didn't stop Ty flinching, however.

He opened his mouth, cleared his throat. This time words tumbled out in a high, strangled pitch. "Um." He swallowed audibly. "I have been told to pass on that these roles are non-negotiable, and a condition of the gifts of house, finances, food, et cetera."

Marcus swallowed. Nodded slowly. Softened his face and responded. "Thank you for pointing that out, Ty. I appreciate that being the messenger is not the easiest job in the world. If I, or any of us, have a problem with the conditions of this contract, we will take it to the Overseer."

Ty let out a ragged sigh. "Thank you. Um." He breathed deeply, stood tall and looked Marcus in the eye again. "He requires your assistance starting tomorrow. He is heading to Philadelphia for a meeting and requests your services to transport him."

"Tomorrow? Philadelphia? What? For how long?" Marcus's splutters dropped from a roar to a whisper.

"You will be back Wednesday. It is a short trip, and he is very grateful for your assistance."

Marcus was as white as a sheet. Kait took his hand in both of hers and leaned in so close she was almost sitting on his lap.

In the booming silence, Ty continued. Looking to his list, he then turned to Kait. "Our PR team have suggested that you would be perfect for their 'Face of Laodicea's Future', a series of media releases and productions that share information and advancements made here in Laodicea in partnership with the Community. Since you have hospital experience, and you are an outsider, they feel you would be perfect to front the medical Futures branch. Interviewing scientists and doctors on medical research and advancements." This time he did stop and allowed Kait's stunned silence to fill the room.

"But... but I was a nurse. And it's been years since I've worked in a hospital. And I don't know anything about the advancements and medical miracles going on here. I am completely unqualified for this role." The whites of Kait's eyes were blending into her paling skin.

"On the contrary. The team feel that with your gracious nature, your knowledge, and your looks, you will not only be a figure that followers will connect with easily, you'll be able to reduce the scientific to layman's terms." He smiled. "They are not trying to connect with the scientific community, but the everyday person. To be transparent and informative of what's going on and the great work being done by the Community. We have a reputation to uphold. They think you will be perfect for the role."

Finally, Kait shut her mouth and dumbly accepted the folder he passed to her. He brushed his hands and rested them on his hips. It was then I twigged. There weren't any more folders. Tessa spoke into the void. "What about Dan and Val? What role does the Community have for them?"

"Well..." Ty swallowed noisily. Great. More bad news. "It seems that Valarie's ability to fight is not one the Community has a need for. Since the enemy is not in Laodicea."

Val had the grace to meet that insult with merely raised eyebrows. Tessa however charged right in. "But what about her knowledge and ability to teach The Way? Surely the Community needs teachers?"

"Yes, of course we do. But all our teachers have graduated from our own Community Seminary. A very extensive program." Ty studied his hands. "Unless she were to enrol in the four-year program, she may then be considered for a position?" He looked at her. But when he saw her face, he continued, "So, sorry, there is no role for you here. But"—his eyes brightened, and he looked her in the eye—"since Marcus will be away from home at times and Kait will be working outside the house, the Overseer thought it would be helpful to have an adult here to help with the children." His head nodded to each of the twins, just in case we weren't aware of who "the children" were.

"But what about Dan?" Tessa was still riding that white charger into battle.

I didn't qualify for dropped eyes or an apologetic look. "Hmm." Some of his former snark snuck out from under his mask. "With Dan's inexperience in the Light and his past practices, the Overseer wanted to allow him some more time to adjust to his new life."

It was like I wasn't even in the room.

"How long? A week, a month?" Tessa had picked up that bone and she was not letting go.

"We'll see."

"But then? What will he do?"

"There are cleaning teams that could use some help." He had the gall to look like this was a positive.

"But why couldn't he join a team now? What's so special about cleaning that he wouldn't be suited for?" Tessa stood in an attempt to meet Ty eye to eye. She didn't quite meet his chin, but it was better than arguing at his crotch.

Ty flicked his eyes to me and then dropped them to the floor.

It was all I needed. I stood and answered her myself. "Because even though the toilet bowls are screwed down, lots of other things aren't. I suspect they fear I will be tempted to lift something that I shouldn't. That's right, isn't it, Ty?" His silence was all I needed for confirmation. A frozen lead balloon socked me in the gut. And all of a sudden, that positive light that had kindled around the man faded and winked out. But like Marcus said, he didn't make the decisions. So, despite the humiliation I was drowning in, I tried to follow my mentors' lead and extend grace. "If these roles"—I pointed to the folders—"are in exchange for the provisions"—I waved to indicate the room in general—"does that mean I have to leave?"

Tessa sucked in a breath beside me.

Ty seemed genuinely affronted. "What? No. Of course not. You are welcome to stay and partake in the provisions."

"But, if the job is payment for the goods, and I'm taking without paying, isn't the Overseer encouraging me to steal?"

His eyes grew at my interpretation. "But... no... the Overseer is extending grace."

I didn't even try to hide my disbelief. "Without a catch? You telling me, all this is for free? For me? A no-good gutter-rat thief?"

The payoff was his red face. "Well"—he cleared his throat again—"it was hoped that this gift of grace would help ease the burden of others' expectations."

Right. Do as you're told, and we'll pretend we're not offended by your dirty thief. Got it. But since I was working at being gracious, I didn't smash the errand boy. "Well, thanks for passing that information on. I will wait till the Overseer and this Community can find a role that I may serve in."

Placing one arm around Tessa's shoulder I swallowed my pride and extended my hand and thanked Ty for taking time out on his Sunday morning to keep us up to date. I was gratified that he didn't leave me hanging.

Val, the least shocked or rocked in the room, escorted Ty to the door and echoed my thanks for coming by.

She came back and we attempted to manage the fall out.

24

MARCUS: DEALING WITH THE SPLATTER

"Well, if that ain't the pig's buttocksials, I don't know what is."

Kait looked around the room, gulped, then tried to focus on the positives. "It isn't all bad. Tessa's assignment sounds very exciting. We should celebrate with her."

"And what about you, hey? Movie star and all." I tried to make light of it.

"You take that smirk off your face this instant. You know very well how I feel about being in the limelight." She smacked me shoulder. It was light, but I could see she was upset. And she was right. Tessa was struggling to keep the sparkle out of her eyes, and she shouldn't have to.

"Before we start dissecting the verdict, I'd like Dan to finish." Val looked at the lad, who had retaken his seat flanked by Tessa and Riah.

Eyes wide and brows up, he returned her look. Blank.

"Your dream. You were just about to share when Ty arrived. I think it's important that we hear what assignment the Light has given you." She nodded, handing the floor over to him.

"Oh. Yeah." He gulped and colour drained from his face. His cup clattered as he placed it on the table. "Someone needs our help."

"Who?" I think Val and Sariah were the only two who didn't jump down his throat.

Dan pressed back into the couch at our attack. His eyes darted to the rest of us as we launched ourselves like dieters at the dessert trolley. "How the hell am I supposed to know?" His shoulders slumped. "Sorry. I don't know. All I know is, there is someone in this city who's calling out for help... over and over and over again."

His eyes bored through the table back into his memory. "A girl. Young. She's hurting. Dying? Sick? I don't know. But she's crying and doesn't have a voice. It's just crazy. The whole dream was in black and white... and every shade of grey." His haunted eyes came back to us. "She's suffering. Crying. Calling. She won't stop. On and on... keening." He took a shaky breath, looking to me, Kait and Val. "We've got to find her."

Kait released an anguished moan. "How can we? The Community has us all tied up." The thought of a child in pain or suffering would be breaking her as much as it was tearing me up.

"Calm down, Kait." Val's warmth brought peace to the room. "Let's talk to the Light about this and then make a plan."

And we did. Remembering to give thanks for bringing us to this place. For Him finding roles for us to help the Community and serve its purpose. For our Badges to be used to pull the oars.

We asked the Light to help the kids at school, to help Kait deal with all the attention, and wisdom in what to do about me job offer. It was good to hand it all over, knowing we were just the soldiers and He was the General making the moves. I didn't know about anyone else, but it sure did help me breathe easier.

Best to take the bull by the horns and ride that sucker all the way through the eight seconds. "Right. What's the plan?"

"Little Master." Val nailed Raph with his nick name for a purpose. I think she was reminding him of who he was to us. "Princess." Sariah, like her brother, was precious in not only our eyes, but in the Light. "Are you up to the challenge?" She quirked an eyebrow at the kids. "Surely this can't be as bad as a library full of demons?"

Clever. She was reminding them of their victories and who they were, then throwing the gauntlet at their feet in direct challenge.

They looked at each other, communicated silently, then Raph slowly turned back to Val and nodded his head with glassy eyes.

The boy was breaking me heart. I wanted to tell him it was going to be alright, that he would be fine. But I knew better than to make promises I couldn't keep. So just went with telling them how I felt. "You know, you two are the apple of me eyes and the stars of me sky. Whatever you do and wherever you are, you're in my mind's eye and heart's light."

Riah tilted her head at me.

Raph screwed up his face, his mouth moving as he repeated me words to himself.

I was never the best with me words. So, I tried again. "We love you and are very proud of you guys for giving this a go." I didn't want them to go. I wanted them home with me, to be safe. But I wasn't even going to be home to protect them. So, I did the only thing I could think of: bargain. "If you hate it, and it doesn't work, you don't have to stay. Okay?"

I was rewarded with a watery smile from Raph, steel from Riah, and a frown and a rewording of me deal from Kait. "Give it three months, if it isn't working, then we'll reconsider," she amended.

Riah sized her up. I suspect seeing how strong Kait's stand was. Then nodded.

Deal.

Three months.

"Right, next. Tessa. You're happy with your role." It wasn't really a question; Val merely stated the obvious. "Before you get too carried away, read through that document and ask lots of questions. If you want help, ask. If you don't understand, ask. If you're not happy, speak up. Understand?"

Tessa's curls took off like a startled flock of geese as she nodded in agreement.

Val moved on. "Kait?"

"Yeah. I know, dear heart. Read, ask, challenge and be sure." She smiled at her sister. I knew Kait would rather eat razor blades than do this role. Truth be, she would rather be at home with the kids. But seemed we were all making sacrifices. And that should not've been a surprise.

It was my turn. "Marcus?" The warmth of Val's voice almost brought me to tears.

I didn't want to leave me family. Especially in a strange city. But what could I do? What choice did I have? "If He wills it, I'll do it. But it breaks me to do so." I wrapped me arm around Kait and held on. I couldn't look at any of them without shedding tears, so I looked to Val who gave me the strength I needed to get through. "I'll do what needs doing Val, you know it."

She nodded in response. Kait buried her face into my side. My shirt absorbing her tears. Val moved on, giving us space. "Dan?"

"What? You heard the guy. I'm just a useless gutter-rat. Useless for anything but thieving."

"Snap out of it, princess. You know very well that's not the case, so stop feeling sorry for yourself. You are here, you are needed, and you have a job to do." Val was good at the verbal slap. I wondered if it was a Badge.

Dan sat up in response.

"The Community may have dished out jobs for everyone else, but the Light has given His own orders."

He tilted his head like a one-eyed dog.

"As of tomorrow. You and I are on the hunt for a young girl who needs our help." The softness of her face turned to iron as Dan met her challenge and, in her words, "manned up".

But then he stooped. "But how are we going to find this girl? Laodicea is huge. She could be anyone... anywhere."

Pride shot out of me like a flamethrower. "Kait will tell you where to go. This is how it works, lad. We get a directive. Kait Knows. Val Sees. I Sense. Easy as peas in a mushy pie."

Tugging hooked me focus. I looked at me wife's white face and felt ill. "What's wrong?"

"I can't help." She looked to us all. More tears flooded her face. "Since we've arrived, I've not been able to fast. I have lost my Badge."

Kait's fasting involved sticking to a vegan diet. It wasn't that she was against eating some kinds of food. Truth be, Kait loved all food. And when I say love, I mean like sugar coated oxygen. She inhaled the stuff. Well, not anymore. But it was a passion and me Kait was a passionate woman. But if she chose to stick to this discipline, her Badge was intensified, and she would hear words that directed and led us in the Light's will.

"But you can still ask. Surely the Light'll understand. Won't He?" I looked at Val.

She shrugged her shoulders. "Worth a try. Any help would be appreciated."

Kait sniffed, then forced a smile. "Enough of this doom and gloom. We all need something to eat, then we can each go through our information and start figuring out what on earth this next chapter is going to look like for our family."

She stood up, shook out her hair and marched to the kitchen. Her grieving was done. And now she was ready to start dealing with the realities and necessities... like lunch. It constantly amazed me how quickly Kait could process and move on. I knew it would keep bubbling away under the surface, but she would put it away for now and pull it out and deal with it at a more appropriate time. She was aiming to set a good example.

Least I could do was to share the load. I stood and held me hand out. "Hey Raph, want to help me make pancakes for breakfast?"

The boy perked up and launched himself off the couch to join me on the way to the kitchen. But as he ran past, I grabbed his waist, spun him around and carried him by the ankles. His squeals of laughter were a tonic for me soul.

"Hang in there, Raph, I'll save you." Tessa crept towards us with her fingers twitching.

"Now hang on a minute, Tess. You tickle me and I'll drop the kid." Me gangster interpretation was woeful, but it was enough to distract her. I gently laid Raph on the carpet then made a swoop to get them both.

Raph scrambled to his feet, bouncing and yelling, as Tess and I faced off. "Run Tessie. Run." And they both scooted out the back door. I played my part by roaring and racing after them but making sure I gave them enough time to get a head start.

How the hell am I going to leave them for days at a time?

I roared louder and gave chase.

SITTING around a table laden with pancakes that Kait and Riah had made, partnered with toppings, fruit and coffee, we made a plan for the day. We'd take our folders and read through them to get an understanding of what was required. Then meet up for lunch to share.

Val, Dan and the twins would pick a movie from the ludicrously large library and chill out in front of the equally large screen, eating their way through a mammoth batch of popcorn. We couldn't stop the tide of tomorrow, but we could plant memories in the sand today that would carry until next weekend.

Please help us get through this.

We hit the hay early, so we could spend Monday morning together before we were all peeled off in different directions.

FOR THE FIRST time I could remember, I was up before dawn and Kait, and started the coffee brewing. I then went back upstairs to watch me wife slowly wake. Lord she was beautiful. A more magnificent human being I'd never had the privilege to meet. And she was me wife. For almost twenty years, since she stopped working shifts at the hospital, I'd not spent a night away from her.

I think the sound of me heart breaking brought her fully awake. "What? What's wrong? Why are you up?"

I leaned down and kissed her, trying to reveal the depth of me sorrow and love. She wiped the tears from me eyes.

I took her hand and gently encouraged her up. "Come on, coffee's brewing. We need to get moving or we won't have a chance to see everyone before we all head out."

She snagged me round the waist and whispered into me chest. "I love you. Always have. Always will. Where you are and what you're doing can't change that. I will miss you"—her voice cracked—"but already, I'm looking forward to your return." Looking up, she smiled. "It'll be alright. We'll be okay."

I kissed her again. What more could I say? I was not doing this for the Community. I'd made it clear to everyone yesterday that me decision to go was based wholly on me love for them and the Light. Since we all felt this was His will, I would do it. I was just pickled as punch that I could let me guard down with Kait, let the pressure cooker of me emotions ease, before ramming the lid on and heading down to morning time with our family.

Tessa, Dan and Val had made the drinks. The twins were not down yet, Dan reported as he handed me a cup. "I think they're in denial."

I nodded. "Right. You go get Riah, I'll get Raph. I am not leaving without having a proper farewell."

Moments later I carried Raph over my shoulder in a fireman's lift. Dan walked behind us, holding Riah by the hand as she dragged her feet and stomped down every step into the lounge. Everyone was waiting to go through our morning routine reflecting on the Light. Then we went outside for an abbreviated version of our sets.

We were sitting around the table, showered, packed and dressed in our specified uniforms, when the first caller came.

I was strangely encouraged knowing the Community's Administrator would be joining us. But then, when I thought about it, it was obvious. "Good morning, Felix. Do you have time for a coffee before we head out?"

"From your machine? Yes. That would be… preferable. Thank you." I was actually beginning to enjoy his drollness.

Dan rose and brewed him a cup. When he returned to the table, Felix produced seven boxes and laid them out on the table. Kait and Tessa were beaming. The rest looked as clueless as chooks in a rowboat.

"Phones." Felix passed one to everyone. "I know this will be... difficult for you all. So, I have arranged for you to have a way to communicate. They are all fully charged and programmed with each other's numbers already." He looked at the boxes and passed them out according to the name handwritten on the top.

When he passed one to Riah, Raph spoke up. "Mr Felix, this is very generous of you. Thank you. But Sariah does not speak." He took his sister's hand, and two sets of black eyes considered the man.

Felix leaned over and made a show of speaking conspiratorially to Raph. "I know. But she can hear."

Riah gasped. Her chair grated across the floor and she dashed around the table to wrap herself around our guest, her shoulders shaking.

Stiff as a board, Felix patted her on the back. "There... there. You can also video call and group chat." Now he was wrapped in two children. If he wasn't careful, he would soon be wrapped in five adults as well.

Even Val had a catch in her voice. "Well, that's very thoughtful of you Felix. Thank you."

The man's alabaster skin darkened to a shade of off-white. "I know this transition is... challenging. I thought these may help." He looked around to us, his eyes pleading for help.

Tessa and Dan helped peel the twins off him so he could drink his coffee. His hands straightened invisible wrinkles in his immaculate suit. "Now"—he pulled a device from his pocket—"just confirming. Kait, Georgie will be by to pick you up at seven o'clock. Tessa, Kari will come and get you at eight. And"—his eyes flicked to the twins—"school starts at eight-thirty." He looked to Val and Dan. "You have a car. Is one of you able to drive, or would you like me to organise someone to collect the children?"

Val put voice to the warmth of our collective heart. "We're good, thanks again for everything, Felix. We really appreciate all that you're doing for us."

The man merely nodded his head and finished his coffee. "Very good." He considered Dan. "Thank you."

Dan shrugged. "No worries."

"Right then." Felix looked around the room. "Unfortunately the inevitable has a way of arriving right on time. And we need to make a move." Turning to me, he continued. "I'll wait outside and give you a chance to say your farewells. We need to pick up the Overseer at seven, so we don't have too long."

I nodded, getting his meaning. "I'll be right out. And thanks."

DRIVING THE SLEEK, black SUV through Laodicea, I flicked me eyes to Felix sitting in the back seat. From the moment we'd left, he'd been tapping away at his laptop or speaking to people through an earpiece. The man didn't stop. And it seemed that there wasn't a part of the Community's business he didn't manage. From the cleaners and the PR to the Shepherds.

I followed the sat-nav to the Overseer's palace and parked in the driveway. As soon as the wheels stopped rolling, Felix was out of the back and knocking on the front door.

A well-fed, older woman answered, dressed in a simple black uniform and a fluorescent white apron. They spoke.

The woman rang her hands and dropped her eyes.

Felix looked at his watch, then nodded to the woman. The door closed and he made his way back to the car. From his seat in the back, he explained. "The Overseer has been... detained. It appears we will have a bit of a wait. My apologies."

"No worries. I'm sorted. What about you? You not going to wait inside the house?" Surely the Community's Administrator should be able to wait in the Overseer's mansion instead of out in the cold?

"No." In the rear vision mirror, I saw one eyebrow quirk. "I have work I can do here."

With that, he readjusted his computer and started working again. I figured since these guys seemed to have money to burn, I'd turn the car on and run the heater. Couldn't see the point of the two of us freezing our butts off as Old Mate worked through his detention. I pulled out a copy of The Way and opened up to where I'd been reading last.

Val had cautioned me to keep up with me routine, even when I was away.

Especially when I was away.

25

FELIX: PHILADELPHIA

I had just got off the phone from, once again, making excuses for the man. Thankfully, Overseer Jonathan was a decent sort of chap and seemed to understand. The main reason we had agreed on the early start was to beat the traffic on the main highway that ran through Philadelphia. The city was relatively new and had become both a hub and a gateway into the three regions it butted up against. All under the governance of the Gerent, of course, but still a place open to trade, investment and innovation. As a result, morning traffic was a bottleneck. That we were now stuck in.

Our new driver didn't seem to mind. Marcus. Blue armour. Blundstones. Husband. Adoptive father of the twins. Fit. Lithe. Forty-one years old. Co-leader of their group... family? Uneducated but skilled. Aggressive? No. Not aggressive, protective and... blunt. Confident. Not a threat. Potential ally? Handled the car well, hadn't baulked at the challenge of a quick start in his role and time away from family. It was obviously a challenge for him... for them all and, as such, a credit in his ledger. Along with his driving skills... and patience.

The Overseer looked up from his device and noted we hadn't moved in the last ten minutes. "Can't you go around this blockage, my man?"

"Well now, I'll agree we're about as stuck as a pig in a fly trap, but unless you want to grow us some wings... me man, you've got about as much chance as Buckley. So, I'd suggest you settle, read your book and next time, chase the worm."

The Overseer and I caught each other's eye in the mirror of the sun visor in front of him. His mouth was agape.

Dear Lord, it was gold. I'd pay to see this expression on my boss's face at least once again before I died.

It was a riddle. I couldn't help myself, my brain was already reeling and working to solve the puzzle of the man's vernacular. It provided a dash of colour to the otherwise tedious trip.

When thought returned to the Overseer, he shifted so he could look at me directly in the middle of the back seat. "Was that English?"

I bit the inside of my cheek and caught Marcus's wink in the rear-view mirror. Fixed my mask and gave the Overseer a nod.

"What did he say?"

"I believe Marcus advised that we can't go around as we are stuck in the middle of a traffic jam. He also offered his condolences that we were unable to leave on time which would have avoided this... delay?" I caught Marcus's eye in the rear-view mirror again.

His grin and nod confirmed I had indeed interpreted his riddle accurately. His credit ledger had just increased tenfold.

"Quite. Yes. Right you are, my man. Right you are. Damned shame. Although, I'm sure it won't be long now? Would you say..." He had been looking at his new driver but at the last moment the Overseer swung his head to me. "Felix?"

Obviously, I had no idea. I had to check with Marcus who nodded to the horizon where life was slowly returning to the car park in which we were becalmed. "Not too long now, Overseer."

"Good. Good job." And he returned to whatever was holding his attention on the device in his lap.

Seventy-three and a quarter minutes late, we arrived at the headquarters of the Community of Light in Philadelphia. The home office of their Overseer and Head Shepherd, Jonathan. The house was simple and neat. Two levels. Brick. I couldn't see the backyard. But I'd estimate a generous eight hundred–plus square–metre block. Level. Well maintained garden out front, large shade trees out the back. Movement from behind the curtains on the top floor.

The Crow stretched and ruffled its feathers. I didn't expect too much trouble from the beast. This Overseer was head of the Community in another city. He seemed reasonable on the phone and in all dealings we'd had so far. As minimal as they'd been. He was no threat to me personally or professionally. I was perfectly capable of holding my own in this situation, as I was in all professional situations. With a whispered cackle the Crow circled, sat and subsided... for now. I had my medication, mouthguard, and new mobile phone to connect with Marlene if it turned tumultuous. I was prepared for all eventualities.

Philadelphia's Overseer himself answered our knock, greeting us in blazing violet armour and well-worn Asics.

"Welcome to Philadelphia, Overseer." He held out his hand.

My Overseer shook it and puffed out his chest.

Next our host turned his open face and fit body towards me and kept his hand extended. "Jonathan. You must be Felix. Welcome."

He shook my hand with a firm grip, then led us through to his office which was off the entrance hall. From what I could see, the house was bright, clean and open. Large glass doors revealed an expanse of grass and garden out the back. I added an extra fifty square metres to my original estimate. Neat. Well maintained. Uncluttered. Welcoming.

Overseer Jonathan ushered us into his office, but before we could sit, he interjected, "Your driver is still in the car?"

My Overseer was seated and already sizing up the room and preening himself. "Yes. Yes, he's fine. No need to worry about him."

Overseer Jonathan hadn't moved from the door. "He is welcome to come in."

Loud thumping came from overhead. Both my Overseer and I froze and looked to the ceiling.

"Sorry about that, Laura is getting Ruby ready to go for a walk."

The Overseer once again chose to speak before he thought to think. "Is Ruby your dog?"

An ocean of shame and humiliation swamped me. From looking around the man's house, even this very office, it was obvious Jonathan had children. The photo on the wall showed him with a woman, four boys and a young girl... and no dog.

Thankfully our host was good natured enough to chuckle. "No, although she's as energetic as a puppy. Ruby is our fifth child and only daughter. The boys are at school."

I had not yet taken my seat and was happy for the opportunity to stretch my legs for a moment longer before committing to sit for the meeting that would follow. "Shall I invite Marcus to come in?"

Moments later, Overseer Jonathan and Marcus stood in the doorway gripping wrists and greeting each other with beaming faces like long lost relatives. Light sparked along their arms where raging violet was engulfed in electric blue.

It was uncanny. "Have you already met?"

They looked at each other and grinned, yet denied prior knowledge of each other.

Our host invited us to make ourselves comfortable then offered refreshments. He then disappeared around the corner, taking Marcus with him. "Laura, honey, we have a guest." It wasn't too long afterwards he returned carrying a tray with three mugs of instant coffee and a plate of homemade biscuits. "I doubt Laura will get out on that walk. She and Marcus are talking ten to the dozen out there."

Overseer Jonathan handed around the victuals then, finally, we began.

"Thank you for coming to meet with me. I know you're busy and quite frankly I am surprised and honoured that both of you would give up your time to come and visit. Can the Community do without both of you for a couple of days?"

My Overseer brushed crumbs off his shirt front. "Yes, I manage a well-oiled machine. And if anyone needs me, I am just a phone call away."

I succeeded in not allowing my inner groan to escape. "How may we be of help, Overseer Jonathan?"

"Jonathan." He replied.

"Yes. Overseer Jonathan."

He laughed. "No. Please, just call me Jonathan."

I nodded, accepting the compliment of camaraderie. His gentle, genuine warmth put the Crow to bed for the meeting.

"As you know, we are a new Community planted in a relatively new city. We have incredible potential and opportunities here to grow and serve." Jonathan went on to give us statistics, plans, goals and his team's vision for the Community in Philadelphia. "But while we are full of passion and ideas, we are poor in resources and capital. We have been seeking the Light in how to proceed and we were encouraged to reach out to the other Communities in our region and seek advice." He stopped, really looked at us, then continued. "The first being you."

The Overseer's, "We shall consult the Light on your behalf," overshadowed my, "I would advise you to invest in local resources."

Jonathan laughed. "Thank you both for your enthusiasm. Overseer...?" He was yet to learn that, unlike himself, our Overseer enjoyed his title in preference to his given name.

"Just Overseer will do."

Again, Jonathan responded with a warm chuckle. "Overseer, thank you for your offer of petition. We will take all of that we can get. And Felix, that is wise counsel, but we have no funds to invest yet."

This time, the Overseer's, "That is a problem, we shall consult the Light on your behalf," slid under my, "We will sort something out. We have the funds invested for this very purpose."

With his eyes wide, Jonathan stuttered. "That is very generous of you. But I suspect it will be a while before we can pay you back."

"No need. It will be a gift." This time I spoke without the Overseer's accompaniment.

Nonetheless, the Overseer's response was speedy. "Why Felix, my boy. I think you mean, loan. We will *loan* Philadelphia the money."

I looked to my boss, then returned my attention to Jonathan. "We can organise a stimulus package. Look at local industry. What is established and what is in the pipeline. Yes, Philadelphia is a relatively new city, considering your well-established neighbours dominating the region, but look to what is a growth industry. Initially I would strongly encourage you to investigate local wineries. Their fame has already blossomed throughout the continent and is spreading worldwide. Look for one that is in need of help; an older one needing a boost or a new one becoming established. Then research what is happening at your universities. What is new and on the rise?"

Now it was the Overseer's turn to stutter. "Yes, very good advice, Felix, but don't get ahead of yourself. Don't overwhelm the poor man."

Jonathan did look overwhelmed. But by the way he was madly jotting down notes, I didn't think it was a negative.

A high-pitched squeal and Marcus's deep roar erupted from the back garden. Instantly I was on alert, horrified that our driver was threatening Overseer Jonathan's child.

But the girl's father didn't flinch. His pen continued to fly across the page. Once the pounding of my heart quietened in my ears, I was able to discern the screeching was accompanied by peals of the child's laughter. I took a deep, calming breath and continued.

"Next, we can offer your people training. We can provide scholarships to worthy contenders for the programs being run at any of our universities. I suggest we get some people into our horticultural and viticultural studies. Our seminary can offer professional development for your team of Shepherds and Waiters." I stopped to think. "I will need to look around and hear more of what you need. But I am sure we can work something out."

Jonathan stopped writing and stared at me with a white face. A watery glint brought a sparkle to his eyes. Like a desperate fish, his mouth opened and closed a couple of times before words tumbled out. "Thank you." He wet his lips. "I was hoping for some assistance, but"—he shook his head—"I wasn't expecting anything like this."

It was now the Overseer's turn to stare. "Yes, well. That's all well and good. But don't forget, Felix"—his glare intensified—"we will need to get the board's approval before we can go ahead with any of these generous offers."

I said nothing because the man didn't know his own organisation. The board had already agreed to the support. That is why we were here. This scenario sat in the Aid Portfolio which was also under my governance. Once the board approved a project, the final word on what and how much—within the pre-approved budget—sat with me. I was well within my rights. We were exceedingly well off and I had established and managed investment portfolios purely for this purpose. I just needed to contact Marlene and it would all be set in motion.

Jonathan was doing his best to hide his disappointment.

So, I did my best to shore up his confidence. "I would appreciate you showing me around your Community and the city. Then we will have a better chance of advising you on how to best invest the stimulus package."

Silence not only entered the room, it squeezed calm and comfort off the table, leaving a definite chill in the air. But underneath its echo I believed the Overseer's seething heart and Jonathan's fluttering hope would soon see the temperature set right.

Another cacophony from Marcus's roars and the girl's shrieks of amusement broke through.

The Overseer's bad mood ratcheted up several levels. "For goodness' sakes. Does that man not know his place?"

Jonathan was already making his way out of the office and stopped by the door. "I'll sort it out. Then, could I show you our city? And perhaps, shout you lunch?"

This seemed to appease the Overseer somewhat. But as soon as our host left the room, he had his phone out and was madly texting. I didn't have to look to know it was a group message to Raymond, Nyle and Edward, the remnant I had not been able to shift over the past twelve years. They continued to be a thorn in my side.

Thankfully they still represented a minority on the High Council. They were his men. Or, I should say, he was theirs.

26

KAITLYN: LEARNING THE ROPES

Georgie was a hoot. He had no armour but he also had no deference towards anyone or anything. How could I help but fall in love with him immediately? I was broken after farewelling Marcus half an hour prior and seeing the twins giving up the attempt to be brave.

Rightly assuming the next caller at our door would be for me, I'd said my goodbyes and thought it best to just get out of the house and make a start. I opened the door to a tall, gorgeous movie star with immaculate skin, hair, nails and shoes. I was kind of jealous.

"Oh honey, the cameras are going to eat you up. You are adorable with a capital, oh. My. Gosh. I want your hair." Georgie winked, looped his arm through mine and led me to his red, sporty, two-seater car. "We are going to have a blast. Today is going to be a bit crazy and overwhelming, and that's just me." He rolled his head back and released a rich baritone laugh that swept me off my feet.

"But honey, in all seriousness..." He stopped, stood in front of me as we reached the car and placed both hands on my shoulders. He bent down to look me in the eye. I lost track of him as my vision blurred with a river threatening to break the banks. "You don't have to worry about a thing. You just stick by me and I'll make sure you're okay."

The dam walls burst in a very unladylike manner and I was mortified. I had promised myself I would not do this.

"Oh sweetie." Before I could sniff, I was wrapped in his strong arms and resting my head on his rock-hard chest. "It's going to be okay. Come on, let's go to the station and hang out in wardrobe and make-up. That's enough to cheer any girl up."

I couldn't help but laugh. How could anyone be sad around this character?

Thank you for this amazing human being and knowing exactly what I needed.

Georgie was right. Meeting the team and seeing the amazing wardrobe and hearing the promises of the make-up crew, I did feel better.

Next on the morning's agenda was the PR weekly planning meeting. With coffees in hand, we walked into a large room on the fourth floor of the Community Headquarters. Extravagantly lush leather chairs circled a massive deep-mahogany table. The whole far wall was a whiteboard, the wall to the left of where we entered was plastered with corking. Flyers, brochures, photographs and colour competed for prominence. It created a wonderful contrast to the stark white walls and floor.

The end furthest away from the door was a screen targeted by a projector attached to the ceiling. The external side of the room had the obligatory wall of windows overlooking the loveliness of Laodicea.

Even though we were assured we weren't late, we were the last to arrive. "Over achievers," Georgie whispered in my ear as he placed a hand on my lower back, guiding me to one of the last vacant chairs. After the introductions, Georgie sat and withdrew his computer from his satchel. As he busied himself and people filled the void by talking among themselves, I took the opportunity to weigh up the room.

Apart from the two of us there were six. Two teams of three if I read the room properly. One team of two men and one woman, and the other, two women and one man. All of them beautiful, men and women alike. All perfectly turned out and presented. I wondered if they visited wardrobe and make-up on their way in, or whether it was just a side effect of working in the industry.

Faint hints of armour whisked about them all, except Georgie. None were alive and vibrant. The sigh that escaped me was noted by the lady on my right. She held out her hand. "Lindy. I know there were introductions, but I suspect you will have forgotten."

She was right. "Thanks. Kait." I gave myself a mental forehead slap. "But I guess *you'd* not forgotten."

Lindy laughed. "No. Not yet. So welcome to the mad house." She nodded to Georgie. "Some madder than others."

I returned her laugh in response.

She wasn't joking.

Then a ninth person entered the room and, like someone had pressed pause, everything stopped. Everyone stilled.

"Welcome, Kait. Great to have you on board. No doubt Georgie will fill you in as we go. He's one of the best, so listen and learn." With no introductions or slowing of his stride, the man marched to the head of the table, hit the control bringing the projector to life and began outlining the week's plan.

Essentially, this part of PR was broken into three teams. Each covering one of Laodicea's main industries: Agriculture, Textiles, Medicine. Behind the scenes were research teams who kept abreast of the latest advancements and discoveries through industry connections. They passed this information on to the planning team, who set up the meetings and scheduled the interviews and created a calendar for the release of information according to current issues and topics.

I was now part of the "face" crew. We went out armed with the information, to meetings arranged by Planning, and interviewed the specialists from a layperson's perspective. The transcripts and taping would then go to production who would touch up, edit, and polish, ready to be released by the media team.

Again, I protested and tried to be as transparent as possible regarding my lack of experience. Our nameless leader listened, then dismissed my arguments. "Are you a nurse?"

"I was. I've not been on the floor in years."

"Do you have a brain?"

Flabbergasted, I tried not to burr up, but noted my armour flared as I answered. "Obviously."

That drew a smile. "You have looks. And a good voice. So, like I said, perfect." And that was the end of that.

Apparently.

Then he dismissed me by turning his back. And then I burred up good and proper. I tried to make a point of pushing my chair back, but the wheels were silent as the lush carpet absorbed all sound. So I slammed my hands on the table as I stood. This guy had crawled under my skin and today was not a day to trifle with me. I missed my husband and my kids.

He turned. Eyes wide and questioning. Maintaining eye contact, I moved around Georgie's chair and prowled to the head of the table. He didn't step back but I noted a twitch in his eye as I met him toe to toe.

By now my green armour was on fire, flickering in time with my fuming heart. One hand on my hip, the other held out, I purred, "We've not formally met. I'm Kait."

His eyes narrowed, his lips twitched, and he slowly started nodding. He took my hand. "Pleased to meet you, Kait. Griffin. And you will be perfect. Just perfect."

I squeezed his hand harder than protocols advised. To his credit, he didn't flinch, but I took a small delight in the tick in his eyes.

"Great to meet you, Griffin."

"Griff."

"Griff," I purred, then turned to face the room of wide-eyed occupants. "I am looking forward to getting to know you all and learning as much as I can. Thank you for inviting me to join your team."

Georgie's face radiated glee.

The others', shock.

Later as we walked to Georgie's... *our* office, he told me, "Girl, no one, and I mean. No. One. Ever. Stands up to Griff. I am now officially one hundred percent your fangirl. And completely in love."

During a lull in the afternoon, I used my family phone and rang Marcus.

"You're going to love Philadelphia. Met the Overseer/Head Shepherd here. He's the ant's pants. His wife, Laura's, a peach. Both of them, armour as thick and bright as the noonday sun. And their little girl, Ruby, is a firecracker. So, what's it like where you are?" His excitement was the perfect medicine. We were going to be okay.

I knew I only had a few moments, so I gushed out everything I could think of. "You should see this place. I have a desk in Georgie's office, another phone, a computer, and a bag to put everything in. Oh, and a card. A credit card. It was for anything to do with work. Shoes, bags, clothes, hairdressers..." I had no room left for being shocked. The constant surprises and learning curves were exhausting.

I hadn't finished but Georgie found me and, with sad eyes, tapped his watch. It was time to go. "We'll face-call you tonight. What time do you finish?" I asked.

"I've got no idea. I can text when I know." He chuckled. "I can't believe I just said that."

"Love you, Bear."

He was silent at my new nickname for him. "Love you too."

"Look, I gotta go. Talk tonight. Love you."

"Have fun and don't spend too much... scratch that, knock yourself out." He signed off.

I hung up and turned to face a grinning Georgie.

"Bear?"

"Yeah, so you better not tell him how much you 'love' me. Or let him hear you say it." I smiled at the thought of what would happen, then sobered. "Yeah, best not to do that."

"Okay honey, I'll keep our love secret. I'm good at secrets." He winked. But he couldn't hide the sadness that clouded his eyes.

The rest of the day I was shown the layout of the building and given a schedule for the week and the transcripts of the facts I'd be covering on Thursday. I was so absorbed looking into the amazing results of the research, I hadn't noted the time and had to be pulled out of intense focus by a shake to the shoulder.

"Come on girl, time to go. We can continue this tomorrow." Georgie had packed his bag and stood ready to leave.

"Oh my goodness, Georgie. Did you know about this stuff? It's amazing." I was scrambling to shuffle all the pages back into their folder. "I cannot believe the things they are achieving in eye surgery."

"Oh honey, I know all right. They're completely amazing. And our job is to share it with the world. What is going on here is changing lives." He held the door open and ushered me out. "You know, you are kind of perfect."

I shot him a glance.

"For the job. Griff is right." He smiled and threw his arm around my shoulders and walked me to his car.

Thank you, thank you, thank you for this great opportunity and this wonderful man. Please help the others to have had a great day. And please keep watching over Marcus.

The car hadn't even come to a stop when the front door of our house burst open. A blur of blue and white erupted from the house. With one leg and half a torso still inside the car, I was swamped by two bodies who attached themselves like limpets. "Georgie, meet my kids, Raphael and Sariah."

"So... they take after their dad?" Backed up against the far door, Georgie raked his eyes over the twins' skin, so many shades darker than my own.

"They're adopted." I hung on tight to the wriggling bundle in my lap. "Well, kind of." I tried to break free, but they weren't budging. But then Sariah rose into the air and was removed from the car. "Georgie, this is Val."

Next, Raph was physically removed from my lap. "And this is Dan."

With Raph hung over his shoulder, Dan bent down to look into the car. "Hey, Georgie. Thanks for bringing Kait home."

"The pleasure is all mine."

I couldn't believe it had only been one day, and already I felt Georgie was part of the family. "Would you like to come in?"

"Thanks sweetie, but I can see you've got a bit of catching up to do. Maybe another time." He ducked his head and waved at us all.

And so, with Raph firmly pinned under Dan's arm and Riah over Val's shoulder, we went into the house.

"Where's Tessa?" I dumped my bag and flicked my shoes near the door.

"She called to say they had to work late." Dan seemed pretty flat. "She didn't know what time she'd be in and she'd eat dinner with her team."

Even though this still didn't really feel like home, it was beginning to grow on me. Especially because this was the place where we could be together and breathe. That, and the fact that Felix ensured we were not going to have strangers walk in on us.

Collapsing on the couch with a twin tucked under each of my wings, I took in the dining room table covered with books, pens, papers, plates and cups. "Homework?" I looked from Raph to Riah. "Already? That's a bit tough."

Raph curled his lip, disdain oozing like an infected wound. "Not really. It is so easy. They are not very smart at that school. They are way behind where we are up to."

"That's not fair, Raph." Val tried to hand me a water, but with both my hands full, she put it on the table. "They have to share their schedule with other things as well as schoolwork. Also, you guys have had a teacher each. And at worst, one teacher between two. These guys have one teacher between a room full of kids."

He turned his head into my shoulder and mumbled, "They are still dumb."

Riah looked up at me, rolled her eyes and nodded. So, I guessed that was the consensus.

Over a late afternoon tea, Val and Dan shared their lack of success. But considering the size of the challenge and their newness to the city, it was hardly surprising. It tore at me that I had not been open to receiving any words to help them in their search. "I'll keep trying, guys. I'm so sorry, but up to now, I have not received any inkling of whom or where our target is."

Val put on a positive voice. "That's okay, we're not wasting our time. It's early days."

With everyone in the dumps, I decided it was a good time to try to face-call Marcus. The room's energy cranked to crackling as I sent him a text. He was in the midst of a dinner with the Shepherds of Philadelphia. But he took our call, excused himself from the table and within moments we were laughing, crying and fighting over the phone to get our faces on the screen. It soon became a competition on who could make the craziest face and embarrass Marcus by making him laugh out loud.

Not surprisingly, Sariah won.

After a gruff accusation from a person seated near him, Marcus rang off with all of us feeling better.

We could do this.

27

FELIX: PARTY OF FIVE

Raymond had suggested that he come through and pick the Overseer up on his way to Sardis. They could catch up on what was happening in the Community there since it was only an extra forty-five minutes down the highway from Philadelphia. They had spent the night accommodated in Sardis and Raymond had agreed to take the Overseer home later today.

I had kept Marcus with me, and our day was to be spent looking around Philadelphia to see how we could best support their fledgling ministry.

Philadelphia truly was a cosmopolitan city with many representatives from all over the continent. A true indicator of its relative infancy. There was a lot of potential here. I might even consider investing on behalf of the Laodicea Community... and myself.

Knowing the limited funds and resources of the Community here, I had booked Marcus and myself into a central hotel and invited the head Shepherds and their team to join us for dinner at the in-house restaurant.

However, I was not anticipating the inability to get separate rooms.

I never shared accommodation space with anyone.

Except Marlene on the very rare occasion I needed her assistance.

The thought of having to occupy my cave for the evening with a stranger had the Crow cackling in preparation for a disaster. The best I was able to organise was a suite. Two separate rooms each with their own private bathrooms joined by a common sitting area overlooking the city below. The walls were solid, and the carpet was thick. So, my plan of attack was to retire early and medicate well.

At dinner, Marcus was instantly welcomed into the fellowship of Philadelphia's Shepherds. As was I. Me, because of my position and what I had to offer. Him, because of his vibrant armour... apparently. Each Shepherd was bedecked in blazing colours of the Light. I felt underdressed for the first time in my life.

Of course, they were all too polite to mention it. But I was intrigued. The brilliance of one's armour seemed to be a ticket to some inner circle, regardless of education or position. I would speak to Marlene about it when I returned. In Laodicea, she and Fleur in their vibrant armour were in the minority. Here, they would not be.

I was glad to see Marcus and his family using the phones I'd purchased. They were funded from my personal account. Not that they needed to know, but their connection intrigued me. Never had I experienced anything like their family unit. I didn't want to intrude or eavesdrop, but I was surprisingly chuffed when I heard Marcus pass my greetings on to his family.

Not only had I not experienced anything like their bond, I had never come across two so... engaging children. Young yet old. Innocent yet affected by life. Out of place in school shoes. I don't know what it was about them, but Raphael and Sariah caused my heart to... tilt.

And then there was Marcus and Kait. I did not consider myself a voyeur, yet I found watching the pair and their connection brought... comfort? No. But a sense of rightness, like when I know Marlene occupies the office next door. Or when at the end of the day, the job is done, and my desk is clear. "Peace" perhaps would be a better word.

And Val...? Strength. Independence. Intelligence in Blundstones. Yes. An admirable woman.

Whatever it was, this family drew me like a magnet. Did I need to be careful or engaged? Again, I would consult Marlene.

~

THE MORNING DAWNED clear and promising. I had slept well with the aid of medication and had awoken at the prescribed hour of four forty-five. This would give me time to catch up on headlines, read my emails, and deal with the business of the day before heading to breakfast with Marcus at 7 am.

Room service had not opened yet, but we had been supplied with instant coffee in our suite. My dilemma was not too intense. I would drink tea for now.

Moving quietly through the apartment so as not to wake Marcus in the other room, I was pulled up short when I noticed the man was already up. His baulking form was taking up most of the balcony and blocking the predawn glow. The thick sliding doors were shut. He wore Adidas, was rugged up in a tracksuit of some description... and was moving as if in the grip of a mild psychotic episode.

I didn't have time for untreated mental health issues in my staff. Heaven knows I had enough trouble dealing with my own. I tapped on the doors.

He stopped, turned and grinned. He didn't look too psychotic. With the doors open a sliver I challenged him. "Are you unwell?"

He barked a laugh. "No, me man." He actually winked at me. "Just doing some morning stretches and preparation."

"Preparation for what?"

"Battle." A face-splitting grin erupted across his countenance. Perhaps I should reassess my previous judgement of psychosis.

"Are we expecting war today?"

"Always, Felix. Always."

"Very good. I am making a cup of tea. Would you care for one?"

"Aye. That I would. Thanks mate. I'll be in soon."

I made myself an Earl Grey, prepared one for him, and adjourned to the table to read the paper that had been left outside the suite's door. However, I must say, Marcus and his... whatever it was... were rather distracting. Trying to work at the table with a hulk of a man dancing like a cautious praying mantis in my line of sight was too much.

In the end I gave up my attempt to concentrate on the news and sat back watching my new driver. After a while I found the combination of the aromatic scent of my tea, combined with the fluidity of Marcus's rhythmic movements, soothing. Hypnotic even. Deciding there would be time for news and emails later, I surrendered to the pull and studied. I allowed my mind to travel with the sweep of his hands and body. It was a shock to discover it had a calming effect on me.

What is it about these people of yours with the thicker armour? They all have a sense of rightness about them. A confidence... and an air of peace. I should like that. Very much. Yet how do I go about it? What must I do to earn this advancement? I think I would like to know more. Can you help? Can this man?

"Do you want to join me?" Marcus's head slotted through the balcony door brought me back from my musing.

"Pardon? Oh. Sorry. Didn't mean to stare."

"You can if you want. Join me that is. It's quite easy to learn."

I seriously considered his invitation but was brought up short when I checked my watch. "Maybe next time. I'll bring more... suitable attire."

"Right you are then. Would you like to join me in The Way over our cuppa, before we begin the day? Tell me how I can petition the Light on your behalf."

"You would do that?"

"Bet your bippy I would. You, in the position you hold? You need all the petition you can get."

"Marlene does that for me. But I'm not sure if anyone else does."

"Well, that's as puzzling to me as Adam on Mother's Day. Count me in. Re-boil the kettle, I'll be back in a jiffy." The paradox of a man passed through to his quarters and soon after, I heard the shower run.

Bet my bippy, indeed.

I stood to follow his request but froze.

In the corner, by the door Marcus had just passed through, was a figure. Faint. But tall, imposing and, quite frankly, very intimidating. It wasn't human. It looked human but there was an "Otherness" about it. And it held a sword. Much like the ones Marlene, Fleur and Marcus carried. However, this one was much... much larger. The tip to the floor, the creature's hands rested on the handle at its waist. It wore army boots.

Surely it was my imagination. Too much mind drifting, watching Marcus and his procedure. Now who was undergoing a psychotic episode? I shook my head to clear the absurdity.

I took a step.

It remained perfectly still. But it tracked me with its eyes. Its blazing eyes. Its sword remained planted on the floor which, I admit, brought a small degree of relief.

I suspected if it wanted to harm me—that is, if it were real—it could do so at any point. So, tentatively, l took another step toward the kettle.

Ridiculous. I was hallucinating, surely. I shook my head... harder this time, planted my eyes front and centre and strode to the kettle to prepare Marcus a cup of tea. I kept my eyes on the bench and placed imaginary blinkers over my eyes, blocking everything in my peripheral vision.

With cup in hand and eyes trained on the carpet, I made my way back to the table but was distracted as Marcus marched through the door.

I am ashamed to say, the cup did not survive.

Behind him was another creature.

We were under attack.

Words tumbled over themselves and formed a bottleneck in my throat. I pointed and, while incapable of being coherent, I believe I may have gurgled.

I was not proud of my response, but I felt I owed it to the man to warn him of his imminent danger.

Of course, because I was not making any sense, Marcus did not understand and, rather than defend himself, rushed to me to fuss over the wretched cup of tea currently soaking into the carpet.

Still incapable of sensical conversation, I tapped wildly on Marcus's shoulder and pointed in a mildly mad manner at the two "Others" that stood watching my shameful performance.

From his position crouched at my feet, Marcus looked to me, then to where my shaking hand was indicating. The infuriating man then laughed. Now I was quite positive he was mad. Any number of emotions and responses would have been both acceptable and appropriate in this situation. And as ashamed as I was of my own reaction, I felt it too was not only acceptable but wholeheartedly understandable.

But laughter? I think not.

"So, you've met your guards then, Felix?"

Finally, the gridlock of words cleared enough to emit one escapee. "Guards?"

"Aye." He stood, clapped a hand on my shoulder and nodded to the two beings in the corner. "Warriors of Light."

They nodded back.

One may have smiled.

It was hard to tell.

Two words made it out. "My guards?" If I kept it up, at this rate I may finish a sentence by breakfast.

"This one has been with you the whole time and he'll stick to you like a barnacle on a ship's buttocksial."

Pointing my still trembling hand, I managed to squeeze out, "But there are two?"

Another laugh. "Aye. The one on the left is with me. That one on the right is yours. And for this trip"—he pointed over my shoulder—"that one is for backup."

Again, I am ashamed to admit a squeak may have escaped as I turned to see a third... "guard" standing in the opposite corner. My head spun back, we were outnumbered and surrounded.

"Guards, you say? We are not in danger?"

"Oh, yes. We are in danger alright, Felix. That's why we have guards. But we're not in danger from them."

The original... *my* guard, nodded and gave me another impression of a smile.

Not wanting to be rude and in order to cover my embarrassment, I extended my hand to greet and welcome him. "Um, sorry about that and thank you for your service—"

The weight of Marcus's hand upon my shoulder stopped my progression across the room. "It's all good, Felix."

My head volleyed between the three: Marcus and the two groupings of guards.

Marcus smiled and the guards nodded.

"They have a job to do and we have a job to do. While we exist in the same space, and we're on the same team, we walk parallel paths."

"Parallel paths?" Oh, dear. I'd thought I'd progressed beyond two-word responses. Never mind, breakfast was still a way off.

"We can't do what we do without them." He nodded some kind of acknowledgement to his guard. "But we don't mingle."

"We don't... mingle?" There I'd done it. Three words.

"Aye. We leave them to do their job and we get on and do ours." Marcus was stomping on a dry cloth, forcing it to absorb my spilt tea. "Thankfully it was without milk and not too strong. I don't think it will stain."

"You're worried about the tea?" I was on a roll. I do believe I was going to be back to normal before my first meeting, or any social interaction outside this room.

"No. Like I said, I don't think it'll stain. Now, how about I make us both a fresh cup and we can have a look in The Way."

Bother. My words had retreated, and I was once again rendered speechless.

28

DANIEL: FREE IN THE CITY

Working hard to be sensitive to the twins' distress, I tried to disguise my joy at what lay ahead of Val and me... after we got the kids to school. I opened the back door and prised Riah out of the back seat.

"Come on, Princess." It was hard to get the words out through the strain of gritted teeth. She was stuck like a sticking plaster to the car. Obviously, I wasn't happy about how much the kids still hated school after seven weeks, but after we'd gone through the production of faking a positive attitude, peeling their fingers off the car doors, and depositing them inside the school grounds, we'd be hitting the streets.

Just thinking about it was like breathing pure oxygen. I was as high as a kite. With everyone else running around like worker ants for the Community, Val and I were on a mission from the Light. Each day we combed the city: this ridiculous, try-hard, city. The place was so fropping clean. It irritated the skrat out of me. It was all so damned fake.

"You will be back to get us at 3:10 pm?" Raph twisted his hands through the shoulder straps of his backpack. The two of them used to hold hands, but since they copped a serious ribbing about it from the other kids, they'd dropped the habit.

"Yeah mate, you know the routine. We'll be here by three and we'll wait by that tree." I pointed to our usual spot that was in line of sight of the main gate and fence. They would be able to see us as soon as the bell went and they were released for the day.

Even here, at the Community's "prestigious" College, the stench of sulphur did my head in. I know it shouldn't have shocked me. If they were in the High Council chambers, and Headquarters, why wouldn't they be at the school? The demons were everywhere. We weren't chasing or looking for them, but they were making themselves fully known.

To me anyway.

No one else saw them. I started to think I was imagining things. They'd flaunt themselves and when I pointed them out, they'd disappear. At home, in a crowd, at the school, in the city; they were everywhere. But apparently, I was the only one who could see them. Talk about a turnaround. Before I came to the Light in Sodom, I was the only one who couldn't see them.

They hadn't attacked or threatened me... yet. But I wasn't about to relax. My guard never left my side. Never. And to me, that meant I needed protection. So, I focused on my training, studied The Way, and tried to keep my eyes on the Light.

But still they came to me often. Well, she did. To taunt, tempt and torment. Why? Why me and no one else? I had no kretting idea.

Having a Warrior shadow my every move freaked me out at first in Sodom. Always having someone watching you... all the time, trailing you... everywhere, it felt like any slip-ups were going to be reported straight back to head office upstairs. But I soon learned that the guy was genuinely there for my protection. He was part of my defence. Now, I would feel naked and completely vulnerable without him.

Cheers for that.

Seriously, after Sodom and seeing what the Dark had up his sleeve, I really appreciated the guard. Plus, these guys had demon-cred and full respect. Hell's minions still threatened, but when the Warriors were around, the bad guys thought twice about making a move.

Maybe because they were skrat scary; tall, broad and fearsome. The kick-butt sword helped their image. Anyway, I was hard-core happy to have mine accompany me everywhere.

Seriously, I mean it. Thanks.

Hitting the streets with my mentor and our two guards was pretty cool. Each day we scoured the city and got a feel of the culture and the lay of the land. The place was massive. And even though the artificial face of the city irritated me like rocks in my socks, I had to admit those aqueducts and canals were pretty cool. If I had to pick a city to be homeless in, my vote was for Laodicea.

Although in saying that, I wanted to know where the homeless were. Where did the darker side live? The part of town where the real people hung out? So even though we were on a search for this black-and-white, voiceless girl, I was eager to find Laodicea's face behind her mask.

So far, we'd had as much luck finding one as the other.

Kait was tearing herself up not being able to help us with her Badge. But things were just too complicated with her work for her to follow her fast. All of us had sat down and tried to nut out a plan of attack to find a girl who was in black and white. Was she in the news industry? Media? Film? Val and I had visited all the major corporations, but not really knowing how to ask for what we were looking for, we mainly scoped the buildings and waited for Val's badge of Seeing to kick in.

After three weeks of that we decided that perhaps the girl wasn't someone who worked in media or film but someone who'd been reported on in the newspapers. Our search then took us to the epic Laodicean library where they had internet records of news going back till the dawn of flopping time. Thankfully we could narrow it down to local news.

And that really helped... not.

The city was humongous, and the news was endless. But at least it gave us a target and somewhere to go.

I had to admit, the costumes the Community had dressed us in made our way easy in the city. The fact that we slept well every night, ate well every meal, and bathed every day made us invisible. We could move in and around the city and no one even blinked at us. If I were still inclined to steal, this place would be a dream come true.

But now that I was sworn off that, and I had two guards watching over me—my Warrior and Val—I was not likely to slip back into that habit. Especially after the apple debacle of Sodom. If only I could burn that memory as good as the Light burned Sodom.

Thanks for that as well.

But that kind of left us with a bit of a problem. We had no money.

The Community controlled everything. They gave us everything we needed, except cash. They held the purse strings... in a vice. So, Val suggested we bring my guitar on our "outings". If I could pull a few coins from busking we could grab a coffee and, if there was anything left over, a bite to eat. And if we were careful, we could start putting a bit away for a rainy day.

This is where fitting the mould also worked. We kind of looked normal. Not as normal as the others, but normal enough that people would pay us. And, because we didn't look like trouble, we could go to the same place each morning, without a licence, and get some regulars. We made sure it was just outside our favourite cafe.

With our schedule locked in around the twins' drop-off and pick-up, our session times were pretty predictable. As it turned out, Serendipity's business benefitted, so they pitched in a free coffee each morning, and a discounted lunch. A truly symbiotic relationship. With their help, we were actually building a good nest egg, enough to buy a new, second-hand guitar and birthday presents for the twins. They turned eleven in a couple of months and we were planning on surprising them with a pass out of school and a day on the town.

So, all in all, our days were looking good. Exploring the city, playing music, and enjoying good food. The only thing that would have made it better was finding our target... and a good fight.

Val was still on edge, never knowing when the Dark Lord's knives were coming back. And she didn't get to see any of my demons to vent her frustrations on. Added to this, she missed sparring with Marcus and Kait. She had to do it with me.

My respect for Marcus shot through the roof. I was sporting a lot of new bruises. And when I say a lot, I mean I freggly hurt all the fragly time. Thankfully she hadn't broken any of my fingers. I could still play. And I couldn't deny I was also getting better. A lot better.

So even though Laodicea was a mysterious woman, it was great to be out on the streets living life again. However, there was one major downside. I missed Tessa.

I also had to admit I missed all of the others too. Yeah, who'd have thought? I missed Marcus and Kait. It's strange, but having them around, living out their role of husband/wife, mum/dad, kind of filled the house with peace and... security.

I know. Weird.

So, things were good, but there were five very distinct holes in my life. But for now, we'd follow the Light, walk the streets, and hunt our prey. But first things first. Play a session at Serendipity.

"Morning guys? Do you need a starter?" Missy had been waiting for us.

Val looked at me and cocked her head. "Can I have one to go, please? I'm going to head straight to the library, the long way round. You don't need me babysitting you. Come meet me when you're done."

She chatted to the staff while she waited for her coffee, and I took my place on a stool they'd set up for me.

Obviously, she was totally capable of taking care of herself. She'd be keeping her eyes peeled going a circular route looking... scouring... begging for any chance of a fight on her way.

And I figured since I was in a very public place, I should be fine too. I did have my guard, so I sat down, tuned up, and began.

The sky was clear, the streets were fresh, the crowds were amiable, it was the perfect day. I tried not to think of the twins locked away in school. And I definitely tried not to think about Tessa. I just wished she could be here to enjoy it with me.

29

KAITLYN: FLYING HIGH

"Nailed it," Georgie whispered in my ear as he leaned over and kissed my cheek.

I couldn't help but smile. We had. The story was filmed, edited and posted. It was going to be another hit. After two months of madness, learning the ropes and finding my feet, Georgie and I had found our groove.

Despite the fluff and bubble he presented to the world, the guy was a maestro. Not only his understanding of the media industry, but also his ability to read people and situations, was a gift. If he'd been wearing armour, I would have suspected it was a Badge.

The lights flicked on in the small theatre and the other two teams started rising, talking among themselves and making notes.

"Nice work." Fletch, lead of the Ag team, nodded as he passed me on the way out. I smiled but stayed silent, studying him for any signs of sarcasm. I still couldn't tell when he was being genuine.

"Keep this up and you won't be easily forgotten." Lindy winked as she passed me.

I almost swooned from this praise from the head of the Textiles team. Sadly, I hadn't managed to re-engage my brain enough to come up with a response before she'd left.

"Come on sweetie, lunch is on me." Lunch was always on Georgie. We made to follow the others but were pulled up short.

"Hold on a sec, guys. I'd like a word." Griffin unfolded himself from the back row and made his way over. His black eyes sparked and glittered, but his face was unreadable. Like a bug under a magnifying glass in the sun, I could feel smoke rising from my shell in his gaze. "You've got a way to go. You're rough and still wet around the edges."

I bristled. I shouldn't have. He was right and I was always the first to admit it. But still, Griffin had a way of flaying my soul with the simplest of words. Like Georgie, he didn't wear armour, but unlike Georgie I'd not yet had the privilege of seeing under the surface.

"But you've got something, Kait. And I like it. I like it a lot." His lips twitched. "Good work."

I gaped in the most unladylike manner.

That actually elicited a chuckle.

"Georgie." Both men, blank faced, regarded each other. "Another success." With a mutual nod, Griffin left us in his wake.

"Should we invite him to lunch?" Even though the man got under my skin, I had a sense that he was lonely. He couldn't be as tough as he made out... all of the time. Surely.

"Oh sweetie. Only you." Georgie's arm was around my shoulders and I was swept out of the theatre. "I'll pass it on that you asked. Griff doesn't socialise with the teams." His voice developed an edge. "Not good for his reputation."

Over lunch we discussed our "success" and started planning our next project. I was still pinching myself daily. I seriously couldn't believe the opportunities Laodicea had offered me. Each week we looked at medical "miracles" developed in the local hospitals and universities. This past assignment had been on the eye salve that restored sight to those who had what would previously have been catalogued as permanent damage. The work had been in the pipeline for years, but finally the initial results had been released.

With this new ointment, sight could be restored to thousands. The complexity was beyond me, but the results weren't. After reading the studies, Georgie and I had visited the developers and recipients.

The results were mind-blowing. And the repercussions were going to be life-altering for millions.

At this point in time the ointment was still too expensive for many, but with further work the developers believed they could bring that price down. And, with the funding and support of the Community, hospitals and government grants, already the sight-giving balm was making its way around Laodicea with amazing affects.

The week prior, we had the opportunity to pull a story together around the latest cochlear implants. Like I said, it was mind-blowing. I just couldn't believe the discoveries being made here and the differences they were making and the differences they could make. Just thinking about how we could get this out to the poor, struggling populace, or even third-world nations was enough to make me giddy.

Georgie was a pro. I didn't understand why the others gave him such a hard time. More often now, he dropped the act when it was just the two of us, and I had the absolute pleasure of getting to know this amazingly gifted, generous human being. Our little team of two was growing in trust and understanding. It'd only been three months, but already I felt I'd known Georgie my whole life.

"Earth to Kait." Warmth engulfing my hand called me back to our lunch celebration/meeting. "Come on sweetie, enough coasting on our past successes, let's look forward." Georgie retracted his hand and produced a folder from his satchel. "Next, we're working on nerve regeneration."

"What?"

"Yep. It's not new, but with the addition to the development in bionics that we'll be covering next week, it will be a good review."

"What? They're already capable of helping paraplegics?" I was sure I'd spent most of my time on this job with my mouth wide open.

"No, sweetie, keep up." He gave me a light-hearted swat. "They don't 'help' paraplegics, they cure them. But like I said, that's old school."

Speechless. I was speechless.

Your work here truly is miraculous. Thank you so much that I get to be at the front of letting people know how you are working in the world and how you are enabling people to live life to the fullest. You truly are an amazing God. Thank you for bringing us to Laodicea.

30

DANIEL: RUNNING THROUGH WET CONCRETE

Another. Wasted. Day.

Another. Failed. Attempt.

You're not. Pulling. Your weight.

Each time my foot punched the pavement the litany started over again. My guard and I were going through the streets after picking up the twins from school. They were barely hanging in there but were doing their best to do their bit.

Everyone was doing their bit.

Marcus was high flying with the Overseer and Felix—mainly Felix—travelling all over the continent playing host and bodyguard.

Kait was hot skrat all over the internet. The hottest new thing bringing the eyes of Laodicea to the work of the hospitals, and programs sponsored or supported by the Community.

Tessa was playing PA to Kari whose team was organising big events that were either run by, sponsored by, or created by the Community. Not that I really knew what she was doing. It'd been three and a half months since she'd walked out the door on Kari's leash. I'd hardly seen her since.

Val was keeping the home fires burning, everyone in line, and the heartbeat and soul of our family pumping.

And me?

Another. Wasted. Day.

Another. Failed. Attempt.

I was supposed to be finding this mute black-and-white girl in a golden city that wouldn't shut up. Her cries haunted me most nights. I was getting desperate. I needed this to end.

My pity party was so engrossing I hadn't noticed her arrival or my guard burring up. But I got one helluva shock when I realised we'd picked up a passenger.

"Hey gorgeous. Rough day, huh?"

Running into the wind had helped mask the sulphur, but once she was in my mind, nothing could mask that body busting out of its lycra. I stumbled. My guard shot me a warning glare. Right. Eyes front. "What do you want?"

"You were looking like you were having a tough time and I thought I'd come and keep you company."

"I have company, thanks. I don't need any more." Eyes front. Breathe. In, in, out. In, in out.

"I don't know why you stay with these guys, you know? You were better off without them. And they obviously don't need you anymore."

I picked up my pace.

"But then, have they ever really 'needed' you?"

In, in, out. Left, right, jab.

"I mean, think about it. From the start, what have you brought them except another mouth to feed?"

Left, right, jab, jab, punch.

"Think of all the opportunities this city has to offer a man with your skills. Seriously, have you seen this place? You could be living the high life in no time."

Push faster. Create a space.

"I have connections, I could help get you started."

Faster.

"The Community doesn't recognise just how talented you are, Dan. I could have you set up in no time."

Faster.

"A nice place of your own. Your own set-up, women, money…"

"Enough." I stopped in my tracks and yelled at her. Well, I would have if I hadn't been out of breath. "Do you ever just… shut up?" I dropped my hands to my knees and raked in breaths. She just stood there, no sweat, no panting, just examining her nails.

"No need to be rude. I was just trying to help."

"Help?" I lifted my eyes and through the rivers of sweat I tried to eyeball her. But when she had my attention, she ran her hands down her curves.

"Yeah, you know. Help take your mind off things. Offer you a way out. Options." She leaned forward and met me eye to eye, knowing full well she was giving me an eyeful. "We all like options, Dan." Slowly she stood like a cat stretching, ran a finger down my lathered cheek then disappeared.

I gave up calling her a twik. She knew already.

Instead, I turned and stumbled my way home.

31

RAPHAEL: PEARS NOT APPLES

The tie choked me, the shirt was starchy, and the people were horrible. It was supposed to be a Community school. A school where parents of the Light sent their children, who were also supposed to be in the Light. We had only been here a few months, so I did not fully understand how things worked.

One thing I did know was that the Light in Laodicea was very different to the Light of Sodom. Maybe the depth of darkness had something to do with the strength of the Light. Maybe it was because they were right and there was no enemy here. Dan and Val told us not to believe this lie. Even though we had not seen hide nor hair of any demons, they said the evidence was everywhere.

Dan had stopped trying to convince me that he saw them all the time. He said they came to him and taunted him. But no one else.

We never saw one.

Ever.

In the three months we had been here we had not seen any demons or had a visit from the Dark Lord. Whatever the reason, it did not matter. Because another thing I knew for certain was that I hated it here. So did Riah. We had to come to school because the Community had given everyone in our family jobs. That is, except for

Val and Dan. The others worked in return for the house, and the car, and the food, and the clothes, and the school fees.

That was another thing that was different here. In Sodom, we had worked for the Light and He had provided for us. In Laodicea, we worked for the Community and they provided for us. So now, instead of following orders from the Light, we obeyed orders from the Community. The grown-ups would not talk openly about this, but I did not think anyone in our family was happy about it.

Regardless of what they thought or did, for us it meant school. We had tried to be strong. They had said it would be good for us to meet other children of the Light, and to have an opportunity to fit in and have a normal life. But if this was normal, we did not want it.

I think the real reason was, now that everyone was busy, we had to stay out of the way, stay out of trouble, and stay under the radar. Whatever that meant. We tried to explain how horrible it was, but they just kept telling us, "It will pass."

"The others just don't understand you," they had explained.

"You need to give them a chance to get to know you," they had pleaded.

We knew we were privileged to come to this very expensive Community College. The staff and Community kept telling us so. But it was so boring. The work was too easy, and the kids were stupid.

And rude. "Soddy", "Plinter", and "Dappin" were just some of the names they threw at us. Even their insults were dumb and lacked imagination.

But worst of all was the way the teachers treated Sariah. Just because she did not speak, they treated her like she had no brain. I tried to explain to them that she was very bright. But every time I brought it up, they put me in a place called Detention. I think it was supposed to be a punishment. But I could not see how. Not that I would tell them that. After I raced through the work they gave me, I was allowed to read a book. I told Sariah that she should try harder to get sent to Detention too.

We stuck at it for months allowing the insults to "flow off our feathers", as Abbot would have said. But lunch times were the worst.

We would sit by ourselves and wait for the other kids to find us and come up with new ways to torment us.

I practised my breathing. It seemed that since escaping Sodom, I was getting better at riding the Dragon. Now, when I saw him coming I was able to head him off before he got a full hold... most times.

Sariah practised her patience. And we both practised pretending the bullies were not there.

Since homework took no time at all, Val and Dan let us spar with them each day after school before we cooled off in the pool for the rest of the afternoon. It all helped us to release the springs that were wound up tightly each and every day. It helped reduce the pressure so we could sleep. And it helped us deal with the next day when it would happen all over again.

As a result, our hand-to-hand and sword skills were getting much better. It was interesting how anger helped me focus at improving my skills in harming others. I had kept my promise not to kill anything... or anyone, not that there was any hunting in Laodicea. But working off my frustration each afternoon was the best part of the day.

Sadly, today had been different in that it was worse than the normal nightmare. Maybe the bullies got sick of us not reacting. Maybe it was the month of the year. Maybe it was the full moon. I had no idea. All I knew was that the hostility in the playground had not died down like everyone promised. It just kept coming. They did not take a break.

I did not understand. As the new kids we had to be patient and accommodating to them. We had to make excuses for them. We had to wait for them to feel better, more comfortable, less intimidated. But they were our hosts. Should they not have been welcoming us? Was that not what hospitality and Community was all about?

"Hey freakoid, I'm speaking to you."

We had just collected our lunches and were heading to our seat for the break. As usual, we did not respond. We kept on walking.

"Hey, dappin girl, didn't you hear me? Are you deaf as well as dumb?"

We both just breathed in deeply. This was an old insult. They were so dimwitted, they could not even come up with anything original or clever. We had learned early on that if I retaliated and used my words to interpret for Sariah, it made things worse. So, we just kept moving, pretending to ignore them.

The big one decided he'd had enough and shoved Riah in the shoulder.

She stopped.

We did not look at them.

I just waited with Riah until she could breathe through the anger. I breathed with her. The foolish boy thought this was an invitation to have another go. He stepped in close and raised his hand to push her again.

"I would not do that if I were you," I tried to warn him. "Do not touch her. She does not like it."

"Yeah? What are you going to do about it, Soddy? Huh?" He kept his eyes on me and shoved Sariah in the back again. Harder.

She stumbled forward.

I begged her, "Ri, remember what we have been told. Do not hurt him."

"Hey, I was talking to you." The boy tried to get in my face.

I ignored him. He was like an annoying fly. I did not care about him. I should have, he was a fellow child of Light, or his parents were. But I was ashamed to admit I was only worried about Riah. If she hit him, she would get in trouble. They would not get in trouble. They never did.

The boy stepped between us and stood over me.

I had to bend my head right back to see his face.

"I said, I. Was. Talk'n. To. You." He punctuated each word with a shove.

I tried to side-step him, he was huge but insignificant, I was only thinking about Riah.

"Hey." He hit me so hard I fell backwards. My lunch scattered and hit some of the bystanders. All his sheep bleated obediently.

But then the screaming started.

One by one the boys fell, clutching their wounded bodies.

When none were left standing, Riah stepped over one and offered me her hand.

But before I could get to her, a teacher stepped out of the shadows and grabbed her shoulder.

"Do not touch her," I yelled. I tried to warn them. Why would they never listen. No one ever listened to us. "She does not like it."

But it was too late. The teacher's screams joined the others when, after months of restraint, stress, anger, and grief, Riah twisted the woman's wrist.

I leapt to my feet and reached for our teacher.

Please, please, please let me fix this? Make her whole? Protect Ri?

I managed to lay my hand on Mrs Wiggan's shoulder for a moment. Immediately, I sensed the injury, a tiny crack in one of the bones. I pictured it healed and whole. As I was offering a word of thanks she spun out of my contact and marched towards the office to report the incident. She still clutched her wrist, but she had stopped her bawling.

We did not have a lot of time. I scampered around the herd rolling on the ground squawking and whining, and gently laid my hands on each of them. I asked that they would all be restored. I had to confess it was not for their sake I was asking.

Our names were called over the loudspeaker. We were to report to the office immediately. Poor Ri. She was still angry, but she knew she had done the wrong thing and now we were going to get into big trouble. And what was worse, so was our family.

I hugged her and we spent some time with the Light working things through and making things right with Him, before we made our way to the office.

"Raphael, you are not needed. Go to the Responsible Thinking Room, they are expecting you," the Deputy said.

"I think I will stay if that is okay, Mrs Wiggan. I will be able to communicate for Sariah so you can hear her side of the story." I sat next to Riah and held her hand.

"That will not be necessary. Please go to the Responsible Thinking Room, now."

"I will stay, thank you, Mrs Wiggan." Val was always polite when she spoke to the Dark Lord, so I thought I should be too.

"At this point in time, you are not in trouble. However, if you stay, I will take up your failure to comply, with the Principal." She turned her sharp grey eyes to Riah. "When the police have finished with your sister."

Riah gasped and I thought I was going to throw up. "P-police?"

"Of course." She glared in glee then turned back to Riah. "You are not in Sodom now, young lady. Such acts of vulgarity and violence are not only unacceptable at Community College, they are unacceptable practices in Laodicea." She smirked at both of us. Her words sounded like she was talking about our actions. Her face looked like she was talking about us.

"Well then, in that case, I think I will definitely stay, thank you, Mrs Wiggan."

"Suit yourself." Sparks of self-satisfied delight shot from her eyes.

I turned my back on the horrible woman and leaned over to whisper in my sister's ear. "Pity she is not a demon, then you could stab her with your sword."

Riah giggled.

Mrs Wiggan roared, "What on earth do you think you have to laugh about? By the time I'm finished with you—"

All three of us jumped when the external doors to the administration building burst open and the walls shuddered. Light exploded through the opening and two silhouettes stopped, turned, then marched toward us. Riah and I were on our feet and running.

Riah launched and wrapped herself around Val like a second breastplate. Dan got down on one knee and opened his arms to enclose me within his fortress. We were safe. They had come for us.

I could hardly see Val and Dan's bodies, their armour was at full colour, fuelled by their readiness for war. Dan often joked about Val's deadly laser eyes. Well, she had Mrs Wiggan in her sights, and she was not joking now.

"What is going on here?" Very quietly, Val spoke over the top of Riah's shoulder.

"Ah, Mrs..." Mrs Wiggan looked down at the clipboard she clasped like a shield.

"Miss."

"Miss...?" Our deputy was no longer sparking with glee.

"Benleukos."

"And Mr...?" She threw her eyes to Dan. The confusion on her face would have been funny if the situation had not been life and death.

"Irrelevant." Val jumped in before Dan could answer. She was spearheading this attack.

"Please come into Mr Blake's office. He is waiting for everyone to arrive." Mrs Wiggan spun on her ridiculously high heel and marched ahead of us.

We were herded into the principal's office where Mr Blake sat behind his mammoth desk. He stayed sitting. He did not hold out his hand to welcome Val and Dan. I guess it would be hard to expect the staff and students to be hospitable and welcoming if the principal was not.

"Please, have a seat," he offered.

Val and Dan sat. Sariah was still firmly attached to Val. I was locked between Dan's legs, both my arms glued to his shoulders.

"Sariah, get off your mother's lap. You two can wait outside." Mrs Wiggan liked bossing people around.

I buried my head in Dan's shoulder and tightened my grip. A gasp made me look up. Mrs Wiggan had stretched her hand out toward Sariah.

"Do not touch her. She does not like it. I believe that should be in her file. We made that very clear when she was enrolled." Val's words, silent knives, each hit their target.

Mrs Wiggan stopped.

Val upped the temperature of her laser eyes. I knew they could not really hurt people, but none the less, Mrs Wiggan took a step back and her hair sprang into small curls around the edge of her sheening face. Her hand dropped and she turned to Mr Blake mumbling, "Doesn't seem too upset about 'touching' people now."

Val did not back down. "Both Sariah and Raphael have survived extraordinary circumstances. It is important that Sariah is free to initiate contact when she feels comfortable and safe. But then you would know this and the nature of these circumstances if you had taken the time to read their file."

Mrs Wiggan did not look at Val, she just continued mumbling. "Gets it from the mother." She snatched her folder from Mr Blake's desk and scratched notes on her ever-present clipboard.

"It's okay, Carla. Geoff will be here soon, and the children will need to be here for his interview."

A shadow fell across the room. A brick wall had stepped into the doorway and stolen the sun.

"Greg, Carla." The wall nodded his head and took the seat next to Val. "What seems to be the problem?"

Mr Blake looked to Dan and Val as he introduced the newcomer. "This is Senior Constable Clarke. He is here to follow appropriate procedure."

"Right you are, Greg. Why don't you give it to me in shorthand and we'll take it from there?"

Our principal, Mr Blake, inclined his head to Mrs Wiggan and invited her to dob us in.

"This girl has wreaked havoc at this school and has severely injured multiple students and wounded me." She switched the pen she had been writing with to her left hand and held out her wrist for inspection.

The room was silent as we all looked at the perfectly formed limb.

"Hmm." Senior Constable Clarke looked from Mrs Wiggan to Sariah. Her dark eyes were large and watering; she clung to Val like a barnacle. A beautiful little sparrow-barnacle surrounded by ferocious shark cats. "I dropped into the infirmary on my way here and checked on the lads." He looked back to Mrs Wiggan. "And I'd say they're in as bad a shape as you are, Carla."

Mrs Wiggan crossed her arms and sent us a grin. She'd just received a bowl of cream.

"So, I'd say, if you offer these folks and me an apology for wasting our time, we could call it a day." Turning to Val he continued, "Is there anything you'd like to add or say at this point?"

Mrs Wiggan had only just begun to realise that the ball was not in her court and she was now mid-air without a leg to stand on. "My wrist. Those boys—"

"Are perfectly fine, Carla." He stood and shook the proffered hand without a whimper of complaint from our deputy. He then turned to Val and Dan and shook both of their hands. "Good day." Then he left the room. And the sun flowed like a river.

Mrs Wiggan and Mr Blake stared, open-mouthed, at the door.

Val spoke quietly and politely. "I would like to lodge a formal complaint. Could you please tell me how to go about that?" She rubbed Riah's back. "Then I'd like you to arrange the paperwork for us to remove our children from this establishment." Mr Blake and Mrs Wiggan did not move. They sat and stared, gaping. "As soon as possible, thank you. Then we too will be on our way."

"Do you mean it? Can we really leave?" My feet were jumping all by themselves. I was hugging Dan, and Riah, and Val, and Dan, and... I may have even squealed... just a little bit. I was very excited. I could not believe a day that started in hell could end in heaven. Dan had to keep readjusting my hands because he said I was choking him. But I could not make my arms let go of his neck.

Riah's face was buried in Val's shoulder. She could not be convinced to let go either, so the paperwork had to be signed and sorted around her. Just in case something happened, and someone changed their mind.

There was no way they were leaving without us. Nor were we ever coming back.

32

CONTESSA: THE BEGINNING OF THE END

"Come on T, time to get moving."

I finished zipping up my Adonis boots and hot-tailed it into the sitting room. I'd stayed over at Kari's again last night. But right from day one, six months ago, I had learned that it wasn't wise to keep Kari waiting. Punctuality was important if you wanted to succeed in this game. And also, stay free from her stink eye and epic grudge-holding superpowers.

So far, so good.

"Yeah," she said as I twirled for her inspection. "Looking good, but I'd go with the Achilles white jeans instead of the skirt today." She laughed at my gasp. "Don't worry, we've got time... just."

Trying not to rip seams in my rush, I followed Kari's advice, then tidied everything away back on their hangers, and gave the room a quick once-over to make sure it was perfect and I had removed all evidence of my stay.

I would more than likely be coming back tonight. But Kari had made it clear it wasn't "my" room, it was just easier for her to have me on hand if she needed me. I made a last check in the mirror in case my hair or make-up had been damaged in the change.

It was really important, as Kari's PA, that I looked good. She said I represented her everywhere I went, so she made sure to approve... well, everything really, before I went in public. She really was so kind and literally a trendsetter. Seriously. People always took note of what she wore and what, and whose, accessories she used.

Why she kept me around and continued to be so lovely, I had no idea. But she did. Everyone told me there were like hundreds of people who'd kill for my job.

I knew. I was so lucky.

She nodded. "Much better. Okay, grab these boxes and let's go."

I. Loved. Laodicea.

And what was even better, Laodicea loved me.

In Sodom, I was constantly attacked and teased about my shape. You see, I kind of didn't have one. Where all the girls in the gangs were well-rounded, I was not. I had often been described as a bean pole—one of the nicer descriptions. But here, in the fashion capital of. The. World. Stick figures were in.

Yay.

Yes, you heard me. For the first time in forever, I was the right size.

And not only that. The crew—Kari and the gang—loved, loved, loved my armour. They kept wanting to touch it.

Sillies. Like they could.

But they were constantly gawking and admiring it. And do you know what else was just the raddest thing ever? This top fashion designer, Achilles, a really good friend of Kari's, had decided to launch a whole new line based on armour. Mine in particular.

I know.

Who'd have thought that so many incredible people were in the Light?

In Sodom, it seemed only the down and outers were in. That sounds pretty harsh. But seriously. Look at us and who we were. We were kind of the dregs. But here, I get to hang out with people like Achilles and meet all these other really amazing people.

Like, they even loved my nuts-o-crazy hair.

No one loves my hair.

Not even me.

Anyway, Kari's apartment was so cool. Right in the middle of the city. Huge windows showcased the spectacular night lights and the aqueducts and canals. She lived there by herself, but sometimes she had team meetings up here. Not the whole crew, just those she called the Inner Circle.

And you guessed it.

I was in.

Over the last six months I had slowly been allowed access to the heart of the group. Well, being Kari's helper helped. Being adored by Achilles also went a long way to getting me a ticket in.

Yep. The. Inner. Circle.

Even though Jason was in, his other boorish friends weren't. We did have to see them from time to time, but since Dan set everyone straight, I wasn't troubled by them anymore.

At the moment we were working on a big fashion show that would officially launch the Spring season. So, not only was I meeting with Achilles and being his "muse", I was learning the ropes of event management.

Far. Flaming. Out.

No wonder they started so early. Like months ahead. I had no idea how much was involved. These guys... I mean we, did everything from organising the big names to sign up, their transport, the venue, the DJs, all the way through to picking the decor, colours and ordering the serviettes.

Kari was a legend. Literally. Everyone knew her and respected her. She had been doing this for a while and said she had a formula. When she started it was a bit tricky, because no one knew her. But her mentor, an old guy, Bertrand, introduced her to everyone and taught her everything. Now, she was almost as famous as the designers and the models. Eeeks. Have you met those girls?

Thankfully we didn't have to organise *them*. Each designer worked with their own stable of clothes horses.

And, Oh. My. Word.

I thought the girls in the gangs were mean. They had nothing on these girls. Some of them were just nasty. They seemed to respect

Kari, though. So I just stuck close to her and tried not to have anything to do with them. Although I watched them and studied how they moved. They were so beautiful and graceful.

As Kari's PA, whatever she wanted I got or organised. Wherever she went, I went too. She even gave me my own laptop and phone. She said she wanted to be able to reach me at all times. She said it was the best way for me to learn the ropes. But on the flip side, she was also like my personal shopper/styler. Every day she was giving me new shoes, bags, and clothes. Not to own or anything, just to wear for the day. She had access to the latest trends and styles... ahead of time... and was allowed to wear it to help promote the latest looks. Or something like that. Anyway, she had a cupboard at her place where she got stuff for me. It all had to go back but I got to look great, All. The. Time. Kari even paid for me to have a makeover by Leonardo.

So now I had a new look. My hair was shaped in the latest cut. My make-up was done in the latest style. And I was walking around in the latest look. People now noticed me and stepped aside when I walked into the room.

The only downside was I didn't get to see my family much anymore. Since we were putting in the long hours for this event, I usually slept over here so we could work late and start early.

I missed them all so much.

But I especially missed Dan.

I tried calling him throughout the day, but whenever I got my phone out to make the call, I'd be needed to run some errand or take some notes. Then, when I was free, it was the middle of the night and I didn't want to disturb him.

We used to text a lot. But now, not so much. Just the thought of him had me pulling my family phone out.

"T, we're running late. Can you carry these boxes to the car? Jason is meeting us in the garage and we're heading over to the Theatre to discuss the menu for the opening night." Kari swept through the room. "You okay?" Her eyes softened as she caught me with my other phone.

"Yeah, I was just texting Dan. I haven't seen or heard from him in ages." I slipped the phone back in my bag. Kari said we shouldn't put phones in our pockets, it ruined the lines of the outfit and stretched the fabric.

"I know it's tough." She placed her perfectly manicured hand on my shoulder and stooped to look me in the eye. "But it isn't forever. As soon as this show is done, we'll have a long break." A rueful smile softened her perfect face. "You going to be okay?" She was so understanding.

"Yeah, thanks. I'll try to contact him later."

"That's my girl." She hooked her arm through mine, and we laughed and tripped as we tried to carry everything through her front door to the lift.

When the doors dinged open, Kari put her professional face on. Walking tall, she led the way to the car where Jason stood waiting, madly flicking through something on his tablet. Without greeting us or looking up, "Flight times," he explained. "Transfers from the airport are going to be tight."

"Get Lawrence onto it." Kari's car beeped as she approached the driver's door.

"Got it." After a few more swipes and flicks, Jason stowed his tablet, looked up and grinned. "Good morning Sunshine." He leaned over and air-kissed my cheek. It had taken a bit of getting used to, but that's how everyone greeted each other. Everyone but Kari. She was more of a hand on the arm or shoulder kind of gal.

Returning the gesture was a bit tricky as I had to negotiate my way around the stacked boxes in my arms and my new Adonis bag. But, true gentleman that he was, Jason helped unburden me and stowed them in the boot.

Then at the passenger door, with a flick of his faux-crocodile-skinned boot, he tipped the seat forward so I could climb into the back. It was a bit of a squeeze with all of Kari's bags, but thankfully I didn't take up much space. Especially since I had lost a bit of weight.

With the radio playing the latest tunes and the roar of the engine, I wasn't able to hear the conversation in the front. So, I took the time to take in the city as we sped through the streets to the Theatre; the latest venue and the site of our big production. With Kari and Jason occupied with details, driving and all the drama, I thought it would be a good time to sneak a text to my family. I pulled my family phone from the depths of my bag and unlocked it.

"We're pulling through for a coffee, what would you like?" Kari was so generous.

I slipped my phone back. "Espresso thanks."

"So, you're a convert?" Jason beamed over his shoulder as Kari zipped through her favourite drive-through cafe.

I hadn't always liked espresso. In fact, it was still a little hard to drink. But everyone else drank them and I didn't want to look immature ordering a big milky cappuccino like a kid.

Because Kari was driving and Jason was tableting, I had to hold the tray of coffees. Not daring to spill any of the black gold, as Kari called it, on my white Achilles pants, I decided I'd video-call the family later on.

We pulled up to the monumental centre. Doormen raced out to greet us. After they'd helped unload they held the doors, and a valet caught the keys and took care of the car. I passed out our coffees and we entered the foyer. The rest of the team were waiting for us. The centre's manager showed us through to our meeting room. And so began another day of meetings with lighting, sound, backstage, caterers, designers, advertising, or programmers. It seemed an endless line of people.

I STRUGGLED TO KEEP UP. But Kari was relentless.

In one of the breaks, I was supposed to be taking everyone's request so I could order coffees. It was late and going to be a lot later before we were wrapped up. The team needed fuel. But I was busy reflecting on all the details we'd just sorted through. Had it only been one day? It was overwhelming.

"Hey." Kari smiled her trademark gorgeousness at me. "You okay?"

"It's just so much. How do you remember all of this... know all of this... stuff? What to ask for, plan or how it will all work?" I looked at her. How could someone so young have so much experience?

"You're just learning, T. It'll come. Just give it time." Her hand was on my arm again. "I once sat where you're sitting now. And that's how I learned. So make notes, ask questions, and be a sponge." She leaned back. "But before you do all of that, could you order coffees? We're wilting." Her gentle laugh was echoed around the room.

I couldn't believe I'd been given this great opportunity to learn. I loved the organising and the planning. The note taking, listening and being like a sponge was the easy bit. But I chose not to entertain the thought of having to do it by myself one day. For starters I would never be in that position. And secondly, it was all kinds of scary.

With the late afternoon tea ordered, I wandered down to the foyer to wait for the delivery. I knew they would send it up, but I just wanted some space to catch my breath. I retreated to the shadows by the concierge and in the lull, thought I could shoot some texts off to my family.

"T, my little Miss Sunshine, there you are." Jason bowled across the foyer. "We're waiting for you. What are you doing down here?"

"I was going to bring the coffee up—"

"Don't be silly, the couriers will do that. You have more important things to do. Come on"—he looped his arm through my mine— "Achilles wants you to drop by. And you know what he's like." We rushed back across the foyer. As we waited for the lift, Jason explained, "You and Kari need to be ready to get out of here in half an hour. So that gives us twenty-five to wrap up and dish out to-do lists."

We exited the lift and dashed back into the room, taking our seats. Kari smiled at me and raised her eyebrows. "You heard?"

I nodded, not even trying to hide my smile.

"Good. Now, let's wrap this up."

33

DANIEL: CLASH OF CLANS

Raph threw himself at me and tried to break me in two. "This is the best birthday ever. Thank you for saving your money to bring us here." His skinny body was a bundle of nerves, shaking with excitement and sugar.

When he relaxed his grip, I moved us out of the doorway to the restrooms and took a knee in front of him, grabbing him by the shoulders. "Little Master, first, it is not 'my money'. The Light gave it to Val and me to share with all of you. Secondly, you're welcome." I winked and softly cuffed him on the shoulder.

His head dropped. "You should not call me that anymore. I am no longer a master of anything. I am not allowed to cook, I cannot practise my Badge, and I am no help to anyone."

I gave him a little shake until he looked me in the eye. "Just because you have not had opportunity to release your awesomeness into the world, doesn't change the fact that that is who you are. You are still all those things. And don't forget, you're definitely getting better at hand-to-hand." I rubbed my thigh in memory of where he had been able to get past my defences this morning in practice with a perfectly executed roundhouse.

His face lit up and I almost landed on my butt as he launched himself at me again, wrapping his arms around my neck. I caught him, set us straight, then he took off down the hill to rejoin Val and Riah. He tried in vain to stop his gangly body from skipping, but the end result made me laugh as his arms and legs flew out at all angles with joy. He reminded me of the baby giraffe we'd just seen frolloping around its mother.

Yeah, you heard me. Giraffe. What other city has a bleeding zoo in the middle of it? Hectares of prime city real estate dedicated to wild, exotic, bizarre animals. Val and I had managed to earn enough money from busking to start saving a little "petty cash", as she called it.

We'd been able to buy second-hand gifts for the twins' birthday today. Not that they'd seen them yet. That was for later tonight. As far as they knew, this was their present; we'd managed to secure a family pass to the zoo for the day. We had a few more surprises in store for them as well, and I was about as buzzed as Raph with excitement. I couldn't wait for them to experience it all.

Kait had said she'd try to be home early so she could set everything up for us and surprise them when we got home this arvo. And Tessa... well, we'd wait and see if she showed up. I doubted it. We no longer ranked as important in her life.

Damn it. I'd promised myself I wouldn't go there. Not today. Today was about the twins. To see their armour back to full force was confirmation taking them out of school had been the right decision. I looked down the hill and saw them bouncing around, totally unable to contain their excitement.

And why should they.

The mountain of pain climbed back behind the wall of my heart and light returned. Those two oozed joy. It was impossible not to be infected.

Val turned to speak to them and right on cue, sulphur crashed my party.

Great.

"Cute little critters, aren't they?" Disgust and disdain dripped from her words.

I turned to look at her. "Seriously? A safari suit?" If you could call it that. She'd poured herself into the child-sized costume.

"You like?" She turned, revealing just how poor a job it was doing covering her... assets.

"No." I hated the way my body responded to her. I was no better than the rutting beasts surrounding us. I hated her. But it made no difference. It was like my brain was at war with my instincts. She knew it too. And she loved it.

She purred and leaned forward to whisper, offering me a view that, I'm ashamed to say, never grew old. "You know she doesn't really respect you. She just keeps you around because it's good for her ego."

"What? Who?" I had to fight to focus on what she was saying.

"Val, of course. The middle-aged, dried-up hag gets a kick out of walking around with a fine young thing like you. It makes her look good."

"What?" The idea was ridiculous, even for her. I turned to look for where Val and the twins had gone. It was time to get back.

"Oh, look. I've dropped my..." The oldest, dumbest trick in the book. She squatted in front of me and of course my stupid eyes were glued to her as she glided her hand up my leg when she stood. Leaning close she whispered, "Lap dog." Her dead eyes sparked with undisguised promises.

"What the...?"

"You're just her little lap dog. She whistles, you come. She points, you go. She commands, you fetch. You're just her very pretty little... lap... dog." She pressed her chest into mine and my wretched body betrayed me. Panting in my ear, she licked my cheek and disappeared.

Frack.

"Anytime. Anywhere. Gorgeous." Her voice bounced around my head as I desperately tried to erase her image. Like that was even possible. And she knew it.

I ducked back into the restroom and threw cold water on my face and wrists. Soaking a hand towel, I sloshed it on the back of my neck, forcing myself to remember her attack on the streets of Sodom and the fight I had barely survived in the pit of Gomorrah. I reminded myself of the final battle for Ebony and forced my body back under control. Deep breaths and focus. She was a demon, not human.

By the time I made it back down to Val, the twins were nowhere in sight.

"You okay?" The warmth in her eyes helped calm my heart and set me right.

"Yeah. Thanks. Sorry about that." Looking around I tried to see where the twins had gone, and *she* appeared. All the self-loathing flooded back. All the failures, wretchedness and shame returned. I couldn't believe her gall. She stood behind Val's right shoulder with her hands bent in front of her chin imitating a dog... panting.

Then, her head snapped back.

Yep. That's right.

Snapped. Back.

If she was human I wouldn't have been surprised if it had come clean off when Val's armoured elbow smashed into her face. It had sounded like a rotten pumpkin hitting concrete. She lost her focus enough to slip her disguise, revealing the hideous stench of evil beneath. That's all "she" had been. Foul, life-sapping, light-trapping evil wrapped in an intoxicating bow.

"I'm getting pretty sick of her. How about you?" Val's sparking eyes never left mine as she returned her arm to her side.

Hissing and spitting erupted behind her as my demon pulled her disguise back together. Now when I looked at it, all I saw was a try-hard. She wasn't appealing, alluring or tempting at all. Surrounded by Warriors of the Light, swords drawn, and Val with her indigo armour on fire, the demon looked pathetic—a joke. How could I have fallen for her?

Val winked at me then turned on the cheese. "I am so sorry. I didn't see you there." Classic Val.

The demon was caught. She'd been playing tricks. Apparently, there was some rule about engaging the enemy. I still had my learner's plates, but I did know we didn't go around starting carnage parties without the call. The easiest way I had of knowing when to act was watching my guard. When he drew his sword, I drew mine. If he didn't, I wasn't in mortal danger and needed to sit tight.

But because the demons, mine in particular, had been playing hide and seek, Val could call ignorance when called to task for physically engaging the enemy, unprovoked. Which is what she did when Suit Dude arrived.

In Sodom, he had stalked me until I'd made my decision to step into the Light. Afterwards, things got a bit nasty. On the day we were celebrating my choice to enlist and sign up with the cool kids, he rocked up and did a fancy dress parade of all his faces and disguises. But for me he presented as Suit Dude; smooth, smart and suave.

This time, he rocked up with a small monkey clinging to his shoulder. It was one of the freaky little beasts that had attacked Val in Sodom. It drooled venom, and played with a heavy, dull knife; one of the many that used to be buried deep in Val's flesh.

"My dearest Valarieee." He approached and everyone froze. The Warriors, the demon, and me. Val dropped her head. "You are walking a ththin line. Do I need to remind you of your weaknessss?"

Val closed her eyes, inhaled deeply, then quietly breathed, "The Light's grace is sufficient for me. His power is made perfect in my weakness."

"Wonderful." The creature disappeared from the Dark Lord's shoulder and reappeared on Val's back with its blade wedged into the gap between her helmet and back plate.

Its shriek of laughter almost covered Val's gasp. She dropped to her knees. The Warriors stiffened but none moved. I was desperate to do something. But before I could move, or think, Suit Dude swore, and he and his pet—both of them—disappeared quick smart.

Summer came back to the air around us, the trees gently moved with the breeze, the white noise of distant conversation and children laughing returned. The extra Warriors disappeared, and our two guards stood down. Mine looked me in the eye then looked to Val. My mind-freeze thawed, and I raced to her side, madly running my hands over the back of her neck and searching her body for more blades.

Was this it?

Were they all coming back now?

Did I need to get help?

Skrat.

Help me know what to do?

"Dan, I appreciate your concern. But could you please stop running your hands over me. It's not only unnecessary, it's really weird." Val chuckled and stood.

"Are you okay? Do I need to call someone?" My heart was racing as fast as my brain was electrocuting my sanity.

"Stop. Breathe. Focus." Val's verbal reminder defibrillated my brain.

"Right. Sure. Okay. What do we do?" I could do this.

"Well, for starters, I suggest we find the twins. I hate to think which animal enclosure Riah has decided to climb into."

"But what about..." For flack's sake, was she not aware of what had just happened? "The thing..." I madly pointed to the back of her neck. Then to mine. Just to make sure she knew what I was talking about.

Turning her back to me, she pointed and clarified. "It's all gone. It was a warning. Nothing more."

"But the... but what... the thing!"

Oh God, oh God, oh God. Hell is coming and I am the only one here. What am I supposed to do?

Val's heavy hand crashed onto my shoulder. I winced, but it provided the anchor I needed. "Dan, it was a petty warning. The Dark Lord and both his minions have gone. He can't reach beyond what the Light allows. The knives will return, but it seems today is not the day." She smiled and the sun came out. "I knew I was walking a boundary, but"—the grin spread across her face and light exploded from her eyes—"it was worth it. Did you hear it? What I would have given to see its face." She shook her head and chuckled.

I couldn't help myself. I joined her. "It was brilliant. She didn't see it coming, then her face exploded."

"It, Dan. It's not she, it's an 'it' dressed up, or undressed, in whatever package is going to get under your skin. The pushback was well worth it." Then the light intensified to laser beams and she nailed me. All laughter gone. "Dan, you made three mistakes. First, you didn't speak. Secondly, you let it speak. And thirdly, you didn't speak."

I wasn't going to tell her she was repeating herself. Or that she wasn't making any sense. I already felt like a complete fool. Obviously, the neon sign that we refer to as my face let her know I did not follow.

"When the Dark approaches, first thing you do is call the Light. The Dark can't stand it, or in it, for that matter, and they will run. Do your best to stay in the Light always. But, regardless, they'll still come at you. Especially when you're weak or, funnily enough, when you're strong.

"Secondly, don't let them speak. Do not engage the enemy. Only novices talk before they shoot. *Always* shoot first. Then, if in doubt, shoot again. And just to make sure, hit it as hard as you can in the guts."

"Hang on. I didn't think we could kill them unless it was some kind of agreed all-in slaughter."

"We have more weapons than just our swords, Dan. Our armour, as you can see, is very effective in repelling unwanted attention." Her car salesman pitch lightened the mood. "We also have our shields, and most effectively our words. Plant the truth of The Way in your head and heart. That is why we study the text daily. Then, when they come at you, and it's not an opportunity for a broadsword hack-and-slash, use your words like a rapier. A sharp needle to the eye, heart, brain, or any other vital organ. Pure gold."

"Okaaay..."

"And thirdly, you didn't speak to us. You didn't let us know you were under attack. We are here to help. And we can. You've got to get it through your thick skull, you are not alone anymore. You are one with us. If you're under attack, we're all under attack."

"I didn't think you'd believe me."

"And why would you think that?" Her hands were on her hips and I had the feeling that any second I was going to feel like a complete fool.

"Well... they are in hiding? I tried telling you guys but got sick of feeling like a complete fool for being the only one in the whole city who could see them. My demon told me no one would believe me, she dared me to tell Tessa. So, I did. The demon was right."

Val raised her eyebrow. Just the one. It was a question.

"Tessa tried to convince me I had been dreaming. It wasn't real. But it was. Everyone saying that there are no demons in Laodicea is complete skrat. And she... it doesn't matter."

"Hmm. Well Tessa isn't in the best place at the moment. But what makes you think the rest of us wouldn't believe you? Even though you can smell them a mile off, doesn't mean the rest of us aren't catching a whiff as well. If there were no demons here, we wouldn't have guards." She turned to acknowledge hers and they both did a chin dip of acknowledgement. She turned back to me. "And we wouldn't be here."

I looked to mine. He did a very good interpretation of Val's one-eyebrow-raise. And boom! There it was. I felt like a flaking fool. "Sorry."

Val clapped me on the back and hung her arm over my shoulder, encouraging me to start walking. "You live and learn; no permanent damage done. But remember, one of the Dark's greatest tactics is divide and conquer. We are called to be a unit, not solitary. Now, let's find the twins and rescue any animal Raph has decided he wants as a pet, and Riah has gone to capture for him."

34

FELIX: FINDING THE WAY

"You up for a session?" Marcus stood in the dim morning glow on the balcony, dressed in his morning workout garb, holding up a pair of boxing gloves.

After the initial accommodation hiccup in Philadelphia, it was a hiccup I made a habit of repeating whenever I travelled with Marcus. This morning we awoke overlooking the Aegean Sea from a suite on the top floor of the Ephesian Princess. Even though we were only an hour and forty-minute drive down the highway from Laodicea, and I had the privilege of a driver, I didn't make it to the sea as often as I would like.

The city was still asleep, but the gulls were not. Their cries accompanied the soft lapping of the ocean, and the cool scent of the sea swirled through the open door, helping to chase the last vestige of sleep away.

The hotel's seminar room was adequate to accommodate the numbers attending the gathering I had convened. It had been well catered, a credit in the resort's ledger, and the gathering had been productive, a credit in the ledger of petitioning the Light. Marcus, Marlene and I had spent considerable time coming before the Light, asking for direction and success in this project. And all things considered, the conference had gone well.

The Overseer, High Council and Shepherds here in Ephesus were agreeable to the idea of forming a group of delegates from each of the seven major Community centres in our region. We were on target to meeting that goal well within the next six months. It had been slow going, visiting all the cities, selling the concept and gaining approval. But on this our last stop in the circuit, with Ephesus "in the bag" as Marcus had put it, we could finally return home to finalise details after a lunch meeting today.

I had a sense this project was a good thing to do, and almost a... compulsion to see it done. This was an opportunity for the Communities of the Seven Cities to support each other. Laodicea had been abundantly blessed with financial resources and the others had been equally equipped in other areas.

The Gerent was tolerant of the Community in Laodicea and Ephesus because we were large, wealthy and didn't rock any political or religious boat. However, the smaller gatherings in other cities did not curry the same favour. Especially in the newer city of Philadelphia. If we could demonstrate solidarity across the region, he may be inclined to be tolerant of all Community groups. But we had to act quickly before any significant ruling was made. Either way, his decision would not easily be revoked.

It was one of the projects the Overseer and I saw eye to eye on, and had both been investing time and energy in over the past six months. The smaller centres were keen. However, a couple of the larger organisations were fearful of having to support the fledglings financially, and having their current "provisional" status revoked due to association.

Personally, I did not understand this thinking. As I had been studying The Way with Marcus, I believed this was the only path for us to follow. So much so, I had asked Marlene, Marcus and his family, and Fleur to join me in petitioning the Light daily to make it happen. But to get the final cities over the line, we had to include a proviso for exit if they felt threatened at any point in time. I struggled to feel... brotherly to these men.

"Hello?" Boxing gloves waving in my face brought me back to the hotel suite.

"Thank you, Marcus." These morning sessions had become a highlight of our time together and I made sure I was prepared whenever work took us out of town.

Wearing my new "workout kit" I was ready to begin: a pair of New Balance—appropriately named I thought—thick sports socks, and black tracksuit, all of which I had personally purchased and took with me everywhere. I had learned the basics of the sets and each morning before work I had started to experiment with the movements on my own at home. I found it helped me prepare for the day.

Since beginning the routines, I also found it easier to sleep. I still needed my medication to manage the Crow, but a few times I had survived a night without them. I had also found the more strenuous exercise helped with clearing my mind and managing my lists.

Not only did we practise sets and sessions each morning, true to his word, as we reposed over coffee and The Way Marcus asked how he could petition the Light on my behalf. Not only that. I knew he passed this information on to his family and they too supported me this fashion. He always asked first, of course, as to what was sensitive and what was for general sharing.

I still found Marcus a paradox of a man, but one whom I had begun to call... friend. What was more surprising was that this friendship of sorts was reciprocated.

I had a male friend.

It was new and... pleasant.

I believe our developing connection moved from acquaintance/work colleague to trusted confidant the night the Crow caught me out in Smyrna. Thankfully the Overseer had been absent. Marcus had been too perceptive and noted my fumbling and what he called my "paler than translucent pallor". I expect the slight tremor and the inability to open the blasted bottle of pills were also key indicators.

I really did have to do something about that.

Trying to convince him that all was well did not go to plan, and in short order he had me and the mounting chaos in hand. Once the point of severity had been breached, I communicated he should connect with Marlene who would give further directives.

She had explained.

Marcus had acted.

And now he was "in the know", so to speak.

Marlene approved, of course. Since then, they'd had that special bonding experience I'd witnessed between Marcus and Jonathan... and Marcus and the Community heads in Philadelphia. I am now convinced it was the armour.

I will be honest and confess that I was happy to see that my own orange armour was developing and thickening considerably. Jonathan noted it last time we were in Philadelphia. I was... chuffed.

The Overseer had also noticed. But he was not quite so impressed.

I turned to acknowledge my guard whom I now took great comfort in.

He nodded back.

"Earth to Felix. You coming out this morning or are you going to waste your time navel gazing?"

"Yes. Yes, of course."

We met on the patio overlooking the ocean. It was a beautiful sight. The breeze carried with the salt air the suggestion that the sun was ready to roll up over the horizon. It wasn't until I had started taking the time to slow down and focus on the Light that I'd started to notice these things.

It was... pleasant. Very pleasant.

After six months, I'd spent a significant amount of time with Marcus and less with the Overseer. It may have been due to the issue of the armour. It may have been due to the personality of Marcus. It may have been due to other interests. But whatever it was, the man was sending me out to undertake the official tasks, while he pursued his own ambition to be known as the "Face of Laodicea"—more out of Laodicea than in.

We had always had different priorities. It had not been an issue as our roles were so different. Yet, it was not hard to identify that the more my friendship with Marcus intensified, the further apart the Overseer and I became. He chose to engage a driver Nyle had suggested, thereby distancing us physically as we pursued our common goal of unifying the Community in our region.

Is it horrible to confess I approved?

I had never liked the man. We were cut from a different cloth, he wasn't quite a Minyetti man, but he was well on his way in Gallis. I respected what he did... to a point. And there was merit in his work. I just wasn't convinced how much of it actually benefited the Community, let alone the Light.

Another interesting result from spending time with Marcus and away from the Overseer was how close I was getting to the Light. This too was... rewarding. I had found it intriguing that the closer I looked at things through the Light, just how different they appeared. This would be deemed logical I suspect. But still, it was eye-opening.

I found it encouraging to have others petition the Light on my behalf. Somehow it caused a feeling of... connectedness. I also found that, in turn, I was prompted to petition the Light on behalf of others, as well as myself. This too was new. And pleasing.

To begin with I was concerned that I would lose time by giving up portions of my mornings to "sets and sessions", as Marcus liked to call them. But on the contrary, this was not the case.

So, this morning, looking out over the Aegean Sea, I allowed Marcus to lace up my gloves and waited for him to don the mitts. And then we began.

I will admit to being thrilled he had promised, as my armour developed, we would begin sword fighting. I had seen him train, and confess that I was more than mildly impressed. I didn't for a moment believe that I would ever gain his skill or experience, but it was invigorating to think that I might wield such an instrument.

"Come on, man, stop dreaming and start hitting."

"Right. Yes. Of course." I really had to get my "head in the game" as the man tended to say. I dropped my weight, breathed deeply, centred my mind, put everything I had into it and gave a quick, one, two. I was rewarded by a grunt from my coach. I do believe I was making progress.

This, too, was rewarding.

35

MARCUS: THE PARTY

I didn't know what was more exciting: seeing the kids again, or surprising them. We were all set up and ready to go. But I had to lay credit where the fees were due. Without Felix's help, none of this would have been possible.

Why he was helping us so much, I didn't know. But I had to admit that he was worth his weight in silver linings. Spending time with him, seeing the load he carried, the way he ran the Community and actually saw and cared about the people he managed, I couldn't help but acknowledge the man's substance. That and his planning. If he wasn't fishing, he was mending nets. The fact that I'd been privileged to see behind the mask and been trusted with the knowledge of his battle was humbling. Felix had grown from an oddity to a true friend whom I admired, appreciated, and enjoyed chewing the fat with.

He had convinced the Overseer that we needed to be back in town today. Obviously, he didn't say it was for the kids' birthday party. But truth be, it was. The man was slick, I had to give him that. He was also generous with a capital $. He knew the system and that we were short on funds, so he had paid for all the froth and bubble for this afternoon's gig.

Kait had been given the afternoon off, and had the go-ahead to

organise a cake, decorations, food and treats, and Felix had paid for it
all. Personally. I was plucked as a speckled hen to know why, but...

*Thank you for bringing the blessings out of the crazy town of Laodicea.
If you'd asked me six months ago what I would be enjoying here, I would
have been drawing blanks. So, thanks from the bottom of me heart. You
know it's true. I'm ever so grateful. Even though it's hurt, it's been good.*

I'd dropped the Overseer off at his palace, taken Felix back to
headquarters, then come home, showered, shaved and changed. It
was strange moving around the vacant house. I'd not been here by
meself before. I indulged by walking through all the rooms, seeing
how everyone had made their presence felt and left their mark.
Taking in how the sterile house had been turned into a home by the
fingerprints. Couldn't help me smile when I saw the sitting area, hall-
ways, and bedrooms wallpapered in butcher's paper with Riah's work.

The kitchen had been rearranged to suit Raph's preferences.
Things in the garage had been moved to give space to the punching
bag. A tight squeeze, but I could just imagine Dan working out his
frustrations pounding the leather.

Kait had bought some perfume, and walking into our room both
warmed me and pierced me heart. I loved her. I missed her. I was so
proud of her. The scent of lavender and rose was all Kait.

The main armchair in the sitting room was partnered with a side
table overflowing with books. A blanket lay over the back and a lamp
watched over the lot. I could just imagine Val perched up, reading.
Never content to read one book at a time. She always had four or five
on the go, at least.

Me heart smiled as I walked around the house and saw how
everyone had made their mark and made the most of what they'd
been dealt here in Laodicea.

Since it was a glorious summer day and the afternoon promised
to be sweet, I set up the outside table and chairs on the patio that
joined the house to the pool. Its roof gave shade from the sun, but
allowed the breeze to flow through the big sliding doors to our sitting
room. After that, there wasn't much to do till Kait got here.

She'd be here soon. I threw my washing in the machine. Straightened any mess I'd made. Checked meself in the mirror. Walked around the house. Checked the machine. Walked around the house. And kept tripping up at the end of me tether.

Adrenaline was electrifying me brain, turning me fingers to thumbs and giving me two left feet. I was walking in circles, fumbling and dropping everything I touched.

She'd be here soon, and the others wouldn't be here till later, much later...

I ran upstairs, threw on me trunks and punished meself in the pool. I wasn't a natural fish, but only because I'd never had the opportunity. But I could swim, so I did. Lap, after lap, after lap, after lap.

Eventually, I couldn't breathe, I could barely move. I was as cooked as a goose in the sun.

I dragged meself to the shallow end and collapsed on the edge, heart pounding, sweat bleeding into the pool. Chlorine filled me senses and tightened me skin. I allowed the gentle, cool waves of the water to rock me body as I dissolved into a puddle of relaxed jelly.

Somewhere in the back of my brain, a flag waved, fluttering on a pole. Something prodded at the edge of me haze. A hint. A memory. A scent.

Lavender and rose.

A hand slid up my back. I froze. Me body tensed. Fire crept from me heart and within a second me calm was as done in as a dead man's dinner. A warm, weighted cloak spread across me back. Skin to skin. Me heart exploded. Arms wrapped around my chest. It was the only thing holding me together.

"Hello, Bear. Welcome home." Soft lips branded me shoulder.

Every nerve in me body took off like a Catherine wheel. I couldn't speak. I turned in her arms and buried me face in her hair and clung on like me life depended on it. 'Cause right then, it did.

When I'd managed to get meself back under control, I kissed her. And when I'd managed to drag meself back under control... again, I led her to our room. Locked the door. And became reacquainted with me wife.

Once again, I was reduced to jelly of contentment. I could stay here forever. Well, until the rest got home. Which would be... I looked at the clock on the bedside table... soon. I launched meself out of bed.

"Hey! Watch it, you big oaf."

I turned back round and scanned the room. Kait had disappeared. Where the...? What the? I climbed back onto the bed and looked over the edge to see my once agreeable wife glaring at me from the carpet. "Come on, no time for mucking around. The kids'll be home soon." The pillow hit me in the back of the head as I scrambled into me jeans. I laughed harder.

Could life get any better? I think not. Thank you!

Pulling a shirt over me head, I ran down the stairs and started to take stock. Then it occurred to me, I had no idea what to do, or how to do it. Kait had bought all the supplies and done all the planning. She bumped my hip, hard, as she walked past.

"What do I do? How are we going to do this? Have you got everything ready? Did you get everything Felix organised?" Marching round the room, I hadn't noticed the drop in temperature until I made me way back to the kitchen bench. Ice was shooting out of her eyes. "Right. So. What do you want me to do?"

She crossed her arms under her perfect chest, raised her perfect eyebrow and gave me the perfect glare. *What do you think? Perhaps the first thing you could do is... think.*

God, I loved this woman. *Be nice.* I couldn't hide me grin. I loved riling her. And as far as I saw it, I had a week's worth of riling to catch up on.

Still saying nothing... out loud, she slid a box across the bench that stood between us. Inside was stuff to decorate the table with. I couldn't hide me sly smile or the heat that returned. I only had to look at her and the heat simmered away.

Hard as she tried, neither could she. *We don't have time for that... now. Get out there and get to work.* With that she turned her perfect butt and dismissed me. I couldn't help it. I slid across the bench, grabbed her from behind and... was interrupted by an alert on her phone.

"Quick. That's Val. They're on their way." She slapped my arms and pushed me out of the kitchen.

I left her to prep the food as I did what I was told. I didn't know who was more excited about this party: me or the twins.

We'd had just enough time to set everything up when we heard a car in the driveway. Kait scooped the rest of the wrappers into the bin with one sweep of her arm and I ducked around the corner and hid. The door burst open and laughter and yells exploded into the house, bringing it to a new level of life.

I listened while Kait welcomed everyone home and tried to sort through Raph's storytelling. The boy jumped from pillar to post, making it hard to follow. I couldn't wait any longer and crept out and stood with Val and Dan. Each gave me a quick silent embrace. We stood watching the show. Raph was trying to tell Kait what they saw and did, but he was constantly interrupted by Riah making him share something else.

Kait pulled them both in and locked her eyes with mine. Yeah, these were the kids the Light had given us in place of the ones we couldn't have ourselves. They looked up to Kait from under her wings and saw she was staring at something. They turned. They both froze. Raph fell silent and Riah squeaked.

We all froze.

That was the first noise she'd made in the three years since they'd been rescued, apart from the miracle song during the battle of Sodom. I dropped to me knees and only had time to throw me arms out before I went down under their scrum. As was always the way, we ended up on the floor, me growling, Raph squealing, Riah shaking.

"Uncle Felix." Raph's cry pulled us all up.

"Uncle?" Felix's eyebrows disappeared into the wrinkles of his forehead.

I tried to cough to cover me gaff.

Raph scrabbled out of me arms. Composed himself and put on his teacher voice. Using his whole hand to indicate who he was referring to. "Marcus is my father, Dan is my brother, and now that you are choosing to wear your armour, you are my uncle." He beamed, his face alight, his chest puffed out; simple.

Felix dropped his eyes and considered his armour. I'd seen him most days and was aware of the gradual but definite increase. The others hadn't been privy to his journey.

"Come on in and join us, we were just about to start." I put Sariah aside and went to welcome me friend, trying to alleviate his discomfort.

"I, ah, shouldn't stay. I don't want to interrupt your family gathering." His hand fidgeted with the colourful bags he was holding. "I just wanted to drop these off."

Kait joined me at Felix's side. "Don't think you're getting out of it that easily, Felix. Haven't you been listening? You are family now." She kissed his flaming cheek and added, just loud enough for the three of us to hear. "Like it or not." She turned and called out, "Raph, honey, pull up another chair."

"But there is one there already."

"That's just in case Tessa can make it, sweetheart." Her lead balloon splattered all over the joy in the room.

"Ah. Yes. Well... thank you. I won't stay long."

The three of us trailed the others out to the patio where the party was ready to begin. Sweet drinks, sugary food and greasy carbohydrates—the essentials for any celebration—littered the table. After the first wave of consumption, I pulled two parcels from beside me chair that I'd planted earlier, placing one in front of each of the kids. "A little something from Ephesus."

Sariah ripped the wrapping off in one move. Raph gently peeled away the tape, reverently unwrapping his package. We all heard the eye roll coming from Sariah as she watched her brother impatiently.

"Riah, you could use this paper in your craft, or the blank side for your drawing. We cannot waste it. What if we run out one day?"

She smiled at her brother.

He graciously accepted her acknowledgement. I crumbled a bit inside. He was so used to going without, he was always saving up for the next rainy day. They both burst into laughter when they saw the ridiculous T-shirts I'd ordered from an instant print place during this last trip to Ephesus. Riah's had a picture of a princess in a crown, jeans, T-shirt and sneakers. The T-shirt read, "Kiss my royal buttooshie". Raph's had a chef's hat and apron, proclaiming, "The Master's in the house".

Kait shook her head, faking disapproval. "Right then, moving along." She nodded to Dan.

His chair almost fell in his rush to get their next presents. Val cleared the place in front of Riah, placing the jug of soda and the flower arrangement on the floor beside her chair. Kait pushed all the decorations in front of Raph to the centre of the table to make way for the large box Dan delivered. He then turned and deposited a badly wrapped bulk in front of Riah. "We didn't have a lot of money, but Val and I found these things and we thought you guys might like them."

Wrapping paper carnage littered the table and floor within seconds. Riah was gaping like a hungry fish, her eyes as wide and wet as ponds, holding a bright red, three-quarter-sized guitar. Tears streamed down her cheeks, her shoulders shook, and her red armour ignited as she clung to that instrument like it was a newborn baby.

I had to clear me throat to dislodge the pile of wood shavings that had wedged in it, making it difficult to swallow.

"Oh Riah!" Raph stopped the painful process of unsticking the cover of his box to watch his sister.

She rubbed her cheeks on her shoulders, not releasing her gift, but nodded her head, indicating he needed to get a move on, unwrapping his. Eventually Raph folded back the lid of the battered box and stood transfixed over the contents. He didn't move or speak. Both very uncommon for him. Riah stamped her foot, demanding he reveal what was within. He looked around the table through the swimming pools in his eyes, then dipped his hands into the box and withdrew a collection of orange cooking bowls and measuring cups.

He picked them up, clung to them, dropped his head and rocked them.

I turned to Felix. "Abbot was the main one who taught Raph to cook, and Riah to garden. He wore orange armour." I didn't have to say any more. Felix knew our story and how Abbot had sacrificed himself in Sodom to save the soul of Ebony. He was aware of how we still grieved for our grandfather and the hole he had left in our lives. At that, Felix dropped his head and noted his own orange armour and how it sparked in the light of the setting sun.

"Perhaps now might be the best time to bring out these." Val lifted a bundle wrapped in cloth and reverently laid it on the table. "Abbot knew for a while he was going to die. He didn't know how, or exactly when..." Val stopped, took a deep breath, then continued. "So, he set these things aside for this—"

Val's speech was interrupted by the sound of our front door opening. "What in the name of all that is good and right in the world is wrong with you people." My chair crashed to the floor as I raced to the sitting room to confront the bleeding intruder. "How bleeding hard is it for you to bleeding knock on the bleeding—"

"Marcus!" A chorus of shouts pulled me up short.

"What?" I turned and released the remainder of me fury at me family. "I've warned them not to walk into our house uninvited or without knocking. I'm sick of it. How dare they?"

Kait raced to the trespasser and put her arms around her.

"I wasn't actually going to hurt her Kait. Come on—"

"Marcus. It's Tessa."

A pin dropped somewhere and it stopped me dead. Life drained from me heart and took me remaining years with them. I was an old man, breathless, speechless, groundless. "What have they done to you?" A whisper was all I had left in me.

36

KAITLYN: FALLOUT

Oh, dear Lord, help us.

I folded our girl into my arms and tried to hold Marcus together with my eyes. Val came and took Tessa upstairs and I tried to deal with my broken husband. He'd not seen her for months, she'd missed face-calls, practically moved out to be on hand for Kari and the team. Her work had been demanding in more ways than one.

Despite our best efforts to keep her encouraged and strong, she'd fallen. Her armour was now as weak as the city that had claimed her. She'd lost her light, her joy, and her spark. Not to mention, lost more weight, colour and health. I understood why Marcus didn't recognise her; the transformation was complete.

We'd been asking her for months to come home. For weeks we'd been begging her to come to the twins' party. She'd never given us a definite answer. But she was here now. We'd make the most of it.

"I should go." Felix pushed his chair back from the table.

"Actually, Felix," I steered my husband back to the gathering, "I'd really appreciate it if you stayed." I gave him the warmest smile I could muster. "It looks like you've got some unfinished business?" The bright bags he'd brought with him sat untouched beside his chair. "And whether you like it or not, we need you. Marcus needs you."

"What?" Just as I had hoped, that snapped some fire back into the man sagging at my side. I winked at him, guided him back to his place at the table, put a donut in one hand and a sweet drink in the other. "Here, sugar will help your shock."

"What happened to her?"

"Six months of dining out on Laodicean skrat." Dan's stony growl from the other end of the table was accompanied by stern nods from the twins standing either side of him. The fallout had been significant.

"Well, she's here now..." I tried to soothe Dan's pain as I made my way back to my seat.

"For how long this time? Just enough to pick up a change of underwear and go again? It's not like she needs anything else here. Kari dresses her, feeds her, treats her like some kind of flocking pet —" Dan's armour went from vibrant Indigo to semitranslucent.

"Language, Dan." Val returned to the table and took her seat beside him.

He looked to Tessa and challenged her. "Well? How long are you here for?"

Tessa, a shadow, followed her. "For good, if you'll... um... have me. She, ah... threw me out." It was half a whisper, half a sob.

"Sweetheart, why? What happened?" Once again, I went to our girl and hugged her as she caved in on herself like a scrunched-up piece of paper.

"I no longer have anything they want. They took it all from me then spat me out." There was fire and pain behind her words, but we could deal with that later.

"The main thing is you are home and in time for the party." My falsetto grated even on my own ears.

Tessa slid into the vacant chair we'd left for her, next to Marcus. He looked to the untouched donut and drink in his hand, passed her the drink and inhaled half the donut, then dragged her closer and wrapped his arm around her shoulders.

Taking the drink in both hands, Tessa collapsed into his embrace and was instantly removed from centrestage.

"Right, now, where were we?" I took charge and did my best to get the show back on the road. "Felix, we appreciate you're busy and that you have taken time out to join us." He jumped into the opening I had created like the professional he was.

"Yes. Thank you." All eyes shifted to him and he artfully manipulated the mood. Much like Abbot would have done.

This man was an onion of significant layers. His droll, dry manner lifted the mood, now that we knew him better. Six months of trying to hide his huge heart and sizzling wit—why? I didn't know—had only made him dearer to us as his friendship with Marcus had developed, along with his impressive armour.

"As you know, I spend a lot of time with Marcus." He paused and looked at the twins conspiratorially. They giggled. "And, as you know, Marcus likes to talk. A lot." More giggles. "On and on about this family he belongs to." He pursed his lips and shook his head theatrically.

Thank you for this precious man and his ability to recapture the magic of this day.

"Apparently, they are special and deserve the world." He could disguise the feelings behind his bored tone, but he could not hide the joy in his eyes. "Well, I don't have the world, but thought this might be a start." He shrugged his shoulders, bent to pick up the bags, and deposited one in front of each of them.

The twins stared at each other without moving, yet we could all see the mind-speak gushing between them. He'd thrown them completely.

He reached out as if to take them back. "But... if you don't want them, I can—"

That was all it took. Riah snatched her bag and withdrew the parcel in a heartbeat and held it to her chest, staring at Felix with wonder in her eyes. Raph placed two hands over the box he'd retrieved from his bag. No one was taking those gifts away. I suspect we were all remembering our first morning months ago when Felix had offered us all gifts, enabling us to stay in touch and cope with the new life we were entering here in Laodicea.

Raph ran his hands over the paper slowly, examining the shape, size and weight of the package. Riah searched for the tape and slowly started peeling away the bindings, stopping every so often to look at Felix. He nodded at her each time. So she continued.

They both arrived at the same point together by some unspoken agreement. The packages were untaped, but still wrapped.

"Oh, for frigate's sake, would you just open the bleeding presents. I want to see what you got." Dan had run out of patience.

Marcus grunted in agreement.

Enjoying her position of control, Riah sassed them both, hands on hips and shifting her chin side to side.

But Raph's gasp had her attention racing back to her gift. He lifted a tablet—a very expensive, latest version, with all the bells and whistles tablet—out of the wrapping.

Riah stood looking at her own gift, completely overwhelmed. Tears washed her face again and her shoulders shook once more. It was an overwhelming night for all of us, it appeared. Riah hadn't even touched the revealed gift. She turned and buried herself into Dan's shoulder and wept silently.

"Would someone please tell me what they got? I can't see." Marcus, still clinging to Tessa, was at a distinct disadvantage.

Wordlessly, Dan held up Riah's package of a tablet, similar to Raph's but with an extra drawing tablet as well.

Marcus's Adam's apple worked furiously.

We all turned to stare at Felix, whose normal pallor had tinged to pink. "Well, I thought it might be helpful if Sariah could store her pictures electronically and, if she wanted to, she could share them online? I know Marcus misses them when he's away, and well... I think she's quite good. I was hoping to encourage her."

Sariah launched herself from Dan to Felix and clung to him like a limpet.

"There... there..." Wide eyed, he looked around the table and woodenly patted her shoulder.

"My sister is very grateful, Uncle Felix. She is saying, 'thank you'."

We all burst out laughing at Raph's understatement.

"Ah... yes... well. Your tablet has been loaded with an encyclopaedia of recipe books. I have had them catalogued into the different traditions of cooking as well as the types of foods, cross referenced with different meals. You know, breakfast, dinner et cetera... Oh dear." Again, Felix searched the table looking for clarification. But by this time there was not a dry eye in the house. Through my own watery veil, I could see even Val wipe a stray tear. And now Felix had two weeping children in his arms.

"If I'd known there would be this much emotion, I would have posted them."

And once again, he'd saved the day and lifted the mood as laughter simmered through the tears.

Thank you.

I pushed my chair out. "I'll put the kettle on. I think it's time for cake." I believed more sugar was needed.

"It would not have made a difference, Uncle Felix." Raph had retreated to Dan's arms. "My sister demonstrates her love by giving gifts. Since we have nothing apart from who we are, in Sodom she spent time creating a beautiful garden for us all to enjoy. She created a masterpiece inside and transformed our house into an art gallery. These were her gifts to us all, to surround us in her love." We all stopped at that point and looked at the wallpaper of Sariah's drawings in the house. "You have given her a gift. You have helped her draw. You have demonstrated great love to her."

"Oh. I see... thank you for explain—"

Raph had not finished. "I like to show my love by spending time with people and cooking for them. You have taken time out of your very busy schedule to spend time with us this afternoon. You have given me a gift to help me cook. You have demonstrated great love to me too, Uncle Felix."

Felix's orange armour flamed with a tinge of pink and hues of red.

"Thank you Raph. That is helpful to know."

"Oh please, get me a bucket. I'm going to be sick." The sarcastic drawl was accompanied by the toxic tang of sulphur.

Gooseflesh covered my body and chills cramped my spine. In all the time we'd been here, there had not been a confrontation or even a sighting. But now the joy of the twins' party was infected by bitterness. And I was in the kitchen, separated from everyone else outside on the patio. Not ideal. "On guard. Now."

I knew they liked to play with their food before going for the kill. I left everything where it was and drew my sword as I dashed round the kitchen bench, skirting the furniture and the pod of demons that had just arrived, giving them as wide a berth as possible, and ducked through the sliding glass doors onto the patio with the rest of my family.

"What's happening?" Tessa was even paler than her new shade of translucent.

"Felix, Raph, Tessa, by the wall." Val pointed to the corner where the solid glass of the sliding door met external palings of the patio wall. Val was armed, ready and on fire. Literally. Her armour was sparking, and her eyes were hungry for the fight. "Sariah, Dan. Guard duty." Using her chin, Val indicated the three now huddled in the corner. She then nodded to me and Marcus, with no words required.

Marcus tried to encourage his friend. "Felix. Draw that thing on your back and aim the pointy end out. Anything that comes close, stick it."

To his credit, the man did what he was told, pale, silent, and shaken.

Dan and Sariah moved to cover the three: Tessa wedged at the back, Raph and Felix standing guard in front of her. Raph reached his hand up and whispered to Felix. Both nodded and turned, ready for a taste of hell.

Their placement wasn't ideal as it didn't leave Dan and Riah a lot of room to move. The space in front of them was cluttered with discarded chairs and the table still laden with food and gifts. But with such short notice, it offered a place to stand in the battle and a boundary line at their backs for the Warriors of Light to defend.

Our guard had increased in number. All of them had also drawn their weapons, taking their place around the perimeter of the death ground… and the roof, by the sounds of it.

Val nodded to her guard. He acknowledged her. Were they both hungry, after a fast from fighting?

"They're here, aren't they?" Tessa was huddled in the corner, her eyes darting around the house and patio. Her armour was so weak, her weapons non-existent and her sight gone.

"Hey, what do you call a newb, a bare-skin, a broken blade, and a dimwit?" The beast nodded to the corner where Felix and the kids stood. It didn't wait for a response. "Easy pickings."

The rest laughed. Then transformed into women of ludicrous proportions, each in body armour a mockery of our own. "Hey gorgeous." The lead looked to Dan. "I told you she was no good for you. Look at her."

They all leered and jeered over Tessa's reduced form.

"She was so easy."

The group all high-fived and hip-bumped. The speaker strutted over to Dan. His face was a mask of rage. But when his lips started moving, it stopped mid-step, yelped, dropped the disguise then returned to its group, spitting insults.

Dan's armour was back to full strength, and he smirked.

The temperature plummeted even further. "Well done, Daniel." Slow, solo clapping circled the room. "Following the adviccce of your handler to rebuff my giffft to you. Your lossss. You could have had it all, you know. *My* promisessss aren't hollow."

Lord help us. The Dark Lord.

"Valarrrie, your boy is learning new tricksss. Congratulations."

His icy hiss slithered through my veins and cracked my defences. Today he came in the guise Dan called Suit Dude; sleek and smooth evil wrapped in elegant style.

I clung to the Light, despite my hope and courage fading with each second of his presence.

"Dan, ssso good to see you again." His minions parted as he entered the fray.

To his credit, Dan stayed quiet. He was learning. His armour was once again full strength. Whatever he was doing, it was working.

Please help him. Help us all.

Darkness stopped in his progress, tilted his head, then his toxic chuckles wrapped around us. "Yes, very good, *my boy*. Now, I think it might be time to make a deal, don't you think?"

Dan refused to be drawn, his eyes fixed on his tormentor.

"I will tell my girls to leave you alone if you relinquish your agreement with Tessa. I mean, seriously, look at her?" And he did. Our poor girl was huddled in a ball, head buried in her knees, arms wrapped around, holding herself together. Her shoulders were shaking, but her armour was tingling. A faint yellow current was surging around her.

Yes! Thank you. Get her back in the game!

"Pathetic," one of the minions spat.

"Rather." The Dark Lord was in agreement but, none the less, continued with his bargaining. "Let's be honest shall we? It's obvious what you really think of her." Soulless eyes raked Dan's flickering armour. "And we can all see what she really thinks of you." Pitiless eyes burned Tessa's stirring form in the corner. "So, what's it to you? Relinquish your agreement with her, and I'll not only call my girls off you, I'll give Contessa some space."

Dan's jaw clenched even tighter. Surely his teeth were in danger of cracking, but he stood firm and mute.

I looked to the whole group sheltered in the corner of the patio wall. Felix stood still, pale and shaking, but firm. His sword was drawn and grasped, white knuckled, with both hands. Raph stood at his side, a scarred hand on Felix's forearm. The boy's head was bowed, and his lips were moving. Sariah stood to Dan's left, eyes, armour and sword dancing and alive with her own vibrant, unconfined red inferno.

The Dark's hand shot out. Dan gasped as his head shot back. "I'll let you think on that, as you... reflect... on all the ways she has deserted you, used you and dropped you into skrat since your arrival."

Felix yelped as Dan fell to his knees.

"Ah yes, the new awakening." The Dark's focus shifted to Marcus. "You have been busy, haven't you?" He stalked toward my husband, a finger tapping on his chin. "What shall I offer for him? More quality time in the pool with your wife?" His chuckle was disgusting and depraved. "To ensure she does not spend more quality time with another man, every day at work, while you are far, far away? Oh, you didn't know about that?"

The Dark Lord spun and speared his accusation at me. "Kait, you naughty girl, not telling *Bear* about George? My, how deceptive. Not like you at all." He looked around the group. "I can see Laodicea has been good for all of you."

"Georgie's a bloke?" It was nothing more than a croak. Marcus searched my face, bereft, broken, betrayed. His armour wavered. His knees buckled briefly.

I sent him my own message back by way of grappling hooks into his heart: *I love you; you are my one and only, do not listen to his lies.* Then gave him a non-verbal slap: *do not doubt me!* I edged closer to my husband. It may have been to present a solid front, but I wasn't beyond punching him for his doubt. But that would come later, after we'd faced this obstacle together.

The smell and feel of death swam around the room.

How much longer, Lord? What is this all about? What is his purpose here? Hold us firm, protect us, be with us, use us and strengthen us.

Sunlight glimmered from the corner of the room. Red faced, tear-stricken, Tessa stood.

37

CONTESSA: HOME COMING

Damn that kret to hell... again.

"Honey, we're working on it, don't you worry about that." The Dark's chuckle set my teeth on edge.

"Not Dan. You."

Here I was, once again. On the wrong end of the you've-stuffed-up-completely stick. Honestly, I was gifted.

Maybe that was one of my Badges. Serving and Stuffing Up.

Nice.

I mean, seriously, I had been working my guts out to help my family stay in this nice house, to be looked after by the Community. Kait, Marcus and I were working like slaves.

For them.

Didn't these guys know we were doing it for them?

To make their life easy.

Just so they could swan around all day having fun, going to the zoo... while the rest of us earned a living?

I didn't get the communal hostility. Seriously. What more did they want? Blood?

"Oh, sweetie, they have no idea what you've done for them. How hard you've worked, slaved, and sacrificed, for them. And what do they do? Shut you out," the Dark crooned, and added fuel to my anger and resentment. "You don't need them, and they don't appreciate you."

He was right.

But he was so very wrong.

I did need them.

I needed them so very, very much.

And I missed them.

I wanted to come home. Walking into a party that I should have been part of, planned, helped prepare...

Breathe.

That's what I had to do.

Just breathe; Light in, me out.

Instead, I'd come in late, broken and blind.

I mean, seriously, a pack of bleeding demons were in the house and I couldn't even bleeding see them, or smell them. That's when I'd realised just how far I'd fallen.

As sick as it sounds, I missed Sodom. Well, not the city, and the stench, and the foul yuckiness. I missed my life there.

And the way it had been.

And the person I had been.

And my family... and Dan.

That's when I realised: when we were living in the middle of the war zone we worked hard. We kept the Dark out and the Light within and we came out on top. The trip out of Sodom had been frightening, but it had been the highlight of my life. I'd had a purpose; I could see the reason for the training, and the discipline, and the sacrifice.

But here, I'd allowed myself to believe the lies and given up the fight. Now, it was the other way around. I'd let the Light go and Dark seep in.

Help? Please? Forgive me? Please? Please!

Breathe. Light in. Me out.

Right. Truth was, I had stuffed up. I threw my eyes around the room to my family. I had gone out to serve them. To help them. I wanted to be the one who was important. The one they counted on, the one who was out there doing my bit. Instead of being stuck at home, helpless. Useless. Baggage.

But I kind of got caught up in it all.

I lost sight of what I was doing and who I was doing it for and ended up in a cage of all kinds of ugly.

Kari had told me that I was better than a cleaner. That she had saved me from being on one of the pleb teams. She had said I was better than a server. I was too good to run around doing other people's washing and cleaning and errands. But in the end, that's all *she'd* used me for.

Once I'd moved out of the Light, it wasn't only my armour that had dimmed, but my Badges as well. Instead of finding and giving joy in what I was called to do, I was a husk. A black hole that absorbed and destroyed all the joy in and around me.

And once I'd lost the lustre, the others hadn't wanted me anymore. I had nothing to offer them. They threw me out. Even Achilles ditched me like a hot spud when my armour faded. They only wanted me for what the Light had given me. When that was gone, I was of no value to them.

But damn it.

No longer.

I opened myself up to the Light and offered all my mistakes and stuff-ups. He took them all. Every one. And gave me back my light. I was crying again. The mountain had moved, my drifting soul found its anchor... just like that, He blasted the dark away and I was clean again. My armour was back, I could see again. I could see my family, Suit Dude, the... women?

Seriously, why are the demons dressed up like... like... bikini models in biker outfits? That's just off. Who are they trying to impress?

Dan!

Oh. My. Word.

How dare they!

"Oh, sweetie, you got nothing. While you've been away, Dan and I have been having a play." One twik of ridiculous proportions sashayed to the front. She was busting out of her biker jacket and the leather was stretched so tight it shone like chrome.

Could it be more cliché?

I still had a long way to go to make it up to my family. To Dan. But I was moving in the right direction.

I stepped past Felix and Raph. I didn't look at anyone. I couldn't. I had the Light's forgiveness and that was enough. In time I'd see where I stood with everyone else.

As I moved forward, she... it... sidled up to Dan, flaunting her assets at me.

Pathetic.

As always, the Dark knew where to hit. I had nothing... but I had everything I needed. With or without Dan's friendship, I knew my family... well, Marcus, Kait and Val would take me back.

She burst out laughing. "You? You're calling me pathetic?"

So, I eyeballed the twik, and took my place at Dan's right. My hopefully-soon-to-be-restored-to-best-friend-status partner looked at me. His eyes full of pain, but the twitch at the corner of his mouth gave me hope. Standing beside him and Sariah, facing the enemy, my heart jolted into a rightness, and a lifeline secured my drifting soul and locked it back onto a purpose.

So, I leaned closer to the demon like I wanted to say something. She bent forward, coming down to my eye level, giving me the best view of what I'd never have. And I punched her as hard as I could in the face.

With my armour renewed and my heart consumed by fury, the smack was good, and the splatter was satisfying. I knew I shouldn't have, but I got in close and gripped the lapel of her stupid jacket. "Stay away from Dan you over-inflated, under-dressed, style-less... twik." Then punched her again... in the throat.

As hard as I could.

The first time, I took it by surprise.

The second time I was skating on thin ice.

And I knew it.

I was all kinds of weak from missing out on six months of training, but I was pretty skitched off. However, I wasn't a complete idiot. So, I jumped back out of reach and drew my sword.

"Sssso be it." And once again, the Dark Lord took off before the uglies hit the fan.

In a way it was good. I kind of sensed there was all kinds of aggression storming around the room. Not least of which was mine. And Val had always said, this was the best way to let off some steam.

I was surprised to see Felix here with his armour so solid. More so than mine. Well, than what mine had been when I came in. But now? Now I was on fire. And really, really angry and hungry for a fight.

Val, Marcus and Kait had moved out to the lawn, standing back-to-back, ready to take on the ten or so demons that followed them out. The Warriors stood guard around us, limiting the number that could get in. Or come at our backs, through the roof and walls... and floor.

As five demons moved in around us the battle began. And even though I was out of practice, and low on condition, and very unfit... it was like I had never left. My body knew exactly what to do, my mind shifted into autopilot, and the three of us presented a unified front to the enemy. Our swords parrying and blocking their initial assault. It was all kinds of amazing.

Until it wasn't. Soon it was super obvious they were just playing with us. And oh. My. Word. I was not going to be able to keep this up. I mean, seriously, not long after the initial adrenaline boost began to wane my arms grew tired and I was running out of breath.

It was so embarrassing.

Here I was, supposedly protecting the two behind me and I felt like asking for time out to take a nanna nap. I can absolutely guarantee there was no finesse in my defence. It soon deteriorated into a very unattractive clunky slash and stab, swing... and a few misses.

Please help me hold my game together.

Thankfully, Dan and Riah, way fitter than me, were doing a far better job of holding their own... as well as a bit of mine. Dan gained some ground and pushed our opposition back. The tide was turning, thanks totally to those two. A small swell of hope began to build and I was going to ride that sweet thing all the way to the finish line.

Or at least I'd hoped to. With every step of ground we gained, the more entangled we became in the bleeding chairs and blocked by the bleeding table. I tried to keep an eye on Dan to follow where he led. We couldn't afford to get divided. But we couldn't stay like this— because even I could see our attackers weren't really trying. They were just holding us in place. Why, I didn't know. But I was confident that I was going to run out of juice before they did.

Finally Dan had had enough. "Riah, stay and defend. Tess and I will draw the others away."

It was a risky move, leaving Sariah, but I trusted Dan to know what he was doing. I mean seriously, I was in no place to argue... or judge.

Please let him be making the right decision. Help us. Protect them.

Dan went out on a limb, faked a parry, then lunged. His sword hit its mark. The one I'd throat-punched fell. Dan leapt over its leather-clad ridiculously-proportioned body as it reverted to true form, a naked humanoid of pure muscle and sinew, its skin a swirling mass of charred black and burning red. I mean, seriously, ew.

Humanoids freaked me out—human-like, but not... human. But I had to follow Dan or the whole plan wouldn't work. I leapt as high as I could to clear the fallen body. But its eyes flew open and it shot a hand out, grabbing my ankle as I made my escape. And I face-planted.

It wouldn't let go. We lay there: it on its side at full stretch grip-ping my ankle in a vice, me on my stomach. It flickered back to a faint glimmer of its former disguise. And smiled. "Gotcha, princess."

That triggered a switch in my brain and I was all action. I kicked and flopped around like a fish out of water, but it wouldn't let go. A new dose of adrenaline took over. I knew it was wounded. It was bleeding out. But even in this state it was far stronger than me.

I couldn't use my sword at this angle. And brawn definitely wasn't going to work. Madly looking around for anything to help I spotted a vase of flowers on the ground under the table, and hurled it at the thing's head. It had no effect but to make it even more skitched. Next to where the vase had been was a jug of soft drink. I pitched the contents it in its face. The demon snarled and scrubbed the icy cold, sticky-sweet liquid from its eyes.

It was just enough to get it to release my foot. And that was all I needed. The pure creepiness of the thing was enough to propel me to my feet. While it was still spitting, cursing, and rubbing its eyes, I drove my sword into the sweet spot where the spine runs into the skull.

It stilled.

Then dissolved.

I exhaled.

"A bit of help here, Tessa? Please?"

While I'd been rolling around with this one, both Dan and Riah had been taking on two each. I followed Dan's call and, still on a high from my kill, stabbed the thing as hard as I could in the back. It's not that easy to kill a demon. There's a lot of hard stuff on the outside you've got to get through before you get to the soft vital bits in the middle. I knew I was out of condition and practice, so I threw everything I had behind my thrust. It did the job. I hung on tight as it fell to its knees, and used its downward movement to help me retrieve my sword.

Had it really been this hard in Sodom?

I don't remember it being this hard.

I'd only killed two here. There I killed... well, I had taken care of heaps. Too much had been going on to keep count.

I watched Dan's other opponent fall as he pushed its body off his dripping sword. I could never do that. He was way taller and stronger, but it did look kind of cool.

We turned to see Riah madly trying to keep her two at bay—they were merely toying with her, laughing at her desperate attempts to keep them away from those she was guarding. We were slapped into action when one snuck past her and moved to play with Felix and Raph.

Felix's sword was drawn, but by the looks of things, he hadn't much of a clue as to what to do with it. Raph hadn't bothered to draw his. It had been broken by the Light, and would have been useless in this situation anyway.

Riah's attack had turned wild. She had lost all control and her tactic was now just thrash and slash as her eyes were constantly drawn to her brother behind her.

Felix wove his sword back and forth in the space in front of Raph and himself like a complete newb. The demon laughed and snapped his hand out and snagged the end. The room froze.

Even Riah's skirmish halted.

Dan leapt the fallen chairs and slowly-dissolving carcasses. His sword made a massive dint in the neck of Riah's opponent.

But the world stopped spinning when Raph's hands wrapped around the arm of the last of our five attackers. As the demon screamed, the gates of hell opened, and the torment of souls ripped the fabric of my sanity. I dropped my sword and covered my ears. It didn't help. Raph's lips moved furiously, his eyes clenched shut.

The demon released Felix's sword in an attempt to dislodge Raph's grip. But the boy hung on, his face getting darker and dripping from the strain.

The demon raked Raph's arms with its free hand. But Raph did not let go.

Felix finally used his sword and buried it deep in the demon's chest, bringing a silence so complete I thought I'd gone deaf.

The others on the lawn had dispatched the last of the enemy.

Apart from the fallen chairs, and the dissolving bodies burning holes in the mats and turf, it seemed there was no damage.

How was that possible?

Felix slid down the wall behind him, wide eyes fixed on his sword still gripped firmly in two shaking hands. Riah clung to her brother, both of them on their knees, Raph's hands, torn to shreds, held up and out to the sides of his sister's body.

Val, Marcus and Kait rushed over, throwing fallen chairs out of the way. Dan came to stand by me, frantically clearing a space from our side of the mess.

Kait was beside herself. "Quick, Sariah, move out of the way. We need to help Raph."

Sariah wouldn't move. She clung to her twin, silently sobbing, her face buried in his shoulder.

Marcus was silent.

"Sariah, come to me now." Val kneeled beside the girl and peeled her reluctant arms away, releasing Raph. "Let him heal."

Sariah's armour had deepened to a new shade of crimson. She spun and clung to Val, but watched on as Kait took over.

"Raph, honey, you know what to do." Kait knelt in front of Raph, eye to eye as he leaned back into Marcus's arms. She couldn't help herself; Kait ran her hands over his face, through his hair, over his shoulders. Marcus, kneeling behind, gripped him around the middle, holding him up, wrapped in both arms.

"I did not let go." Raph's overly bright eyes looked at us all, his face flushed, voice high and excited. "I hung on and did not let go. I won. I did it." Then he looked at his hands and blanched. "Oh." He swallowed. "Oh." He turned green. "Oh." Marcus turned him to the side, and supported him as Raph vomited, collapsed, then groaned.

Far. Flaming. Out. The stench was putrid. With the fading sulphur, Raph's burned flesh, and the smell of vomit, I was about ready to join him. My stomach turned. I breathed through my mouth and tried not to embarrass myself any more than I already had this evening. I handed Kait a handful of paper napkins from the table.

"Raph, honey. How about you have a go at healing yourself again?" She wiped Raph's face. She crooned and fussed. Marcus rocked and hugged, careful not to touch his wounded arms.

Raph continued to hold his hands out like a surgeon after scrubbing and prepping for surgery. He shut his eyes, mumbled something, then passed out. The skin on his arms miraculously knit, reformed and healed.

"Did I just see what I think I just saw?"

We all turned to look at Felix who had been flying completely under the radar in the corner.

38

DANIEL: MOP UP

"I'll put the kettle on." Tessa dashed inside. I don't think she realised she was still holding her sword. She skipped and jumped over fallen furniture and darted to the kitchen. It was the most life I'd seen in her for months. Hell, this past evening was the most I'd *seen* of her in months.

I didn't know how I felt. I was hurt. I was angry. I was relieved. I was on a high. It was the best feeling in the world having her by my side in the fight again. And to watch her take on that demon, her tiny yellow body sparking with green flames. Getting in close, then smacking it in the head with a truckload of venom. Pure Tessa. Golden.

But then, every time I looked at her, I felt betrayal. Hard. Cold. And distant.

I know that's what the Dark wanted. So, I had to get around that. But I didn't know how. Or if I could. Or, deep down, if I wanted to.

"Don't just stand there, help pick up the mess. We're moving inside." He sounded gruff, but Marcus's arm around my shoulder pulling me close told the truth. He knew. He understood.

I sheathed my sword and followed orders.

Raph had been placed on a couch in the sitting room with a blanket, conscious, but spent. Riah sat pretty much on top of him cradling both his injured hands in hers, staring at him. Poor kid. When you don't speak and you are used to using body language to communicate, you are even more voiceless when no one looks at you.

Felix had been placed in one of the recliners, also with a blanket, for the shock. Soon, Tessa would give him a hot cup of something sweet.

The rest of us righted furniture and brought in food and gifts from outside. With the doors shut, and everybody settled with hot drinks, we were ready to help Felix come to terms with his introduction to the uncensored version of living in the Light.

Val leaned forward in her chair, ready to lead proceedings. "That, Felix, is what we've been trying to explain since we got here." She smiled with eyes still radiating her post-battle-buzz. "That is a small part of our reality. And that is why we work so hard at keeping our armour strong."

"But we don't have... demons... in Laodicea."

I couldn't hold in my laugh. "Yeah, you keep telling yourself that." Felix was still in the denial phase. I had been lucky when I was hit with the reality—I had Raph's gift to help deal with the shock. But for now, Raph was busy dealing with his own shock. "But that's obviously a load of skr— ubbish." I flicked my eyes to Val.

Sorry. I'm just sick of this place. And its stupid ignorance. I'm frustrated that we haven't found the girl we're looking for. And for feeling so bloody useless... and for... well, you know... everything.

I continued sharing the reality of life in the Light. "They're here. They're everywhere. You can smell them, even if you can't see them."

"Is that what I can... could smell?" Felix sniffed the air.

He was right, the smell had gone with the last demons dissolving. Although there was still a hint of melted mat in the air. Thankfully, the coffee was stronger.

"The carpets." He looked to each of us, eyes wide. "That was real. Wasn't it?"

Marcus smiled at his friend. "You can bet your bippy that was real. Welcome to the Light, me friend."

"All those things you have been showing me, teaching me... it's all real isn't it? I mean, I know it's real. I know the Light is real... but..." He looked at us all, then his eyes landed on the twins. Raph's hands, still red and inflamed, held by Riah. "Everything."

Wonder and awe removed the final traces of droll from his voice. Felix put his cup down, removed his blanket and went to kneel on the cold tiles by the twins. "You both saved my life." His whisper carried around to us all. "You are mere children. But you saved me. Thank you." He shook his head, then swivelled and looked at me. "And you." I know it wasn't meant to be an accusation. I think. "You, and..." He found Tessa. "Wait a minute... your armour is back. How is that possible?" Felix sunk his butt to the tiles and leaned against the arm of the couch, drew his knees up and shook his head before burying it in his hands.

"It is okay, Uncle Felix; it will all be okay." Raph freed one of his hands and laid it gingerly on the man's head.

Kait stood. "Right. Well. A few of us have gone to a lot of trouble to make a very special birthday party for a couple of pretty special kids. And I for one am not prepared to let that cake go to waste." She then started directing traffic. "Marcus, could you bring the cake over? Dan, the plates and serviettes? Tessa, I think Raph is ready for his hot chocolate now, thank you. Val, I believe you had something to do before you were interrupted earlier on this evening?" With her hands on her hips, Kait surveyed the room to make sure everyone was moving.

"Riah, help get Felix resettled in his chair." Satisfied we all had tasks to do, finally she exhaled, and I saw the landslide fall off her shoulders.

I put my load down, wrapped my arms around her and whispered in her ear. "All your chicks are okay, Mama Bear. We survived, and we're all going to be okay." I winced as she gripped me tighter than I thought possible. Once again, I was reminded not to underestimate the strength of this woman, physical or emotional.

The sugar from the cake and the caffeine from the hot chocolate and coffee did the trick. Apart from the adrenaline crash—which would take a while to get over—we had all perked up, or chilled out, or whatever. We were in the green zone. In a lull of benign conversation, until Val pulled a battered box from beside her chair into everyone's focus at her feet.

"Felix, you've heard us speak of Abbot?" After he nodded, she continued, "The Light gave him warning before he died. He knew he wasn't going to make it out of Sodom, so he made preparations."

At the mention of his name, a reverent silence filled the room. Even though I hadn't known him long, the time I had spent with him had a huge impact on me. He had inked his mark on my soul. Again, I was a cocktail of warmth, humour, pain and loss at his memory.

"He left something for each of us and asked that the twins be given his gift on their next birthday."

Raph was now sitting, Riah holding both their cups, their faces once again damp. I was surprised they had any tears left after the tsunami of emotion this afternoon turned out to be. Riah sat tall and stoic. Raph bent over, his hands still gently laid, palms up, on his lap.

Val reached into the box and drew out a stack of letters and a parcel wrapped in cloth. "Raph, Abbot asked that you be given this."

Felix offered to take the twins' cups as Riah went to claim the gift on her brother's behalf. We all waited for them to finish their wild, unspoken conversation as she laid it on Raph's lap.

Tentatively, edge by edge, Raph gently peeled away the fabric to reveal an ancient book. He looked up to Val with his mouth as wide as a cave.

We all knew straight away what it was.

But for Felix's sake, I guess, Val explained. "It's his original copy of The Way. He received this from his mother when he left home as a young man. As you know, he spent time in there every day of his life; reading it, writing in it, studying it, and battling with it—and over it—constantly. It is fragile and falling apart, but it is alive with his connection in the Light."

Raph picked it up in his red, swollen hands and held it close to his heart. Riah threw her arm around his shoulders and held him tight.

Then Val continued. "Riah, as you know, Abbot grew up in a

family who knew and loved the Light. As a young boy he was given a symbol of the Light that he wore around his neck every day of his life. Sometimes he needed to hide it, but he never took it off until the day we left Sodom. In his note, he asked that you accept this and wear it in remembrance, not only of the Light, but of Abbot, and his love for you."

Val reached into the box and pulled out a small bundle. She unfolded its cloth wrapping and showed us all a silver symbol of the Light, hung on an old, worn chain. It was a bit smaller than my little finger and ornately carved with vines and flowers. The symbolism was not lost on any of us, least of all Riah, who stood to retrieve it with shaking hands. But before she could grasp it, Val stood and placed the long chain over the girl's bent head. The emblem came to rest just under her ribs. Sariah returned to the couch and settled close to her brother; violet and red light danced over each of them independently, but both were tinged with pink.

"Now. We were going to hold off giving out the other gifts, but considering the circumstances, I think we might go ahead." Val smiled as she looked to Tessa sitting next to Marcus, and at me, sitting on a stool by the kitchen bench.

I began to worry.

"But first, Marcus and Kait." She pulled out a folded letter and read, "*Dear hearts...*" Val stopped, took a deep breath. Flicked some invisible fluff off her jeans, then continued.

"I know that wherever the Light has led you, you are safe in Him. And that is all I need to know. So, as I write, I am content, that even though I cannot be with you all right now, He is, and that is all I ask.

Now, I beg of you to have a little patience for an old man's whimsy, but as I sit here and look out on our beautiful garden in our wonderful home, I think what I may leave you. Considering, of course, that I have nothing to give.

And so it is, I ask that I may leave you a legacy. As such, with all gifts, one has the choice to take it up or leave it lie. And this is such a case.

In my family there was a tradition. Every first-born male would take the middle name of Joseph, and every first-born girl would be gifted the middle name Naomi. You are all children of my heart. But I was hoping I may impose my claim on you even more and ask that you accept these names in partnership with the ones you already carry, as a sign that indeed you are dear to me as my own, and the first two I had the blessed privilege of journeying with out of the darkness of Zoar into the Light.

Of course, I shall be none the wiser if you choose to accept this gift or not. But it gladdens my heart now, even as I listen to the bustle of you all coming in from one of your outings, to think of you as more than children of my heart, but children in name as well.

Know that I love you both dearly, eternally and with the fierce love of a father,

Abbot"

Pregnant, heavy, painful silence smothered us all. Kait was wrapped in Marcus's arms and together they wept openly. I guess it had something to do with not being able to have kids. Something Abbot had understood—and, come to think of it, probably Val as well. Even Felix sitting quietly out of the limelight, subtly wiped his face with a flick of his hand.

Val reached over and gave the letter to Marcus, who still held a liquified Kait in his other arm. Breathing deeply, Val took a big swig of her coffee, shook herself and dived back into the box. A smile chased her tears away as she pulled out two more small parcels. But it was the gleam in her eyes that had me worried the most. That, and knowing deep down, Abbot had been a cunning fox... in the nicest possible way of course. But he was always up to something.

"Tessa," Val began.

Blotchy faced, Tessa sat up and paid attention. Her lips trembled.

Before I thought about it, I had started to rise to go to her. But when my brain caught up with me, I shuffled and sat back down, pretending that I was just readjusting my seat.

"Abbot has left you a gift as well." She picked up a tiny bundle and held it out for Tessa to come and take.

Standing in the middle of the circle, Tessa let the cloth wrapping drop to the floor and looked to Val with a puzzled face. She held out a golden ring. "I never saw him wear this."

"It was his father's wedding ring," Val explained. "His mother gave it to him the day she died. The day we left Hormah."

Tessa slipped the ring on each of her fingers in turn. "It's beautiful"—she twisted the plain gold band around each finger then held it in the palm of her hand—"but it's too big."

I looked around the room and noticed the way the grown-ups looked at each other. Something was up. Kait sat tall and looked at Val, eyes alight with their own secret language. "Try it on your thumb."

Tessa did as she was told and gave a satisfactory huff as it fit. She then gave her hand a test flick and it stayed in place. "Cool." Staring at it, she returned to sit by Kait's side and showed it off.

"Dan." Val couldn't keep the sly smile from sliding across her face as she held out another tiny gift.

Intrigued, I claimed it, unwrapped it. Then got the joke. "Nice one, Val. You mixed the gifts up."

"Why, what did you get?" Tessa was on her feet and looking at the tiny ring set I held on my palm. She gasped. "They're beautiful." She went to touch it but snapped her hand back and made a fist at her chest. "What's their story, Val?"

"These belonged to Abbot's mum. One of the last things she did before she died was to remove them and give them to him with her husband's ring."

"Oh, that's so beautiful," Tessa gushed.

I had to be honest. "And kind of daft."

"Dan." Tessa burred up. It was just like old days.

"What?"

"She gave the symbols of her and her husband's love and lifelong commitment to each other to her only son before she died. That"—predator bird had returned—"is beautiful." She actually growled.

It was all I could do to fight the smile forcing its way across my face. But I did. "And he gave the bloke's ring to you and the chick's ring to me." *Check.*

"Oh, you're right."

What?

No fight?

What was wrong with her?

Tessa had moved on and forgotten me. "Val, are you sure you got this right?"

"Perfectly. There are letters here explaining everything." She handed a letter each to Raph and Sariah. Then passed one to me. "Could you give this to Kait and Marcus?"

Val had several other letters in her hand. I saw one had my name on it so put my hand out to receive it.

"Not yet. You have to wait."

"Till when?"

"Till the time is right."

"When will that be?"

She winked. "I'll let you know."

"What am I gonna do with these?" I held up the tiny chick rings. They were beautiful. Dark blue stones sort of sat in a cluster-kind-of-ring arrangement, around a diamond. The other was a plain, thin gold band. I tried to fit the band on my pinky, but it didn't fit.

"I suggest you keep them safe. I think they're worth a bit. Abbot's parents were loaded."

Skrat. What if I lose them?

"Here, take this." Val reached into her box of tricks and pulled out a long silver chain, much like the one Sariah now wore. "He kept the three of them on this."

"Do I have to give mine up? I'd rather not." Tessa clutched her hand to her chest. She looked at me as I threaded the rings. "If that's okay, I mean."

"It's yours to do with as you will, Tessa. It's all explained in your letter." Val held up an envelope then placed it in the box with mine.

"Val?"

"You will also receive your letter at the appropriate time."

For the first time ever, I was happy to see the predatory bird take over Tessa's face. Mainly because it wasn't targeting me. But it had no effect on Val.

"And finally, Felix."

I think the man's Badge was invisibility. Once again, he'd merged into the background. Watching. But his cool facade had once again cracked. "Me!" Thankfully his cup was empty, otherwise he and I would have worn it as he sat up with a start. "Are you trying to say there is something in there... for me?"

"Yes, actually, I am. There is another parcel that has been sitting here with no name. And I believe it's for you." Val pulled out another package. I stretched to take it and pass it to Felix.

"But what about you, Val? Isn't this your gift?" He still held the parcel at arm's length, trying to give it back.

"No. Mine is still in here." She smiled, holding up a faded photograph. End of story.

We all turned and watched as, finally, our new brother relaxed back into his chair and unwrapped his gift.

It was another copy of The Way. Plain cover, medium size, it didn't look particularly special. But sitting inside the front cover was a letter. Felix carefully unfolded it and read it to himself. His face shifted from shock, to smiling, then dissolved to watery, then was set in grim determination. He meticulously refolded the paper, placed it back in the envelope, and closed the book. He placed both hands on the cover, leaned back in his chair and clenched his jaw as his armour exploded into a raging orange inferno.

Yeah, I reckon she'd got it right. Abbot meant the gift for Felix.

39

IZABAAL: FULL HOUSE

I t had been a long night... and day. But finally the baby had arrived, and both Genni and bub were resting. It was a tricky birth, three weeks ahead of schedule. But thankfully Lottie and the others had all been on hand to help.

I couldn't believe it. Our first girl. She was going to be spoiled rotten.

Ten-year-old Joko was a bit upset. He had wanted another boy to join his warrior clan. Thankfully Kazi wasn't around to hear his complaint. But when I pointed out his mum was the fiercest warrior of all, he forgave Genni and started planning.

But now, in the dim light of evening, I farewelled Indy and Mina as they set off. Indy to share the news with Ben and Tomi. Mina to let the girls at the Temple know that Genni and her baby were fine. Still under the radar, of course.

I could not describe the joy I felt at being in a position to help and support my sisters as they were discarded from the Temple as Greyscales. No more were we left to die in the streets. There was somewhere to go. There was someone who cared. But, as of today, we were fifteen. Since Amber and Genni arrived six months ago, all our rooms were taken by my sisters and their children.

In the fading light and post-birth high, I was wandering around our home trying to see how we could accommodate more women. Crazy, I know. We lived in a factory—a contaminated factory that had not produced any ill effects for seven years, mind you—you'd think there'd be room. But "rooms" we didn't have. Nor privacy.

As much as I hated it, it had been inevitable. With our numbers growing it was impossible to keep our family a secret. Especially since Lily chose to keep up her "skills" in order to provide her contribution.

Obviously, we told her she didn't need to do that and rathered she didn't. We would be alright without her earnings. I didn't want anyone to be part of that life anymore. We would make do with what Indy could supply and with the generosity of Kerm and Helen.

But she insisted. However, Lily understood she was strictly forbidden to bring any worshippers on site. But I was so scared for her. I believed she had found someone who "arranged" meetings for her. I hated it. Hated it. It literally made me sick that she was putting herself back under the management of someone who exploited her.

While I waited for Indy to return, I was exploring the old office space in Warehouse One, considering how we might utilise it, when a commotion started.

As soon as I heard Amber's cry, I was running. She was struggling with a worshipper. Hitching my skirts higher, I ran for all I was worth.

"I said, I got good money, whore, and I want to worship the goddess."

Amber was trying to fend the man off, but he was overpowering her. "Leave me alone. I do not serve the goddess. You must leave."

Under the streetlights near the entry, the man had seen that Amber's scales, limited to her wrist and ankle, weren't actually grey like everyone else's. She'd been liberated from the Temple when the fade started, but her scales hadn't progressed fully to grey. She hadn't been pregnant. None of us had ever seen anything like it. It had been enough to rouse the punter to think he was on a winner.

"Stop." I threw myself at the intruder. "Amber, run. You know what to do." It was a drill we practised regularly. It gave me peace to know everyone would be okay. At the signal, sisters and children entered their cabins, locked the doors, and made sure all lights were extinguished. Then, sitting silently in their rooms, all would wait for the next signal to be given that it was safe to come out. We made sure to practise this regularly, because sitting still and quiet, we learned very quickly, was almost impossible for little boys. But they were angels, all of them, and knew what to do and how important it was.

Climbing to my feet I gave myself a quick once-over to see what I'd hurt—just an elbow and two knees—nothing serious. I brushed myself off, wrapped my Chief Priestess cloak around me and demanded the man leave.

"Well, well, well." He was drunk and reeked of fumes. But not drunk enough to stay down.

Bother.

He staggered to his feet. "What have we got here?" His eyes combed my scales.

Sadly, the "Chief Priestess cloak" I used was metaphorical. I would really have appreciated some significant covering right now. And a very big brick wall between him and me.

Chin up, I looked down my nose at this filth and tried not to dry retch at the memory of having to serve similar leeches. "You are not welcome here. If you wish to make a contribution to the goddess, you will need to go to the Temple. We no longer serve Ashera. You must leave."

"Don't need to be so coy, lovely. And you don't need to play tricks. I got good money and I want to make an offering to the goddess. I thought the other one was a pretty find, but you, now." He licked his lips.

My stomach lurched. Thankfully it was empty. But I needed to keep my barrier up. It was very important not to show fear or weakness. That was an aphrodisiac to some. "Step away from me. I told you, I no longer work for the Temple."

He leered and ran his hands up and down his lean stomach. This one was not soft. Nor did he appear to be one who enjoyed fear. Rather, the opposite seemed to be true: he enjoyed a bit of "spirit", or so they called it.

I flicked my eyes over him. Bedraggled, mildly inebriated, but strong.

I was in trouble. Both Indy and Mina were out and not scheduled to be home for a while yet. All the ladies were in their rooms keeping the children quiet. "You must leave now." The cloak slipped and my voice wavered. It was his green light.

"I said I got money I wanna spend, so shut up, twik, and come with me, now."

Why did he have to come on site?

I tried to remember the moves and the strategies.

But I was flustered.

I had to think.

Fight him. I had to fight him. Try to throw him off balance.

Be heavy.

Stop him.

Hurt him.

The slap across my face actually helped. It brought clarity and stirred my anger. Indy said: eyes and groin—disable then run. Extending my fingers, I jabbed him in the eye, but he had already got a swing away. As I connected to the softness of his eyeball, his fist connected to my cheek. Why couldn't my scales be a bit more substantial? Since so many men were right-handed, I could do with the extra protection.

The man's gurgled yell gave me the satisfaction that I had wounded him.

But a light flashed in my head as his hand connected. I stumbled. The pain brought a fresh wave of nausea. I turned to run, but not fast enough. With his hand over his eye, the man thrust his foot out and tripped me in my attempt to flee.

Instinctively, I rolled into a ball, expecting his boot.

He didn't disappoint.

After the second or third kick to the back, my stomach rebelled and purged itself.

"Move away. Now." A quiet voice overrode the screaming static in my head.

"Well, hello darling. Aren't you an ugly one? But you gonna have to wait your turn, I do believe I have earned the right to go first. Although I can't see a gimp like you being able to do the deed." His laughter stopped when Indy spoke.

"Move. Away. Now." His voice held authority and the distinct threat of violence.

"I think you got tabs on yourself, boy. Skitch off and go play with your own kind."

I could feel his attention come back to me, obviously dismissing Indy as inconsequential. It was the second major mistake he'd made. I listened as wheels coasted across the distance, then waited. It would be over soon.

A muffled cry. A thump. Followed by a primal scream. I rolled over and saw the man on his knees, with fingers, hand, arm and shoulder all being held in an agonisingly unnatural position. Using minimal effort, Indy ignored the man's screams and looked to me. "Are you alrig—" He saw my face and what I suspected was blood that I could feel trickling down my cheek. He could probably also smell the vomit. I could. It was almost enough to make me gag again.

Indy flicked his wrist, and, over the strangled cries of the man, I heard several cracks as all the strained joints were pushed past their limits. He released my attacker and leant down to help me up, then sat me in his lap as he wheeled me home.

As I clung to him, I felt the heat of his anger and the racing of his fear.

"He attacked Amber. I had to stop him, Indy."

He didn't say a word; we would speak later. For now, he would take me home where we would be safe, and I would heal. My surroundings dissolved into the inferno blazing in my lower back and head. The slight jar of the wheels hitting the ramp to our cabin sent electricity coursing through my body. I couldn't hold in my gasp. Nor could I remember it being this bad before.

I just needed to go home where we were safe. To go to bed and fall into one of Lottie's famous oblivions. Anything to escape this all-encompassing fire.

Once we were inside, Indy shut the door. Now I knew we were safe. No one had ever crossed through the barrier of our door unless invited. From the moment I stepped into the room seven years ago, I knew it was special, I knew it would keep us safe.

Indy helped me into bed, but before he could leave to get Lottie, he was stopped on our porch.

"What is this?" Mina was home.

"Intruder got Iza. Going to get Lottie and then finish the kret off, yeh?"

Silence sang like a siren. It joined the throbbing of my body's pain. I could not see Mina or Indy. I could not confirm what was passing between them, but I had a good idea. Indy's voice trailed as he scooted down the ramp. "Please, check on Amber. Get Lottie. Make sure that everyone's safe, eh?"

Mina stood in our doorway, her back to me, but her voice was loud and clear. "He is gone. I took care of him. How could you let this happen?"

"Yeah, nah. Not this time, Mina. I am not to blame for this."

The constant battle between the two of them would be the end of me. I didn't have the energy to sustain the ache in my heart as well as in my body. I called out to them in a whisper. "Please. Not now. Amber. Lottie. The signal." Then everything else was too much. I curled into a ball as a fire spread across my back and through my body. I didn't hear them speak. I didn't hear Mina leave. I only heard the pain as it spread and consumed me.

Soon, familiar hands examined my body. When she had finished, Lottie made up one of her potions and I did my best to keep it down. Then she left Indy to cleanse my wounds with salt water. Lottie's potions were a wonder. I had no idea what was in them, and I didn't care. I trusted her with my life and took whatever she gave me. Thick, sluggish darkness crept into my mind. I was leaving the pain behind and racing into the void her elixir offered. But before I left altogether, I was aware of Indy shuffling in behind me and shutting the world out.

I gripped his arms and pulled them tightly about me. I knew he would leave to check on everything once I was out. But I wanted to make sure he stayed as long as possible. He had to stay. I could live with many things, but I couldn't live without him.

It was to a symphony of kisses on my shoulder and in my hair that I finally let the blessed darkness take me.

40

INDIGO: A DEAL'S A DEAL

O kay, Light, I'll do you a deal, yeh? You get her out of this and make her better and I'll come have a serious chat to you like Dad asked, eh? But I tell you what, chat or no chat, I am killing the next kret that comes onto this site. I'll fracking kill 'em all.

I'm sick of this warped city. I'm sick of the warped people who live here. And I hate this kret of a chair.

Yeah, alright. I am happy to be doing something to help those poor kids who've been screwed up, spat out, and left to die as sport and playthings of this twisted town. But after seven years it's still the same. No change at all. Iza still can't go out in public. The girls are still hunted. We're all still targeted.

I just feel utterly fracked. Plain and simple.

At least the gangs here are pretty skitch-weak. They wouldn't've lasted a night in Gomorrah. That's one good thing. Idiots still haven't figured out how to fight a gimp in a chair. So, yeah. Thanks for that too.

I suppose while I'm at it, I should thank you for Iza as well. And for escaping the hell of Gomorrah. And the other things, like Kerm... and Ben... and Kazi.

Yeah, alright, so you've been around a bit and that's cool, yeh? So, like I *said, if you can help Iza out, you and I will sit down and have a proper chat.*

Can you let Dad know I'm thinking of him and miss the hell out of him? And any of the others out there... or however it works. If you managed to get hold of Dan, say g'day to him too. I still miss them both as much as I miss my legs.

But these kids you brought along are sweet as. They and Iza are going a long way to filling all kinds of gaps.

But I tell you what, you can keep your bleeding Community. If I have to hang out with the likes of those stuck-up krets, all talks are off.

How is that supposed to work, huh? Dad says, find the Light. So, we swallow our pride, seek out the Light, and what do we find?

Rejection, judgement and a very clear, "We are here to help. But not the likes of you." An ex-servant of the Temple—a Chief Priestess, to say the least—and me, a crippled, cut-up, black kid from the bowels of hell itself, Gomorrah. I don't know who they hated more—Iza for escaping or me for breathing.

I don't know what they do or who they do it for. But we weren't welcome. As far as I'm concerned, frack them. Frack the lot of them.

So, like I said, if we have to do life with the likes of them, all bets are off, yeh?

Except the one where you fix Iza... please.

I GREW up in the heart of the city—my city, Gomorrah—and that's where I felt safest. But even after seven years, this still wasn't my town. The soul of a city is revealed in its dark side. Laodicea was rich and pretty on the top, but she was a heartless twik at the core. But we'd carved out a home for ourselves and the Greyscales. Those who were caught between the bright face and the dark heart of the Temple: the untouchables. Well, untouchable for "proper" society. But bleeding touchable for the scum who wanted servicing at a discount rate.

My heart broke for these girls. And that's exactly what they were:

girls. Lily was seventeen when she arrived, losing the baby shortly afterward. But the worst of the lot was Amber, who managed to get out at the age of thirteen. These kids were bought as youngsters and babies, then taught the trade of pleasuring others.

As they grew, they were pumped full of hormones to make sure they developed in all the right ways, then fed on drugs to immunise them against pregnancy. Which I found baffling when Asherah was a Mother Goddess of fertility. Go figure, yeh?

And for some equally weird reason she was represented as a mash-up combo of a tri-coloured snake and a curvaceous chick. And what was even crazier, over time, through surgery, medication and training, her acolytes were transformed to take on her appearance. It's said that in her left hand a priestess holds the hand of the goddess, and in her right, the hand of humanity. Through the girls' sacrifice, the goddess communes with humanity—men—for plea-sure... for a price.

But it was a trap. Their scales were highly sensitive to some hormone. Iza told me, I forget what they call it. But when one of them slipped up, or their meds did, and they got pregnant, this hormone faded the colours from blue, purple and gold, to grey. To start with, the lustre of the full colour died down, but over time it eventually leaked away altogether, leaving the scales grey.

Apparently, it was a crime for the conduit of the goddess to incu-bate something as offensive as human flesh. As acolytes they were pampered and adored by a salivating society. When they were rejected, they were hated and scorned. None of it was their choice.

Some of the girls tried to terminate, with varying levels of success. I didn't blame them. Knowing what lay ahead, it would be a tough call to bring a kid into a world that promised nothing but hardship and hatred. Listening to Vashti and Shauna's stories was enough to break the hardest of hearts.

Others did all they could to keep their babies. I kind of admired them. They got the concept of hope. Hope for something better. Hope of change.

Stupid, kretting hope that kept you going when you knew that, in reality, hope was a gutless fairy tale for stupid fools like me, who just couldn't give up. Hope was a curse.

I had lost everything except the freedom to give up. I had to keep going. Iza would be lost without me. And to be honest, I'd be lost without her. So, that twik of a muse, Hope, kept leading me up the garden path by the nose.

And like a fool, I kept following.

Even after that instant, seven years ago on the bridge when, acting from instinct not thought, I lost everything. Saving Iza had cost me my legs but given me purpose. We were as useless as each other; she needed my smarts to survive in the jungle, I needed her for... everything.

She had helped me navigate my new life in this chair. She restored my pride by needing me. She instilled value by respecting me.

I saved her life but, in reality, she made mine worthy of living. She wouldn't let me tell her I loved her, so I showed her in everything I did. But the cool thing about Iza was that she got it.

Izabaal was different to all the others. She left by choice. She didn't intend to survive her defection, but she left none the less. She still had her colours which was why she kept getting hassled. But I was ridiculously proud of her for walking away, yeh?

Helping the Greyscales and their kids was our way of sticking it to the system. Giving the finger to the Temples and the krets who ran them. They dined on human souls and spat out the waste to die on the streets.

Well, not if we could help it.

But the scum who came after the Greyscales, even after they'd been kicked to the kerb, they were another matter.

"Come now laddie, let me look at her." Now that Iza had passed out, Lottie could give her a proper inspection.

I eased my arms out from around her. I froze when she groaned, but after I'd counted to five she'd stilled. Lottie gave me room to get into my chair and stepped back as I rolled out.

Amina was waiting out on the tarmac.

But I jumped in before she had a chance. "That's it. No more. Lily makes a choice, yeh? Work the street or live here. She can't have it both ways anymore."

"You do not tell her—them—what to do." Amina's nostrils flared as she spat her words.

"How dare you accuse me of not protecting Iza, but then stand in the way when I am doing what needs to be done?" I'd had a gut full of Amina and her skrat.

"Lily's actions are not the cause of your incompetence, boy."

"Damn it, Amina, you know bleeding well they are." My body shook and my volume increased. I couldn't stop it, even if I'd wanted to. "She's like a twik on heat. And that plinter she works for, lining up every mongrel, kret, slime ball from every corner of this neighbourhood—"

"Enough lad, that's not fair." Lottie stood on the porch and slowly shut the door behind her.

I had to force the cool night air into the deep corners of my lungs to stop myself from screaming at the both of them. I waited, counted to ten. Then did it again. In the end I had to admit, in a way, she was right. And I was ashamed enough to admit it. I knew she was "doing her bit" the only way she knew how. She also needed a purpose. Didn't mean I had to like it. Or agree with it. So, I changed the topic. "How is she?"

The old woman hobbled down the ramp and came and stood with Amina and me. We may have hated each other, but the love Amina and I had for Iza was a bond we couldn't deny.

Lottie pulled one of the disgusting cigarette butts out of her pocket and sucked a deep breath. "Not good. I'll be honest with you both, she's in a bad way. We may need to take her to a hospital. Or at least call her mother."

"Hell, Lottie. Iza will kill us." I flicked my eyes between the two women standing over me.

For the first time since I'd met her, I saw fear in Amina's eyes.

Lottie spat the butt to the ground and hacked up a lung. "Aye, that she might. But at least she'd be alive enough to do so."

I remembered my deal with the Light. Was this part of his answer? I knew I mirrored Mina's fear 'cause it ate me from the inside out. "How long do we have before we have to make a decision?"

Lottie didn't answer straight away but swallowed deeply and ran the back of her arm over her eyes. "Not long laddie. Not long. But the medication I've given her will make it hard for the medicos to check her over properly." She looked away. "But if we don't move her tonight, we'll have to transport her in the daylight. Not ideal."

"Kerm and Helen will drive her, or Ben... if she needs to go." Again, I looked to both of the women standing like sentinels either side of me. "Can we wait and see how she is in the morning? Wait till the meds wear off so she can have some say in this?"

"She will not go." Amina spoke the truth. "Even if it will kill her, she will not go. We need to make this decision for her."

Lottie just nodded.

Okay, Light, if you're there, you make it very clear what we're to do?

I waited.

The two women stared at me.

I wanted some kind of signal. Some sign to tell me what to do.

But I got no inspiration. No feeling. No message. Nothing.

I wanted someone... something... anyone to tell me what to do. To take this weight from me. But I'd already learned the hard way, that's what life was all about. There was no one else. The buck stopped with me. But I needed time to think. "We wait till morning. Check everyone stays in lockdown for tonight. That fool may have friends who could come round wanting a frack or a fight." I eyeballed Mina. "You make sure the girls stay in tonight." She rolled her lips between her teeth as her nostrils flared. "I mean it Mina, so help me. If anyone goes out tonight, I will not be held responsible for what happens to them or what they bring back, yeh?"

Not waiting to hear their arguments I pushed past and made my way back into our home. After shutting and locking the door—firmly, but not so firmly as to wake Iza—I climbed in beside my soulmate and hung on for all I was worth. In the darkness, alone, I let the pressure of my fear escape through tears. I just could not lose her.

You promise me, damn it. You fix her and make this right, yeh? And I promise you, I'll kill the next kret that walks onto this property.

We had a deal.

41

FELIX: ON THE ROAD AGAIN

I opened the door to my office and settled in behind my desk. The clock by the door blinked. Three am. I hadn't slept. Not because I hadn't taken my medication. Actually, I hadn't taken my tablets—because I hadn't wanted to sleep. There was too much to process.

The battle.

The demons.

Those children.

That letter.

Emotions, thoughts, fears and thrills rampaged through my mind and the cocktail was invigorating. I wasn't ready to let go because I had never felt so alive. I was scared that if I slept, I would lose it. I would wake up and discover it was all a dream. At first, I'd assumed the stirrings was the waking of the Crow.

But I'd been wrong. My thorn was still and silent.

I looked to my guard and was fortified and comforted by his presence. He had been there. He had seen it. "It was real, wasn't it?"

He nodded, grinned and... did he just wink at me?

It was real. I had faced a demon.

And not only that. I had stuck the blighter with my very own sword.

We, Raphael and I, had survived an attack.

A horde.

The Dark Lord.

My sword.

Raphael's hands.

The letter.

How could a letter from a man I had never met, who had died six months ago, have been so personal. So... frightening. Exciting. Electrifying.

No, I hadn't slept because I hadn't wanted to let it go. The electricity, the memories... Those things had actually happened, they were locked into the vault of time. No one could ever take that away from me. The vividness of life that surrounded me was like a drug. I was on a high and didn't want to come down. I didn't want to slide back into the mutiny of the mundane. I had stepped fully through a portal and wanted the door shut and sealed behind me, barring mediocrity from infecting my life again. Reality was more radiant, more fanciful, and far scarier than fiction. My eyes were now open... burned open. Never to be shut again.

It was not the Crow that haunted me now. It was the Light's blinding revelation.

I found it hard to believe that I had lived my life on the threshold, hovering in the void between two realms. Neither in nor out, hot nor cold. Lukewarm.

Existing, not living.

I pulled the letter from my pocket again. The feel of worn, creased parchment spurred my confidence; it was not my imagination.

You are His appointed. I had been confident it wasn't for me. But as I read on, what my mind denied, my stirring spirit embraced.

I will give you every place you set your foot. Did that mean the treaty would work? Would my plan for the Seven Cities succeed?

No one will be able to stand against you all the days of your life. I will never leave you nor forsake you. Did that mean in my role as administrator? Or in my battle against the Dark?

Be strong and courageous, because you will lead these people to inherit the blessings I swore to their ancestors to give them. I did not understand this. But the command to be strong and courageous scared me. I knew in my heart the struggles I fought daily. The fear that one day I would be discovered as the fraud I truly was. It would be revealed to all that I was, in truth, incapable. Inadequate. An imposter.

Be strong and very courageous. There it was again. Mocking me.

Be careful to obey all the law. Do not turn from it to the right or to the left, that you may be successful wherever you go. Was this the key? It had to be. I would speak to Marcus about it.

Keep this Book of the Law always on your lips; meditate on it day and night, so that you may be careful to do everything written in it. Then you will be prosperous and successful. Had we not been doing this? Had I not already felt the benefits? It had to be the answer.

Have I not commanded you? Be strong and courageous. Do not be afraid; do not be discouraged, for I, the Light, will be with you wherever you go. The continued, relentless command to be strong and coura-geous both shamed me and confirmed the truth. This letter had to be for me. It highlighted my biggest failing.

The phone interrupted my musing.

"It's done. I tried ringing you last night, but obviously you were off-duty."

"Good morning, Overseer. You're not usually up this early." I flicked my eyes to the clock again; 4 am. I'd not ever known the man to rise before seven.

"Up? Damn it man, I've not been to bed. I've been up putting out fires all night."

"Fires?"

"Your free-loading Sodomite associates have blown their last chance. We're in agreement, they have to go."

"Who exactly are 'we'?"

"The whole council. Kari made a complaint last night. The High Council met, and a decision was made."

"Why wasn't I informed of this?" I'd had my phone on me all night, and even though I was... socialising, I'd kept an eye on it.

"Raymond rang your home, and you weren't there. Marlene told us you had no meetings scheduled. How were we to know where you were?"

"There was no message on my landline, and I had my mobile with me at all times. Why was I not informed of this?"

"You have climbed above your station, Felix. You have a vote on the Council, but this is not your say. We have voted and even if you were to have cast your lot, you still would have lost." The man did not even stop to draw a breath, yet he could not disguise the glee escaping with his declaration. "They are out. Today."

"You will not even give them the chance to find alternate accommodation before you evict them?"

"They have had six months. I think that is long enough."

I was left holding a dead phone. After declaring his victory, he'd hung up, leaving me to deal with the fallout. I had one hour before they would be up and preparing for their morning routine at the house in the Jacaranda District. One hour to ring around and try to reverse the situation.

I replaced the receiver and pressed speed dial to start my petition, member by member, to the High Council. I suspected if the Overseer had been up all night, he would have ensured he was not alone. The whir of my brain, my planning and list making was brought to a halt when the whole building shook.

I waited.

A second minor wave rattled the windows.

Should I evacuate?

The breath captured in my lungs burned and I slowly released it, straining my ears to hear any indication of significant damage. My nerves stretched to pick up any evidence of more tremors or resulting damage.

We lived in a volatile region and tremors were not uncommon. But that was more than a tremor. That was a significant shake.

Night lights and reflections from the canals still lit the scene out my windows. Power was still connected. No emergency vehicles took to the streets. No sirens broke through the silence. Several minutes passed and I began to wonder if I had imagined it.

Returning to my desk, I focused again on the task at hand. Could the majority of the Council be persuaded to reverse their decision within the next fifty minutes? Jarvis was an agreeable fellow. I'd start with him.

42

RAPHAEL: A NEW DAY

It was early. The faintest glow was peeking in through the tiny gap between the blind and the wall.

"Good morning, LM." Dan moved out of the shadows and sat on the edge of my bed.

"LM?" I still had croaky sleep voice.

"Little Master, although, with the way you're sprouting, I think we'll be calling you Tall Master, soon." I could hear the laughter in his voice. But it was not mean. "How are your hands this morning?"

"Oh." It was funny, as soon as he mentioned them, the memory of last night and the dull throb came to mind. "Not too bad."

He reached over and flicked my bedside light on. I squinted against the light. By the time I could open my eyes, Dan had finished looking at my hands and was staring at my face.

"What? Did I get demon splatter on my face too?"

"No. I just can't believe how bleeding amazing that was. The way you took hold of that thing and hung on. Mate. Did you hear it scream?" He shook his head.

"No. I just remember hanging on and asking, and asking, and asking that I might be able to hang on and not let go." I remembered the burning. "It hurt a lot. But..." I looked at the scars caused by my sword's binding—raised, thick, white lines lacing across my palms, now buried by fresh, red welts—and remembered the night I had received them in Sodom. "I hung on."

"What made you do it? I mean, what gave you the idea?"

"I do not know. But Uncle Felix was scared, and the creature grabbed his sword. Mine is broken and I know I am not to kill them. So, I thought I would lay my hands on it and speak to the Light about what I might do to help." It was hard to remember what had actually happened, but I could easily remember the feelings. I looked back to Dan. "The demon did not like that."

Dan roared with laughter and I had to join in. We stopped when there was a knock at the door.

Sariah peeked through and, seeing the light was on, came in and climbed up between me and the wall. She picked up my hands, turned them over and ran her fingers over my old and new scars that ran up my wrists. Her fingers were warm feathers. Her face was hidden behind the curtain of her hair. But I could tell she was upset even before I heard the sniff or felt the tears plink onto my arm.

"I am okay Ri. Dan and I were just remembering what happened and—"

She jerked her head and glared at Dan. She stared at him; her armour was so dark it was tinged with black. The snarl on her face was like a wild cat.

I knew it was in defence of me. My sister was very protective. When we lived in Sodom, we had pretended it was me who looked out for her. But always it had been the other way around. I knew her rage bubbled up out of fear, but I was worried that Dan might take it the wrong way. "Riah does not mean to be rude, she was worried about me. That is all." I looked to Dan and saw he was mirroring her expression. "Oh dear. I now have two of you."

"Three." Tessa stood in the threshold of the room, not entering.

"Six." Marcus's voice trailed down the hallway. "Now, stop lying in, you lazy brat, it's time to get moving. War hero or not."

Tessa peeled away and disappeared into the hallway. I was so happy to see her in armour again.

Riah and Dan exchanged nods, then my sister leapt from the bed and twirled out of the room.

"Come on mate, everyone is going to want to check out your cool new scars." Dan threw some tracksuit pants at me and waited. With his arm around my shoulder, we went to have our morning "coffee" (although mine and Riah's was still hot chocolate), in preparation for sets.

Dan was right. Kait was the first to put me through the magnifying glass of her inspection. Val checked me over, with Marcus looking over her shoulder. Then, once everyone was finished and I had some space, Tessa edged closer and asked if she could take a look too.

She was skin and bone. The black circles under her dark eyes reminded me of the days when she first joined our family a couple of years ago. A white daisy with dark, sunken eyes. Her skin was so pale she was almost see-through. Back in her normal "Tessa" clothes, it was obvious how much weight she had lost; she was a skeleton. Her beautiful golden hair was dull and flat. But her armour was back. Without her painted mask she did not look like stupid Kari's "T" anymore. She had started to smell like our Tessa again.

It hurt to see her so empty. But it also hurt that she had chosen them over us. She had left us. It was then I noticed that the lakes in her eyes were about to overflow. And my heart broke that she was so sad. Yes, she had left us. But she was back now. I knew her heart was pure and that she loved me. But most important of all, that I loved her.

Abbot had always said love is a one-way river. A river does not care if the land is thirsty or full. It does not matter if the land gives or takes. A river just flows because it is full and alive and that is what it does. The only time a river does not flow is if it is dried up or blocked. Then it does terrible damage. First, it starves the land around it, and secondly, when the dam bursts, it destroys everything in its path. So, Abbot would say, best to keep that river running young man.

Tessa looked like she had been in a drought, so I threw my arms around her and tried to love a river back into her soul.

She sobbed and clung to me in return.

My hands ached and throbbed, but I pressed them firmly to her back and asked the Light that He might make her right again and return things to the way they had been before... but better. An image was forming in my mind. It was blurry. I was trying to grasp the edges of it, so I could straighten it out.

But a knock at the front door pulled Tessa out of my arms. She sniffed a snuffly "Thank you" and grabbed some tissues on her way to see who it was. It was still early, the sun was not up, so it was odd that we would be receiving guests.

I moved to the couch and sat between Marcus and Kait, and took the cup Riah passed me as she nestled on the other side of Marcus. It burned a bit to hold, but I did not want to make a fuss.

"Perfect timing, Felix." Val poured him a cup and invited him to join us in the sitting room. His armour was still flickering, and he carried his gift under his arm.

"Thank you for taking time to see me this morning." His eyes drifted around the room and settled on me, Marcus and Ri. He shook his head, then took his cup and joined the circle. "I trust you all slept... well?" His droll was back and it made me smile.

"Looks like you've not slept at all." I loved the way Marcus's growl vibrated through my ribs. I leaned in harder.

"Perceptive as always, Marcus." His eyes dropped to the book on his lap, then again went around the room, making contact with everyone. "Thank you for what you have given me. Thank you for what you have shown me." He took his cup in both hands. "And thank you for how you have welcomed me." He breathed deeply then looked up, and an avalanche of sadness rolled out of his eyes. "I have bad news."

The silence echoed so loud my ears hurt.

"While I was here last night, reports were coming in and, evidently, Kari has decided that she will no longer require Tessa's help on the Events team."

"Yeah, she kicked me to the kerb yesterday. Told me that maybe I was better off in a cleaning team..." Tessa breathed a heavy, watery sigh. "So, I guess I'll need a new uniform?"

"Sweetheart, you don't have to do this. You know that." Kait rolled out the same speech she had been giving Tessa for months.

"And like I keep saying, Kait, I'm doing this for you guys. We need to work for this house, for the food, to pay the bills. We don't have a choice." Her face became fierce. Her focus flicked to Dan before hopelessness came over her and she came back to Kait.

"We always have a choice, Tessa." Val's soft words broke the steel in Tessa's back.

She slumped. "I wish that were true."

"Unfortunately, in this case, it seems the decision has been made for you." We all looked back to Felix. "As I said, 'reports'... plural, came in last night. And since I wasn't there to deal with it, the Overseer called the High Council to intervene and... overreact. It appears, now, with only two of you actively working, and five not"—he looked at Ri and me again—"taking advantage of the Community's... generosity, they have decided the viable option is to"—he looked to the ceiling, skewed his lips to the side of his face, then looked back at Marcus with dark, angry eyes—"retract the offer of lodgings."

"Ha, the cagey coots, they finally got the vote passed, hey?" Rather than shocked like me, Marcus seemed at ease with the bomb that Felix had just launched.

"With my vote off the table, as I was... otherwise entertained, they rushed the motion through last night and it was carried." The anger leached from his body and he slumped back in his chair. "I have been on the phone for an hour trying to work alternate arrangements, but my hands are tied. He is, after all, the Overseer and has final say. I don't know what the final straw was."

Val, Kait and Marcus looked to each other and Val smirked, nodding her head at Felix's swirling armour alive with vibrant flames. "I could hazard a guess."

"But what does this mean for us?" Tessa's voice rose and her breaths came short and fast.

"Simple, we move out." Val stated it like it was as easy as making toast. But like Tessa, I was having trouble accepting this as anything less complicated than a bearnaise sauce.

"We can't move out." It was hard to believe Tessa's pale skin was even paler. "Where will we go? How will we live? How…"

Dan was not smiling when he crossed the room and took the cup from her trembling hands. "Breathe, Tessa. This is where I come in handy, remember? I'm the expert." He collected a few other cups, dropped them in the kitchen, then headed outdoors to the back lawn and faced the east. "At least it's not winter."

We followed him out and made space for Uncle Felix. It was sad that he had accepted our invitation to join us for morning sets, and we were being taken away from him. Who would train him now? Who would take care of him when the attacks came? He was all by himself.

I watched him take a place near the back and checked out his guard. The Warrior turned his head to me, and nodded, then turned his attention back to Uncle Felix.

Thank you that you are the One who watches over us. That it is you who keeps us safe. Please take care of him and protect him against the Overseer.

After breakfast and showers, we had to pack up our house.

Again.

At least this time the world was not going to go up in a ball of flames. We just had to move out to the streets. I tried not to think of this too much, because it was an open invitation for the Dragon to visit. But I had been learning how to put a handle on the beast. It still bucked me off, but I remained standing. He had not won yet.

I stopped.

Breathed: Light in, me out, Light in, doubt out.

It didn't take the fire away completely, but it put a damper on it. I had learned that looking at my hands helped. When I really needed an anchor, I traced the raised scars with my fingers.

Each battle, every victory was tied to a line. Today I added new victories to my list. In my hands, I had all I needed to survive, to win, and to be okay.

And I had more. I had been given the gift of helping others with these hands.

And I had more. I had been given others who could help me.

And I had even more. I had One who watched over me, loved me and had a purpose for me. Breathe; light in, me out. In... Two... Three... Out... Two... Three...

If only I could lay my hands on the Dragon. Then I'd show it a thing or two. But as of yet, I could not. It was too slippery. But it was enough that I could coast with the wave and wait till it left me in peace once again.

Even though we had lived here for more than six months, there was not too much for us to pack. Most of the things we brought with us were still in the truck. The Community had provided everything. But I had snuck some of my things into the kitchen. I was sad that I was not going to try out my new cooking set, experimenting with new recipes. "Maybe we could find a place that has a kitchen?"

Riah stopped packing utensils, looked at me, and rolled her eyes.

"Yes, well. I guess not many homeless people have the luxury of a kitchen... or the money to buy food..." Breathe: in... two... three... out... two... three...

Fingers running back and forth across white ridges. Scarred hands running over swollen wrists. A scaled tail flicked, and a toothy mouth grinned. Light in, me out. "It's going to be okay, Ri." Eyes clamped against the heat rising. "We're going to be okay."

Bands of iron wrapped around my back and shoulders to hold me from flying apart. A blanket of peace settled behind my aching eyes. A cool cheek rested on mine and a cushion of deep, steady breathing rose and fell behind me. One by one, the talons that pierced my heart withdrew. A steady beat returned with my sanity.

Then a wet, slobbery finger was inserted in my ear.

"Eww, Ri, you are so gross." I was madly wiping the spit away as my sister roared silently with laughter.

"She get you again, LM?" But instead of offering me support, Dan walked past me and high-fived my brat of a sister.

We all stopped and stared as there was another knock at our door.

43

KAITLYN: TRANSITION

Convergence

"Darling, is it true?" Georgie had me encased in his arms on the doorstep. "I came as soon as I heard." I tried but couldn't get a word out. "Griff's seriously skitched. You should have seen him. He's storming the castle later this morning. The others aren't happy either." He took me by the shoulders. "I can't bear it, how am I going to go on without you?"

A cough from the hallway pulled him up.

"You must be Marcus. Oh god, are you okay?"

Before I could stop him, Georgie launched himself at my husband and threw his arms around him. "You poor, poor things." With one arm on Marcus's shoulder and my hand engulfed in his free hand, he continued without missing a beat. "What do you need? What can I do?"

Marcus looked to me, to Georgie, then to the hand resting on his shoulder.

Taking the hint and finally feeling the frost that had settled in the air, Georgie removed his hand from Marcus's shoulder and offered it in greeting. "So sorry, sometimes I do get a bit carried away. I'm Georgie."

Marcus's eyes found mine as I stood to the side of my partner's back. I raised an eyebrow and dared him to be rude. *Drop your leg and stop marking your territory.*

What did you say?

You heard me, put the club back in the cave and behave yourself.

Or what?

Or I will make your life a living hell. That's a promise.

"Pleased to finally make your acquaintance... Georgie." Marcus raised an eyebrow, *Good enough?*

I raised one back, *For now. But you can do better.*

"Oh. My. God. You two are simply adorable." Georgie slipped his arm through Marcus's clenched elbow.

Speechless, my husband looked at me, *What the...?*

Trying to hide my smile, *Behave and invite him for coffee.*

We don't have time for this.

Let me remind you of two words, my love... living... hell.

Skrat. "Do you have time for a coffee, Georgie?"

"Kaitie, darling, if he wasn't wearing that ring of yours, I would snatch him up in a heartbeat."

"Kaitie", did he just call you Kaitie? I'll kill him.

Coffee. Now.

"Come through and I'll brew you a cup, Georgie." My beloved husband turned his back on me and led my colleague through the house.

Georgie looked over his shoulder and winked. It was then I just about lost it. My heart curled in on itself. The Community could keep the house, the product, and the clothes. They could even keep the job I'd grown to love. But I was going to miss this man so very, very much.

My sorrow was drowned out by a scream of joy. "Georgie!"

At least the twins knew how to welcome a guest properly.

I entered the kitchen and saw that the crew had taken Georgie's visit as a sign for a coffee break. Everyone was getting comfy around the kitchen island, with Georgie held hostage by a twin on each side of him.

Marcus looked me in the eye. *Well, he's quite the welcomed... guest.*

Because they all know and love him.

Love him?

He's here a lot. We do work together you know.

Only just now... Kaitie. How come I didn't know he was a bloke?

Because I knew you'd carry on like a pork chop, just like you are now!

Without taking his eyes off mine, Marcus played with fire. "So tell me, Georgie, what's *Kaitie* been like to work with?"

Georgie had been watching us, his face alight with undisguised glee. "Well, *Bear*, where to start..."

Marcus glared at me. *I believe the terms of this agreement were, how did you put it? Living hell?*

I groaned. Time to pay.

44

FELIX: HOLED UP

I made my way home, quick smart. Showered, shaved, ate and prepared for what was going to be a long day. I removed the letter from the front of my new, gifted copy of The Way and placed it in a small, sealed plastic bag and inserted it in the inner pocket of my suit jacket.

I had organised a driver and filled Marlene in on my way to the office. She would meet me there at 7 am and we would form a plan of attack. First thing on the agenda was finding Marcus and his family a place to live. Next, I would call in favours and find employment... outside the Community, for at least Kait and Marcus to start with, and the others as time went on.

Marlene was already in her office and I only rang off with her as I approached the lift at Community Head Office. Out of the lift and stalking down the hallway, my mind cycling through lists, planning, organising, I ran straight into Edward. Or the person I thought of as Edward.

My armour connected with his stationary form. He gasped and his appearance shuddered. Underneath, something else was revealed.

Shocked. Frozen. My mind pivoted off into a tailspin in a completely different direction. "Edward?"

Out of the shadows, Raymond and Nyle moved to flank him. I was aware of movement behind me. Without taking my eyes off the trio, I tilted my head, and my heart followed my mind into the whirlwind.

My guard had unsheathed his sword.

Oh. Dear. Oh dear, oh dear... oh dear.

The Crow stirred. But now was not a suitable time for bargains, lists and silence. The Crow would just have to take a number and get in line.

"It has been noted, Felix, that you have become somewhat of a nuisance." Edward spoke, but Nyle rolled his shoulders and Raymond shook out his arms. All actions reminded me of Marcus preparing to train.

Oh. Dear.

I was out of my depth. The faint cackle of the Crow echoing in my vacant mind caused nausea to swirl in distinct black-green paisley behind my eyes. I had my guard at my back, and I trusted his ability completely. Mine, not quite as much. Actually... not at all. And I stood between my protector and my assailant.

I also had a confidence that the three that faced me were not completely human and very capable of doing me great harm. If they were in league with the Dark Lord and were in any way similar to those we faced last night, then I was also confident this was not going to end well.

"Now that all depends on whose side you're on, doesn't it?" Nyle invoked the other's chuckles.

For once, we were all in agreement. In some irrational part of my brain, I felt vindicated that I had never liked these men.

"Believe us, Felix, the feeling is completely mutual." Edward dropped his disguise entirely and stepped forward. "You were always annoying, but you were useful. Now you are becoming... a problem."

I could neither stop nor hide my shaking. The humanoid creature was similar to those last night. It was coated with mottled swirls of blackened, raw flesh. Soulless black eyes devoured my hope as long bony fingers reached out and flicked my tie. A talon tapped my chest.

"You have become a serious pain in my butt." It used a perfect imitation of my own voice. It was... unnerving.

The point of its claw stilled my heart. Its sulphuric stench brought tears to my eyes and burned my sinuses.

They all cawed at my fear. "So, tell me Felix, how's that 'strong and courageous' working out for you?"

The letter. He knew about the letter. And what was *in* the letter. How was that possible?

"Foolish man, you have no idea what is not possible and the infinite options that are." Raymond had maneuvered himself to my side and as I stood in the midst of them, the noose tightened.

What on earth was I thinking. A life of excitement and exhilaration? What a joke. I was fooling myself. At last, my biggest fear had been realised. I was a fraud and I had been found out.

The other two had also dropped their disguises. I was done for. I would not be able to help the others relocate, I could not even help myself.

"The truth sucks, doesn't it... my man." Again, with the laughter. They were savage cats playing with their prey before the kill.

Claws pricked my heart.

As outnumbered and out-skilled as I was, I would be too ashamed if Marcus found my dead body without my sword drawn. I wasn't sure how to use it, but I remembered his advice that was supposed to work until we got around to training: "Hang on to the handle and point the sharp end at the uglies."

That I could do. With full effect, apparently. It had worked last night. My only hope was that as I flailed and fell, I might also take one of these with me.

A sharp beak pecked the inside of my right eye.

Enough! Damn you, wretched bird. I do not have time or space to deal with you right now. You will jolly well just have to wait till I can process surviving this next nightmare. When I am good and ready, I will get to you.

The silence was refreshing but also disconcerting. I now drifted in a void. I had postponed an attack from the Crow. But I was also incapable of forming any ideas on how I might problem-solve my way out of this mess.

Keep The Way on your lips always and you will be successful.

Okay. I could do that too. Only that morning we had read, *the light shines in the darkness and the Dark has not overcome it.* Well, I was in the Light. And they were Dark. So, that was a start.

They faltered.

A sliver of hope resurrected itself.

I couldn't think of any other direct quotes from The Way, but I was rather fond of the bit in the letter that read, *No one will be able to stand against you, for I, the Light, am with you always.* I also thought it was particularly apt as I had three very intimidating beings standing against me right now.

They faltered again.

In fact, they took a step back.

Everything stopped as a door further down the hallway opened. "Felix?"

They couldn't hurt Marlene. "Stay back." *No. Not Marlene. You must protect her.*

The three spun and... froze.

I will admit, I did too. For Marlene had not listened to me. Rather, she had done the exact opposite. Flanked not by one but two guards, unsheathing her sword, she ran... towards us... saying some very unladylike things... in Louboutins. Forthwith, she impaled the thing that had been Nyle. Next, Raymond fell. Then—I was unsure who was more surprised—Edward ran backwards, into... onto my still-raised, shaking sword. I planted my feet and dropped my weight and lunged forward as Marcus had told me and made sure the job was done.

The stench and horror warred with my senses.

Which was worse? Seeing the creatures disintegrate into pools of black tar, or the reeking smell they gave off?

I had seen it last night. But again... today... in broad daylight... outside my office, was a whole new thing. I needed to sit down. And I felt the hallway was an extremely suitable place to do so. I backed into the wall and slid down to the carpet. The burned carpet. We would have to get that fixed. Fleur. Blazing red armour. Black, wide-heeled, low pumps. Head of all our cleaning crews. Fifteen for domestic and nine for commercial...

"Come on now. Up you get." Marlene was not going to let me rest. The slave driver led me to my office, shut the door and was on the phone as she directed me to my chair. "Fleur, cleaning job. Carpet. Head office. Seventh floor. Yes, the usual. Thanks, dear."

"What?" I stared at my aide. "What was that?"

"Nothing dear, just taking care of business. Cup of tea? I think coffee may be a bit too stimulating, don't you?" She disappeared through to her office and came back a moment later followed by Gem. His gold-green eyes considered me from the doorway.

"You've done this before?"

"Well of course, Felix. But I will admit, I do enjoy the opportunity to take any or all of that particular trio down. Well done by the way. Was that your first?"

"But you just killed two people." My stomach protested. "And I just killed a man... another man." I bolted to the bathroom and emptied my stomach. The face that confronted me in the mirror was a brutally honest portrayal of how I felt: overwrought, exhausted, and washed out.

"Not people, dear, demons. You killed a demon. And I am proud of you." The woman I thought I knew stood in the doorway of the bathroom, beaming.

Gem stalked across the room, head butted Marlene's legs then sat on the floor and blinked.

"What do we tell people?"

"Nothing, not our job. Fleur will have sent a team by now; the carpet will be replaced within the hour. No one will know a thing."

"But Edward, Raymond and Nyle—"

"Don't exist, dear. The Dark Lord will have their replacements installed sooner than we have the new carpet laid. Now, more importantly, what are we going to do about our friends?"

Before I could pull my thoughts back to our original plan,

Marlene left to make the tea. My mind once again ran through lists: people, possibilities, properties.

Absentmindedly I patted Gem, who was now perched on the corner of my desk with one hand, and with the other answered the phone lighting up.

"I want you in Philadelphia immediately."

"Overseer?"

"There's been an earthquake. The city's a mess."

"Absolutely. Thank you, Overseer. I'll head over later today once I've cleared my schedule and sorted a few issues here."

"You will go immediately. You created this mess and now you will fix it."

"With all due respect—"

"I think it's a bit late for that, don't you, Felix? You promised these people aid. They are now in need and are asking for another hand-out. And sizeable, no doubt. I told you, you were being too generous. Now you get yourself over there and manage the fallout. I don't want to have to be supporting the rebuild of the whole blasted city because of your overinflated sense of blasted righteousness and unrealistic generosity."

"I will go, Overseer. But you have just fired our main driver. Shall I reinstall Marcus?"

"Don't play your games with me, boy. I will deal with them this morning. You deal with the debacle you have created in blasted Philadelphia. I do not want their Community bleeding us dry. You have created an epic mistake here, Felix. Do not come back until it is fixed."

"I cannot see the advantage of heading out at..." I looked to the clock again. Seven-thirty. How could so much have happened in such a short amount of time? "...such an early hour. I will make some calls, work out a plan and get on the road after the traffic is cleared. That way I'll know what's needed, put some things in place and be better prepared when I get there."

He was silent. I could feel a new level of animosity channelling down the line. "Do not overstep your boundaries." For the first time in the twelve years I had known him, the Overseer's voice took on an edge I didn't know he possessed. "I am still your employer and you are not irreplaceable." His voice maintained the vehemence and became quieter. "You will go now and if you cannot find a driver, you will drive yourself. And." A pause. A breath. A command. "You will take Marlene."

Again, the man hung up on me.

I looked up to Marlene sipping her tea while she waited for me to finish the call. Still, two guards flanked her. I looked to mine.

Why does she have two?

"Everything alright dear?"

"Philadelphia has been hit by an earthquake."

She gasped.

"I'm to go and help the Community."

"That's uncharacteristically noble of the Overseer."

"Jonathan must have reached out for help. The Overseer is not happy and fears they will drain our coffers."

At this she guffawed. "What's the real reason then?" She continued sipping her tea. Not much came between Marlene and her tea, except possibly Gem.

"He wants us out of here for the showdown I suspect."

"Us?"

"Yes... dear." I struggled to hide my smile. "You're coming with me."

The one small pinprick of light of the morning was the look of utter horror on her face.

"And you'd best pack a bag. We might be a while."

Marlene did not enjoy travel. Even if it was just an hour or so down the road. But, as I suspect the Overseer designed it, it would take several hours to navigate the traffic into a devastated city. That is, of course, if we could actually get in. Then at least a few days to gain information regarding needs, aid and assistance. But then, there may be nowhere to stay. Hmm. Best be prepared for all possibilities.

Marlene was still standing frozen, her teacup halfway to her mouth. "What about Gem?"

"He'll have to come with us."

"He won't be happy about that."

45

KAITLYN: LOCKING HORNS

The lightness and fun of the morning had slowly evaporated, the closer we came to Community Head Office. All of us squeezed into the elevator brought back memories of the last time we rode up here. Battle-weary, ignorant and hopeful. Now we were on high alert, enlightened and ready for a fight.

The elevator pinged open in time to hear a slammed door down the hallway. Like a set of skittles, we were almost bowled over by an enraged Griffin as he stormed into the foyer. "You've not heard the end of this Kait. I am not happy with this"—he looked to the children and Tessa—"incompetent... ignorant... fool of a man." Bypassing the lift, he smashed through the fire escape, his curses and temper echoing through the stairwell until they were silenced by the slam of the door.

I had never seen Griffin lose his temper. Granted, I'd only known him six months and only at staff meetings. But never had he removed the cover from his emotions. Shocked to the core, I realised I was going to miss him and his dry, sharp genius as well.

A quiet buzz brought my attention around to a blonde woman cloaked in cream, sitting behind a pale desk in front of a cream wall. No wonder I hadn't seen her, she was invisible.

"The Overseer has asked if you could please take a seat. He will see you in a moment."

"Waiting for the Overseer, now that's something new."

"Marcus." It was one thing to share our opinion in our own home, but to disrespect the man in front of his staff, in front of the kids, was not okay.

"Kait, if you only knew how much of my time and extra work Felix has to do to cover this man's behind because he can't ever keep a schedule..." He didn't continue. He stormed to the couch and sat down. Then stood and paced.

I guess that was a deep pool of ugly I'd have to deal with later, in a less public place. But for now, we'd wait.

And wait we did. The Overseer kept us waiting for two hours. Another reminder of our first day here. Hopefully this time he'd not keep us *all* day. After we'd seen him, returned the keys and severed our agreements, we still had to find somewhere to camp for tonight. I wouldn't be so ungracious as to say he knew this and kept us waiting regardless. I'm sure he was being held up with very important business.

Well, I tried to keep thinking that. But after the fourth tray of snacks had been taken into his office, I found it hard to think the Overseer was working too hard. Or the meeting he was in was too serious if they had time to keep stopping and eating.

And finally, we received our summons. "Ah, do come in."

We'd waited, deflated and deflected in the hours we'd been made to cool our heels. It took me back to my years at school and the number of times I'd had to wait to see my principal.

As a group, we stood in his presence with a very different dynamic to that with which we arrived. The Overseer had played his cards well. "Glad to see you all looking so well. Felix sprouted some nonsense at me this morning, but you all look just fine to me."

Val waded into the conversation. "Thank you. Where is Felix?" Val looked to the stranger standing in silhouette at the Overseer's shoulder.

"Urgent business came up this morning and I had to send him to Philadelphia to sort it out."

Marcus grunted something incoherent. Probably best none of us heard. But it was enough to draw the Overseer's attention.

"You. After all I did for you." It must have been a morning for revelations. The Overseer pulled back his congenial mask and unleashed hostility at Marcus. "This is how you repay me."

Marcus was as shocked as the rest of us. "Excuse me?"

"I give you a home, I give you all jobs, I send your kids to the best school in the city"—his glare turned to disdain as his eyes travelled over the twins—"and I give you the most honoured job of all. And you repay me by ruining my aide. You've ruined him." Anger drew the Overseer out of his chair. Leaning over his desk he shook his fist at my husband.

The move was subtle, but the seven of us eased apart, loosened up and upped the focus. I guided Raph behind my left hip.

"Don't you threaten me. Did you see that?" The Overseer turned to the shadow at his right. "Did you see that?"

Obviously, we were not subtle enough. It wasn't meant to be threatening, it was a natural response to being challenged.

"Maybe I should call for refreshments, sir. You've had a busy night and a full morning."

The strain evident on his face, the Overseer turned his back on us and instead looked out the wall of windows as the afternoon sun bathed the city outside. The scene of the vast glass kingdom beyond must have brought him comfort. His breathing slowed and after a count he faced us again. Back in control of his emotions, he began pacing and preaching from behind his desk. "When you arrived in my city, you had nothing. I gave you everything." He vaguely waved his hand indicating the city beyond the window. "I place two of you in honoured jobs."

He switched to counting off facts on his fingers. "I allowed Kari to persuade me to permit an untried, inexperienced... girl in a prominent position. I offered your children a place at the most elite school in the country. I overlooked the criminal past and the hostile behaviour of two of your group, and allowed them to have a free ride, contributing nothing. I put you up in one of our best houses in an exclusive suburb, gave you vehicles, clothes, food, finances... I paid all your bills." By now, the Overseer had run out of fingers. "I have opened my coffers and showered you in my wealth and this is how you repay me?"

He stopped pacing and drew his fist once again, jabbing a sausage finger at each of us in turn, emphasising his case. "You two walk the streets everyday causing havoc. You two undisciplined..."—he chewed on his words, couldn't find the right one, so stumbled on without it—"... fought, were rude, unyielding, unteachable, and were expelled from Community College."

He turned on Tessa. ""You became a burden on one of our most valued team members. You were assigned beautiful living quarters but you refused to stay in them. You shamelessly forced your way upon Kari's goodwill. You are a leech."

Before any of us could make a reply, he turned on Marcus. "And you. Yours is the greatest betrayal. You took my generosity and in return have destroyed Felix and his position here.

"I make a place for you upon our boat and rather than pull your oars, you have been worse than dead weight. You have done your best to sink us. You have consumed precious resources and offered nothing in return. Is it fair that others clean your house, cook your food, while you give nothing? Do nothing?"

As he ramped up, his confidence in his case transformed his rage into self-righteous grandstanding.

We waited till he got it all out and let him purge the wound. Pleased with his summing argument, he faced us, inflated and self-confident.

"Are you quite finished?" Val's quiet steel chilled the room.

"You." It didn't take long to tip the scales back to angry. "You do not speak in this office. You do nothing, have nothing, offer nothing but trouble. You *are* nothing but trouble." He turned to face Marcus.

Marcus did not say a word. He deferred to Val, silently asking her the question, *How do you want to play this?*

"Do not look to her. I am talking to you."

Marcus simply shook his head. And again, looked to Val.

"I have a message for you." Unsurprisingly, Val's quiet words did nothing to calm the situation. On the contrary, they were fuel for the fire.

"You do not speak to me." Spittle erupted from the Overseer's mouth. He held his hand up as if to physically block Val's presence. "Don't think I don't know you are the one behind all of this."

All of a sudden, the large, opulent office seemed very small.

Mouth agape, even the new aide who had been trying to blend in with the expensive furniture stared at Val, waiting for the eruption.

It didn't come, but the light sparking from Val's narrowed eyes were just an extension of the inferno consuming her armour. And then, the corner of her mouth lifted. "Thank you. However, I'm afraid I cannot take the credit."

"You are an interfering, controlling woman. Don't think I don't know. I've heard the reports from here and Sodom." An overstuffed manila folder was lifted, waved and then thrown back down on the table again, punctuating his point. "It's about time you learned your place, learned to toe the line and learned to contribute."

I do believe Val was starting to enjoy herself. Very calmly she responded, "I offered my services when we arrived, but was told you were not in need of the skills I had to offer."

"Fighting. Warfare. Hand to hand combat. What kind of woman indulges in these pursuits?" He glared at Marcus. "And what kind of man allows it."

Oh dear. I do believe we have turned from ugly and are teetering on the verge of unresolvable. Help please!

White-faced, Marcus threw his arms up in surrender and stepped backwards, completely thrown. "I don't allow or disallow Val anything. She is her own woman and me trainer, mentor and sister. That is not me place."

"I suspect that is the main problem in your household. You have no control over your wild, undisciplined children, savage ward"—he looked to Dan—"and irresponsible charge"—this to Tessa. "Even

your wife is reported to have unhealthy connections with her...
colleague. No wonder you could not fit in here."

Marcus went from white to red to purple, his eyes bulging like a
chihuahua's. Thankfully he could not voice the words I saw racing
through his mind.

"Enough." Val drew her sword and pointed it to the Overseer. "Do
you not have eyes to see that which is in front of you?" Indigo fire
with a crimson heart danced down her blade.

Thrown back in his chair, I suspected the answer was yes.

"Do you not have ears to hear the message of truth I have for
you?" There was no answer, so Val continued. Her volume decreased
but the steel intensified. "Achan, I know—"

"How do you know my given name? You will address me by my
title." Even under attack, his pride knew no limit.

"Achan," Val repeated, "I know the secrets stashed beneath your
floorboards. I have seen into your heart and know the lust and greed
that live there."

A fish out of water, the Overseer's mouth opened and closed.
Neither sound nor air escaped.

"Great responsibility has been gifted to you and you have squan-
dered the blessing. As a leader you should serve, as a servant you
should love. But you, the Shepherd, have fed off your sheep. Justice is
a foreign language, the oppressed are trampled underfoot, the father-
less are cast aside and the widows are neglected.

"You say you are rich, that you have acquired wealth and do not
require anything. But you do not realise that you are wretched, poor,
blind and naked. I counsel you to buy from the Light gold refined in
the fire, so you can become rich; and white clothes to wear, so you
can cover your shameful nakedness; and salve to put on your eyes, so
you can see.

"Weep and wail because of the misery that is coming on you. Your
wealth has rotted, and moths will eat your clothes. Your gold and
silver are corroding, and their corrosion will testify against you and
eat your flesh like fire. You have hoarded wealth in the last
days. Look! The wages you failed to pay the workers are crying out

against you. The cries of the harvesters have reached the ears of the Light. You have lived on earth in luxury and self-indulgence. You have fattened yourselves in the day of slaughter. You have condemned and murdered the innocent one, who was not opposing you."

"How... how dare you? What on earth are you talking about, you delusional woman? What has the Light got to do with anything we do here? *I* have slaved for years, dragging the reputation of the Community up into the realms of public acceptance. *I* have the approval of the Gerent to operate, and on *my* coat-tails, smaller Communities are sliding in under the goodwill *I* have earned."

The man stood. "The Light? What good was the Light in Sodom? You say you were the only survivors; that the world turned against you, that the demons ran amok, and they ran the town. Well, look around you, woman, there are no demons here; the world is not against us here. Why? Because of what *I* have done. Me."

The Overseer's sickening blindness was complete. "We are not in danger of being attacked or persecuted. The world loves us and what we do. We are helping people, saving people, teaching people and creating better lives. Look at what we have. Look at what *I* have achieved. Look at where we are, for crying out loud." He threw his hand to the window again.

Val's sword cracked with Indigo flame. "You are being given one more chance to return to the Light: to acknowledge His authority and His place of honour here. Now. Turn back to Him, or you will be spat out of this city with nothing but the clothes on your back. You will be lucky if you escape with your life.

"You say, 'What has the Light got to do with what's going on here?' The Light is everything you do here. If He isn't, then you have no part in it. The office of Overseer is for a child of Light, living in the Light, to govern by the grace and in the wisdom of the Light, serving the people of the Light. You are not the head of the Community. You have no right to claim that name; you are the head of a worldly organisation."

The Overseer was so shocked he couldn't speak into Val's silence. Just as well. She hadn't finished. "Admit it and free yourself from the guilt of lying, at least. In your role of Overseer, you have failed, and if you do not change your ways you will be judged accordingly. You foolish, arrogant man, it is bad enough you are heading for oblivion, but your crime is so much worse for the multitude you lead into Abaddon behind you. You have been warned."

"Get out. Get out and never show your faces here again. Jones, take their keys, their phones... everything."

"But Uncle Felix said we could keep our phones."

"Boy"—anger had turned the Overseer's words to a vibration that shook the air—"you came with nothing and if I could strip the clothes from your back so you leave with nothing, I would." His roar shook the room and spittle sprayed his desk. "But I will do everything I can to ensure you leave here like the beggars you are."

46

CONTESSA: CAST ADRIFT

I was dumbstruck. Seriously. I couldn't say a word. That man was all kinds of horrid.

Val led us out of the room and out of the building.

We followed like sheep.

Silent sheep.

Shocked, silent sheep.

Well, at least I was.

What were we going to do? Where were we going to stay?

This was all my fault. I hadn't been good enough for Kari or been able to keep Achilles' interest. We would still be safe and have somewhere to live if I had done my job better... been better.

We couldn't survive on the streets.

Dan might be able to.

But I couldn't.

I mean, a girl needs a bathroom for goodness' sake.

I didn't want to even think about it.

Oh Lord. I'm going to be sick.

The pressure built up in my heart and kind of leaked out my eyes, but I was quiet about it. I was a good, quiet, crying sheep. No one else seemed to be too upset. And I couldn't understand why on earth they weren't.

I know I've just come back. But please help me have their kind of calm. I am so sorry that I stuffed up. Please help us find somewhere to live and be safe.

We hadn't got out of the office till after lunch and I was starving. I know, I was sick to the stomach *and* starving. I didn't normally get too hungry, but I was stressed. And, well, you know. In these extreme circumstances a girl needed food. Carbs preferably... or chocolate... chocolatey carbs would be ideal.

We all climbed back into the truck and Marcus drove us a few blocks away from the Community Headquarters and parked up so we could breathe. With the back door lifted, we all gathered around our belongings that had once again been stuffed into transit. I nestled in Sariah's beanbag. And as our new reality hit, exhaustion swept over me like a suffocating blanket.

I couldn't think civilly, let alone behave that way. So, I didn't say much. With a lot of ground to make up, I didn't want to ruin any grace that was remaining in my credit by bringing out the Twik Princess that was raging beneath my frazzled exterior.

Instead, I chose to sit and listen. Apparently, that's what I did best: sitting silently, listening to others make plans, for me to run and fulfil like an obedient, silent, sheep.

But that was the bitter talking. These guys weren't Kari. These guys were the ones who were going to save my butt. So, I sat, silenced the twik, and let my family make a plan for the immediate future... because it included me.

For now, I was just relieved that I was back with them and they would know what to do.

After making a plan, with truckloads of possiblys, maybes and hopefullys, we decided someone should hunt for food.

Daniel looked at me. His eyes were still guarded but at least they weren't hostile. "You guys stay with the truck; we'll go and get something for lunch." He turned, and Val and the twins disappeared after him.

Already he was saving the day and soon I would have something to eat. So, I did the next best thing and curled deeper into Riah's bean bag and let the suffocating blanket of exhaustion smother me into nothingness.

Well, I tried to.

I had just sorted the lumps and bumps when bashing on the siding had me on high alert. The back door had been closed, but the doors of the cab were open. Even though the voices were muffled, I got the gist of the conversation. We couldn't stay. We had to move on. I climbed over the mounds of furniture and boxes to listen.

"There is no signage saying it's illegal to park here." Marcus pointed out the obvious.

"You blind? You can't see the yellow line painted on the side of the road?" The voice drifted further to the front of the truck.

"You awake back there, Tessa?" Kait called through the hole in the front.

"Yeee." I had to clear the sleep out of my throat and try again. "Yeah."

"I've got some lunch for you if you're hungry."

"What? How? Where did that come from." I burrowed further through the storage boxes to get to the passage into the front of the truck. I flopped through the hole in the cab wall onto the bench-seat, with the help of Kait who delivered me from the squeeze.

"The others came back a while ago, but we didn't want to wake you."

I was about to argue that I hadn't actually gone to sleep and that, in fact, no time had passed. At. All. But at the mention of food, my argument was washed away when the heavenly scent of burger and chips hit me like a brick. With a waterfall of saliva threatening to flood the truck, I'll admit I may have snatched the food from the box on the dicky-seat and stuffed my face. Because sometimes a girl's gotta do what a girl's gotta do. Right?

Irrelevant.

I was starving.

Thankfully, Kait was as gracious as she was understanding and looked the other way as I consumed the cold, soggy burger. Done. I didn't even bother trying to hold back the groan of satisfaction.

"It's a bit cold, but better than nothing." The smile in her eyes made it clear that she understood, perfectly, that it had been far better than nothing. It had been perfect.

But since I'd started on the cold, congealed chips I could only nod. Looking around, I noticed the sun was setting. "What time is it?" Well, that was what I intended to say—it didn't come out quite as clean as that.

But Kait put two and two together and deciphered my chip-induced-mumbling.

Her eyes were out the front window watching Marcus negotiate with the traffic warden but she answered without moving her head. "Coming up to five o'clock. Val and Dan went back out with the kids to try and find a place for us to set up camp." She looked at me with a slight smile. "For tonight at least, if not for longer." She handed me a takeaway cup that held a warm chocolate milkshake. "I don't know what this will be like, but it might help fill you up."

I looked inside but found the warm soup unappealing. "Do we have any water?"

She just smiled and handed me a bottle. After I'd drained most of it, I started to feel more myself. It was then panic set in. "Any toilets around here?"

"Yes, thank the Light. Just around the corn—"

"We have to move." Marcus hauled himself up into the cab, gave me a wink. "Good to see you've made it back from Nod." Then proceeded to drown my immediate need with the roar of the old engine as it echoed around the narrow alley.

"It's okay, though. The guy told me I can stop for a bit down on the main road. Parking restrictions have almost ended, so we can perch up there for a while and still keep an eye out for the others."

I crossed my legs as the truck came to life with a bladder-torturing shake and rattle, then rumbled back out on the main street. "Parking just around the corner" was all very good in theory, but there were no spaces and Marcus had to drive a fair way before he found any spot big enough to get our big, fat, ugly truck in. I was already missing Kari's little red car. But not Kari.

By this stage, it wasn't just my legs that were crossed. My toes were curled, my fingers were knotted, and my eyes were spinning circles and swimming.

Thankfully we were near some kind of green space and a sign for public toilets pointed down a shadowy path. I just hoped they were free and... free. One way Laodicea kept unsightlies out of public places was putting a fee on the conveniences. Now that we were on the street, were we now unsightlies too? I would consider this new identity as soon as I had dealt with my current emergency.

Even before the engine was off, I scrambled over Kait and was out the door and running... in a crouch. Tears were streaming from pain and relief as the dim lighting revealed the large metal gates were unlocked and open and the doors did not require a coin. But it wasn't until I was finished that I noticed the condition of the block and the smell. Seriously. It was the most disgusting thing ever. Well, for Laodicea that was.

This was the first "unlovely" thing I'd seen in this city.

Even when we had scouted all sorts of places for fashion shows and other events that needed an edgier atmosphere, everything without exception was... orderly, neat, sanitary. I didn't know the right word. But it was a given; in Laodicea, no messiness was allowed. Nothing undesirable was permissible. It was the polar opposite to what I had become accustomed to at home in Sodom.

I rinsed my hands and left the building and walked straight into a broad, solid chest. "I'm so sorry, I didn't see you there."

The light was fading quickly now and the lamp outside the gate spluttered. Stepping to the left, I tried to move past the body I presumed was a man. He didn't say anything. He moved with me, so my way was blocked.

"I'm sorry, but this is the ladies', I think the men's is on the other side." Smiling, I tried to sidestep again.

He moved with me.

Again. "Umm, excuse me. I'd like to get past."

"How much?" It was more of a grunt than anything.

"Pardon?"

He leaned forward and growled in my ear. "How much?"

I must have misheard him. Obviously, I didn't have anything to sell. I wasn't carrying a bag or anything.

"What's your rate?"

"I beg your pardon?"

He pulled out a wad of cash from his back pocket.

Understanding dawned. I could feel heat rising up my neck. "Oh! Um..."

"You new here? I've not seen you working the park before." He was in silhouette, but I could hear a grin in his voice.

"I'm not... I don't... I mean, I just..." I pointed back to the block to illustrate my point. "The loo."

"I've got good money. How much?" His voice dropped.

So did my stomach.

"I am not... I mean, I don't... not... for sale, so please let me past." I thought tough thoughts and desperately tried to impersonate Val. But my shaky legs and wobbly voice kind of gave me away.

"I've offered to pay, but if you'd rather the other way, I can do that too." He stepped closer.

Any further and I'd be trapped within the shelter. I couldn't let that happen. It'd been months since I'd been to training, but thanks to my minor workout the night before and sessions this morning, my body quickly remembered what it was supposed to do.

As he reached out to grab me, my ugly took over. I couldn't use my sword, it wouldn't have worked on him anyway, but I had plenty of hard pointy bits that were just as effective: knees, elbows, fingers.

Within moments he was on the ground cussing and moaning. But he still blocked the entrance. And while he was conscious, he was still a danger. It was only last night I had been reminded of that lesson. But this time it was a human.

"You okay in there, Tessa?" Kait's voice came from the shadows into the light of the entrance. In a heartbeat, she'd assessed the situation and was on guard. She darted over, reached out and offered me her hand. "Come on sweetheart, the others are on their way."

Holding tight, I leapt over my attacker. On take-off, my foot slipped on something I'd rather not think about and before I knew it, I was lying sprawled out on top of him.

Eww, yuck. Damn.

He grunted. "Enthusiastic one, aren't you."

I gagged. He stank and his hands were crawling down my back and grabbing my butt.

I'd like to say that it was instinct and months of hard training and discipline that got me out of the mess.

But that would be a lie.

I was just angry.

Cold, tired... exhausted, and I just wanted to go home.

I hated Laodicea.

I hated the Community and what they'd done to us.

I hated being out of sorts with my family.

And, right now, most of all, I hated how this guy made me feel and what he was doing. I was taken back to the gangs in Sodom. Once again, I was goods to be used, swapped, or taken.

And, well... I kind of lost it.

I vomited all my anger and frustration from the past six months—and possibly a bit I hadn't dealt with from my previous life—out onto the lump under me.

Well, not literally, of course.

That would have been gross.

But all the emotional bile I'd been carrying erupted.

There may have been a bit of screaming and possibly a bit of swearing... and maybe a hint of spittle—not intended. There was definitely some hair pulling.

His, not mine.

And absolutely no style or technique whatsoever.

I vented all my grief and angst. Just as well my sword wouldn't work on him and I didn't carry a knife, like Dan. I really wanted to hurt the guy. But I probably would have felt sad if I'd killed him... at some point.

Finally, two sets of hands gently pulled my exhausted body up and cradled me back to the truck. Later, Kait told me the poor guy was left in the foetal position with his hands over his head, bruised, broken and bleeding. He may have been whimpering a bit as well.

I wasn't proud. But I did hope he had learned his lesson.

No meant no.

47

MARCUS: FINDING HAVEN

Kicked from pillar to post like a junkyard dog. This city and the Community here were as backward as a pack of cards. I knew we'd be okay. It'd be a bit tough for a while, but the Light'd see us through. No doubt about that. How we were going to find that way, though, I'd no idea. I guess that's what faith's all about. But sometimes, like today, that was as appealing as choosing door number three dressed only in swimmers and flip flops.

But enough of the pity party. It would take a while, but we'd work our way back. First up, make sure I was on solid ground with Kait. Then find us a place to stay.

Kait and I would be right as rain. I was just gutted that she'd felt she couldn't tell me Georgie was a bloke. What did she really think I'd do? I trusted her and it hurt that she didn't trust me to trust her.

But for now, we needed a place to pull up for the night. Everyone was walking on eggshells on the crumbling edge of a cliff, exhausted, hurting, and hungry. Praise the Light, Val and Dan hadn't been twiddling their toes this year. Every day scouring the city, getting the lie of the land, they'd found a possible place. But it was a last resort. Which is why we'd spent the afternoon trying to figure out a better option.

Definitely short-term. Possibly longer. However, there was a significant problem. It was dangerous.

Kait was now mothering Tessa in the back. The twins were laid out across the bench behind the seats of the cab. Dan and Val were up front. Dan had been kind enough to let me drive. After learning how to, he wasn't too keen on relinquishing control. But he was happy enough to navigate the way to our potential stopover. The streetslights were in full force as the city changed guard for the night.

Everything here was quiet, clean, and... weird, as usual. Nothing seemed normal in this city. Not that I'd call Sodom normal. But every city had an underbelly. I'm sure Laodicea had one too, but she was a prim little lady, keeping her skirts secured.

We cruised across town. Streetlights, shop signs and car signals burst to life as twilight merged into night. Dan had me follow the main arterial as it hemmed the heart of the city. We crossed a bridge, and I was directed to take a sharp right, and then another. We pulled up outside a disused milk factory.

From left to right a high, solid brick wall ran each way into the darkness. Directly in front, the truck lights bounced back from a sign and two large, chained gates. A piece of ply hanging from one corner told us that the Bovait Factory had closed and would remain closed. Bonus for us.

Due to contamination. Not so good.

With the engine purring, I tried to take in the immensity and absurdity of what I was looking at. A huge chunk of prime real estate, settled under one of the main bridges heading into the city, was shut down. With no intention of opening in the foreseeable future. Maybe it was too dirty for the City Council to touch.

Or perhaps it had something to do with the yellow and black symbols everywhere telling us it was contaminated. But why would authorities leave a huge contamination threat next to a canal?

The headlights, boosted by an old spotlight on site, partially illuminated a large shed. Possibly another two slept in the shadows. Lights from the city rainbowed across the aqueduct above, splattering bits and pieces of bright colours across the top of the buildings on the site.

I could just make out a few smaller buildings, possibly offices or workers' accommodation? Heaps of room for parking. The underside of the bridge's off-ramp offered shelter for the truck from sight and weather. I worked at keeping me excitement at bay as I started to consider the problem of the locked gate.

And the contamination.

"You like?" The pride in Dan's voice was warranted. They'd done good.

"Perfect." Before I could ask, "Have you got a way in?" he was opening the gate to let me through. Maybe this was one of the times I didn't ask about his past. Or remind him that breaking and entering was illegal. He was still touchy about his past, especially considering the way the Community had treated and judged him. And we really needed this. So, I stopped thinking about the illegal aspects of what we were doing and started giving thanks for the potential of a safe haven for the night, or maybe two.

I echoed the truck's sigh as I turned the engine off for the night. Tucked away, as close to the roof of the off-ramp as possible, I took the opportunity to breathe. I wasn't hitching my wagon to a star, but I had me hopes on this place. Until the Light told us it was time to leave.

It was all very well and good for the Overseer to share his opinion with us so enthusiastically. It was the most life I'd seen in the man over the past six months. He was literally as mad as a bag of wet cats. I wasn't sad that I'd not be working for him anymore. But I surely to goodness would miss Felix. I was confident though that the world was small enough and we'd be meeting up again at some point.

We'd just wait and see where and when the Light sent us.

But for now, like Tessa and Kait, I just wanted to sleep for a million years and deal with tomorrow next week.

"Come on, Old Man." Val had come round and opened me door. "The sooner we look around the sooner we can make a plan, and hopefully down tools for the night."

I slid out of the truck and went to join the quiet huddle conferring out the back. With minimal light, there wasn't too much we could do tonight apart from a basic reconnoitre. We'd left the twins dozing in the cab.

"Well?" I looked to each of them.

Val, Dan and Tessa looked to Kait.

She lifted her eyes. Even though she was in silhouette, I could feel tension building like a morning mist. "I think I have heard a message, but I can't be sure." Her head dropped to her chest. "I'm so out of touch, I can't tell between wishful thinking and a Word." Kait had always been our ears to the Light. Her badge of Hearing had saved our buttooshies more times than I can remember. It was something that I had taken for granted... once I'd gotten over the shock that she could do it.

I looked to the rest of the group, some in shadow, some illuminated.

"What do you think you're hearing, Kait?" Val asked.

Her head turned and hope infiltrated her voice. "That it's safe. That this is a safe place for us; our new Soteria House." Her silhouetted head turned to take us all in. "I'm not yet back on track. Intention is one thing but following through with the discipline is something altogether different. I don't know how long it will take before I'm discerning with confidence. It's up to you. Take it or leave it. I'm not prepared to make the call."

Val didn't pull her punch. "Not good enough, Kait. Based on what you're feeling, make the call."

She took a step back. Val's words may as well have been a physical blow.

"I can't. It's too big a call: too much at stake."

"This is not about you. This is not you. It's your Badge, but not your power." Firm and direct. I don't think Val knew any other way. But that was okay. It's what we needed. In a softer voice, she encouraged me wife. "Make the call."

In the following silence we heard the echo from the city bouncing over the water of the neighbouring canal and the looming void of the huge sheds that surrounded us.

"We look around and if it's suitable, we set up camp. This is it."

"Good." Val turned to the rest of us and dished out the agenda. "Tessa, stay with the twins in the truck. Don't rouse them unless we have to. Kait with me. Dan, Marcus, check out the smaller buildings. Meet back here in ten." Val turned and Kait followed to scout the sheds. Tessa peeled off and returned to the cab.

Dan and I headed to the two short rows of smaller buildings. They were our best hope for shelter for the night, other than the truck.

Using reflected light, we made our way onto the old porch stretched along the first row of demountable cabins facing the front gate. Dan was smooth and stealthy as a panther. We'd all decided to be completely silent. It didn't look like anyone was here, but we weren't going to take our chances of forcing a fight before we were ready. And after the day we'd had, and the evening before, we weren't ready.

I welcomed the cool breeze running over me face. It dimmed the rising heat of adrenaline fuelled by hope. Combined, it helped keep me awake. But I could do without the hints of city life—exhaust, trash, and fried food—the breeze brought with it.

On the way in, we'd passed some warehouses, corner stores, and a few worker's cottages dotted in between. I also noted a couple of small shop fronts. If the Light was calling us to stay in Laodicea, and *if* we could set up stumps here, these would be handy.

It was an interesting area. Seems the shadow of the city had kept the light of development away. That, or the contamination. For now, that suited us just fine.

Thankfully, it wasn't winter. With that security fence, there was the possibility of sleeping under the stars if need be. I'll admit though, with Dan rubbernecking as much as me, I was on high alert. But I'll confess there was a vein of solid hope beating beneath.

Is this too good to be true? Have you brought us here?

Wooden boards creaked under our combined weight. Then,

together, we froze. It wasn't so much the silence. But the lack of echo that should have been in an empty space; a solid void holding itself in check.

We weren't alone.

All time stopped and we were back in Sodom. Once again, pulling as a team. No words needed. Dan waited, and I moved to the other side of the door of the occupied room. I started unfolding my fingers in a count, when we heard soft footfalls across the tarmac. The girls were making their way over.

Abort.

Dan and I locked eyes in agreement. This time we jumped the railing and landed softly on a stretch of grass, not wanting our steps tracked. We met up with Kait and Val and let body language and hand-signals tell our tale. Val intimated that they'd also suspected life on the base.

Possibly a tail.

They were being slightly obvious in the hope of drawing him, her, or them, out.

We returned to the truck, woke the twins and shared our intel with Tessa. After a quick, quiet consult with the Light, we made a plan. Best to be bold and up front. We were in someone else's territory—and home?—and we wanted in. So we'd add "polite" to that list as well.

All seven of us made our way back to the demountable and formed up outside the door we suspected was inhabited. After a collective low breath, I knocked.

48

DANIEL: COMING HOME

Marcus's knock sounded like a shotgun.

Silence.

He knocked again and called out. "Hello?"

There was movement in the room. But no answer.

Raph whispered from behind my left shoulder. "What do we do? Can we pick another room that is not being used?"

"Well, if someone is using this place as their home, we want to ask permission to stay. We can't just barge in." Val's voice was a beacon of reason.

Kait stepped into what had become a huddle. "We found a separate building to the side, closer to the canal. It's medium sized and looks like it could be suitable. How about we go check that one out?"

We moved off in agreement and let her lead the way, her silhouette clear in the moonlight. Behind her, Tessa's skeletal form followed. It was great to see her armour back. But I still didn't know how I felt about her. I mean, the way she stood up to that demon was classic Tess. And the way her armour went from zero-to-full-on in a heartbeat was pretty impressive. So, she must've sorted some of that skrat out. But I was still feeling the wounds from her burns.

It sucked that we'd ended up in this place, here and now, in a dump, on the street and at odds. But at least we weren't stuck in that hellhole anymore. After a while, the luxury had felt toxic. Especially when you knew what it cost.

Bit skratty we couldn't trust Kait's Knowledge anymore. Val seemed solid. Right now, I was following her lead as she followed Kait's, rather than the other way around. Kait'd saved us in the past. Hell, she sent them out to save me at the start of all this craziness. But now? I didn't know how long it would take for her Touch to return. But if Kait chose to get back on the fasting wagon, I'd be a lot happier to have her insider information.

But one thing I did know: living back on the street with family would be far better than in that castle with hostility. And I was damned happy to be away from the freaky Overseer and his frecking circus. But I was going to miss Felix. I wondered if we could get a message to him when he got back from Philadelphia.

We moved as a group, staying close. The hairs on the back of my neck were up. Val and Kait had said they thought we were being followed, or at least watched.

I felt it too.

Were we walking into a trap?

I guess we had little choice. The sooner we could get a place we could defend, the better. But as the seconds pulsed, I was convinced we were surrounded.

We kept Raph and Tessa on the inside. Although, after the birthday party, I was pretty impressed and relieved Raph wasn't left without some form of defence. And Tessa retained some form. But after watching her go ape-skrat over that freak in the park this afternoon, it was obvious that, today at least, she was out past her limit.

We circled our way round the area, keeping our backs to the warehouses. Our target stood by itself, closer to the canal wall, surrounded by a neat garden. We were going to have to leave the shadows and risk further exposure to approach.

It was decided that Kait and Marcus would stay with Tessa and the kids in the shadows. Val and I would check it out before the others joined us.

It was pointless trying to be invisible; they already knew we were there. But we weren't going to make it easy for them either. Before we launched ourselves across the clearing, we waited. And yep. There it was.

At least one set of footsteps to the right, between us and the truck. Straining to see into the shadows, I was sure I could see movement across from us, on the other side of the clearing. Our objective was off to the left, towards the canal. The city provided a constant backdrop of noise as it echoed across the water. It made it hard to guess how many others were out there.

At least I could confirm, apart from the constant white noise of demon stench that was everywhere all the time in this flecked city, there was nothing more intense: our company was human. At least I knew what weapons to use. I kept my sword sheathed and palmed my knife.

Heading off on different tangents, Val and I intended to meet up at the far side of the hut. I took the factory side. Val took the canal front. As the building took her from my sight, I tuned into the Light and went on high alert. But I'd have had to be unconscious to miss the action happening on Val's side of the building.

Scuffling, grunting, then the walls of the building shuddered. Pitching caution to the wind, I bolted and arrived just in time for the show.

"Twik." A slurred yell erupted from a lump as it rolled away from the building.

The city lights illuminated Val standing at ease, one eyebrow raised.

"You kretting twik. You think you're too good for me? I got money. You and your Greyscaled twiks aren't worth skrat, but I got money." The fool rolled to his hands and knees and attempted to stand.

"Stay down. Sleep it off." Val was surprisingly reasonable considering the idiot's manner.

"Skitch of a whore." He screamed and lurched himself at her, swinging like a scarecrow and falling like a bag of potatoes as he met Val's fist, again. I suspect this time she didn't pull her punch. He went down. Stayed down. And snored? At least he was still breathing. Using her boot, she rolled him onto his side and kicked his legs and arms into the recovery position.

Drunken idiot.

Mistaking Val for a temple prostitute would be like mistaking a Sherman tank for a Corvette.

We checked he was out cold, and safe, finished circling the building, and signalled the others to join us. Kait touched Val's shoulder and Riah wrapped her arm around Val's waist. She was fine, but they were acknowledging we were back in the real world.

"Always the battle hog," Marcus breathed as he passed her on his way to the front door.

"You still owe me dinner, Old Man." And with that, we were good again... well, almost. It was interesting how external conflict brought us back together. I guess we couldn't afford to focus on ourselves when we were fighting for a common goal, or against a common enemy.

Back on guard, we waited as Marcus approached the door to knock. You could have blown me over with a whisper when Ri raced up and put her hand on his arm, stopping him. After a quick shake of her head, he dropped his arm. She pulled her sword out and used it to point to me.

She had us all confused. "What's up?"

Riah used her blade to point to the handle sticking up over my shoulder.

"You want me to use this?"

With an eye roll, she told me to stop being so thick. I tell you, she was eleven going on obnoxious brat.

Marcus shrugged his shoulders and moved aside, making room.

I ruffled Riah's hair as I passed because she hated it. And received a swat on my arm in response. All fell quiet again. I paused and breathed in the peace.

Regardless of the situation, our circumstance, and the yawning unknown, this place held peace.

It was time to move. I drew my sword and ran it down the join in the doors, like Marcus had taught me a lifetime ago in Sodom. I looked to Riah and accepted her smirk as we all heard the click of the door unlocking. This was a Soteria House.

This was our new home until the Light led us to somewhere else. *Thank you.*

Along with everyone else, I relaxed. I didn't even look through the door as I pulled it open. With one hand over my head guiding my blade home, and the other widening the opening, I was completely bowled over by a blow to the gut from a bull.

I was ridden down the ramp like a sled. Tarmac slammed into the back of my head and a brick wall pinned me to the ground. A flecking strong brick wall with ten arms. Blows came at me from every angle. I was still seeing stars from the fall and trying to regain some air.

Matching screams split the night. One inside the hut. One out.

One second, I was trying to defend myself, the next, the weight was being prised off. Not a lot was making sense. But I was completely aware of Tessa standing astride my prone body swinging like a banshee. And by the sound of it, landing a few hits along the way. Val and Marcus held the guy between them. Kait tried to constrain Tessa.

She may have been weak and out of condition but the earlier scare in the park must have triggered something. She was as wild as a berserker, managing to get past Kait's restraints. I actually started to feel sorry for the guy. I knew what it was to be on the receiving end of her attacks. I crawled out from between her legs and wrapped my arms around her and breathed into her ear, "It's okay Tessa. Let it go."

She spun and stared at me. Her eyes wide and unseeing, her hands everywhere: my face, head, shoulders, arms.

Wincing and wheezing, I gripped her hands. "Tessa." This time, my quiet challenge brought her back.

A soft light coming from inside the hut revealed her eyelashes beating like hummingbird wings. Then, with a quick flick of her head, she looked at her fists, dropped them back by her sides, apologised and nestled under my arm. It was instinctive.

With her calmed down, I turned to face my attacker. He slumped between Val and Marcus. He was silhouetted by the light from the open door. His skin blended with the night and, at first, all I could see were the whites of his eyes. I froze as they grew. I'd know those eyes anywhere.

"Indy?"

"Dan?"

I couldn't breathe. A hand squeezed my chest, expelling all my air. All senses were dimmed by the fireworks frying my brain. I dropped to my knees. Someone scooted a... a wheelchair? A wheelchair was placed under him and he collapsed into it. *What the frack?* "What the frack?" I was drawn closer to the mirage.

It said, "Well frack a fracking fracked cat. What the frackety frack?"

"Indigo. Please." Again, a weak pitiful cry came from inside the hut. This time a splinter of steel laced the pain.

I looked to the door, trying to make out who was inside. Indy's eyes never left my face. Like a wet dog, he shook his head and with a watery voice he whispered, "You're dead. You died... you're dead..." Wonder, grief, surprise blended with the tears rolling down his scarred cheeks.

My voice came with a roll of anger that boiled over, threatening to consume me and anyone else standing too close. "What happened to you? What's with the chair? Who did this to you?" I was a raging inferno ready for blood. "Are they here? In Laodicea? Are they still alive?" Standing and shaking out my limbs I prepared for action. "I'll kill the krets. Who did this? Where are they, Indy?"

"Dan, let's go inside and talk." I flinched when Val's hand rested on my shoulder.

"I'll fracking kill 'em, Val." I looked to Indy again. "Is Abraham here? Is he safe?"

The river of tears turned to a flood. "They killed him, Dan. They waited for us. Cowards waited till it was dark, then took us. We didn't stand a chance."

I pointed to the chair. "Who, Indy?" Fire was sparking along every synapse. I not only welcomed the rage, I opened up and ushered it in.

Crouching by his chair, a fracking wheelchair, I ran my hand over the wheels. This was not real. It was impossible.

"No, Dan." He looked at me, the whites of his eyes full. "No. You don't understand." Then he was gone again, he dropped his head. "It's too much, too heavy." My soul-brother slumped back into his prison, broken, hopeless and wretched.

I rocked back on my heels, frozen and speechless. I was incapable of thought. Surely this was a dream. It couldn't be real. How was this possible. He was lost. Dead. But now, here he was. In front of me. In the flesh. The throbbing pain in my face and body attested to the fact I wasn't dreaming. He might be in a chair, but Indy was sure as hell not defenceless. Never defenceless.

"Indy!" the Siren inside warned again.

It snapped my brain into some form of action. Clarity came back like a bucket of icy water. Everyone was standing around watching. Waiting. Indy just stared blankly at his hands.

"Indy." There was an extra edge in the plea from inside the hut. Pain? Fear? Need?

He turned his chair and rolled up the ramp into the hut. "Come inside and meet Iza."

AFTERWORD

A note to my readers

Thank you so much for joining me on the second leg of this adventure into the Light. I hope you have enjoyed getting to know more of the family and a bit more of the backstory as much as I have. This book and these people are as real to me as my family and it is a pleasure to bring them to life on the page and share them with you.

If you have enjoyed this book, please consider leaving a review. It would inspire others to pick it up as well as encourage me to write some more. Although, that's not too hard to do.

To keep up to date with more books in the series and other news, sign up to my newsletter at donitabundy.com

Donita Bundy

BLINDING REVELATION PLAY LIST

Laodicea theme song: Zion & Babylon – *Josh Garrels*
Valarie: Trouble – *Matthew S. Nelson & Dan Haseltine*
Izabaal: Hurt – *Johnny Cash*
Indigo: I Like to Be With Me When I'm With You –
 Drew Holcomb
Daniel: Keep Me – *Crowder*
Kaitlyn: There's a Light – *Liz Vice*
Marcus: Heaven's Knife – *Josh Garrels*
Contessa: Fighter – *Tyrone Wells*
Sariah: Where Were You – *Francesca Battistelli*
Raphael: Train Song – *Josh Garrels*
Felix: Whom Shall I Fear – *Chris Tomlin*
Family: Forever On Your Side – *NeedToBreathe*

ABOUT THE AUTHOR

Donita Bundy was the inaugural Somerset Writer in Residence (Queensland Australia). Along with monthly short stories with the Somerset Writers Group, Donita blogs regularly on her website and contributes to the Gracewriters Podcast. When she's not writing or teaching, she enjoys photographing the local area as well as designing book covers.

To connect, follow her blog, listen to the podcast, check out the gallery or just keep up to date with what's going on, go to her website and sign up to the newsletter at www.donitabundy.com.

ACKNOWLEDGEMENTS

I would like to acknowledge my husband, Simon, and our two boys, who have not only survived but coped surprisingly well with my juggling of (too) many projects. Their patience and grace has made the production of this book possible.

Secondly, I would like to thank my support crew, who are such an integral part of this journey:

Belinda Pollard, my friend, sister-in-arms, and editor, I couldn't have done it without you. For culling commas, cheering from the sidelines, and for the smilies and suggestions in the margins, thank you.

Alix Kwan, the most amazing proofreader of all time, thank you for carving time out of your very busy life and breaking the sound barrier in your efforts to support this team effort.

Ella Green and Lee Cawthray, the loudest, steadfast-est supporters cheering me on when I was merely a shadow in the cave tapping away madly, or lost, out on a limb of the unknown. For your unyielding enthusiasm and confidence, thank you.

To Sarah and Ella, who have shared laughs, tears and coffee. Who have understood weeks on end of radio silence, and have stood beside me through bushfires, droughts, famine and pandemics.

For my Beta Reader Crew, who not only survived round one, but came back for more to provide support, perspective and feedback, thank you:

- Lee Cawthray
- Ella Green

- Belinda Pollard
- Jennie Del Mastro.

To the Somerset Writers Group, the most amazingly diverse group of creatives, with immense hearts and fearless spirits, thank you for your company and encouragement on the journey.

To Rob and Ruth Elliott, for your medical advice and pointers on paraplegia, thank you. And to Bill Fuller, for giving me helpful insights into wheelchair handling and generously sharing his perspective as a wheelchair user, thank you.

To my family at our own Soteria House, for your constant prayers, support and encouragement, thank you.

And finally, and most importantly, I give thanks to God, who has inspired, carried, prompted and prodded this book over the line. This story, and the library of others associated with it, have been with me most of my life. It is told through the lens of my life experiences, yet it is not my story. It is His. My prayer is that you, dear reader, will find inspiration, challenge and encouragement to keep journeying the incredible adventure in, and with, the Light.

ARMOUR OF LIGHT SERIES

Book 1: Dangerous Salvation

What if your saviour was more dangerous than your enemy?

Lonely and living on the streets, forced to steal clothes to survive another bitter winter, Daniel has an encounter that turns his world upside-down.

Confronted by two strangers who tell him things about himself that no human could possibly know, Daniel is offered a choice: to stay where he is and face the dangers of the street, or accept the invitation of a warm bed, a family... and to join their war.

Can he trust the safety this "family" appears to offer? Or will he give in to the temptations of the Dark Lord?

He must make a decision. Fast.

ISBN:
Print: 978-0-6487423-0-8
Mobi: 978-0-6487823-2-2
EPub: 978-0-6487823-1-5

www.ingramcontent.com/pod-product-compliance
Lightning Source LLC
Chambersburg PA
CBHW020258120726
47904CB00001B/256